# PROPHET'S MERCY

## PROPHET OF THE BADLANDS BOOK 2

### MATTHEW S. COX

DIVISION ZERO PRESS

Prophet's Mercy
Prophet of the Badlands Book 2
© 2020 Matthew S. Cox
All Rights Reserved

# DIVERGENT FATES
### —A— —NOVEL—

Cover illustration: Jackson Tjota • Cover formatting: Alexandria Thompson • Interior art: Ricky Gunawan

ISBN (ebook): 978-1-950738-44-1

ISBN (paperback): 978-1-950738-45-8

# CONTENTS

1. Quieter    1
2. Coronado Pond    19
3. Round Rocks and Wooden Pegs    35
4. The Bird of Death    51
5. Ordinary... Almost    65
6. Worlds Apart    82
7. Contagious    93
8. Love    102
9. Far and Wide    106
10. The Expedition    117
11. A Danger to the Innocent    135
12. Superstition and Darkness    142
13. Trader Makko    148
14. Cursed    167
15. Afbee    199
16. The Tracker    219
17. Claimed    225
18. Opportunity    233
19. A New Legend    239
20. Driver's Education    254
21. The Spirit Talker    269
22. The Spoils of War... or Kidnapping    277
23. Breach    280
24. Almost Spirits    288
25. Nerd Word    304
26. The Rat of Death    311
27. Ginger Ale    317
28. The Un-Hospital    329
29. Too Innocent for the World    334
30. Out of the Slime, Into the Fire    343
31. A Common Misconception    349

32. The Line Between Help and Harm      361

33. Lesser Evil      370

34. Triage      374

35. Dreams      382

36. Benevolence      390

*Acknowledgments*      395

*About the Author*      396

*Other books by Matthew S. Cox*      397

# QUIETER

Adapting to new situations didn't often fluster Althea, but having friends felt weird.

It seemed like forever ago she drifted across the Badlands wherever the whims of raiders or circumstance dragged her. Abduction had been a way of life ever since she'd tried to help the Wagon Man, as she called him. Soon after she'd discovered her ability to heal, he'd stumbled into the village where she'd grown from infant to around five or six. The man suffered an attack from wildlife of some kind, likely bonedogs or soldier scorpions. Without her, he'd have died—or so she remembered. The details of his injuries faded long ago into a morass of hazy memory, though she distinctly recalled saving his life.

For her kindness, she spent the next few years locked in a cage in his wagon, carted around while he charged other people pay-things to let them visit her to have their sicks and hurts cured. Thanks to him, every marauder, raider, bandit, scrag, and settler knew about The Prophet. His final irony came in that the cage he'd put her in prevented her from saving his life when a bunch of raiders refused to pay

for healing and simply shot him and his two hired guards...
then stole her.

At no point in the five or so years she'd spent mostly as
someone's captive had she ever thought about having
friends or doing anything more than using her abilities to
help everyone she could. It didn't matter if villagers found
her and treated her well or bandits kidnapped her, as long
as she could still help those who needed it. Knowing the
raiders she healed would only run off and harm others
bothered her to a point, but she couldn't let anyone suffer,
not even bad people.

Althea hadn't cared who took her... until she made a
friend. A boy named Den in a tribe of scrags decided to
treat her as a person, not the 'Prophet.' So what if his tribe
also took her by force and kept her in a cage for a few
months? They eventually trusted her promise not to run
away and let her out. She liked Den, and it hurt when
raiders took her from the tribe. For the first time, she wept
over being kidnapped. Still, she couldn't bring herself to do
anything but obey her new captors. The Prophet never
tried to run, never put up a fight. Everyone knew she was
an easy capture — or at least used to be.

'The Prophet' never resisted because she had no reason
to, nothing to fight for. She should have refused to go with
the raiders who took her from Den. It would have been
easily within her power to do so, except for being afraid. It
took arriving here — and finding a family — to overcome her
doubts and insecurities. Karina and Father opened their
home to her, treated her like family for no reason other than
she needed one. Despite her fame, the people of Querq
somehow hadn't heard about her. No one wanted to claim
her as a great prize. In fact, the town elders nearly exiled
her over an idiot's ravings.

Father did not want her to leave, but thought it better

than allow her to be sold back into slavery. He'd been ready to leave Querq with her, but Althea refused to abandon her home. She knew The Many influenced the people, making them angry so they didn't think. His corruption would not harm this place again.

The arrival of The Prophet hadn't been the only change to the village. A mean and somewhat crazy man called Archon from the fancy big city in the west decided he needed her to help his great plan… and so she'd been kidnapped yet again, this time to a glittering electronic hell full of awful emotions. She still couldn't understand how *so* many people could exist in one place and never talk to each other. Everyone rushed by in a hurry to be somewhere else, all the while staring at small handheld devices or looking without seeing—their consciousness in an alternate electronic reality. Her foray into what some called 'the modern world' resulted in the city police taking a big interest in her.

They'd followed her back to Querq.

While no one could call it the biggest or grandest settlement in the Badlands, Querq had a well-organized Watch and defensive wall. The city police brought some 'technology' stuff. She worried they would try to make it more like the bad place in the west, but thus far, things like 'electricity' hadn't rapidly turned everyone sad or angry. She used to believe her abilities came from magic, but multiple adults told her she had 'psionic' powers. Archon claimed her something he called an 'Awakened' psionic, much more powerful than a normal one.

Althea frowned to herself. She didn't like being worshiped as The Prophet, nor did Archon's attitude about being Awakened sit well with her. He thought himself better than other people because of it. The word felt arrogant and bad, so she didn't use it.

People treating her like a real person, not the Prophet, not some rare and powerful psionic whatever, thrilled her, setting off a warm, fuzzy feeling inside her chest. It didn't seem possible for normality to ever feel normal. She'd taken kidnapping after kidnapping in stride, adjusting to new places to live, possibly a cage or leash, with no difficulty. Except for when Archon's people stole her from Father and Karina, no abduction bothered her as much as sitting here talking to her friends.

She didn't know how to deal with being just another girl.

Like some manner of ordinary person, Althea hung out with a small group who she'd become somewhat close to: Kim, Paama, and Esmerelda. Kim, almost fifteen now, used to live in the big city. She'd been tricked into joining Archon's 'psionic army,' not understanding his true craziness. The girl's father told her to go away because she had psionic abilities. For no reason Kim understood, the man *hated* psionics and thought them some kind of evil creations needing to be destroyed. He'd spent years ranting about them and a relatively small, but highly vocal—and violent—group of people did something called 'voting' for him because he hated psionics. Something about his being a 'senator' was more important to him than his child. She covered her sadness with anger, but here in Querq, with adoptive parents, she'd become much happier.

Paama came from up north—an area the modern city people said used to be called Detroit—along with her entire village, the Transit Tribe, fleeing the dangerous areas full of killing machines. They clustered together in a district of sorts at the northwestern part of Querq, essentially recreating their former home on the surface instead of in underground tunnels. Her tribe stood out among the locals. Paama, and about a third of them, looked like Althea: pale skinned. The rest had much darker skin, more so even than Rachel. People from the Transit Tribe knew even less Spanish than her. Some had difficulty adjusting to the warmer climate, but regarded it as a small price to pay not to worry about robots. For now, she and Althea were the same age, twelve, though the girl would have a birthday four months ahead of her.

Esmerelda lived in Querq for all ten of her years. Despite being the youngest, she wasn't the smallest of their friend group, a title belonging to Althea. The city police thought the way her healing power worked consumed energy she otherwise would have used to grow. A life in captivity without being given enough food to compensate certainly hadn't helped. She didn't really mind being undersized or looking younger than her age—it made it less likely anyone would try to wife her.

A few months ago, while playing a kick-the-ball game, Esmerelda used her size to plow down smaller kids, being a bit mean about it as well. Althea asked her to stop, which set off a fight. Scrag kids often got into scraps, behavior encouraged by parents as it helped prepare them to defend the village as adults. Althea adored being treated like an ordinary kid, but as soon as Esmerelda noticed her glowing blue eyes—that she'd struck the Prophet—the poor girl nearly dropped dead from fear. Her father almost punished her severely, believing that mistreating the great 'Prophet' would bring bad luck on their family. Althea compelled him not to punish her, and for that, Esmerelda had become her friend.

They sat around some old concrete benches and tables on the property of what might've once been a school building. According to Officer David from the city police, this area had been called Albuquerque before something known as the 'Corporate War.' The people who established this settlement in the rubble of the former city must have found a damaged sign where only the middle part 'querq' remained readable. She didn't like to think about the thousands of people who used to live here or what happened to them three centuries ago during the war.

Another change in her life—knowing her age. She'd spent the past year considering herself twelve. The city police had been right about 'corporations' wanting to take her. Two different ones tried. During the first attempt, she read the thoughts of a man who knew the day she'd been born. He belonged to the same corporation her real mother used to work for. In truth, Althea had been eleven at the time. At least she could now truthfully claim to be twelve.

The second time a corporation tried to abduct her, it ended with her bringing Paama and the girl's entire tribe back to Querq as well as making a strange new friend, a synthetic woman named Teal. Althea thought the 'friend' concept confusing. She considered Teal a friend but not in the same way as the other girls her age. Teal didn't hang out with them, want to play, sit for hours talking. She acted much like any other adult in the city. How could 'friend' mean both the girls she spent time with as well as an adult she'd become fond of?

Worse, the whole 'boyfriend' idea her sister Karina brought up in regard to Den.

Althea struggled to learn the 'proper speaking' the city people—and Father—wanted her to. For example, she considered Pedro, Santiago, and Diego friends. They happened to be boys, too. But for some reason, she couldn't call them boyfriends. Some of the words didn't make any sense.

Kim thought it strange for Althea to hang out with boys and do 'boy stuff' like go exploring the Old City outside Querq or play the game with the ball and the goal things.

As far as she thought, a girl should only spend time with *one* boy and wrapped it up in an entirely different emotional quality than simply being friends. Paama and Esmerelda shared Althea's opinion—kids were kids.

Althea still smiled whenever she thought about Kim's reaction to the first time they went swimming in the river. They'd gone with a group of twenty or more, ranging in age from later teens to little kids. Apparently, Kim had expected some weird things called 'bathing suits' and hadn't been prepared to see everyone, especially the older boys, take their clothing off and jump in the water. This led to Althea explaining to her how clothing is more a symbol of status as a scavenger or hunter in scrag tribes. Except in cases like Paama's group who lived in the colder north, scrags tended to wear whatever they could find, if anything at all, and primarily for decorative purposes.

The city girl had trouble understanding when Althea told her she hadn't owned any clothing at all until she'd made herself a skirt around age ten. She called it 'tribal' and thought it strange. Still, the girl had somewhat adjusted to life in Querq. People there probably counted as 'settlers' more than scrags. For one thing, they organized more like a prewar city and less like a tribe of primitives. For another, the locals put more emphasis on clothing than scrag tribes, the same way people in the big city had the strange notion people *needed* them even in warm weather. To Althea, the people of Querq tried to re-create the way society had been in the Before-Time. Perhaps scrag tribes would, too, if they knew any better, but most of the time, simply staying alive proved more important than anything else.

Having the city police bring electricity-making boxes and other modern conveniences further elevated Querq, likely turning it into a 'town' rather than a village. Between Althea's presence here diminishing the power of The Many over the area as well as the influx of technology and interest from the big city, Querq had become a veritable fortress in the Badlands.

The girls spent the past hour or so talking about boys... or three of them had. Althea mostly listened, trying to understand the strange emotions surrounding her friends. Kim gave off a distinctly different sense than the others. Thanks to her lessons with Officer David, who also possessed the psionic power they called Telempathy, she understood the emotion coming from her friend to be something called lust. Or, at least, a far more innocent form of how raiders felt when they wanted to wife someone. Kim's emotion mixed it with love. The raiders didn't combine their lust with any love, rather greed and a sense of enjoying the power they had over a weaker person. Some of them gave off similar emotions while killing rival raider groups or each other during contests and duels. Those raiders tended to frighten Althea.

Talking about boys made Paama and Esmerelda giddy and embarrassed. Mostly, Paama appeared miserable at the heat. The poor girl sweat heavily, even in a thin linen dress. They all wore basically the same manner of garment, since the people who made clothing here didn't care about fashion. Kim had even gotten into the habit of going barefoot like most kids in Querq.

Paama fluttered her thin dress to let air under it. "Ugh. It's so hot."

"You'll get used to it." Kim, who also sweat a little, shrugged. "It's not *so* bad."

"I'm thinking about hot because it's all I have to think about." Paama leaned forward, folding her arms across her knees. "They don't want me scouting. They treat me like a kid."

"You *are* a kid." Kim chuckled. "You shouldn't be running around with a gun doing dangerous stuff."

Paama scrunched her nose. "I didn't have a gun. I had a spear."

"Oh, even better." Kim rolled her eyes. "You aren't super primitive anymore. Be a kid. Have fun. At least you get to do it. My dad used to keep me on a really short leash."

Althea scowled. "Mean. I hate leashes. Did he put it on your leg or your neck?"

"Huh?" Kim blinked at her. "Oh! No... not an actual leash. It's just a phrase. He never let me do anything. I couldn't have friends. One of his 'people' constantly monitored my NetMini to see what I did."

"Oh." Althea fidgeted at her dress, squeezing two handfuls of fabric above her knees. Not understanding how words sometimes didn't mean what they said kinda embarrassed her, but at least she could be happy no one put a real leash on her friend.

"It *was* fun hiding from robots and looking for stuff." Paama fanned herself. "I'm not a little kid anymore. I want to help. What are we supposed to do? I feel lazy just sitting around."

Esmerelda shrugged. "Learn how to make food or take care of babies."

Paama shot her a 'yeah right' look.

Kim scoffed. "What century are you living in? Girls aren't stuck sewing and cooking and making babies anymore."

"It's what Papa wants." Esmerelda brushed some sand off her foot. "I'm going to be a mama someday and take good care of my babies."

Contempt wafted from Kim. She made a face as if she'd eaten something questionable.

"What's wrong?" asked Althea.

Kim gestured randomly. "Her father shouldn't be forcing her to do that stuff. Girls don't *have* to cook, clean, and make babies. Screw that backward stuff."

"I'm not backward." Esmeralda folded her arms. "I'm not a scrag."

Paama smirked at her. "I'm not backward either."

"Your tribe prays to old corporations." Kim laughed. "But at least you guys know what clothing is."

"Corporations…" Paama made a face like she wanted to be angry and confused at the same time. Since arriving in Querq, her people learned all the 'ancient glyphs' inscribed everywhere around where they used to live came from ancient companies, not long-lost gods. "I… umm."

"You guys aren't scrags anymore." Kim patted Paama on the arm. "You've come back to the modern world… sort of. Querq isn't exactly there, but it's nice. Just saying, forcing girls to only do 'girl stuff' is backward and wrong."

Paama shook her head. "My people didn't do that. I used to be a scout. I can fight and sneak and track."

"They don't force." Althea shook her head and rambled about the various villages and raider groups she'd been with between her time with the Wagon Man and finding Querq. Only a few of the 'nicer' settlements demanded girls only do 'girl stuff' and boys only do 'boy stuff.' Most places, especially the raider groups, had a fairly even mix. Strangely, female raiders tended to be more violent and vicious than the men. For the most part, people did whatever they wanted and could handle. Of course, among the raiders, weakness of any kind got exploited. "The Ravens don't *make* anyone do anything they don't want to do."

"Ravens?" Kim raised both eyebrows. "You're talking to birds now?"

Althea laughed. She adored feeling so happy, so she laughed again. "No, the council. I call them ravens 'cause they're all in black and scary."

"Oh… the judges." Kim nodded once. "Or the people who dress up like judges. Pretty sure they didn't go to law school."

"But I want to be a mama." Esmerelda's eyes widened. "What is wrong with doing girl stuff? I also like playing the games with the ball and running."

"You run over most of the boys." Althea grinned.

"What's wrong with it?" Kim stared in shock. "There's *so* much else to do other than cooking, cleaning, and having babies. You could be a scientist, a doctor, a lawyer, a pilot, a starship engineer or…"

Althea, Esmerelda, and Paama exchanged confused glances.

Kim smacked herself in the head. "Or not. Okay, dumb of me. Wow. I keep forgetting where I am. Guess you guys aren't thinking about college."

Paama tilted her head. "What's college?"

"More school. You won't need it if you stay out here." Kim looked down. "Only if you go to the city."

Althea cringed. Her experience in West City left her no interest in returning. True, she'd been abducted there against her will, then left stranded on the street in an overwhelming, confusing, indifferent place full of people and technology she'd neither seen before nor imagined possible. Up until Kim ran away from home, her life there had been completely different.

"What do friends do?" Althea glanced at Kim.

"Umm. Well… hang out—which we're doing now—or go to the mall, or play video games. Maybe watch a holo-vid," said Kim.

Again, Althea and the others stared at her.

"Right. Like I said." Kim stretched. "Totally different world. I really have no idea what friends do in a place like Querq. We've basically jumped a thousand years into the past."

"Did you have friends in the city?" asked Paama.

Kim tilted her hand in a so-so gesture. "Not really. Because of who my dad is, they didn't let anyone get close to me for security reasons."

"We'd play games," said Paama. "Hide and find in the tunnels, or robot. Had some toys, too. And story time."

"What's robot?" asked Esmerelda.

Paama stretched her legs out and again fluffed at her dress to get some air moving under it. "I'm melting. Umm, robot is a game for kids. We're a little old for it. One kid is the robot and they try to find and kill everyone else before the time ends. The 'people' have to hide and not let the robot find them."

Kim gasped. "I hope you don't really mean kill."

Paama laughed. "No. It's just pretend. But it's a teaching game. Where we used to live had real robots on the surface. It's why we lived in the tunnels."

Esmerelda spoke of hide and seek, a favorite of the kids here in Querq. Paama commented it similar to 'robot' except any kid the seeker found had to lie in place and pretend to be dead until the game ended. Also, if one of the 'people' could sneak up on the robot unnoticed and touch their back, the robot 'died.' Kim thought them too old for such a 'childish' game, but then lamented the lack of video games out here. This, of course, led to her trying to explain to the others what video games were.

"What's a holo-vid?" asked Esmerelda.

Kim held a finger up. "One sec. Let me think of how to explain it to you. Umm. You know what stories are, right?"

"Of course. I'm not dumb." Esmerelda tried to thump

her on the arm.

Kim dodged. "Heh. Okay. Basically, a holo-vid is like a story but instead of reading it, you watch it happen on a screen."

"Like play acting?" asked Paama.

"Yeah, but they aren't real people, just computers."

"Huh?" Althea scrunched her nose.

Kim sighed. "This is going to be hard to explain to you since you don't understand anything about the modern world, but I'll try. A long time ago, actual people called actors pretended to be characters in holo-vids. When technology reached the point where AI could mimic humans perfectly, they stopped using live actors because it cost way too much money. I learned in school some actors would earn millions and millions of credits for *one* holo-vid. It's way cheaper to do everything computer-generated. An AI character isn't an actor pretending to be someone else, they really think they *are* the character, so the 'performance' is genuine. And, they can make them look exactly like they're supposed to. Also, AI characters don't do things like break the law, get messy with politics, or ask for even more money, or demand 'creative control' over the story."

"I don't understand," said Esmerelda. "Nothing."

Paama sat there staring at Kim with an expression like she just stepped in something unpleasant. "You know strange things."

"It's not strange. It's the real world." Kim waved her arm around. "The whole planet isn't like this. Civilization isn't gone. I really don't understand why they let the middle of the continent stay like this."

Althea sighed. "The Many won't let them have it back. People have tried. The robots where Paama used to live were supposed to get rid of monsters, but they became monsters."

"Yeah, I remember that from school. Cybernetic Reclamation Project or something." Kim frowned. "It's weird, they just gave up on so much land. My dad used to say it wasn't 'cost effective' and we didn't need the farm space anymore since most of our food comes from hydroponic factories."

A group of kids and teens went by, Den among them — though he carried a rifle since he'd joined the Watch. He appeared to be escorting the others, probably out to the river for swimming. The areas outside the wall close to Querq tended to be fairly safe, but the Watch usually sent at least one person along for safety. Considering Den had been allowed to join the watch much younger than normal at fourteen, they often gave him 'easy' assignments without too much danger.

Paama and Esmerelda got to talking about the boys. Again, Althea listened without comment, smiling and waving at Den who grinned back at her. The boy fit right in with the locals from Querq, dark sienna skin, black hair, more Spanish than English in his words. He'd fled from his tribe despite being the chieftain's son so he could be with her. His father chose another girl, Yala, to be Den's wife… but he wanted Althea.

It confused her to hear him use the term 'wife' differently from how she thought of it. To Althea, 'wifeing' was a horrible thing raiders did to women they kidnapped. To Den, it meant he wanted to spend the rest of his life with her. According to the silly electronic device they made her learn words from, 'wife' didn't count as one of those 'verb' things the way Althea used it. She didn't really care. She knew what her words meant.

"Kim?" asked Althea, interrupting a discussion of Santiago's cuteness.

"Hmm?"

"Why isn't being friends with a boy the same as having a boyfriend?"

Esmerelda and Paama giggled.

"You're too little for a boyfriend." Kim pressed a fist into her shoulder and gave her a nudge. "Don't worry about it. If you have to ask, you aren't ready."

Althea flailed her arms. "How do you know if he's a friend or a boyfriend? Is it the lip-touching thing?"

The girls giggled again.

"It's more than that." Kim put an arm around her shoulders. "You're the telempath from hell. You should understand emotions."

Althea frowned. "I'm not from hell."

Kim laughed. "It's just a saying. I mean, your powers are really strong. Go look at how people in love feel about each other. If you feel the same way about a boy and he feels the same way about you, he's your boyfriend. If you're just hanging out with them doing fun stuff, then normal friend."

"Oh." Althea stared down her legs at her feet, watching a tiny beetle crawl over her toes.

"You already knew the answer." Kim squeezed her. "It's okay. You're afraid because you don't feel that way about Den, right?"

Althea exhaled out her nose. "I don't know. The rest of his tribe are afraid of me. Den treated me like a person. I really like him, but it doesn't feel the same as, you know."

"Because you're too young." Kim winked. "Another two years or so and you'll definitely know."

"Gotta be four." Althea grumbled. "Father said he'd throw Den off the wall if he didn't wait until I had sixteen birthdays."

"Wait for what?" asked Esmerelda.

"Nothing important. Don't worry about it." Kim waved

dismissively at her while radiating embarrassment. "So, what do you guys want to do? Can't really go to the mall or funzones. Well… maybe we could if the cops gave us a ride back to the city. But I don't think you would like it."

"Funzone?" asked Paama in a hesitant voice.

Kim sighed. "Yeah… umm, so like, most of the modern world is in virtual reality. People are all connected to fake worlds inside computers. Most kids stay home all the time because there are so many people and so little space. And it's dangerous in some areas. Kids go to school in VR, play games in VR, hang out with their friends in VR… basically everyone spends all their time inside their homes. Lots of adults even work virtually. Some egghead got the idea to make places called funzones where parents can take their kids to meet in person and do like physical games and stuff. It's pretty cool. But… you guys don't really need it out here since *all* your games are physical stuff."

"Bleh." Althea stuck out her tongue. "I don't like being in the big city."

"It's not that bad. You were kidnapped and didn't see it the right way." Kim patted her on the back.

"More." Althea twirled a finger around her ear. "I feel how lonely, sad, and angry everyone is. I hate being there because it makes me sad."

Kim winced. "Ack. Didn't even think about that. You know, not *everyone* in the city is in a permanent bad mood, but I suppose there are a lot of people who aren't happy. And yeah, I guess to a telepath as strong as you are, it's gotta be rough."

"If they're not happy, why are they there?" asked Paama.

"Because they are used to it and afraid to do anything else." Kim swiped her hair off her face, tucking it behind one ear. "Honestly, most people wouldn't want to live in the middle of nowhere without technology. It's so damn quiet here. In the city, you can't get away from advert bots always playing music, or traffic noise, or something happening."

"Aren't you scared of raiders?" asked Esmerelda.

"Nah. It happens in the city, too. I mean, not like slavers and raiders, but there are gangs who aren't much different. They don't like take slaves, but they'll do horrible stuff to people. Not sure which is more dangerous, to be honest, there or here. I used to have it pretty easy since my parents are rich… but then I had to leave, so… living on the streets in the city is almost *more* dangerous than being in the Badlands. I totally feel safer here than I did in Archon's place or the street."

Althea hugged her legs to her chest, burying her face in her knees, hating how much suffering existed in the world. At least in the Badlands, the evil made some degree of sense. Out here, The Many caused people to turn dark if they lacked the willpower to keep him out of their minds. Those he couldn't influence, he'd torment in other ways. The big city had far too many people for him to affect. She didn't really understand how it worked, nor did Officer David, or the city police. Worse, they didn't take her story all too seriously. Ghosts, demons, and things of that nature, even other psionics often regarded as not real. The idea of a malignant entity formed from the tormented souls of everyone killed during the Corporate War sounded, to them, as silly as the ramblings of a primitive scrag who worshiped corporations.

"Cheer up." Kim nudged her again. "Talk about something nice. Querq is a better place to live than on the street in the city, even if it can be a bit boring."

Althea lifted her head and pulled her hair back over her shoulder. "What are we supposed to do with boyfriends?"

Paama smiled. "Hunt together."

"Mama said to go for walks by the river." Esmerelda twirled some of her lush, black hair around her finger. "Maybe sit and watch the sunset. Talk. Hold hands. Kiss, and some other stuff she won't tell me about until I'm older."

Althea felt no rush to explore the 'other stuff' yet—in no small part because she didn't want Father throwing Den off the city wall. However, spending time with Den, walking by the river, and holding hands already happened. She enjoyed being with him in a different way than hanging out with Diego, Santiago, and Pedro. Being with those three often made her feel more like their frantic mother trying to keep them safe. With Den... not the same. Perhaps she *did* have a boyfriend after all.

"Let's go swimming." Paama stood. "I'm too hot."

A mild waft of embarrassment came from Kim, but not enough to stop her. "If you guys want. Not like there's much else to do here." *Althea, can you make me not blush please?*

Althea nodded in response to the telepathic request, grinning.

"Okay." Esmerelda got up.

No one would panic, scream, freak out, or otherwise react much to Althea wanting to go outside the wall to the river, beyond the same need to keep a protective eye on any other kid. Thrilled at the sense of normality, Althea jumped to her feet. Her elation seemed to leak out over all of Querq. Usually, she tried not to let her emotions broadcast, but figured a little happiness wouldn't bother anyone. Even the Water Man only pretended to be grumpy.

*Oops.* She snickered to herself and ran after her friends to the gate.

## 2

## CORONADO POND

Althea continued thinking about Den over the next few days.

He definitely felt like more than a simple friend. The boy had been the first crack in her indifference to all the raiders of the Badlands kidnapping her. Because of him, she allowed herself to believe another reality could be possible. She'd been too afraid of being burned to death as a mystic to dare use her psionic abilities to protect herself. Thinking back on it, she doubted anyone would have tried to kill her for refusing to let people be mean to her. Mystics—a scrag word for psionic—couldn't heal anyone. They took over people's minds and stole their thoughts, which made them terrifying. Althea would never turn anyone into a mind slave or make them do bad things. Commanding a person to 'go away' certainly wouldn't result in the same kind of fear.

And she had something they wanted: the ability to heal.

But no one had to *steal* her. She would readily help anyone who asked for it. Raiders did not have to own her. She'd told the Watch to let anyone in who needed help, even raiders, but only a few at a time and not with weapons. The Ravens believed that once word spread anyone (who behaved) could come here for healing, it would make Querq prosperous. While they said nothing about asking pay-things in exchange for healing, Althea would never allow them to do it. They most likely believed most of the people who came to see her would end up trading while here. Settlers might even relocate. At last, her presence in a place would bring prosperity, not ruin.

She decided to consider Den her boyfriend. The love he felt around her came from a genuine place and resonated inside her as well. Other emotions and stuff would most likely happen later, once she became older. Althea kind of dreaded the idea she might experience lust at some point. She definitely didn't have any desire to rush. In four years, she might no longer be afraid to do the wifeing thing — assuming it didn't resemble anything like what she saw in raider camps. Of course, it would obviously be different. Althea wouldn't be trying to fight and escape the whole time.

It didn't seem possible for wifeing to be something nice since those women and even some men fought so hard to stop it. The way some of the slaves screamed, Althea expected it to hurt a great deal and couldn't imagine someone *wanting* to do it. However, since living in Querq, she'd stumbled on at least three couples doing the deed without any screaming. She told Karina seeing them 'gave her a confuse.'

Karina explained the stuff about where babies came from. It explained both why people here did 'wifeing' and liked it and added another reason to why the women taken by raiders fought so hard: they didn't want to have a baby and watch the raiders enslave or harm the child. Prior to the conversation with her sister, she'd assumed babies spontaneously happened as soon as a woman wanted a kid.

Her week had been nice, aside from a few meetings with Officer David and some others in their special building—a giant metal box known as a drop pod the city police had flown in soon after deciding to 'support' Querq, basically a big box on spring legs. She thought it looked like an enormous version of the containers the 'cheeseburger' things came in from the big city. They kept it super cold inside. Officer David called it 'air conditioning.' She called it annoying.

As far as the city police went, she trusted Officer David as well as Kate, another Awakened psionic who could make fire. The others, not so much. While they told her corporations would steal her because they thought she could make money for them, the people in charge of the city police had become fascinated by her powers and also wanted to study her. Their motivation appeared to be a mixture of curiosity and a general interest in learning, so she accepted dealing with them whenever necessary. A few times, they asked her to fly back to the big city and visit fancy places. She didn't enjoy doing so, but caved in. Mostly, they asked her to sit in chairs and tolerate having small items stuck to her, lay on tables and have machines 'scan' her, and sometimes, they asked her to use her abilities. She disliked those tests the most, since it almost always involved a person deliberately harming themselves so she could fix it.

Father thought she put up with the police's requests in much the same way as how she used to allow people to kidnap her, because she could still help people. Althea accepted the poking and prodding of Division Zero—the city police—in exchange for the help they gave Querq. Having a genuine home, a place she truly felt safe and welcome, made her willing to do whatever she could to keep it safe. Unlike the raiders, Division Zero wouldn't *force* her to do anything. She could say no, but chose not to. They did, after all, help everyone living here. Apparently, as 'police,' people in the city *had* to do what they told them to. She figured they served as the Watch for the big city, another reason she generally did as they asked. It felt wrong to disobey them. Also, according to David, they still technically had authority out here, even if they didn't enforce it often.

Den impressed the people in charge of Querq by surviving a walk of several hundred miles to find Althea, most of the reason they'd let him join the Watch so young. Dr. Ruiz estimated he could be fourteen or fifteen. Den didn't know for sure. He already started to look more like a man than a boy in some ways, except when standing near actual adults. Generally, someone had to be sixteen or older to join the Watch, except in times of crisis such as a raider attack. They made an exception for him since he wanted to help in some way but had no skills other than hunting, tracking, and survival. He'd been one of the best Seekers of the tribe, braving the ruins of the Lost Place over and over again. Despite never having touched a functional rifle before arriving in Querq, he'd become rather good at shooting it in a short amount of time. Thankfully, as yet, he'd only shot practice targets and the occasional dust hopper for hunting.

Althea wondered what became of the tribe after he left. Had Braga, his father, realized he'd made a mistake commanding Den to take Yala as wife? She hoped the girl hadn't been punished too harshly for betraying her to raiders, hoping to eliminate her as a rival. If they found out, the rest of the tribe would certainly blame Yala for The Prophet no longer being there.

Wonder about the old tribe swirled around in her head like the dust she swept off the porch. She paused, squinting at the distant sunlit horizon. A light breeze washed over the porch, offering a welcome, if temporary, reprieve from the hot, painted wood under her feet. Intermittent voices echoed from random directions. Querq seemed quiet, peaceful. She had the house to herself at present. Karina worked on the farm for most of the daylight hours. Father would be with the Watch somewhere.

She soon stopped thinking about anything more than the repetitive swoosh of bristles over the porch. Sweeping the dirt away seemed as pointless as trying to make The Many leave the Badlands alone. No matter how much she cleaned, more dirt always came back. Having chores to do further made her feel like a real person, so she never complained about them. Kim constantly grumbled about her new parents making her do stuff like sweep, prepare food, and do laundry. The girl especially hated washing clothes. She thought perching on the rocks by the river's edge 'stupid and primitive' and couldn't wait for 'machines' to arrive.

Once Althea finished her chores, she sat on the porch steps and watched people. Not long after she set the broom down, Den emerged from a gap between two buildings at the end of the block. His hopeful expression turned into a full-on smile when he spotted her. He still looked a bit weird wearing modern clothing, things the adults called 'pants and a T-shirt.' It impressed her he had the ability to accept a gift of clothing from the town. Among scrags, giving someone items found from scavenging amounted to calling them unable to fend for themselves—or courting them. When he'd given her the chest cloth, he'd basically asked her to be his girlfriend. Seekers provided for their mates if their mates couldn't or chose not to explore the

Lost Place. Strangely, Den never complained about feeling less than a man for accepting the garments. Maybe because the Watch considered it a uniform, or perhaps because he understood the rules of Querq society didn't match the rules of the tribe. For a boy who once considered a crowbar a 'magic opener,' he'd certainly adjusted to city technology quite fast.

People here, after all, weren't scrags. They understood some technology, didn't worship random artifacts from the past, and generally wore clothing as a matter of politeness rather than need or social status. Most of the citizens even welcomed the help from the city police and loved having electricity. As much as she feared the approach of modern society turning Querq into as dark a place as West City emotionally, she couldn't deny some things made life much easier... such as instant hot water without having to make a fire.

Althea stood and rushed over, meeting him in the middle of the street. Since she'd frequently observed Corinne and other women greeting their husbands and boyfriends in the same way, she leaned up and touched lips with him. Karina called it 'kissing.' Den gave off a surge of loving emotion. Alas, he still harbored a nagging sense of shame over not being much of a protector.

A few months earlier, The Many influenced an Awakened psionic named Mamoru, tricking him into thinking she was evil and sending him to kill her. He nearly succeeded. The man's psionic abilities made him far stronger and faster than people should be. Even the greatest warrior of the Badlands would've struggled to survive a fight with him. That he almost killed Den in mere seconds should not be a point of shame. Between failing to stop Mamoru and watching Althea use her powers to protect herself, the boy fell into a state of sadness, feeling useless.

She tried to make him understand she didn't care if he could protect her or not; she loved being with him.

At least, he no longer appeared consumed by shame and started to act normal again.

"Hey. Are you busy?" asked Den once they stopped kissing.

"No. I'm finished what I have to do."

He smiled. "I'm on a rest day. Want to walk by the river?"

"Yes." She smiled and took his hand.

His excited nervousness and love fed into hers, leaving her on the verge of giggling the whole time they walked across town to the gate. People they passed waved in greeting. Since the city police brought an electric machine capable of opening and closing the gate much faster than men pulling on a chain could move it, the Watch generally left it open. If danger appeared in the distance, the gate would close in roughly fifteen seconds, forcing any raiders intent on attacking Querq to climb a fourteen-foot-high wall of concrete and metal. Also, the Watch standing on top of said wall with city rifles would have something to say about anyone trying to climb it.

Officer David said life out here reminded him of Earth's ancient history, when kingdoms existed and people lived in fortified towns surrounded by walls. It seemed true what he said about human nature leading to violence, but at least large settlements didn't attack each other for land and conquest anymore. Hostilities didn't come from neighboring towns. People trying to be civilized merely needed to worry about opportunistic raiders. A place as well-defended as Querq proved unappealing to even try attacking. The city police also gave the Watch modern weapons, armored vests, and training. Any firearms in the hands of raiders would be as ancient as the Corporate War, or crude devices made from pipes. Raider weapons couldn't penetrate modern armor, and raider armor did no good against the city guns.

Thankfully, there hadn't been too many attacks since. The one significant assault ended in a matter of seconds with over thirty raiders dead and a mere handful running like hell. She hated the endless violence and death, but hoped the survivors would spread stories and scare other raiders away from attacking Querq.

Warm dirt underfoot gave way to hot, dusty metal plating as she followed Den into the short tunnel through the ten-foot-thick wall. They passed under the elevated walkway upon which members of the Watch stood guard on their way out into the Old City. Albuquerque had been many, many times bigger than Querq, though the old war reduced it to a vast swath of ruined buildings and rubble.

Creatures and other dangers existed outside the walls, though they tended to avoid the area right by the gate. Also, Althea's presence here somehow diminished the influence of The Many on the surrounding land. Fewer and fewer bonedogs, giant millipedes, and other mutated creatures hid among the shadows of former Albuquerque. She felt as though she'd made something of a deal with him. He left Querq alone and she wouldn't run around the Badlands trying to destroy him.

Of course, she never wanted to *destroy* him, merely help him—but to him, help equaled destruction. He—or they—loved being angry and wanted revenge… even though no people left alive now had anything to do with the war. He'd become jealous of the living, especially if they knew happiness.

Den and Althea meandered down a crumbling street, past buildings ravaged by three centuries of abandonment, weather, and warfare. The electronic devices Father made her use to do 'school stuff' contained various classes, some of which included history. Althea cried her way through the lessons about where the Badlands came from. Centuries ago, private corporations and public government got into a literal war over money called tax. The corporations, having established private security forces, refused to pay taxes, declaring themselves independent of government. People started shooting at each other. Horrible weapons including nuclear bombs, chemical agents, robots, mutated soldiers, and mutated animals rampaged up and down the continent, functionally destroying a vast swath of land in the center of what had once been called North America. Most of the surviving people fled to the coasts, eventually forming two massive cities. The corporations who started the war largely left the area, chased away by government forces. They'd collected in a place called Mexico to the south as well as parts of Europe. Some of the Division Zero people told her East City had a 'worse attitude' than West, which they referred to as 'laid back.' Althea had no desire to ever see East City.

"Palik and the others couldn't imagine this." Den gestured at the ruins. "It's just like the Lost Place."

"There are many lost places." Althea bowed her head out of respect for those who died.

"Yes. I understand. My tribe was small. We did not travel far. Before I left, my world was small, too. I went to the big city."

Althea gasped, staring up at him. "You did?"

"Yes. I wanted to see it. Asked one of the police. They brought me there, to a place they called a hospital. Gave me some medicines so I don't get sick."

She squeezed his hand. "I won't let you get sick."

"They don't understand that." He grinned. "Their world is so much different. The police told me they try to 'rescue' scrags and bring us back to civilization if they find us."

"Because." Althea frowned. "They think it's wrong to be simple. I don't know why they want to make everyone have technology. It's so loud. And mean. And stuff everywhere. Blinking lights."

He nodded, though his emotions revealed he found it fascinating.

"You liked it," she whispered.

"Yeah. But I don't have your gift. Being near sad people doesn't make me sad."

They turned left at a street corner, stepping around the wreckage of a military machine with a huge pipe sticking out of it. She suspected it had been some manner of killing device, but after rotting here for centuries, it couldn't hurt anyone ever again.

"Do you want to go there?" Althea traced a line in the dirt with her big toe. "To the big city?"

"I've daydreamed about what I could learn there, what I could see. Other planets even." He exhaled. "But I could end up being shot dead in an alley."

"What's an alley?"

"A small street no one uses." Den crouched and drew some boxes and lines in the dirt, none of which made much sense to her. "Like a space between the big huts where they put trash boxes."

She nodded once. "Oh. What's a trash box?"

"A box they put trash in."

Althea stuck out her tongue at him. "Silly."

"They're real. Giant metal boxes."

She peeked into his thoughts at a memory of a conversation with a female Division Zero officer who took him on a tour of the city. They stood on a corner near an alley about to get 'Chinese food' from a store. Den spotted the trash boxes and asked what they were. Althea remembered seeing them while stuck in the city. "Oh, those things."

A few minutes of walking in no great hurry brought them to the edge of the ruined city. A few hundred feet of relatively open ground stood between them and the river. Thanks to her electronic school, she knew people once called it the Rio Grande. Or at least, this river branched off from the one named that. Maps hadn't been updated in a long time. No one in the modern city really cared about the Badlands anymore.

A giant bomb landed here centuries ago, forming the place they all went swimming: Coronado Pond. It didn't exist before the war, so no maps showed it. Althea had mixed feelings about it. The weapon of death had been so massive it made a hole in the ground almost a quarter mile across. However, it resulted in the formation of a lake-slash-pond beneficial to the area. She didn't understand the difference since people named it Coronado Pond but referred to it as 'the lake'. True, it took centuries to form after the blast, but now it teemed with life and provided a place to swim and have fun. Even Dr. Ruiz considered the fish brought from the lake to be safe as food.

The only problem came from various denizens of the Badlands coming to the pond for water and hunting. It tended to attract bears and mountain lions along with canid mutants, thus the rule about having an armed escort for larger groups. An individual adult they trusted to be able to recognize and avoid danger. A group of children, not so much. Althea found it somewhat amusing how children from the Transit Tribe—including Paama—could show so little fear in the face of killer robots, but the sight of a big bear made them scream and run.

They stopped walking at a nice spot not far from the shore. Den sat on the ground, resting his rifle beside him on a chunk of concrete to keep it out of the dirt. His 'city rifle' looked like a magic object, so clean... boxy, and totally unlike any gun belonging out here.

Althea sat next to him and gazed up at the clear, blue sky. The day promised to be nice.

He continued telling her about his visit to the city. She got the feeling he'd become fascinated by it and wanted to learn more about the modern world. Den appeared to reject the primitivism of his home tribe, perhaps out of spite for the way they treated him, and developed a curiosity for what the 'real world' could show him. He also seemed frightened by it. Lots of people in the city carried guns. Almost everyone, in fact, even some children. Officer David blamed it on uncontrolled gang violence. The police could only do so much. People wanted guns to protect themselves against other people with guns, and the government didn't really care if gang members ended up shooting each other or being shot by citizens.

Althea nearly threw up from the sickening thought of a society where murder became a 'necessary means of preserving order.'

She gazed off at the heat blur dancing over the scrubland around Coronado Pond. A group of about twenty a third the way around the shore from where Den stopped, mostly younger kids, swam and played in the water. Three adults, one part of the Watch, kept tabs on them. This spot afforded Den and Althea a little privacy to have time together. If Den decided to go to the big city for a while, she'd be sad. She wouldn't ask him not to go. He deserved to be happy. His fear of the overwhelming nature of the place plus the rampant violence might be enough to convince him not to bother. Seeing other planets or fancy technology might be fun, but she didn't need any of it. Happiness didn't come from technology, or pay-things, or fancy stuff. It came from a place no person could put a price on or explain. The same way Althea could never be happy in West City, some people could never be happy in Querq, or the Badlands.

"I dunno. It's like we've been eating sandroot our entire life and not knowing about boar meat." Den chuckled. "But what if the meat's got poison in it?"

Althea spent a moment fixated on a tilting shattered skyscraper on the far side of the river, lost in a non-thought. A steady, soft whisper came from a far-away breeze swirling among the dead buildings. Sunlight made the beige monolith practically glow, except for the dark vacuous holes of former windows. As with most places in the Old City beyond Querq, the building itself gave off a sense of presence, as if it looked right back at her. Occasionally, a shadow in one of the windows would shift, either the wind moving an old piece of office furniture or something alive creeping around.

With a sigh, she looked away from the distant ruins, making eye contact. "I want you to have the happy. I mean…" She sighed. "I want, umm. I want you to be happy. If you want to go live in the big city and learn the fancy stuff, do it if it will make you happy."

"Do you want me to go?" He brushed his fingers over her cheek, staring into her eyes.

"I want you to be happy. If it means you must go, then I will feel bad for stopping you from hav — being happy."

"You're talking strange."

"Stupid learnings." She sighed. "I got the speaking wrong. I'm s'posed to speak different. I have the stupid."

"You don't."

"I mean." She clenched her fists and snarled playfully. "Did it again. It's *am* stupid or am being stupid. Can't have a stupid. The stupid tablet said so."

"You're getting angry."

"Frustrated." She folded her arms. "I don't care if people think I'm a dust flea."

"What's a dust flea?"

She rolled her eyes. "Something asshole called me."

"Huh? Your butt speaks?"

She stared at him. "What?"

"That word you just said. It means butt."

"Oh. Well. Archon was a butt." She sighed out her nose. "He called me something mean. I don't know what a dust flea is, but he called me one because I didn't want to live in his big fancy city."

Den laughed. "Okay. I will stay here."

"I will feel bad if you aren't happy."

"Maybe I'll visit the big city, but I will *live* here. You can't go there because it hurts you in here." He placed a hand over her heart. "I couldn't ask you to live there. Querq needs you too much, anyway. The city people have fancy machines to do medicine. And you'll be sad if I go."

She leaned against him. True, she would be sad if he left. She'd also be sad if she kept him from chasing his dream. "It's shiny, but I don't think it is better. If you go and you learn stuff and get one of those job things, then you will complain all the time about how much you hate the job and how annoying it is. Will you really be happier?"

"How do you know this?"

"The city police ask me to visit many times. When I am there, I sometimes look at what people think. Most of the city police are happy with their job things, but everyone else hates having a job thing. They don't like them at all, but have no choice. Like slaves forced to work. If they don't do the job thing, they will die." She scowled. "I do not understand how the job thing makes food. The people do not work at farms. They sit and push buttons."

Den scrunched up his face, equally as confused.

"Officer David talks about the city all the time. Some of them think it's bad to let me grow up out here, like I'm being deprivated or something."

"Deprivated?"

Althea furrowed her brows. "Umm. New speaking stuff." She mulled, trying to remember the word. "Umm. Deprived?"

"What's that mean?"

"They think people *have* to learn all stuff about technology and go live there. I am happy here." She stretched her arms out to either side, leaning against him, grinning.

Den wrapped her in a hug, resting his chin on her shoulder and holding her close. She closed her eyes, sensing the beat of his heart against her back. In seconds, her heart matched pace with his, not that he noticed. Unlike all the frenetic people in the big city, she could spend hours sitting there beside the lake in his arms doing nothing more than enjoying life and be happy. She didn't need constant flashing lights or distraction.

He told her about his trip into the city. She remembered some things, like the little machines flying everywhere and the dangerous cars zooming by depending on what color the floating lights turned. As they talked, she continued to ponder his being a boyfriend or an ordinary friend. He definitely seemed to be more than an ordinary friend. She had no desire to lean against any other boy like this. Still, her feelings toward him didn't quite match those of, say, Corinne and her husband. Again, she blamed age—and decided to stop worrying about it. As Father often said, 'give it time.' She eventually stopped eating enchiladas with her hands. So, too, would she eventually understand the nature of her feelings about Den. No sense worrying about it.

Karina told her people generally don't kiss 'ordinary friends.' Althea not minding the lip touching with Den had to mean something. She wouldn't do it with Kim, Paama, or Esmerelda. She also wouldn't do it with Santiago, Diego, or Pedro. Exploring the ruins with them could be fun, though they had a bad habit of getting hurt while wandering the Old City. Even after a giant millipede almost ate them, they continued sneaking out whenever they couldn't get an adult to go with them, despite it being against the rules.

The idea of doing something fun made her want to get into a splash war with Den.

She stood and pulled her dress off over her head.

A strong sense of nervousness emanated from him, as if he'd seen a giant mauler—a cybernetically weaponized bear—sneaking up behind her.

Althea dropped the dress on the ground by her feet and gave him a quizzical look. "Is something dangerous here?"

"Uhh…" He kept staring at her.

"What?"

He blinked. "Why did you take your dress off?"

*Boys are weird.* "You want to go swimming?"

His nervousness evaporated in an instant. "Oh! Yeah."

He scrambled out of his clothes, took her hand, and ran with her to the pond.

Giggling, Althea dove in.

## 3

## ROUND ROCKS AND WOODEN PEGS

While helping Karina cook dinner that night, Althea talked about Den.

"He probably wanted you to talk him out of going to the big city." Karina handed her a spoon to stir the pot.

Althea took it and stuck it into the stew. "Why would he do that?"

"Boys never say what they really mean. He saw something shiny and thinks he wants it, but knows he doesn't. He also knows he can't have it and stay with you."

Althea glanced over at her. "So he couldn't decide?"

"Nah." Karina chuckled. "He decided already. The boy's still here, right? He's talking about it so you know he chose you over the city."

"Should I feel bad?"

"Did he seem sad?"

"No. Not at all."

"Then don't." Karina patted her on the head. "You got all this power. Use it and stop worrying. He's more boyfriend than not, but you should take it slow until you're older."

Althea had no idea what 'it' she should take slow, but assumed her sister meant wifeing. If so, Karina had nothing to worry about. "I will. If you're afraid he's going to wife me, I don't wanna do that. Eww."

Karina laughed.

Althea blushed. "What?"

"Oh, Thea." Karina hugged her. "One day, probably not too long from now, you're going to wake up and boys are going to stop being 'eww' and start being something else."

"Boys aren't 'eww.' Wifeing is 'eww.'"

Karina winked. "That's what I mean."

"Ugh. You aren't making any sense." Althea sighed.

"Give it time."

She glanced at the far corner of the kitchen. "What's that?"

When Karina looked, she snuck a piece of chicken out of the pot and ate it. Her sister continued staring at the obviously empty corner, certainly aware of what went on. Both of them ended up laughing.

THE NEXT DAY, ALTHEA STRETCHED OUT ON THE SOFA IN the living room working on an e-learn module.

She still disliked having to talk to a machine instead of a real person teaching her. At least this one didn't sound so insulting. It attempted to teach her more difficult information than the other devices; however, the AI voice no longer spoke as if trying to talk to a four-year-old. This made it easier to tolerate, except for times it scolded her for not speaking properly. Even if it made her do math or history stuff, if she said something it didn't like, it would switch and start teaching her speaking stuff.

It particularly disliked her saying 'I have the stupid.'

Althea now understood the lessons came in steps called grades. Despite being eleven when they made her start working on them, she'd been doing lessons intended for kids half her age, mostly about speaking stuff, writing, and reading, along with basic math. The material in her hands at the moment equated to sixth grade, roughly about where a kid her age ought to be according to the city police. Despite thinking it pointless, she tolerated it because it made Father happy and out of hope she might soon be allowed to go to the actual school with real kids.

Officer David told her children in the big city don't go to schools for real. Everyone sits at home and puts on a special helmet so they dream about being in a room with other kids. Still, it *felt* like they got to be with other people. In Querq, they had a real school but didn't teach much beyond the basics, far less than what the kids in the modern world had to learn. The arrival of people from the big city trying to 'modernize' Querq also affected the school. Althea suspected they wanted to find any 'smart' people and try to trick them into going to the big city… but perhaps some people deserved to do so. No one who would be truly content here would leave.

A rapid, but soft knock came from the front door.

Happy for a chance to take a break from the tedious lessons, Althea said, "Pause" and set the datapad down before rushing to answer.

Diego, Santiago, and Pedro stood on the porch grinning at her. Their jeans, multicolored T-shirts, and sneakers looked battle weary from all the roaming they did in the ruins. The three fourteen-year-olds gave off a sense of mischief and eagerness. While all the same age, they didn't exactly look it. Santiago had a few inches of height over his friends. Due to his waist-long hair and slender build, some people mistook him for a girl from behind. Diego, the shortest and smartest, looked a few years younger than his actual age, and often got teased for it. He tended to be the most cautious of the trio when it came to doing dangerous things. Pedro wound up in the middle height wise, seemed average for smarts, and also on the strong side. When the three of them got together, something crazy often happened… a problem since the boys spent as much time as possible hanging out.

"We wanna go to the Old City," said Santiago.

"Watch is busy." Pedro frowned.

"You could go with us." Diego tried to take advantage of his childlike appearance via pleading stare.

Althea fidgeted, annoyed at herself for being so tempted to go with them despite it being a bending of rules. The Ravens relaxed their order about going outside the wall due to dangerous creatures apparently retreating from the area around Querq… however, they still required at least a single armed adult to be part of any group wandering the ruins. Althea did not count as an adult, nor would she carry a weapon. However, her psionic abilities fulfilled the spirit of the requirement for protection if not the letter.

She looked at the boys, torn between temptation and duty to finish her schoolwork… until an inexplicable sense of worry came out of nowhere. Strange moods manifested often enough for her to recognize as a clairvoyant warning. The time she spent working with Division Zero's people to understand her psionic abilities also helped her interpret and recognize a message from her abilities as opposed to random normal moods — mostly.

"Something dangerous is going to happen," said Althea.

"If I say we shouldn't go today, I know you three will sneak out there anyway and get hurt. So, okay."

The boys cheered.

"It can't be too dangerous." Diego scratched at his hair. "Otherwise, you'd be demanding we stay here."

She sighed and walked out, pulling the door closed behind her. "You really ought to. I don't know *how* dangerous it is… only that something bad is probably going to happen if I don't go with you."

They walked in a group down the street, the boys talking about random subjects like new food the city people brought here, primarily stuff they referred to as 'snacks.' Little cakes, chips, and so forth. Food meant to be eaten at no particular time straight out of whatever container it came in, no cooking needed. It sounded odd, but couldn't be any worse than eating grubs, worms, or the slop some of the raiders who kidnapped her used to feed her. She doubted it would be as good as the meat and vegetables from the farm, though. But these 'snacks' didn't seem meant to replace meals, merely lessen hunger between them.

The Watch people at the gate gave the boys suspicious looks, as they had a reputation for sneaking out and getting into trouble, though didn't bother to stop them, likely due to Althea being with them. She stood a little taller, keeping her attention on their surroundings. The boys might be older than her by two years, but she definitely felt like their caretaker. She also had more experience surviving in the wild, thanks to a few months she'd spent living with a kindly man when she'd been around eight. He'd taught her about survival, and likely intended to look after her until she grew up… only he died trying to protect her from raiders.

Althea sighed, momentarily overcome with guilt. If she hadn't been such a chicken, she could have protected him.

Alas, she couldn't do anything to change the past, and maybe her powers lacked the strength to do what she could now back then.

Pedro led the way, going northeast from the gate. Althea hadn't spent much time looking at maps, but generally knew Querq occupied a relatively small area compared to the size Albuquerque had been a few decades over 300 years ago. The Old City extended as a network of interlocking streets, crumbling ruins, and towering steel remnants of former high-rises for several miles in all directions. Most useful stuff had undoubtedly been scavenged by the original settlers already, but the boys found endless hours of fun exploring the old world. Althea learned from the datapad AI the Corporate War started in the year 2092. Her schoolwork didn't mention Albuquerque specifically, so she had no idea when, exactly, it had been destroyed. However, considering the current year was 2419, it didn't make too much difference if the war hit this area right away or ten years after it started.

A central area of massive high-rise buildings stood a little over a mile northeast of Querq's wall, many of the old towers reduced to skeletal frames. Some still had pieces of artificial beige stone cladding or other decorative siding. The fake rocks routinely broke off in chunks and fell to the ground, responsible for almost constant random *cracks* echoing over the area every so often. A fair number of high-rises had already collapsed. The rest could fall at any moment. For obvious reasons, people weren't supposed to go there. Elevated tramrail tracks looped around much of the Old City, some even passing through taller buildings. The boys no longer believed giant worms crawled on them after they found one of the old trains lying on its side at ground level, partially smashed from falling twenty feet.

On a whim, the boys decided to climb a crumbled heap

of former building up to the tram path and walk on it. Being two stories up on an ancient concrete ribbon didn't seem like the safest idea. However, she didn't get a bad feeling, and the elevation offered some protection against bonedogs or other vermin, so she followed them without protest, scaling the mountain of concrete rocks easily.

The tramway had a mostly flat surface except for a pair of grooves near each edge and a raised center spine of metal blocks, many of which had gone missing, exposing wiring underneath. Powdery beige sand coated everything, gathering in the grooves and wisping around whenever the wind picked up. The boys walked on the open flat space between a groove and the middle, an area roughly three feet across. Pedro kicked the occasional concrete chip off the side as they followed the tram route into eastern Old City.

The boys wondered aloud how fast the old machine used to move, primarily to determine if it would have been dangerous to walk on this track years ago.

"I think so," said Althea.

All three looked back at her.

"When they took me to the big city, I saw cars. They went even faster than raider buggies. If a car hit someone, they'd probably die. The machine that used to drive on this sky road probably went as fast as a car."

"It would also be bigger," said Diego. "It carried a lot of people at once."

"So?" asked Santiago. "Big things are slow."

"Maybe, but they also have more power." Diego pointed at Althea. "What would hurt more? Althea running as fast as she could and crashing into you... or Tito doing it?"

Santiago and Pedro cringed.

"Definitely Tito." Pedro whistled.

"Nah. Althea running into us would hurt more." Santiago laughed. "Tito can't run."

The other two laughed.

"I'm not going to hit anyone," said Althea. "And it's not nice to make fun of Tito. Someone tricked him."

The boys stopped walking to look at her in confusion.

"Tricked him?" asked Diego.

"Yes." She nodded. "They plugged the hose into his belly and blew him up."

The boys laughed so hard they almost fell off the tramway.

Althea glowered at them. "What?"

"Wow, Thea." Santiago gasped for air. "Someone's messing with you."

"Yeah. No one blew Tito up with air. He's just fat." Diego wiped tears from his eyes. "He eats too much food."

"Fat..." Althea furrowed her brows.

Pedro stood back up. "Yeah. You've never seen a fat kid before?"

She shook her head. "No. What's fat?"

"Tito," said all three boys at the same time.

"Is it a sick?" Hope she might be able to fix him widened her eyes.

They shrugged.

"He don't seem bothered by it." Diego resumed walking.

"It's not right he takes so much food." Pedro punted another hunk of concrete off the tramway.

"He doesn't." Santiago jumped the center ridge to walk on the other flat spot. "He eats the same as anyone else. Some people are just fat."

"How can you never see a fat person?" asked Diego.

"I dunno." Althea rambled on about raider groups and marauders she'd been forced to live with most of her life. Only a handful attempted to farm or grow food, often at the behest of slave labor. Most relied on stealing food and supplies from settlements, so they tended not to have much. Also, if fat people—as the boys implied—were slow and couldn't run, they wouldn't live long as raiders.

When they reached a spot where a huge collapsed light pole had fallen to lean on the tramway, the boys walked down it to street level. Althea held her arms out for balance and followed, biting her lip at the heat of the metal under her feet. Once she reached the ground, she paused to make sure she hadn't burned herself. Pedro darted across the road, bee-lining for a doorway into a huge, wide building only one story tall.

"Oh, yeah, this place is fun." Santiago waved for Althea to catch up, then raced after Pedro.

Althea followed cautiously, looking around to make sure nothing dangerous approached. Once she felt confident no creatures, raiders, or other threats spotted them, she entered the building.

Rotting brown carpet crumbled to dust wherever her feet touched. To the left, a big glass window bore the words 'pro shop,' like the front of a store despite being inside another building. On the right, a large area contained numerous strange cabinets decorated in multiple colors. Most of them had buttons and little control sticks. Some had steering wheels. They appeared to be machines in need of the 'lectric to work, but this place had none. In front of her, the wide foyer opened to a vast room where multiple clusters of white plastic chairs and tables stood in a line from left to right. Beyond them, the cavernous room contained long paths made of wood, like a bunch of corridors without walls. Each one ended at a dark opening only about as high up as her waist.

She crept forward over the crumbling rug. Once out of the foyer, she peered left down the concourse at a counter like the one from Tumbleweed's bar. The word 'beer' hung on the wall above it in giant white letters. Past it, another bar-like counter bore the label 'shoe rental.' Large drinking glasses lay scattered all over near the two bars.

At the nearer end of one of the bizarre wooden paths, Pedro and Santiago examined a strange shelf containing multiple rounded stones. Diego walked along the wooden pathway to the hole at the far wall. Without hesitation, he got down on his hands and knees and crawled into the dark space. Confused, she padded over to the boys, gazing around at the twenty or so such tracks. Some of the holes at the ends contained a scattering of objects resembling fat bottles.

"What is this place?" whispered Althea.

"Fun." Santiago held up one of the round stones. "All the stuff that needed magic doesn't work anymore... but this doesn't need magic."

"It's not magic," yelled Diego from the end of the lane. "It's 'lectricity like we have now."

She shrugged and sat in a nearby plastic chair.

Diego arranged a bunch of the white bottles in a triangle formation in the hollow at the end of the path. Once he'd set them up and moved out of the way, Santiago rolled the stone ball down the lane into the bottles, knocking some over. Diego sent the stone back to them and stood the bottles up again. As soon as Diego got out of the way, Pedro rolled the stone, knocking over two more than Santiago had.

"Hah! I win." Pedro made finger guns at him.

"Not yet you didn't," shouted Diego. "My turn."

The smallest boy put all the bottles back up, jogged down the lane, and rolled the ball. He knocked over some of the white bottles, but not as many as Pedro.

"Okay, fine." Diego playfully punched Santiago in the arm. "You win the first match."

Althea contented herself to stand there watching the boys roll the stone again and again. Diego apparently did all the crawling into the hole due to his smaller size. He didn't appear to mind the extra work, finding the game of rolling the ball fun. Whoever knocked down the most bottles won each round. After the ninth time the boys repeated the process, she sighed.

They looked at her.

"Why do you bother putting them back up just to knock them over again?"

"It's the game," said Santiago. "Balling."

"This is a balling alley." Pedro nodded. "It's what people used to do here. Roll the balls and knock the pins over."

"Those aren't pins. They're bottles." Althea folded her arms.

"Not bottles. They're made of wood or something." Diego jogged down the lane to stand the pins back up yet again. "It's a game. See how many we can knock down."

Althea swished her feet back and forth. "It looks annoying to have to keep putting them back up."

"When they had the 'lectric," said Pedro, "a machine did it. There's a big metal thing with all these holes above them. We think it used to somehow pick them up."

"It's fun." Santiago smiled.

Again, Althea shrugged. "If you say so."

Santiago walked over and offered her the ball. "Here. You try it."

Althea took the ball in both hands. Unprepared for its weight, she almost fell to her knees in her effort not to drop it on her foot. "Oof... it's heavy! This isn't a ball, it's a stone."

"Stones aren't this round." Pedro patted it. "They call them balling balls."

She examined it, noting three holes in a triangular formation. "What are the holes for?"

"Makes it roll better," said Santiago.

"I think the holes are for weight," called Diego from the end of the lane. "They drilled out some stuff to make it weigh a little less. Or maybe it makes it spin."

*This is way too heavy.* Althea concentrated on sending extra blood into her arm and leg muscles, making herself stronger. The balling ball still felt ponderous, but she no longer struggled to hold it up.

"Okay, you can't step past this line here." Pedro tapped his foot on the floor. "If you go past it, the score doesn't count. Also, you gotta *roll* the ball. No throwing."

She padded over to the line, careful to keep her toes from crossing it. "Okay. So, I just roll it down and try to hit the bottles? Umm, pins?"

The boys nodded at her.

Althea turned somewhat sideways, struggling to hold the ball up in both hands. It took her a moment of test swinging to get a feel for a good way to send the heavy thing down the lane without dropping it. As soon as she thought she had a reasonable enough form, she took two steps back, then charged forward, swinging the ball so it made contact with the floor before she let go of it, hurling it as hard as she could. Throw-shoving such a heavy, ponderous object caused her to fly off her feet and land on her chest.

The heavy stone rocketed down the lane and shaved a little over half the pins off the left side of the formation, leaving four standing.

"She went over the line," said Pedro. "Doesn't count."

"*After* she let go of the ball. It's fine." Santiago shook his head. "Also, her feet didn't go over the line. Rule says *feet* can't go over the line."

"Wow." Diego whistled. "You're pretty strong for a little girl."

Althea pushed herself upright and shrugged. *Okay, it's a lot more fun to play than watch.* "How did I do?"

"You got six." Diego jogged down the lane, crawled into the space at the end, then shoved the ball back toward them before setting the pins back up.

They continued playing for a while. Hurling such a cumbersome, heavy object made balance tricky, but she figured it out on her fourth try. From then on, she no longer fell over when letting go.

Althea stood behind Pedro, biting her lip and hoping he didn't beat her last throw of eight. She'd knocked down all but the two outermost pins at the back of the triangle. Santiago got lucky the past two rounds and managed to get all ten twice in a row, but this round he only hit three.

Pedro sent the ball down the lane.

Diego's scream came from the left.

She, Pedro, and Santiago all turned to look.

A cloud of dust bloomed into the air from behind the 'beer' bar.

"Diego?" shouted Althea.

The ball crashed into the pins.

"I'm okay," called the boy. "Fell through the floor."

"Damn." Pedro kicked the weird shelf holding the other balls. "Five. Althea won the round."

She hurried toward the dust cloud, unconcerned with points.

"Wait," shouted Diego. "No, I'm not okay. Help!"

Althea broke into a run. She zoomed down a carpeted path of chairs and tables, up three steps to a higher area by the bar, and promptly vaulted up onto it. She crouched, gripping the edge of the bar, and peered down a hole where most of the floor behind it had collapsed into the basement.

Diego stood atop the rubble of the former floor, surrounded by three soldier scorpions, the jet-black insects as big as dogs. Each one tried to jab their dagger-sized tail stings at him. The boy did his best to defend himself using a long wooden pole. Within a second of Althea taking in the situation, a scorpion nailed him in the back of the right thigh. Diego shrieked. Before the other two could sting him in the face and chest, Althea gave off a pulse of telempathic calm, directing it at the scorpions. The insects relaxed. Diego fell to his knees, whimpering, clutching the wound in his leg.

Pedro went behind the bar, approaching the hole in the floor, which creaked under his weight.

"Careful," whispered Santiago.

"I am careful." Pedro dropped down to hang off the broken floor, then let go, dropping to the basement. After taking a moment to look around, he pointed. "I see stairs. We're okay." He scooped Diego up and carried him out of view.

Althea continued concentrating on projecting calm over the scorpions until the boys emerged from a door a short distance to the left of the bar. With intruders no longer in the basement, the scorpions had no reason to be agitated... hopefully. They didn't show aggression when she stopped focusing on them. Regardless, Santiago propped a chair against the door in case the scorpions decided to come up the stairs.

Pedro set Diego on the bar next to Althea.

She shifted from crouching to kneeling, grabbed his hand, closed her eyes, and concentrated on his life shapes. Amid the black-and-red sense of his body floating in her mind, a sickly green seep spread outward from a narrow puncture wound. Soldier scorpions injected so much venom, and it spread so rapidly, she'd already lost the ability to simply purge it back out of the wound. She commanded his body to disregard pain, then concentrated on removing all the venom from his life shapes, concentrating it in his bladder. That done, she forced his body to mend the stinger wound.

Diego groaned. "Ow, that hurt."

Althea opened her eyes. "There is poison. You need to let it out."

He grabbed himself between the legs. "It burns."

"Yes. It will burn a little." She nodded. "You must let it out."

Diego scrambled to stand on the bar and proceeded to pee into the hole, gasping, squirming, and moaning the entire time.

Santiago and Pedro cringed in sympathetic pain.

Althea had rid herself of venom several times. Sure it burned, but hardly bad enough to warrant the show of misery coming from the boy. Sicks burned far worse than venom. It seemed mean to make fun of him or even ask why he let such a mild pain bother him so much, so she kept quiet. Then again, most of the raiders she cured of poison tended to moan the same way… perhaps it hurt boys more? Feeling guilty, she put a hand on his arm and turned off his ability to feel pain.

"Ahhh…" Diego relaxed and easily let the rest of the poison out. "Thanks."

She glanced back at the other two. "We really shouldn't be out here."

To her complete dismay, being stung hadn't done much to dissuade Diego from exploring. He still gave off a strong sense of curiosity and excitement.

"It's okay. You're too scared of stuff." Pedro waved for her to follow. "Why be alive if we can't have fun."

"I'm kinda bored with balling," said Santiago.

Diego pulled his pants back up. "At least we know what the danger was. So, we're safe now. Hey, let's show her the giant bird."

"Good idea." Santiago jogged toward the way out.

"Okay." Pedro reached up to help Althea down from the bar. "Let's do that."

"Giant bird?" Althea didn't need the help, but she also adored human contact, so jumped into his arms. "Is it going to try and bite us?"

Pedro set her on her feet, then hurried off after Santiago.

"Nah, it's not really a bird. C'mon, it's awesome." Diego waved for her to follow and rushed off.

## 4

## THE BIRD OF DEATH

Althea peered back at the building as they left to make sure the scorpions didn't try to ambush them.

A line of huge bullet holes tracked across the front wall, some bigger around than her arms. Only their shape and arrangement said 'bullet holes,' though she'd never seen any bullets capable of doing so much damage to a stone wall. It confused her as much as how the Before-Time people could make such perfectly block-shaped stones. After a moment and no scorpions appearing, she turned to face forward and followed the boys.

Strong late morning sunlight shone through the warped metal bones of the distant high-rise buildings and cast long, stretched shadows from the shorter structures around them. Every so often, an echoing *clack* announced another piece of some former tower falling to the ground. Once, since she'd been in Querq, an entire high-rise collapsed. It sounded like thunder and created a giant dust cloud over the Old City. No one knew if a person, animal, creature, or merely the wind had stressed the ancient construction past its breaking point.

She gazed around at the ruins, pausing momentarily to stare at anything colorful. A few bits and pieces of the former society still hinted at how it might have looked centuries ago. One small building still had an orange awning. A blue plastic... something stuck out of a pile of rubble. The streets around them held an uncountable number of small plastic bottles, cans, and bones—both human and animal. Nothing close to a whole skeleton remained, merely a scrap here or there. She didn't think these bones came from the big war, since it had been too long ago.

Santiago took the lead, walking fast like he knew exactly where to go.

All three boys brimmed with excitement. They certainly believed Althea would like whatever they wanted to show her. At the next corner, they had to climb a seven-foot-high mound of concrete chunks and dirt blocking the road. Upon reaching the top, she gazed down a long slope into a crater approximately twenty feet deep at the middle. An entire house could fit in the hole, and its roof would still only be as tall as the street. Fragments of old pipe jutted out of the dirt on either side like ragged, broken veins hanging from a ghastly wound. The path ahead appeared to be unobstructed. All three boys rushed ahead, either unconcerned or unaware of any danger. In the crater, the ground became much cooler thanks to the shade. Ordinary scorpions hid in the smaller bits of rubble inside the hole. A handful of snakes sunned themselves wherever they could. The boys had plenty of room to avoid the creatures, and did so.

Althea scaled the far side of the crater, walking a little more than halfway before needing to grab onto rocks and debris to climb. She beat the boys to the ridge at the top by a good twenty seconds and stood there grinning at them.

Pedro pulled himself up beside her. "How did you climb so fast?"

She raised her arms out to either side and let them flap against her body. "Still strong from the ball. I don't have a lot of weigh. Easy to climb. Sometimes, I'd try to hide from being taken and I climbed a lot."

Diego, surprisingly, finished the climb second, powered by fear of scorpions. A concrete hunk Santiago grabbed plucked loose, causing him to slide most of the way back down into the hole.

"Hide?" Pedro scrunched up his nose.

"You have the remembering of what I told you about raiders? How they used to always take me?"

He nodded, as did Diego.

"Sometimes, other raiders would attack and everyone would die. So, I'd be alone."

"You didn't help them?"

Althea bowed her head. "I wanted to, but if the thinking shape goes splat, I can't make the hurt go away."

They resumed walking. Althea rambled about times when raider groups fighting over her wiped each other out to the last person, leaving her alone, sometimes chained to a heavy object or locked in a cage where she couldn't reach anyone to help. Whenever she managed to escape, or at times they didn't tie her, she would leave in search of nice people who needed help. Though she'd try to avoid being spotted by raiders or mean people, she didn't often succeed for long. The longest she remembered being free had been the time she ran away from Zhar and the other former slaves when the women had gone to sleep... not long before Father and some of the Querq Watch found her. She'd been on her own for roughly a week as best she could remember.

Santiago stopped short at the end of the street, hiding against the corner of a thick, reinforced building made from dark grey magic stone. Father called it 'concrete,' but Althea thought of it as magic stone due to the way the ancient ones could shape it any way they wanted. The walls angled inward toward the top, making it look like the bottom two stories of a ten-story pyramid. A recess in the front formed an alcove around a pair of thick metal doors, which appeared to have suffered extensive damage from gunfire and explosions. Half-height walls at the front appeared to be defensive positions where people shot rifles from.

No sooner did Althea look at the structure than a sense of melancholy fell over her. Fighting happened here. People died. Awful, but she could do nothing for them. She closed her eyes, let the sorrow wash over her, and exhaled a long, slow breath out her nose. Since Santiago didn't give off any sense of caution or fear, she remained standing out in the open. The boy peered around the corner, his excitement growing.

"What are you hiding from?" she asked.

"It's there." He pointed. "Are you ready?"

She sighed. "I suppose."

"Halt," crackled a male voice.

The boys exchanged confused glances.

A spark leapt from a small metal panel on the fortress by the door.

"Who's talking?" asked Diego.

"This is a restricted"—buzzing came from the panel —"rest-restric—ted area. Authori-za-za-za-zation not detected. You have-ve-ve ten seconds to evacuate the area or lethal for-for-force will be used."

Two, much larger, square metal panels above the entrance opened. Robotic arms extended, bearing the

mangled remains of long-ago destroyed machinery. A strip
of bullets dangled from one, suggesting the broken junk had
once been some form of gun... probably one meant to fire
lots and lots of bullets quite fast.

"Are you smart or just a voice?" asked Althea.

"Five-ve-ve sec-c-c-c-onds," crackled the panel.

"It's stupid." She pointed at the broken guns. "Can't
hurt anyone."

"This is United Sta-tay-tay-taytes Government
property. You have ten sec-c-c-c-onds to comply."

Pedro tilted his head. "Didn't we already stand here for
ten seconds?"

"It's broken." Diego chuckled. "Maybe it knows it's
boom machines don't work, so it's still just talking."

"We should look inside." Santiago flashed a mischievous
grin.

Althea shook her head. "No. Aren't you listening? We
don't have an autha-mi-zation. We're not allowed in."

The boys broke into laughter.

"What?" She glowered. "Rules are important."

Santiago gestured at the building. "Those rules are older
than my grandma's grandma. The people who made them
are gone. You don't have to listen to old rules."

"Why not?" She ground her toe into the dirt.

"Because. They're old rules. It's just a busted-up
computer." Diego rolled his eyes.

Suspicious, Althea crossed her arms. "You don't listen to
new rules either."

"Non-compliance detected. Security notified," said the
panel.

Bursts of sparks erupted from both robot arms.

"I think it just tried to shoot us." Pedro pretended to be
afraid.

"Someone already busted in there and tore the place

up." Santiago pointed at the doors. "Forget it for now. The bird's right here."

"Okay." Diego nodded.

Santiago went around the corner of the fortress building. Pedro and Diego brimmed with excitement. They flanked Althea as if escorting her up to claim some great prize. She crept to the edge and peeked around at a street littered with debris. Old drive machines as well as the smashed remains of smaller devices like the flying machines all over the big city, the ones that kept trying to make people buy stuff. However, her attention went straight to a giant metal warbird sitting in the street about two hundred yards away.

She'd seen enough of the modern world to understand it had once been a flying machine, something the ancient people made in the Before-Time. It didn't look anything like the city police's 'hovercars.' It somewhat resembled a bird frozen with its wings stretched out to either side. A clear glass-like bubble near the front end covered a chair sunken in a hollow space. The machine appeared to have landed on wheels, but since collapsed. It didn't look to have suffered much damage from striking the ground, though the back end had been chewed up. A missing fin plus a few huge holes in the side told her it had likely been shot at.

"Come on!" Diego ran down the street toward it. "You can lift the front and sit inside, push buttons and stuff."

"Umm. It's okay." Althea leaned back. "I don't really want to."

"What's wrong?" asked Pedro.

"It's a war machine." She kicked at the dirt. "The ancient ones used it to kill people. I don't want to touch it. I'll see horrible things."

The boys stared at her for a moment.

"Okay." Santiago gave off a sense of apology. "Sorry. We thought you'd like it."

"It's okay. Most people probably would." She swiped at her hair, pulling it out of her eyes. "I get sad too easy."

Pedro jogged down the street toward it, as did Diego.

She reluctantly followed, not wanting to let them run off. Even if the Old City had become less dangerous, she didn't want to be too far away to help if the boys got into trouble.

When she came within a hundred feet of the old warbird, a sick feeling exploded in her stomach. For an instant, she felt as scared as if some raider raised an axe to smash open her head. The dread fear evaporated seconds later, fading to a creepy sense the old flying machine knew she looked at it.

"Stop!" yelled Althea. "Get away from it."

All three boys froze in their tracks, Santiago only a few steps ahead of her. Pedro paused a mere ten feet from the old machine, Diego about halfway between his friends.

"What's wrong?" asked Pedro.

"This machine killed many people who didn't deserve to die. Stay back. It wants to kill us."

Diego flailed his arms. "Aww, come on. It's a machine. A broken machine. It doesn't want to do anything."

"D, back up." Santiago beckoned his friends away from the old fly machine. "Althea isn't saying it's alive and wants to kill us. She's a shaman. It's how they feel things. Maybe it's got the 'lectric in it still and it can shock us. Remember what the city man said about touching the boxes?"

Pedro made a buzzing noise while pretending to be electrocuted.

Althea stared at the old flying machine. It slumped down on its nose, tilted to the left like a dying bird, far from threatening... yet it still gave off a palpable sense of malice like a raider playing dead, waiting to stab the first person to let their guard down and get close. Another presence felt as though it watched her from an alleyway off to the left. She looked, finding only debris and old trash boxes. Still, the spot felt as though someone stood there.

*A ghost?*

A moment after she focused on her desire to see spirits, a glowing man in a pale blue jumpsuit appeared standing in the alley. After a few seconds of looking transparent, his form solidified into—visually—a real person. Officer David didn't know much about the psionic ability he called 'Astral Sense,' other than it could allow her to see spirits. He'd said not many people had it. Division 0 only knew of four or five individuals between both big cities who had it. Aurora told her she had the 'soul of an angel' in a human body. Althea didn't understand what it meant, only that her mother worked as a scientist trying to make a machine so spaceships could go fast. Somehow, their machine went wrong and 'opened a gate' into another place for a split second. Energy rushed through into her pregnant mother… and gave Althea her powers.

Or so they said.

As soon as the spirit realized Althea looked directly at him, he rushed up to her. Numerous bullet holes riddled his chest. A patch on the left breast pocket had frozen speech: 'Cline.' Other patches on each shoulder said "Walmart."

"You can see me?" asked the ghost.

"Yes." Althea nodded once.

"Help me. I'm stuck here. Gotta get somewhere else, but I can't leave until I pay."

"Pay?" She tilted her head. "You can't pay. You're a spirit. Ghosts don't need pay-things."

He bowed his head, causing the breathing mask dangling from his helmet to flop back and forth. "I was supposed to take out a government command facility a couple blocks from here. The anti-aircraft fire was intense. My first bomb overshot the target, hit the wrong building. Monroe told me I'd have to pay for the wasted ordinance since it was my fault... but I don't have eight hundred grand. They're gonna dock my pay!"

"I don't understand..." Althea waved dismissively. "It doesn't matter. You are dead. You don't need to stay here."

"Who are you talking to?" Santiago crept up to her.

Althea glanced at him.

The boys all leaned back together.

"Whoa, Althea..." Diego pointed at her. "Your eyes are really bright."

"Yeah. Way brighter than they usually are." Pedro approached and held a hand in front of her face, admiring the blue glow on his fingers. "It's really pretty."

"I'm doing the ghost-seeing. That's why."

"A ghost?" Santiago scratched his head. "What's that?"

Diego shivered. "Spirit."

Santiago also shivered. "Serious?"

"Yes." Althea faced the spirit. "I can help you go where you need to go."

He pressed a hand to his forehead, emitting a groan of worry. "But I can't go anywhere. I owe the company money... and I can't leave my Hurricane just sitting there. If someone steals it, they'll expect me to pay for it, too."

"The weather's nice." Althea blinked.

The spirit's anguished expression gave way to a momentary laugh. "No, kid. 'Hurricane' is the name for the type of aircraft I fly... or flew. Dammit! I knew I shouldn't have tried to make the second pass in hover mode. Too damn slow to avoid the defensive fire. When Monroe told me they were going to charge me for the missed bomb, I decided to quit. Screw the company. Never should've gone to war with the government in the first place. Figured I'd just land and surrender, defect to the other side... but the bastards dragged me into that alley back there and shot me."

"I'm sorry." She looked down. "You don't need to stay here. The war is over. I need to help you go where you belong before The Many finds you."

"I don't owe them for the bomb?"

"No. They're gone, too."

He stood a little taller and smiled. "Wow. I never thought I'd escape that debt. Still, I can't just leave the Hurricane there with three blue light specials left."

"What?"

He gestured at the old plane. "See those big pods under the wings?"

Althea looked. Two long, cylindrical objects hung from a strut beneath the left wing. The right wing had a similar strut, but only one pod remained. Each one had to be eight feet long and about a foot thick, with fins at one end and a pointy nose. All showed signs of severe weathering, dents, and some sort of chemical residue leaking from seams in their metal housing. Seconds after looking specifically at the pods, the same dread fear hit her again, making her gasp.

"W-988B, 2000-pound bomb. Walmart's kinda cheap. They have their ordinance made in like Pakistan or something... so like one in five never explodes... or explodes when they shouldn't. I don't know how the heck the other three haven't gone off yet. If a fly farts too hard on them, they're going to explode... probably flatten a 300-meter area."

"Eep!"

The boys jumped.

Althea grabbed Diego and Pedro by the hand and

dragged them around behind her. "Do not touch the war machine. It's gonna turn into lots of fire."

The boys backed away from it.

"Spirit, please go where you can find peace." Althea concentrated on him the same way she did for the ghosts on top of Archon's building, wanting to let him through to the spirit realm.

A silvery shimmer appeared in the air behind him. The former pilot stammered in confusion before vanishing into the opening, which promptly closed. All three boys gave a collective gasp of awe.

"I saw light," whispered Pedro.

"Me, too." Santiago eyed Althea. "Did you do that?"

"Just a flash. The sun?" Diego spun, looking around.

"The spirit is gone." Althea stared warily at the old fly machine.

She closed her eyes and concentrated on Officer David, trying to project her desire for him to find her out into the world. He'd referred to the ability as 'clairvoyant summoning.' She'd first used it without understanding how she did to call a nice canid mutant after a slave catcher kidnapped her. The city police helped her understand her abilities more than she once thought possible. Focusing the ability on Officer David would give him a potent urge to find her and also helped guide him to her location. The ability didn't force anyone to do anything, but the stronger her connection to the person and the more powerful her emotional state, the more urgent the call would be. David, being a psionic cop who also knew she had this power, would recognize she called for him and not waste time questioning why he randomly felt like finding her. Hopefully, he'd rush out here as fast as he could.

Considering she presently shook in terror at the idea of

ancient bombs splattering her, the boys, and half of Querq, she figured Officer David would be here soon.

"You okay?" asked Santiago.

Althea nodded. "Yes. I'm getting help."

"You're just standing there." Diego poked her.

"She's doing shaman stuff." Pedro smacked Diego's hand away.

Althea opened her eyes, continuing to psionically call out for Officer David.

Part of her wanted to run away from the war machine. Part of her feared if she moved so much as one finger, it would explode. However, it sat here for centuries already and hadn't done anything. She had no doubt The Many would make it go off if he could when it would destroy her, so she projected her... presence at the plane, trying to shield it from him. While she had reasonable confidence being near it would chase him away, her strange energy wouldn't do anything about ordinary bad luck.

A moment later, the high-pitched whine of a Division Zero hovercar came from overhead.

The boys looked up at the boxy, black machine.

Althea continued focusing on the plane. The large hovercar dropped into view in front of her, blocking the old aircraft. Dust and small rocks blasted out from under the cyan glow of four ion thrusters, one at each corner of the large vehicle. Compared to the old drive machines littered around the Badlands, the city police cars were much wider and a little longer. They appeared heavy with armor plates, but somehow still managed to fly despite being far from bird-shaped.

Both doors opened upward. Officer David and Officer Jess—a girl only a year older than Karina—hopped out. Jess radiated relative calm plus curiosity. Worried, David rushed to Althea, looked around, then relaxed.

"Oh… you're all right." He fake wiped sweat from his forehead. "I thought you were in big trouble."

"We are." Althea pointed. "The fly machine is going to blow up."

"What?" Jess blinked, glancing at the patrol craft.

"No. Not your car. The fly machine behind it." Althea walked to the side so she could point past the patrol craft at the dead plane. "The ghost said the bombs are gonna destroy three hundred meters." She flailed her arms. "An' it's gonna hurt people, not just break the meters."

David swiveled to peer at the old plane. "That thing? It's been here for years." He raised his left arm. A holographic panel appeared above the shiny black bracer around his forearm. He walked right up to the ancient machine, holding his arm out to it while staring at the floating screen. "Hmm." A moment later, his emotions shifted to extreme worry.

"Told you," said Althea.

"Kids, in the car, now." David backed away from the wreck.

"Three-century old ordinance is still dangerous?" asked Jess.

"Crazy things happen out here." David ushered the boys to the patrol craft. "We need to get those bombs away from town. Move them to a safe distance and destroy them before they go off on their own. This close to Querq, it's a danger. Probably won't flatten us, but it'll most likely kill some people and do a lot of damage."

"Bad." Althea scrambled into the back seat, settling down between Pedro and Diego.

The car had enough room for all four of them to sit in a row and not be squished into each other. David and Jess got in, pulled the doors shut, and lifted off. Althea grabbed her stomach at the feeling of zooming straight up. Flying in a car still unnerved her, but it no longer scared her. Her ability to manifest astral energy 'wings' eliminated her fear of heights. Though she couldn't truly fly using them, the power let her drift safely to the ground. She no longer feared falling, but remained nervous at being stuck inside a car if it decided to drop out of the sky.

However, the patrol craft worried her *far* less than being near three big bombs.

## 5

## ORDINARY... ALMOST

They didn't get in trouble for going to the Old City, which somewhat surprised Althea.

Evidently, the Watch considered her enough protection for the boys, perhaps even more than a person with a rifle. The soldier scorpion sting Diego suffered might have killed him before anyone could have carried him back to town and found her. She tried not to think too much about how he only survived because she had been right there with him. Whether her premonition to follow the boys into the city came from the sting or from the old war machine and its bombs, she didn't know.

A few hours after the city police learned of the danger, a heavy explosion went off in the distance to the east. It shook the ground, but didn't do any real damage in Querq. She assumed the bombs had been moved far away and destroyed where they couldn't hurt anyone. For the first time in her life, the wrath of an explosion made her feel better, knowing the horrible weapon could no longer do any harm.

The next day, Althea loaded up dirty clothes in a pull

cart and made her way out to the river to wash laundry. A few other women and boys at the riverside also washed clothes. Most sat or knelt at the water's edge, using the fancy 'city soap' the Division Zero police gave them. Althea, too, had a plastic bottle of the green slimy stuff. Despite being 'modern,' it didn't bother her too much.

Althea waded in up to her knees and proceeded to wash all the clothes she, Father, and Karina dirtied over the past week. She tended to wear the same dress every day until or unless Karina nagged her to put on a clean one, which she didn't always do. Since she'd been wearing her current dress for nearly the entire week, she decided to wash it with the rest of the laundry. Some of the women chuckled as she matter-of-factly removed it and proceeded to scrub it in the river. One older woman gave off the same sort of emotion people did upon seeing a puppy.

She didn't mind being thought of as 'adorable.' Much better that than worshiped.

Respect didn't bother her. If the people of Querq thought of her the way they thought of Dr. Ruiz—someone there to help them if they needed it—great. A few people here did try to worship her as the Prophet. One woman even kissed her feet months ago. That, she hated. It made her feel awkward and embarrassed. In the past, she occasionally ended up at a village of scrags or settlers who *didn't* kidnap her or keep her tied, rather treated her like some great spirit. Althea loathed being carried around on a special chair revered like some kind of goddess they begged to do things she couldn't—like make the crops grow better.

Standing waist-deep in the river washing clothes made her happy and feel like just another village girl, even if no one else thought to wash the clothes they presently had on.

The city soap made her nose—and most of her face—tingle, but she had no name for the scent. It didn't smell like anything real, though somewhat reminded her of the unnatural trees she'd found growing where they shouldn't be... the ones with needles for leaves.

After finishing all the clothes, Althea loaded the wagon with the wet garments and towed it back home. A few people she passed smiled and waved at her. Upon arriving home, she lugged the wagon into the yard behind the house and hung the clothes on the line. By then, she'd dried off, so she went inside to put on a clean dress, then flopped on the sofa with the frustrating e-learning device.

AT BREAKFAST THE FOLLOWING MORNING, FATHER'S excitement made Althea suspicious.

He didn't do a great job of acting normal, unable to hide his smile. Karina also gave off a sense of being thrilled.

*They want to surprise me with something nice.*

She pretended not to notice anything unusual while smearing another strange, new arrival from the city all over her hunk of toast. The reddish-purple slime tasted sweet, like berries. Despite where it came from, she liked it. Not *everything* about the giant city in the west was bad... only most of it, especially the overwhelming negative emotions saturating the place. She'd started to accept her uniquely potent powers of empathy made the city more intolerable to her than it would be for anyone else. Even Officer David, also a telempath, didn't mind being there. The people in the police building who studied her and helped her practice using her abilities couldn't explain why she lacked the ability to 'turn it off' and stop picking up on the emotions of people around her.

Division Zero didn't know much about 'Awakened' psionics. Aurora told her they all had strange quirks, as she called them, like the way Althea's eyes constantly glowed bright blue or Aurora had pure white skin and onyx-black eyes. Anna couldn't control her Electrokinesis, setting off sparks and so on whenever she experienced an emotion. Maybe Althea's extreme sensitivity came from that, too.

"Well, this is not working." Father chuckled. "She obviously knows."

"I will pretend to be surprised." Althea grinned.

Karina laughed. "Just tell her."

"You got a good enough result on the tablet." Father grinned. "If you want to go to the school, you can start today."

Althea bounced in her chair. "Really?"

Karina and Father nodded.

"Who will do chores if I'm at school?"

"You can do them after. School is not all day," said Father. "You'll go after breakfast and be done an hour after lunch. They will give you food there."

Althea grinned, unable to sit still from excitement at being free from the annoying electronic teacher. Sitting alone in the house listening to a machine make fun of her for being stupid had almost been worse than raiders locking her in a room.

"You're so happy *I* can feel it." Karina laughed.

"The whole town feels it." Father reached over and patted her shoulder.

"It happens." Althea offered a sheepish grin.

For the remainder of breakfast, she chattered eagerly with Karina, thrilled to finally overcome the one remaining way everyone treated her differently from other people in Querq. Even if they didn't do it because of her being 'The Prophet,' but due to her having no education whatsoever, it still bothered her. The stupid datapads helped her learn enough to be able to go to school with the other children.

Most of them started learning at school around age six... when she'd been stuck in the Wagon Man's cage. Raiders, bandits, and worshipful villagers didn't bother trying to teach her anything. Then again, scrags didn't have school. Parents taught their kids how to survive. They didn't need to learn the frozen speaking, or how to math, or what happened in the past. Scrags needed to know what they could eat, what would kill them, and how to tell what the weather would do.

The people of Querq, however, weren't scrags. They always had a school.

After they cleaned the dishes, Karina and Father walked with Althea to the classroom. In the Before-Time, the building had been something called an office. The people of Querq added to it, creating a structure part new, part ruin, but solid enough to serve as a place to teach children. Before the arrival of the city police, kids finished school around age ten and went on to learn whatever else they needed to learn from apprenticeships for a particular job. One of the things the Ravens had to agree to in exchange for help had been changing the way kids learned. Now, children needed to be in school for much longer. The adults planned to extend teaching all the way to age eighteen... twelve 'grades,' but the older kids already worked jobs too vital to stop. The Ravens decided to require the long school only for new students. Any teen already working a job wouldn't be forced back into a classroom, but the kids still too young for jobs wouldn't get one until after they finished twelve grades.

Father and Karina went inside with her. In the front room, they met a fiftyish woman with greying black hair named Maya Perez, the person in charge of the whole school.

"Hello, Althea." Maya stood from her chair and walked

around the desk to shake her hand. "Welcome. It is good to finally see you here."

"Hi." She grinned. "I'm really happy I can go to school now."

"You'll be with Nadia's group for now." Maya patted a datapad on her desk. "I'm still trying to get used to all these strange devices and their new ways of doing things."

"It's definitely a challenge." Father chuckled. "A good one, I think. Keeps us all safe."

Maya shrugged. "It might. The outsiders think being safe means they bring us all back to their city, as if we needed to be 'saved' from this place."

"They don't understand." Karina sighed. "We don't need fancy things to be happy."

"Yes." Maya clucked her tongue. "They think we are happy only because we don't know what their land is like. Technology is not everything. Look at what it did here so long ago. All the destruction."

Althea looked down, taken by momentary sadness at the idea of war.

Father and Karina hugged her at the same time.

"I have to go to the farm," said Karina. "I know you will do well here."

"No need to worry." Father patted both girls on the shoulder. "If she can learn from the talking machine, she can learn from a person."

Maya went over to a tall metal cabinet, opened it, and pulled out yet another tablet.

Althea's heart sank. "Ugh…"

"This is a datapad." Maya offered it to her. "It's not an automatic teacher. It contains the textbooks and materials you will need for class. The world apparently does not make books anymore."

"What happened to the books?" asked Karina. "I learned from books."

Maya smiled at her. "You did. And we still have all six of them. They've nearly fallen apart, and the information is old. The outsiders have given us these supplies. Every child has their own 'book' now, even if they aren't really books. They're also looking for a few more teachers. Seems they're having trouble finding people willing to come out here. So, for the time being, the police are doing it."

"They're teaching?" Father raised both eyebrows.

Althea stood there clutching her new datapad, not fully trusting it, half-listening to Maya explain to Father how they've split the children up into grades by age rather than having all the kids in one room learning from Nadia, who now worked with the 'seventh grade' class. Division Zero people from the big city taught the other levels, except for the youngest kids who learned from Julieta, a girl Karina's age learning to be a teacher.

Eventually, Father and Karina had to leave. Maya led Althea down the hallway to the fifth room on the left. She'd been expecting a larger classroom, but it turned out to be a relatively small space with a long table at the center. A mixture of old padded chairs, metal folding chairs, and handmade seats surrounded the table, six on each side and two at each end. Seven other kids sat there, including Paama and Ooru.

Diego, Santiago, and Pedro belonged to the eighth-grade group. Kim, despite being fourteen, didn't have to go. She'd already completed something called 'high school' using those electronic devices. Althea suspected her friend might want to go back to the big city, since she missed technology. The city police had been trying to get her to join them because she had psionic abilities. Kim wanted to do it, but feared her father finding out and trying to hurt her.

Maya nudged Althea into the room. "A new one for you."

The kids all glanced over at her. Paama and Ooru grinned.

Nadia looked up from her datapad. "Oh! Althea! It's about time."

"Sorry." She beamed. "I wanted to be here, but they wouldn't let me before."

Thrilled, she ran over and jumped in the open seat closest to Paama and Ooru. She already knew all the kids in the room. Being here with them to learn felt like getting to play and have fun. She still had chores for later, but they could wait.

⚖ ⚶ 🏛 ◒ ♋

THE NEXT SEVERAL DAYS WENT BY SO FAST THEY MADE Althea dizzy.

School proved wonderful. Not only did everyone treat her like an ordinary person, she had a real teacher to ask questions of, not a frustrating machine… and other kids to talk to. At lunch, all the kids met in one big room and got to do whatever they wanted for a little less than an hour. Along with Nadia and Julieta, she met other teachers, all part of the city police, though not the same way as Officer David. They didn't do the same thing as the Watch or enforce laws, they belonged to something called 'Admin.' They worked for the police but didn't have guns, nor did they go out to stop bad people. A violet-haired man named Luca, one of the outside teachers, explained the 'admin' group basically allowed psionic individuals to become part of Division Zero without being exposed to the dangers of police work. According to him, they did mostly 'office stuff'—not that she had any idea what it meant. Still, they had skills enough to serve as teachers, and being technically part of the military, could be ordered to go out here. Thankfully, command asked for volunteers first.

Althea didn't bother telling him another 'technically.' Due to her unusual abilities, Division Zero considered her something called a 'Tech Officer.' David assured her and Father the city police officially added her to the ranks purely as a means to stop other parts of the government— something called C-Branch—from trying to steal her. Another reason she didn't want much to do with the modern world: different parts of the people in charge couldn't even trust each other. It reminded her of raider groups, how the sub-chiefs usually schemed to eliminate the chief and take power. Here in Querq, the Ravens didn't always agree, but they never tried to kill each other.

For the most part, she found being in school the second most wonderful thing to happen in her life, right after finding Karina and Father. Keeping up with the work proved to be a struggle, but she didn't mind it too much. If she couldn't quite understand something, she read Nadia's mind—something she couldn't do with a datapad teacher.

She had to learn strange things seemingly without purpose, like math, history, new words no real person would ever use, and science. Some things she thought she understood about reality proved false. For instance, ancestor spirits didn't drink any water left lying around, it disappeared due to something called evaporation. Lightning and thunder also didn't come from sky spirits, merely the air becoming angry... and something with clouds.

They also learned a giant world existed outside the Badlands. Two cities, as well as other entire places called nations, some of which didn't like the one she lived in.

People even made cities on the Moon and another entire world called Mars. Althea tolerated learning, even if she'd never need to know any of it.

☙ ❦ ▣ ◈ ♔

ROUGHLY THREE WEEKS INTO ALTHEA ATTENDING REAL school, Den barged into the classroom minutes after lunch, out of breath.

The lesson stopped short, Nadia and the kids all staring at him.

He hurried over to Althea, forcing words between gasps for air. "Roberto hurt himself at the farm. They can't move him without killing him."

Althea set her datapad on the table and took his hand. She commanded his body to release a burst of energy, ridding him of his fatigue. He'd likely sprinted the whole way from the farm. "All right." She looked at Nadia. "I need to go."

"Of course. They warned me this might happen. Go, help Roberto." Nadia smiled. "Day's almost over, anyway."

Paama grabbed Althea's datapad. "I'll put this at your house for you."

"Thank you!" She jumped out of her chair, ran straight across the table, and darted out the door, channeling power into her legs.

She once thought of it as sending 'blood presence' to parts of her body, because it felt as if more blood gathered where she wanted it to. The city police said her healing ability could 'overwork' her muscles, whatever that meant. Regardless of the reasons, the power had the same effect: she could run really fast for a little while. Not until she found a home in Querq did she stop to think about how raiders or bandits could never catch her when she ran to help someone who got hurt. It made her feel foolish all over again at the thought she could easily have escaped any number of times from any number of places.

But it didn't matter anymore. She would never again be kidnapped.

Althea zoomed across Querq, heading for the farm in the northwest. The giant copper-and-steel metal mushroom shape of the Water Man's house appeared in the distance, at the edge of the farm, close to the path of the river. Machines inside helped clean dirty stuff out of the water before sending it into the fields. A man's agonized wailing came from up ahead. She headed toward the screaming, still sprinting as fast as she could make herself go. If Roberto had been hurt so much Dr. Ruiz didn't want to move him, even a few seconds of delay could kill him.

Karina and other farm workers gathered in a cluster at the edge of the field. A man who happened to be looking back toward town spotted Althea and gave a happy shout. The entire crowd shifted to look at her and broke out in cheers. They parted, making an opening. Karina rushed out, blocking the path and waving for her to stop.

Althea slowed to a jog, then a fast walk. Before she could ask why her sister tried to stop her, she remembered the deep ditch surrounding the farm. Father mentioned they relied on it as a defense before the wall existed. A trench fifteen feet across and ten feet deep contained all manner of dangerous concrete rubble studded with rebar spikes. A chunk of missing dirt at the top indicated where the ground gave out and dumped Roberto over the edge.

He'd landed facing down, his body suspended several inches off the ground, impaled on multiple rebar spikes. One pierced his cheek, sticking out behind his left ear. Four metal rods stuck out of his back. Two skewered his right thigh. He appeared conscious, struggling to brace his weight on his arms and left leg. Dr. Ruiz crouched beside him along with Officer Jess and Teal.

Althea blinked in surprise at seeing the former mercenary standing by an injured man, but figured the adults had a reason for asking her to be here. Only a few people knew the truth about Teal, that she'd originally come here to kidnap Althea because a corporation paid her to… but experienced a change of heart. Ironically, she needed to hide out in the Badlands so the same corporation didn't try to attack her for failing. Teal didn't seem to mind. As a synthetic, the woman wouldn't grow older. She'd simply wait until everyone at the corporation who knew her died, quit, or forgot about her.

"Eep!" yelled Althea.

Dr. Ruiz looked up at her squeak. His emotions crashed from helpless worry to relief.

Teal smiled at her, raising her arms in an offer to catch her.

A ten-foot drop didn't require wings, so Althea leapt without hesitation. Teal caught her easily and set her on her feet, balanced atop a block of concrete.

"Careful where you step. There's smashed glass and sharp crap everywhere." Teal shot a sideways glance at Dr. Ruiz. "Why is this death trap still here?"

"Because no one's wanted to put in the work to be rid of it." Dr. Ruiz grumbled. "I guess they think it's still useful in case raiders get past the wall."

Althea squatted on the giant rubble block and placed both hands on Roberto's bare shoulder. Sweat drenched his tank top, turning it grey. She first told his mind to ignore pain. He gave a deep sigh of relief, relaxed, and sank an inch or so deeper on the spikes. Blood dribbled down the rusting metal, pooling on the dirty concrete from which the rods sprouted.

"Althea," said Dr. Ruiz. "The bar in his head is close to his brain, important nerves, and a major artery. I need you to stop him from bleeding. Teal has a Nano knife. She's going to cut the rebar and lift him off once you stabilize him. Then we can get him to the hospital... and I'm being an idiot."

Teal laughed.

Althea peered at him. "Idiot?"

"You're here. Don't need to risk delicate head surgery... you can fix him."

She smiled, then looked up at Teal. "Wait one minute after I start, then cut the metal under him and pull the piece out."

"Which one?" asked Teal.

"Start with the bad one." Althea pointed at the rebar impaling Roberto's head. "When the hurt goes away, pull another one out."

"Wait." Dr. Ruiz raised a finger. "He's suspended on them. His weight is distributed over several bars. Better she cuts all the rebar away and we carry him up top before you remove anything. If you go one at a time, the others will do more damage."

Althea studied the situation. True, all his weight hung on the spikes; at least fourteen inches separated his body from the concrete. Removing one rod at a time would twist the metal inside the body elsewhere. "You're right."

"Here." Teal handed Dr. Ruiz a knife with a crystalline blue blade. "You know the drill. Stupid sharp. Don't need my strength to slice rebar with it. Let me get my arms under him, then cut."

Dr. Ruiz nodded.

Teal moved around to stand beside Roberto, squatted, and eased her arms under him for support. "Okay. Cut."

Althea linked her consciousness to Roberto's essence at

a shallow level. Not so much she plunged fully into the dreamlike state of seeing a person's life shapes floating in void and lost awareness of the world outside, but enough to make sure his blood did not leave his body.

With Teal supporting the man's weight, Dr. Ruiz sliced the steel rods with somewhat more effort than needed to cut carrots.

"Sorry," rasped Roberto. "Damn ground fell out from under me. I shouldn't have been so close."

Teal lifted Roberto once the doctor severed the last spike.

"What were you doing so close to the edge, anyway?" asked Teal.

From her position crouching nearby as Teal lifted him, Althea couldn't help but notice a rather obvious part of Roberto's body sticking out of his pants. "He was peeing."

"Ugh." Teal cringed. "He's dangling, isn't he?"

"Yes." Althea nodded.

Teal stood, easily lifting a man bigger than her. Many of the villagers watching from above whistled or gasped in shock, neither aware synthetics existed nor that Teal was one. Althea didn't truly understand it either, only that the woman had a body made from plastisteel and other stuff never alive in a biological sense. Psionic powers like Telepathy or Telempathy didn't work on her at all, precisely why the corporation hired her to kidnap Althea. Regardless of the electronic nature of her brain, she possessed something close to real humanity. A true robot wouldn't have changed its mind after Althea risked her life to save it. As far as she cared, Teal was a person.

Althea climbed out of the trench, doing her best to avoid stepping on sharp glass while rushing. Breaking contact with Roberto interrupted her ability to make him stop feeling pain. He'd only have about fifteen seconds after her hand slipped away before being in agony again. She made it to the top with only three small bits of glass in her foot, easy enough to deal with later.

Teal eased Roberto down on his side, careful not to disturb any of the rebar bits sticking out in front and back. Althea rushed over, knelt beside him, and rested her hands on either side of the metal rod sticking out of his head.

"Count to ten and pull it out slow," said Althea.

Dr. Ruiz handed the knife back to Teal, then helped Roberto by tucking him back into his pants.

Teal took a knee and gripped the rebar fragment impaling the head. "Got it."

Althea closed her eyes and dove into Roberto's life essence. His heart shape worked too hard, so she told it to slow down, then concentrated on the spot where a half-inch-thick black line cut through his head. Soon, she sensed the abrasion of the rod moving against flesh and bone. At the urging of her power, his body regenerated itself. Thin white lines she now understood to be nerves had been close to the injury but thanks to luck, survived undamaged. Teal must have understood the situation well. Thanks to her inhumanly high dexterity, she managed to extract the spike without tearing up any of the important things near the injury. Muscle grew back at Althea's urging. Tiny fragments of bone dissolved, reabsorbed by Roberto's body. New bone formed where she directed it to. She closed the skin last so Teal would know when to pull out the next spike.

Two passed through his airbag. One penetrated a kidney, another skewered all the squiggly bits in the lower stomach. As soon as the second rebar fragment pulled away, she got to work fixing the damage it caused.

After what felt like an hour, she finished. Dirt and rust on the metal acted like a poison, so she sent it all to his bladder as she usually did with bad stuff. Ironically, needing to pee got him hurt in the first place... and he'd have to go again right away. Hopefully, he'd find a safer spot.

She opened her eyes.

"Damn, kiddo. You are amazing." Teal patted her on the head. "You don't even look tired."

"Small holes. I didn't really have to work hard." Althea sat back on her butt, pulled her left foot into her lap, then plucked glass out of her sole before mending the cuts.

Roberto groaned. "Not again."

"It's poison. You have to." Althea exhaled. "But not here."

He laughed. "Aye. Never again. Stupid lazy... figured I'd save a few minutes walking."

"Stupid glass." Althea held up a piece she'd removed from her foot. "It shouldn't be left where it can hurt people."

"It's put there *to* hurt people," said one of the farmers in mostly Spanish. "The trench is supposed to be dangerous to stop raids."

Althea sighed at the trench. Less than twenty feet past it stood the formidable wall encircling Querq. She could think of no good reason to keep such a dangerous trap anymore. They didn't need it. The spikes and shattered glass posed more of a threat to innocent people than to raiders. Any attack on Querq capable of getting past the Watch and their new city rifles to even come close to the wall, much less over it, would pose a much bigger problem than a ditch could solve. Worse, it only circled the outside edge of the farm. All invaders needed to do in order to avoid it entirely would be to attack from another angle.

She checked her other foot for glass and found none. "I'm going to talk to the Ravens."

"Good luck with that," said Dr. Ruiz, chuckling.

Karina fussed over her. "You hurt yourself."

"Small cuts. I'm okay." Althea stood.

"Why bother the council?" asked Karina.

"This is dangerous and they need to fix it."

Karina shrugged. "It's always been here. They won't want to do anything. They think it's necessary to defend us."

Althea tapped a finger to her chin, debating if it would be wrong to use her abilities to help convince the Ravens to do something about the ditch. She wouldn't command them, merely play on their emotions a little. After a moment, she sighed, guilty. Using her powers like that *did* seem wrong. However, she could still try talking to them. Even if she couldn't convince them to fill in the trench with dirt, maybe they'd be willing to consider a fence or something on the inside.

"You should get back to school. You're not quite done for the day." Karina hugged her. "Don't worry about the farm. We can handle it."

"Okay." She sighed. True, she *was* supposed to be in school now. Permission to leave class and go help someone didn't include spending time complaining to the Ravens. "I will."

## 6

## WORLDS APART

A few weeks after Roberto's fall, Althea settled into a strange routine.

She went to school after breakfast, spending time with other kids and learning, then returned home to do her chores before having the late afternoon into early evening to herself. From talking to her friends, mostly Kim, this new reality they lived in blended two entirely different societies. The ordinary schedule of school, chores, and free time sounded much like how people in the modern city lived, yet Althea and the others did so out here in the wild Badlands. No one back in West City could fling their clothes off and jump in a river to swim, nor run around kicking a ball in the street, or wander wherever they cared to play.

Not only did the big city not have rivers, gangs and other sorts of bad people made the streets too dangerous for unsupervised children to go anywhere. Some parts of the city—like where Kim once lived—had enough security and niceness to be safe for anyone. *Most* of the city, though, didn't have such luxury.

Althea, Kim, Paama, Ooru, Den, Eem, and Esmeralda sat around the porch of Althea's home playing a sort of game, talking about the differences between the two places. Kim's stories of flying delivery bots, being able to 'order' anything she wanted and have it show up within minutes sounded like magic. Despite being in Querq for some time, Ooru remained quite pale. The thirteen-year-old had blue eyes like Althea, but they didn't glow. She'd finally told Paama the boy liked her the same way Den liked Althea. At first, Paama didn't believe her, thinking he wanted to play a mean trick on her. Most of the young people from the Transit Tribe disliked Paama, finding her bossy and abrasive. It made sense to a point, considering the first time the girl spoke to her, she threatened to beat Althea up for her magic ankle bracelets, not realizing she'd been stuck in electronic handcuffs.

Fear did strange things to people. Paama's attitude came mostly from being in a constant state of terror over killer robots. The girl didn't like being scared, so she acted angry. After a few months in Querq, she'd finally accepted the truth that no robots would find them here. Her personality gradually changed. She and Ooru often spent time together and even did the lip touching thing. Eem, Ooru's scrawny, eleven-year-old best friend with long blonde hair, teased him constantly for being in love. Paama often retaliated by calling him girly... until he pointed out she was a girl and she basically insulted herself whenever she used 'girly' as a mean thing to say.

"No raiders in big city," said Esmerelda, radiating fear.

Almost every settler or scrag in the Badlands, especially girls, lived in fear of raiders. The people of Querq hadn't been immune to the worry, though suffered it less than other places.

Kim shook her head. "No. Gangs don't kidnap people.

Usually, they just rob or shoot them. Sometimes, the gangs start fights with each other and bystanders get shot."

"I don't understand." Den leaned forward. "You said they have pay-things that don't really exist."

"It's called credits." Kim laughed. "Not pay-things. Or money. No one really calls it money anymore, only lawyers. But yeah. What's confusing?"

Den grabbed at the air. "How can the gangs steal something that isn't real? People don't carry credits around, right?"

"Oh." Kim exhaled. "Yeah, I get how that's confusing to you. You guys think of money as like stuff you hold. Real objects. Okay, so... credits are just numbers in a computer somewhere. But, some people carry credsticks, which umm... think of them like electronic coins. Those can be stolen. It's how people spend money when they don't want to be traced to an account. Gangs usually force people to buy stuff and have it sent to wherever they are. It's not really stealing credits, but threatening to kill someone if they don't buy them stuff. Some of them have devices called 'skimmers.' If they get close to you, it hacks your NetMini and steals a few credits."

Paama and Ooru stared blank-faced. Eem shrugged, either not caring at all or getting it right away. Den made a face like a caveman encountering fire for the first time, but his bewilderment gradually shifted to comprehension.

Sensing a bit of sadness from Kim, Althea nudged her. "Do you miss being there?"

"A little." Kim shrugged. "I don't miss the city really, just the GlobeNet. Video games. If the Division Zero people could get us online here, this place would be perfect. Never really thought about how awesome it is to be able to buy stuff from a NetMini and have it show up whenever I want it. It's *so* different not to be able to do that. It still feels weird to go to the 'store' here and just ask for stuff and they give it to you."

"You live here," says Esmerelda. "Outsiders have to trade."

"Yeah… everyone working to help everyone, I get it." Kim stretched out on her back, fingers laced behind her head, and gazed up at the porch roof. "Can't really go there anyway, even if I sell out and join Division Zero. My asshole senator dad will kill me."

"Let him be angry." Den sat up straight. "My father is furious at me for leaving. It does not bother me."

Kim scoffed. "I don't mean 'kill me' like be angry. I mean literally try to shoot me. Well, *he* won't do it. He'll pay someone to."

The others gasped.

Althea frowned, having heard the story already. "He can't hate you that much. He's still your father."

"You don't get it. Wow, you're so innocent." Kim sat up. "He *hates* psionics. The man's one of those crazy people who think there's a god and stuff. To him, psionics are some kind of evil thing his god wants him to destroy. There are two reasons he isn't sending people after me out here. One, he doesn't know I'm out here. Two, no one in the world knows his daughter is a psionic… except him."

"Which god?" asked Eem. "Sounds like something MasterCard would do. Or Internet."

"Those aren't real gods, remember?" Ooru elbowed him. "We learned bad stories."

"How did he find out you're psionic?" asked Den.

Kim scowled. "Because I'm a complete idiot. I thought telling him might change his attitude, even if it made him stop campaigning against psionics and not support them. But nope. The bastard tried to kill me. If I didn't have Telekinesis, he'd have choked me to death."

Althea gawked in horror.

"Wha's that?" Eem went wide-eyed. "I'm not gonna even try sayin' it."

Kim sat cross-legged, faced Eem, and stared at him. Seconds later, the diminutive boy levitated off the porch.

He squeaked.

Den, Paama, Ooru, and Esmerelda gawked at him.

"How are you doing that?" Ooru tugged on the boy, causing him to spin in place. Finding this amusing, he pushed harder, spinning Eem faster.

"Stop!" yelled Eem, laughing.

"Telekinesis lets me move stuff by looking at it." Kim stopped the boy from spinning and set him down. "I didn't tell my dad what I could do, only that I was psionic. When he attacked me, I told him his god would be mad at him if he hurt me and made his cross thing fly off the wall and hit him on the head. He still thinks his stupid imaginary god threw it at him."

"Cross thing?" Paama furrowed her eyebrows.

"Some dead guy stuck on boards or something." Kim shrugged. "I dunno. He really likes it. Kinda morbid, if you ask me. It's like the logo for his god. Like you know how CyberBurger has the little cheeseburger with eyes? Cheebo? The mascot? Same thing. Their mascot is a dead guy nailed to a tree. Pretty twisted, if you ask me."

Everyone stared at her.

"Umm, guess not." Kim rolled her eyes. "Yeah, dumb. Why would you guys know about CyberBurger?"

"So you hurt him?" Den raised both eyebrows.

"No. The cross thing is small. But seeing it move on its own scared the crap out of him. He legit screamed and ran out. I grabbed some of my stuff and took off before he came back. Couple hours later, some anonymous dude left a voice message on my NetMini saying not to tell anyone what or who I was in any way that connected back to my father or I'd end up dead. Also, he told me not to bother trying to go home." She scoffed. "As if I'd be that stupid."

Althea hugged her. "I'm sorry."

"Maybe I could change my last name." Kim rested her chin on both hands. "The cops keep trying to talk me into joining them. Don't trust them, though. I lived on the streets for a couple months. Saw what cops are really like to people with nothing. Don't wanna be one of them."

Sensing shame and fear, Althea kept hugging her. "Officer David is really nice. I don't think every cop is mean."

Kim grumbled.

Eem made a brief whistle like a small bird. Paama and Ooru instantly shifted mood from relaxed to guarded. They looked at the smaller boy, then followed his stare to a man in a hooded brown cloak walking down the street toward them. He clearly approached the house, walking at an angle to the road.

Fear and frustration came from Paama. She grumbled about not having her spear while grasping the knife tied to her leg. Ooru also gripped his blade. Eem never went anywhere without his spear, being quite proud of it. He jumped to his feet, holding the weapon sideways in a ready stance.

Den acted casual, watching the stranger approach. Being 'off duty' at the moment, he'd left his rifle at the Watch house. Esmerelda appeared confused at everyone's reaction. Eem had sensed something about the man's body language, putting him on edge.

Althea focused on the man, who hadn't yet come close enough for her to pick up emotion without a deliberate effort to. As soon as she looked at him, she sensed excitement tinged with mania... the exact same feeling most raiders gave off when they realized they'd found The Prophet.

She sighed, annoyed.

Den glanced at her. "What?"

Althea rested her elbow on her knee, chin in her hand. "He wants to kidnap me."

Paama and Ooru gave her side eye.

"I'ma stick him." Eem pointed his spear at the man.

"Don't. It's okay." Althea sighed again.

"You're not going with him." Den rested his hand on her arm.

"No. I'm not." She pressed her hand atop his. "I got rid of the stupid."

When the man reached the base of the porch steps, he yanked his arm out from under his poncho, raising a gun in the general direction of the kids on the porch. "I claim the Prophet. Come with me or I shoot little ones."

"*Lower the gun,*" said Althea, using Suggestion. The light emanating from her eyes flickered brighter for an instant in time with her words.

The man stood motionless for a moment before his arm began shaking, then lowered as if an invisible person wrestled it down.

"Want me to take his gun?" asked Kim.

"Yeah, do it." Den nodded.

Kim raised her arm, fingers splayed. The man's weapon twisted out of his grasp and flew into her waiting hand.

"Whoa…" Eem gawked at her. "Show me how to do that magic."

"Can't." Kim sighed, glancing at him. "You have to be psionic. And you're… holy crap."

"I'm holy crap?" Eem blinked. "What does that mean?"

Kim shifted her gaze back to the man in the brown hooded cloak. "Later. Gotta deal with an idiot first."

Althea lifted her chin off her hand, stood, and walked to the edge of the porch, gazing down at the man at the bottom of the steps. "Go home to wherever you live and don't try to kidnap me again. If you do, I will make you so scared you'll hide in a hole for the rest of your life, afraid of air."

The grizzled, bearded guy looked about Father's age, his face marked by knife scars. Few raiders lived into their forties, typically only cowards, the extremely skilled, or the extremely lucky. Still, he had the feel of an opportunistic raider to him. Clearly, he thought of her as a thing to be taken and owned. His thoughts swam in confusion at why the Prophet didn't simply go with him.

"You not supposed ta say no," rasped the man. "You s'posed ta obey."

Althea set her hands on her hips. "No. Things have changed. I am a person not a... umm, what did Officer David say?" She tapped her foot, trying to remember. "Oh. I'm a person, not a stimpak with legs. If you are hurt, I will help you, but no one kidnaps me anymore."

He reached for her.

Eem and Den jumped in front of her. The tiny boy thrust his spear at the man's neck in a warning gesture, pushing him back without drawing blood.

Althea sighed at the man's stupidity. His thoughts said he still wanted to take her by force.

"Esmee, go get the Watch," said Kim.

Esmerelda jumped to her feet.

"No... he needs to go away so he can tell others." Althea glared at the man, twisting his emotion into fear. "No one kidnaps me." *Except synthetics...* She let her hands slide off her hips and hang limp.

The man screamed in terror, tripped over himself in an

attempt to run backward, then scrambled to his feet and sprinted off down the street.

"Why did you let him go?" Den tilted his head at her. "He tried to steal you."

"Yeah. The Watch should get him." Esmerelda nodded.

Althea went back to where she'd been sitting before. "It's not his fault he is stupid and believes wrong legends. I want him to tell raiders they cannot take me."

"He's a raider?" Esmerelda shivered. "How did he get inside?"

"Probably walked." Ooru chuckled.

"Raiders don't usually go anywhere alone." Den sat next to Althea. "He thought he could act like a trader, get into Querq, and take you."

"How would he take her?" Ooru sat beside Paama. "The Watch wouldn't let him leave with her."

Althea rolled her eyes. "He'd probably point his gun at me and say he'd shoot me if they tried to stop us. Or maybe he thought he'd put me in a box. Maybe he's too stupid and didn't even think of a way to get out."

Her friends laughed.

Den put an arm around her, his mood drifting between annoyed and glum.

She stared into his jade green eyes, smiling. *Don't be sad. I still need someone to protect me from bad synthetics. My powers don't work on them.*

He blinked, then got an 'oh yeah' expression. He shook off the gloom and flashed a genuine smile.

"What's a holy crap?" asked Eem.

Kim waved for him to come closer, then grasped his face in both hands, staring into his eyes, nose to nose. After a moment, she let go. "Kid, you're psionic. Not telekinetic, though."

Eem blinked. "I got magic?"

"Basically." Kim smiled. "But I'm not good enough to tell what kind. If you had TK, I'd know, but you don't."

Althea stared at Eem. The Division Zero people taught her how to recognize another psionic using telepathy. Their brains felt different. Almost any person with psionic abilities, and telepathy, could tell if another person had psionic abilities. Having the same ability as someone made it easier to find it. Althea got the feeling Eem possessed the healing power, too... but not like her. He could only use it on himself. She didn't sense telepathy in him, and thought he might have some other ability she couldn't recognize.

"Talk to the city police." Althea smiled at him. "They can figure out what kind of magic you have. You don't get sick much, do you?"

"Nope. Never!" Eem grinned broadly.

"See how skinny he is?" asked Althea.

Paama and Ooru laughed.

Eem blushed. "I'm not skinny. I'm quick!"

"He heals fast." Althea leaned against Den.

"Eem's a prophet?" Ooru gawked.

"No," said Althea. "He can only heal himself."

The eleven-year-old looked around at everyone, perplexed. He glanced down at his left arm, then sliced his spear across it, making a minor cut.

"Stop!" yelled Paama. "Dumb! What are you doing?"

Blood dripped to the porch.

"Not healing," said Eem.

"Don't be stupid." Ooru swatted him on the head.

"Not stupid. Althea can fix. It not hurt." Eem shoved his arm in Ooru's face. "Just a small cut. Don't baby."

Althea opened a telepathic link to Eem's brain. Instead of speaking, she sent thoughts of how it felt when she concentrated on healing herself. "Think like that. *Want* it to heal."

The boy made faces at his arm. Finally, after about ten minutes, the small cut sealed and shrank to a faint red line.

Paama and Ooru gawked.

"There." Althea nodded. "You're kinda skinny because making hurts and sicks go away uses food."

"You're skinny, too!" yelled Eem.

"Exactly." Ooru swatted him on the head again. "She heals. Althea's not saying you're skinny to be mean."

Eem rubbed the back of his head. "Oh… yeah."

"*I'm* saying he's skinny to be mean." Paama poked him in the side, laughing.

The boy stuck his tongue out at her.

Rapid footsteps in the street made Althea look over at a teenage boy, Miguel, running toward the house. He gave off worry and urgency, a likely sign he'd come to fetch her.

Althea stood. "Someone's hurt. I need to go help them."

Miguel ran up onto the porch. "Althea, Dr. Ruiz needs you at the hospital."

The other kids all got up, apparently intent on following her.

"Okay. I'll go right now. Who's hurt?"

"I don't know." Miguel shrugged. "Dr. Ruiz just saw me going by outside and asked me to find you. Didn't say anything about who is hurt, just he needed your help."

"All right." She hurried down the stairs and started toward the hospital.

It had to be somewhat serious if he *needed* her, but he didn't call it an emergency. No reason to run. Den, Kim, Paama, Ooru, Eem, and Esmerelda followed. Making a person's hurts or sicks go away didn't usually take long. If someone had significant injuries, helping them might knock her out for a few hours. The doctor's lack of urgency made it seem unlikely for a serious problem to be waiting for her.

Or so she hoped.

## 7

CONTAGIOUS

A warning sense came over Althea the instant she looked at the hospital.

She stopped walking in the middle of the street and scanned the area. Nothing dangerous or unusual appeared to be lurking in the gaps between buildings. Being able to understand the frozen speaking—or writing as the teachers insisted she call it—made this part of Querq seem strange. People's homes had odd words on them like 'hardware' or 'pizza' or 'first savings.' The words had nothing to do with anyone living there, so they must be from the Before-Time. Even the hospital had the strange phrase 'Desert Dental' on the front window, the letters not so much painted on as still-shiny glass where paint had once been, while the rest of the window appeared smoky due to grime and centuries of windblown sand scuffing it.

"What's wrong?" asked Den. "You have the face again."

Althea shifted her gaze back to the hospital and again felt a sense of warning. She pondered the strange tingling in her stomach. Clairvoyance, according to the city police, could be tricky to use and even trickier to understand. They felt confident she did not have precognition, so lacked any ability to see the future, at least the future more than a few seconds away. Clairvoyance could, in some cases, provide warning of immediate threat when the threat happened as a result of an action.

The test they gave her involved a series of metal buttons, some of which would zap her finger with an unpleasant but not really painful shock. If she got a funny feeling right before she pushed the button, she refused to touch it, confirming she had the ability. Focusing on the buttons with no intention to push them didn't give her the same sense.

She thought about going into the hospital again, and the feeling strengthened.

"Please wait here. There is something bad inside." Althea pointed at the building.

The others exchanged glances, shrugged, and moved off the street into the shade of Tumbleweed's bar. Althea's warning sense weakened, but remained, telling her if she went inside the hospital, something mildly bad would happen to her. It didn't seem at all likely Dr. Ruiz sent for her so he could do something mean. She figured the sick person might lash out and smack her... or perhaps have a nasty sick she would catch, too. No big deal. It only meant she'd need to cure herself, too. Since the time she spent in the Wagon Man's cage, she'd caught so many sicks, her body practically cleaned itself automatically. Most of the time, she never noticed she'd picked up a sick unless peeing hurt a little. Her body purged it before she felt bad enough to notice she'd caught something.

She mentally prepared herself to be cautious, then walked the rest of the way down the block to the hospital and went inside. Renata, the nurse, looked up from the desk in the front room. She appeared exhausted. One of her eyes only opened halfway.

Renata smiled. "Hello, Althea. Eduardo is waiting for you."

"Are you sick?"

"Am I?" She tried to blink, but her right eye stayed shut. "Feels like I'm floating outside myself."

Althea walked over and took her hand, closed her eyes, and concentrated on the woman's life essence. In seconds, the form of Renata's body appeared as if suspended in a black void. Red blobs hinted at the shapes of muscles, white lines traced nerve routes. Bones appeared dark grey. The blood presence looked like clusters of tiny glowing red tree branches or long noodles. A dull green sick spread throughout her body, vaporous tendrils extending everywhere. Her air-bags contained a bunch of little dots that shouldn't be there, damage caused by the sick.

Thread by thread, Althea forced the unnatural haze out of Renata's body, compressing the ghostly wisps into the bladder. Next, she repaired the air-bags, which made the woman cough. Already, small threads of sick tried to get into Althea's body. She refused to let it take hold.

When Althea opened her eyes, Renata wore a pained expression as though she'd been stabbed.

"What did you do, child?" gasped the nurse.

"You had a bad sick and must make water." Althea squeezed her hand. "Do not make water in the normal place. Put it in a bucket so it can be burned. It is danger."

Renata braced her hands on the desk while rising to her feet. The discomfort from the sick prevented her from standing fully upright. "I... the man they brought in is very sick. I must have caught it from him." She stumbled across the room like a boy who'd been kicked in the groin.

Althea went down the hall, peeking into the various

rooms in search of the doctor. She found him in the second room on the right. He, too, appeared exhausted and sick. The man lying in the bed definitely did not come from Querq, but also didn't look like a city person. He reminded her a bit of Rachel, 'black' as she called it. Sweat dripped down his face and made his short, curly hair glisten. The room smelled like death.

"Thank you," whispered Dr. Ruiz. "I've never seen this before. It's... whatever he's got is pretty rough. I think I've caught it, too. We haven't let anyone else in the building."

"Miss Renata had it. She is better now." Althea approached the bed and rested her hands on the man's forearm, linking her consciousness to his life essence.

The same wispy, dull green sick existed all throughout his body, more opaque and denser than it appeared in the nurse, no doubt because he'd been ill longer. He also had a broken toe and a sprained ankle, trivialities she could tend to after the sick. As she did for the nurse, she forced the disease to retreat from his various life shapes and gather where it could be disposed of. That done, she mended all the little breaks and tiny hurts before releasing the psionic link.

The man awoke yowling in pain and clutching himself between the legs.

By now, Dr. Ruiz had become familiar with the routine and already had a bucket ready.

"Fire!" yelled the man.

Althea opened her eyes. "Yes. We will need to burn it."

He turned his head to look at her. His emotions exploded into joy and relief, a much more welcome mood spike upon seeing her than the greedy triumph of a raider finding a prize. This man clearly recognized her. He'd come here hoping for her help, realized he'd succeeded, and experienced such a burst of gratitude, he cried.

She grinned back at him, overjoyed to be able to heal him.

"I... you're..." He leaned over and hugged her, weeping for a moment or two before he collected himself enough to speak. "I mean... my... uhh." Joy shifted to strong embarrassment.

Althea smirked. Most men didn't like to talk about their boy parts around her for some reason, even raiders. "You had a sick. I put it all where you can get rid of it. You must pee."

The man groaned, shifting to sit sideways on the bed. "Where's the John?"

"There's no one here named that." Althea shrugged. "Do you mean Juan?"

Dr. Ruiz handed him the bucket. "Your urine will be extremely toxic. We have to destroy it. Also, I should warn you, it tends to be quite painful. It's something about the way she purges disease. If you like, she can make you not feel pain... but she needs to be close."

His embarrassment deepened.

"I won't watch." Althea grabbed his left hand and closed her eyes. "It will hurt so much you will scream if I don't." She told his body to ignore pain. Also, the sick had begun to spread upward from the bladder already... so she forced it down again.

"Uhh... all right." The man coughed.

Althea decided to help by taking away his embarrassment. She glanced away because he wanted her to as he emptied the toxic green fluid into the bucket. Once the last of it left his body, she released the psionic link. The man slumped back to sit on the edge of the bed. Althea shifted her attention to Dr. Ruiz, purging the sick from him as well. When she finished, he limp-ran off to find a container to hold the toxic urine he desperately needed to get rid of.

She shook her head at the stupid. They had the bucket right there. Already, a bit of sick vapor gathered around her nose, mouth, and lungs. She cleansed herself, then added to the bucket on the floor. The man's non-reaction to her using the bucket out in the open confirmed he came from a scrag tribe, even though he didn't really talk like one. City people became embarrassed if she made water in front of them. Dr. Ruiz, red faced and sweating, returned carrying a glass container in one hand and a fat rifle in the other. He walked in, stopping short the instant he spotted her using the bucket. He shook his head chuckling.

She looked at him. *I'm not being primitive. It's a bad sick. We shouldn't move it around. You should have let me stop pain. It burns bad.*

Redness and sweating proved her right, though Dr. Ruiz pretended it hadn't hurt much at all. He poured the contents of his flask into the metal pail. "Back away. Preferably out into the hall."

Althea took the formerly sick visitor by the hand and guided him out of the room.

The *fwoosh* of a flamethrower accompanied the room glowing with orange light. Certainly, such a device made for a bizarre addition to a doctor's toolkit. However, almost every disease Althea cured ended up as either abnormally viscous pee or a horrifying glop of slime someone threw up. In either case, the discharge remained a danger to anyone who could catch the same sick from it. Burning it proved to be the fastest, safest way to clean up.

Dr. Ruiz emerged from the room, flame rifle balanced back over his right shoulder. "Well, that's that. Thank you, Althea. I feel much better. We still have a problem."

She blinked. "What?"

"Whatever sickness this man had, it's — "

"My name is Kellis," said the visitor.

Dr. Ruiz nodded in greeting. "Welcome to Querq. I'm Dr. Ruiz. This is Althea."

"I don't believe..." Kellis hugged Althea off her feet, squeezing her a little too hard to be comfortable.

The overwhelming sense of relief, gratitude, and love coming from the man stopped Althea from protesting the crushing grip. He knew she'd saved his life. Also, the 'love' surrounding him didn't come off as worshipful, so didn't make her feel too awkward, no more so than a man twice her age giving off the same emotion a little boy might after his mother saved him from being eaten by a giant millipede.

After he set her down, she took a few deep breaths, then checked everyone again for sickness, finding none. Without the disease in him, the man appeared younger, likely in his middle twenties. His lack of shirt revealed prominent ribs and a few small scars from hunting or small creature attacks. His pants, made from relatively intact grey linen, smelled foul and sickly, sweat-stained and grimy.

"What problem?" asked Althea.

"Whatever disease this man had is all over the room." Dr. Ruiz gestured at the door. "It is also in his clothing and more than likely on his skin. We already destroyed his tunic since it had dried, infectious vomit crusted into it. You'll need to clean up right away and we'll get you something else to wear."

Kellis promptly removed his pants and stood there naked, giving off only a mild sense of disappointment at losing a possession. "You will destroy my things?"

Dr. Ruiz nodded. "We must. This disease is highly contagious. We will give you something to replace them."

"All right." Kellis looked around. "Where can I wash?"

"Renata had the sick, too," said Althea.

As if responding to her name, the nurse appeared at the corner of the hall, carrying a bucket. She paused, staring at Kellis, and threw off a mixture of shock, embarrassment, interest, and a small bit of lust, though kept a perfectly straight face.

Dr. Ruiz beckoned her over and patted the flame rifle.

"Are you going to burn the room, too?" asked Althea.

"No. But it will need to be disinfected. At least we have proper supplies now, thanks to you."

She furrowed her brows. "I didn't get supplies."

Renata carried the bucket containing her sick into the contaminated room and set it on the floor next to the other pail.

"Everything the police are doing here is because of you." Dr. Ruiz smiled and flicked the safety off the flame rifle. "One moment."

Althea sighed to herself as the doctor went in to burn the contents of the second bucket. Sometimes, it *did* feel like the city police wanted to 'have' her the same way raiders did. Only, instead of taking her away somewhere to own, they brought themselves here to where she lived. Maybe it didn't quite count as the same thing. The city police didn't worship her, either... though they did often make her feel like a strange creature whenever they studied her. Still, they gave off genuine curiosity and a desire to help... and she could tell them to go away if they ever broke her trust.

Ruiz emerged from the room, a wisp of fire sputtering at the barrel of the bulky rifle. "This is not good. Althea, I have to ask you to check everyone who came into contact with Kellis, mostly the Watch who found him unconscious on the ground a short distance from the gate and brought him here... plus anyone who's spent more than a few minutes around them. Whatever disease he had is extremely contagious. I'll clean up in here."

Althea squeezed her hands into fists. "Okay. Going right now!"

She raced down the hall, out the door, and sprinted as fast as she could to the gate.

## 8

# LOVE

Althea stared at the ceiling of the bedroom she shared with Karina, unable to sleep.

Her sister lay next to her, also still awake. They'd only made it dark a few minutes ago. Lights they could turn on and off using buttons felt odd to have in Querq, but not terribly strange in general. Some raider camps had loud machines like the engines of their buggies that turned ethanol into electricity. The unusual part came from the boxes the city police brought here for power. They didn't make much sound at all, merely a faint whirring.

No sense wasting time trying to understand how the big city devices could produce the 'lectric without roaring like a raider buggy zooming across the desert. She had bigger problems: like why she couldn't fall asleep.

"I don't understand."

Karina stirred. "What is bothering you?"

"Why can't I sleep? I'm so tired I don't wanna move."

"You were quiet at dinner. Is something wrong?"

"I don't know." Althea yawned. "Lots of people had a bad sick. A man came here trying to find me for help. The sick in him attacked like twenty people. I made it go away, but"—she yawned—"I wanna sleep now and can't."

"Twenty people?" Karina rolled on her side, facing her. "That's a lot."

"Yeah. Dr. Ruiz said it's really tagious. He asked the city police for help."

Karina rolled her eyes. "What are they going to do about a disease? They can't shoot it."

Althea grinned, then yawned again.

"Sometimes, when you get really tired, it's hard to fall asleep. I don't know why. Maybe you are worried about the sick."

"No. It's gone. I fixed it."

Karina poked her in the side. "Then it must be something else keeping you up. What are you thinking about?"

"Den."

"Oh?" Karina grinned. "What about him?"

She huffed. "I don't know if he's a boyfriend or a friend. Why is boyfriend not the same as a boy who is a friend?"

"Do you love him?"

Althea swished her feet back and forth. "I love everyone. How can I tell if he's different?"

Chuckling, Karina rolled onto her back again. "Oh, you'll know. Trust me."

"Grr. Everyone keeps saying I'll know, but I don't." She pretend-fumed.

"You are only twelve, *mija*."

Althea grumbled. "I know. Almost too old to find a seeker."

"Thea…" Karina nudged her. "You're not a scrag anymore. There's no reason for you to get married so young. They only live to like thirty, so they have to start when they're still kids."

She sighed. "No… they get old, too."

"I know some do get old, but they start families when they are too young because it's so easy to die out there. You know the law here, right?"

"Yeah."

Althea shifted her eyes around, moving the light spots they projected around the ceiling as a sort of game. The Ravens wouldn't let a boy and girl become a family until they had sixteen birthdays. In tribes like the one Den came from, most already had a mate by fourteen. Some of the other girls made fun of Yala for being sixteen and not having a husband. Althea considered talking to Officer David or maybe Officer Jess about how things worked in the modern city, but decided against it.

"What I'm saying is, stop worrying about it. You'll know when the time is right." Karina nudged her. "I didn't care about boys at all until a couple years ago. I'm not really sure how or why they went from annoying and smelly and not wanting to be around them to frustrating."

"Frustrating?"

"The boys I liked, I couldn't be with." She frowned. "The council keeps track of families. It's bad to love someone you're sorta related to."

"Oh. I remember. No inbeading."

Karina laughed. "Okay. I have an idea. Look at my feelings now."

Her sister radiated an unfamiliar sort of emotion combining love, lust, and a little embarrassment with a sense of longing, wonder, and uncertainty.

"Umm…"

Karina covered her mouth to mute a laugh. "I'm thinking about Axton. Not sure if it's just a crush or real love yet. But… if you start feeling the same way about Den, then he's definitely your boyfriend."

"Why do you want to crush him if you like him?"

"Thea…" Karina barked a laugh, then pulled her into a hug, kissing her atop the head. "Please don't ever change. You are too cute."

Althea giggled. "What?"

Karina tried her best to explain what it meant to have a crush. It mostly made sense, even though Althea hadn't yet experienced anything like it. The strong love her sister felt for her put a huge smile on her face and calmed her worries about the bad sick. She decided to stop fretting over her feelings toward Den or anything else and simply let life happen. For now, she wanted to be happy as long as she got to share a bedroom with her sister.

It probably wouldn't be too much longer before Karina ended up like Corinne and lived in a different house with a man so he could put babies inside her. She once said Althea absorbed love like a sponge since she hadn't known any for most of her life. Truth being, this time she spent with her sister made her so happy she often cried a little. When the day finally arrived and she could no longer sleep in the same bed beside her sister, Althea would miss it terribly. But… she refused to complain. Karina deserved to be happy, too. Also, it probably wouldn't be long after they no longer shared a bed that Karina had a baby for Althea to help love.

Content to focus on the present rather than become upset at the future, Althea closed her eyes and snuggled close. Running back and forth across Querq tired her out more than cleaning sick out of so many people. Her anxiety over Den solved for the time being, she finally drifted off to sleep.

## 9

## FAR AND WIDE

On the way out of the school the following afternoon, Althea spotted Father waiting for her.

She ran ahead of the crowd of kids all scrambling off in different directions and hugged him, despite worrying what his serious mood meant.

"Did you enjoy learning today?" asked Father.

"Yes." She grinned. "I love it."

He smiled. The joy coming from her echoed in his emotions as well, but not for long. Seriousness returned along with his smile going away.

"Something is wrong."

"Not exactly wrong. I don't agree with them, but they want you to be part of a meeting even though you are a child."

"A meeting?" She blinked.

"Because you are able to heal the sickness the man Kellis brought here."

She shivered. "It's back?"

"As far as we know, it has not returned. We are confident you cured everyone." Father took her hand, walking with her toward the center of town. "Kellis has told the council he is from a village called Afbee. Everyone there is sick. Dr. Ruiz is not surprised considering how fast it started to spread here. He said if we didn't have you, everyone in Querq would have been ill within days. You stopped it early."

"Oh, no... a whole village has the sick?" Althea's chest tightened in pity. "Can I go there to help them?"

Father's mood darkened. "This is why I am not happy."

"Oh." She looked down. "They want me to go."

"The council doesn't want you to go, nor have they said you cannot. I think they are not opposed to the idea, but haven't yet decided if you should go."

"You don't want me to." She jogged, trying to keep up with his long strides. "Even if to help people?"

"I do not want you to be hurt or lost." He made a noise part sigh, part chuckle. "I now understand raiders are no threat to you. The powers you have are scary."

She stuck her tongue out. "I am not scary. I'm determined."

"That you are, Thea." He squeezed her hand. "That you definitely are."

Althea followed him to the big building at the almost center of Querq where the Ravens held counsel. Officer David said the place had once been something called a 'theater.' He figured they probably decided to make it the council chambers because it had lots of seats for people to come listen to the judges talk about stuff. The fancy building seemed older than everything around it, the walls decorated in flaking plaster and little statues of babies with wings. Father went past a heavy curtain into the massive room full of ancient red-cushioned chairs, down a narrow aisle to the spot of bare floor in front of the tall judge desk.

The two women and three men there hadn't changed

much since the last time she spoke to the Ravens. She still thought of them as such due to the long, scary shadows they cast on the wall behind them. Each one sat behind a little block of wood bearing a name. She hadn't been here to see them since learning how the frozen speaking worked. Karina told her the blocks held the 'judge names,' which someone took upon becoming part of the council regardless of whatever name they had from birth. Leftmost, a thirtyish woman sat behind the name Rivera. The eldest man next to her, Althea thought of as nice and grandfatherly. His block read 'Barton.' In the middle, the man with the long beak-like nose, Granville. To his right sat Warrick, a short, somewhat pudgy man who always gave off irritation and impatience. Finally, Whitmore, a grey-haired woman. She, as much as Althea had seen, appeared to be the wisest of the judges.

Dr. Ruiz, Kellis, Officer David, and an unfamiliar woman in a city police uniform stood in a group before the judge desk. The strange woman didn't carry a weapon, so she must be one of those 'admin' people who didn't fight bad guys. Various bits of tech hung from her belt, all the gadgets blinking or glowing from little lights. She seemed young, but older than twenty, and gave off a sense of smart. Though not as pale as some of the Transit Tribe, she didn't look like someone native to Querq, either, having the same shade of light brown skin as Officer David. Everyone radiated varying degrees of concern, though Dr. Ruiz and the strange woman gave off the most.

Althea stepped from the carpeted aisle onto the smooth floor studded with sparkling flecks like chips of shiny copper frozen in ice, though the clear substance had to be a kind of plastic as it didn't melt nor feel cold. The way the metallic bits glinted wherever she looked proved mesmerizing and distracting.

"Well, now that she is here," said Warrick, "We can repeat everything all over again."

Whitmore shot him a cautionary look. "I am sure she is well aware of the situation already." The elder woman smiled at her. "I understand you are attending school."

"Yes." Althea smiled. "Thank you for letting me go. I love it."

Barton cleared his throat. "The visitor, Kellis, speaks of this disease in his home village of Afbee. He tells us he learned of Querq, specifically your presence here, from a passing trader, and came to ask for help."

Kellis nodded. "My village is cursed. I fear we have made the spirits angry and they punish us with sickness. When the trader, Mako, told me he found The Prophet here, I knew the spirits sent me a message."

She tensed at the word 'prophet.' It bothered her for many reasons, the biggest being raiders. For five years, she'd been 'The Prophet,' an object to be taken as a prize. Being called that reminded her of captivity. Second, and far pettier, a prophet could see the future. She couldn't, so it didn't even make sense.

At least Kellis didn't use the name in a bad way. Truth be told, most everyone in the Badlands smart enough to speak in complete sentences knew of her as The Prophet. She'd have to change its meaning, starting with what it meant inside her head. Anyone who thought of her as a prize would be in for a shock.

"You had a sick." Althea looked up at the judges while gesturing at Dr. Ruiz. "He got it. Renata, too. And people on the Watch."

"It's quite contagious." Dr. Ruiz glanced down at a datapad. "I don't have the equipment here to study it, but thanks to our friends from the city, it's being looked into."

"Initial testing confirms it is a viral pathogen, though

not one we have seen before." The woman in the black police clothes activated a holographic screen over her left arm. "The lab is preparing to study it, though due to the nature of the virus, they are taking extreme precautions."

Althea gasped. "You sent the sick to the big city? Why!"

Officer David approached and put a hand on her shoulder. "We have medical personnel who are trained in ways to handle dangerous substances. A small amount of this man's blood was transported to a lab for evaluation. This stuff is out there. We need to know how to cope with it if it ever manages to reach the city in an uncontrolled manner."

"Oh." She bit her lip. "I don't think I can help the big city. There are too many people."

"Likely true. The agent spreads too fast." Dr. Ruiz cringed. "I've been talking with Phoenix about her findings." He indicated the woman in the city police uniform. "Our theory is it may be some sort of biological weapon used by either the corporates or the old government during the war. The villagers at Afbee must have stumbled on an old facility or perhaps an unexploded munition and accidentally released the agent."

"I'm not sure I follow," said Warrick. "Agents? What is a 'biological weapon'?"

Dr. Ruiz and Phoenix exchanged a glance, both giving off frustration.

"Let me try to explain." Phoenix took a deep breath. "Do you understand the idea of germs and viruses?"

Granville and Barton nodded. The other judges appeared confused.

"All right. Basic biology then. Germs and viruses are tiny living organisms. They are so small they can't be seen by a person without the use of microscopes, machines that let us see extremely tiny things. Whenever a person becomes sick, it's because some manner of germ or virus invaded their body and their immune system is trying to fight it off."

Althea thought about the way she 'saw' sick inside a person. She didn't perceive a bunch of tiny little bugs, more a cloud of color that didn't belong. Probably the same thing. The woman made sense. Bad things got into a body to hurt it and Althea kicked them out.

Phoenix paused to let the judges ask questions, but none did. "Some germs and viruses are natural. I'm sure most of you have experienced a cold."

Once she explained what 'a cold' was, the judges nodded.

"A biological weapon is a virus or germ that people deliberately make more dangerous and then introduce to an enemy population in hopes of sickening them, possibly causing death. The civilized world has more or less discontinued their use as they are cruel and unpredictable. However, the society of 327 years ago was not so enlightened. Our history has documented cases, mostly coming from the corporate side, where they used biological agents to infect a population in hopes of turning their loyalty."

"All right, now I have a question." Judge Whitmore held her hand up. "How would making people sick cause them to become friendly to the side making them sick?"

"The cure." Phoenix clasped her hands in front of herself. "The corporates bombed areas with disease, then pretended not to know where the sickness came from while offering the victims a cure either for free or at low cost. The people didn't know who made them sick, so they saw one side as helping them where the government could not."

"Evil." Althea scowled. "If the people where Kellis came from found an old sick, I want to help them."

"This could be a trick." Father grasped Althea's shoulder protectively. "To lure her from the safety of Querq."

Althea looked at Kellis. "Are you trying to trick me?"

"No, Prophet. On the spirits themselves, I swear it." Kellis knelt before her.

His emotions rang true: adoration, gratitude, and hope. She also peeked into his thoughts. He left his home, not expecting to survive the trip to Querq. He still reeled in shock at having made it alive, and worried a little how someone named 'Durango' would react to his bringing her there—if she went. His recent memory contained images of people dressed in dingy grey tunics, some with matching pants, others wearing extremely ratty Before-Time clothes, a handful dressed only in scraps or body paint. They occupied a fairly typical looking village of junk huts, all seeming weary and sick. A bearded man with dark brown skin and clothing much closer to stuff from the modern world appeared in another memory, sitting beside a big pull-wagon loaded with stuff. His long coat, pants, and various bits of armor proved him not a scrag nor part of the village. The man said, 'she is in Querq and will help any who ask' over and over again. Kellis had burned the concept of The Prophet being in Querq into his mind so much, a five-second event replayed continuously in his memory.

She tried to telepathically dig deeper around the idea of Durango's identity. An image of a man in his later thirties appeared, dressed in a strange bluish jumpsuit more patchwork repair than original material. Kellis thought of him as the leader of their group, proud, stubborn, and extremely wary of angering the spirits. Nothing she hadn't seen before or couldn't handle.

"Please don't bow to me." Althea cringed. "I don't like it or want to be worshiped."

Kellis scrambled to his feet. "Sorry."

She looked up at Father. "He speaks true. His people need help. Can we go?"

"It is dangerous." Dr. Ruiz winced. "We don't know the full extent of the disease's capability. Anyone, except maybe for Althea, who goes there might not return. We're confident she can avoid becoming sick and will be able to fully rid herself of any disease before returning to Querq."

"You mean to send her out there alone?" Judge Barton blinked. "She is too small."

"But capable." Judge Warrick gestured at her. "The raiders who attacked us a month ago, she sent them all away. Not one Watch fired a shot. She will not be alone. Kellis will be showing her the way."

All five Ravens stared at her, their emotions swirling between fear and awe. Weeks earlier, Althea happened to be near enough to the gate to hear an alarm go out of raiders planning to attack. In hopes of making sure no one, not even raiders, died, she rushed outside the wall before the gate closed. The sight of The Prophet walking out to meet them alone made some of the raiders laugh at how easy their conquest would be... until she sent them scurrying off into the Badlands, screaming in terror.

No one would kidnap her again.

Ever since she'd done that, the Watch no longer constantly worried someone might sneak in and abduct her. She'd gone from protectee to protector, a change she didn't necessarily mind. Karina and Father made her feel safe enough not to need the entire town constantly defending her. Her only true worry came from the modern city: synthetics. If someone else like Teal showed up to kidnap her, she'd be as defenseless as any ordinary unarmed twelve-year-old. Even her ability to run fast wouldn't help. She couldn't outrun one of them.

"I will go with her," said Father.

"But..." Althea hugged him. "Karina would be too worried if we both left. She needs you, too."

"Count me in," said Teal, as she emerged from the curtain at the entrance.

Everyone shifted to look at her. She stood out among the people of Querq not only for her nearly pure white skin but also her violet eyes and neon-blue hair. Though she looked barely midway into her twenties, she projected an attitude more like someone twice her age. Her preference for modern city clothes, mostly black, only added to the effect. The woman strolled down the aisle between seats to the open area in front of the judge desk.

"Was going by outside, heard someone talking about biological weapons, so I got curious, wondering what sort of mess went on." Teal nodded in greeting to Father. "I can't get sick."

He still regarded her warily, one of the few people in town who knew the truth of her initial reason for visiting. Althea had completely forgiven her for the kidnapping. She couldn't read any emotions from a synthetic psionically, but as far as ordinary human perception went, Teal radiated sincerity.

Kellis gawked at her.

Althea peeked into his head. The man thought her simultaneously beautiful, terrifying, and alien. He'd never seen anyone with blue hair before, and only a handful of pale people, but none as white as her. The man thought of her as a spirit come to visit the living. He said nothing, too frightened she'd be angry with him for daring to think her pretty.

"I don't know..." Father rubbed his forehead.

"What?" Teal raised an azure eyebrow at him. "There's nothing out there I can't handle."

"Not you. I mean... I don't know what to do with myself." He chuckled. "She is right. Karina would be upset."

Father's strong urge to protect Althea wet her eyes. She didn't want him to be hurt out in the Badlands, nor could she let Karina spend the next several days crying all the time. Her sister couldn't possibly cope with *both* of them leaving. She gave him a gentle psionic prod to accept the idea of staying here to watch over Karina, and trust Althea to keep herself safe.

"You will have her with you," said Judge Barton. "If you become sick, she can make you well."

"By that logic..." Officer David exhaled hard. "I will go along as well. Fernando is needed here, both for the sake of his elder daughter and his duties with the Watch."

Discussion went back and forth among the adults. They all agreed if an expedition were to happen, Althea needed to go since no one else could do anything about the disease. Phoenix had technical knowledge about medicine stuff, but the idea of going into an area affected by uncontained viruses terrified her, despite everyone telling her Althea could cure it right away. Officer David didn't mind the risk. Teal simply could not become sick to a biological virus.

Eventually, the council decided to send only Teal, David, Althea, and Phoenix, with Kellis accompanying them to show the way as well as return to his home. They'd drive in an ethanol-burning buggy left behind by a defeated raider attack due to no one really caring if the vehicle ended up lost or destroyed. The people who told Officer David what to do didn't want to risk one of their flying cars becoming contaminated with virus and needing to be abandoned.

"There is a good chance we might have to burn everything we take with us," said Phoenix, her voice shaky. "It depends on how nasty this stuff is. We can't risk bringing it back here. Anything porous must be thoroughly disinfected or burned. The vehicle, we either park a safe distance from his village and walk in, or we go over it with a flamethrower a mile or two from Querq on the way back."

Althea shrugged, thinking them overly scared. The sick already came to Querq once and she beat it.

## 10

# THE EXPEDITION

**P**reparations for the trip took a full day.

Torn between her need to rush off and help people in dire need and her guilt at making Karina and Father worry, Althea felt as if twenty-four hours took the time of forty. She barely concentrated on school and spent the rest of the day shadowing Karina. Once it got dark, she curled up on the sofa between Father and Karina. He read a story to himself from a datapad the city police brought here while Karina practiced knitting. Father remarked at how Althea behaved like a lonely cat, so she obligingly meowed a few times.

The delay came from David requesting additional supplies from the big city to help with decontamination. Phoenix took a hovercar back to the big city to collect everything, and they needed to wait for her return. If the worst happened and their entire group ended up 'drenched in virus,' she feared they would all need to scrub down, then sit out in the desert naked for a while as their clothing basked in an inflatable gas tent—a small price to pay not to have to burn everything they carried.

The buggy, however, they'd likely abandon if they couldn't leave it at a safe distance from Afbee. Phoenix brought back fancy city machines, little handheld blinking gadgets, capable of 'seeing' viruses on surfaces. She would be able to tell if their stuff needed to be cleaned or left behind.

Althea continually reassured Karina she could protect herself from anything in the Badlands... except perhaps robots, but Teal and two city police would be going with her. Karina still worried, as big sisters tended to do, but managed not to panic.

Over breakfast the morning they planned to set out for Afbee, Father and Karina debated going with her. While Father had the skills and experience necessary to navigate the world outside Querq, Karina didn't know how to fight or use a gun. Paama, four years her junior, would be more of a benefit to the group. Then again, Karina hadn't grown up as a scrag, forced to learn how to fight, hunt, and hide.

Besides, Althea didn't want her sister getting sick or hurt.

After breakfast, Father and Karina walked with her to the garage. Two dirt-covered women and three men lived and worked in a giant Before-Time building, doing what they could to keep a handful of extremely old vehicles working. The garage had five huge doors big enough for drive machines. Parts of the dirt-brown structure lost to time and war damage had long since been repaired by various pieces of scrap metal or concrete. A strong odor of alcohol and grease saturated the air, powerful enough to taste along with the stink of ethanol and decaying farm waste. The mechanics also produced Querq's supply of fuel: ethanol as well as something they called bio-diesel. Althea didn't care to understand how drive machines worked or what they ate. If she could ride in one, okay. If she had to walk, okay. Nothing with a smell as bad as what clung to the mechanic's building *needed* to exist.

Metal-on-metal hammering and a stream of bad words echoed inside the garage. She didn't think yelling at a machine would make it work, but the men sure seemed to believe it helped.

Two of the mechanics, Jacinda and Greg, grew up in Querq. The other three arrived more recently, after word of Althea's presence here spread, attracting people in search of safety. In addition to the drive machines, the mechanics also repaired other things like the Water Man's pumps, the gate motor, basically anything with gears. Lately, they'd been tinkering on a number of vehicles left behind by the raiders Althea scared off. The ones closest to her experienced such a crash of telempathic fear they leapt out of their buggies and ran off on foot. She didn't mind, not considering it stealing. If the raiders lost their buggies, it would make it less likely they could roam around and hurt people.

Generally, the sorts of vehicles raiders built tended to be quite dangerous, and came in two basic types: 'fast buggies,' little more than scrap metal (often old pipes) bolted together into a wedge-shaped frame with an engine, seat, and wheels—and what they called 'war wagons,' much larger vehicles often covered in scrap metal armor. No two raider buggies looked alike, though the fast ones usually had giant back wheels and tiny front wheels. The war wagons more closely resembled Before-Time drive machines with a bunch of extra (often pointy) parts added to them.

Only the larger raider groups had the intelligence and resources to use buggies at all—unless they got lucky and found some as well as the ethanol to run them on. The largest marauder bands sometimes even captured settlers who knew how to make things out of metal, so their buggies looked less like rolling piles of junk and more like vehicles. The city police people couldn't explain how any machinery from before the war remained in working order, but Althea knew: The Many. If someone wanted to use a machine to spread pain and suffering, *he* would make sure it worked.

Fast buggies typically had only one or two seats plus a space in the back for a shooter or captured slave. Sometimes, raiders stood on side boards or behind the engine—though they often fell off. She'd healed countless men and women who ended up losing their grip and eating the ground at high speed.

Jacinda stood by a large raider buggy, one firmly in the category of war wagon because all four of its wheels were the same size and it had an actual cabin with seats. She mentioned to Officer David and Phoenix they didn't need to worry about getting something called a 'flat' because the tires were solid. Raiders melted down junk tires to make them. Althea didn't like the tires, specifically because of the spikes all over them. Raiders certainly intended to run people over, though the spiky metal bits sticking out from the tread didn't look long enough to kill anyone.

The elevated body had an almost egg-like shape when viewed from the side, a pod suspended on springy metal legs. David remarked it looked like a 'passenger car raised up on truck tires.' The interior looked to have almost the same amount of room as a city police hovercar, two seats up front and a bench in back. Rusty metal plates welded on the outside gave it more of a substantial body than a cage of aluminum tubes.

*It's different...* Althea wandered around it, then walked under the cabin, having to duck only a little. She remembered the vehicle from the attack. A month ago, a whole bunch of nasty spikes covered the main body, making it look like a giant burr. The mechanics must have removed the bloodstained metal shards, probably using them to reinforce the body plating.

"So how far is this thing going to take us?" asked Officer David.

"Far enough." Jacinda patted the back end. "For its size, the engine's kind of small. Guess it's all they had to put in it. You got two fifty-gallon drums on here for the ethanol. Used to be just hanging on the ass end. We put some plating around them, but they still make for a huge target. Try not to get shot at from behind unless you like being on fire."

Phoenix cringed. "I don't really..." She side-eyed David. "Why aren't we taking a patrol craft?"

He sighed. "You know. It's not an operational emergency, so command isn't willing to risk losing a PC to viral contamination *or* one of those mysterious disappearance events. Besides, a PC would scare the hell out of the locals. Kellis is from a scrag tribe. If they saw a flying car come out of the sky, they'd either run or start worshiping us as gods."

"Your... car... flies?" Kellis raised both eyebrows.

The man didn't look any more primitive than anyone else in Querq. They'd given him a white shirt, plain pants, and shoes. However, he still possessed a slightly feral glint in his eye. Althea sensed fear on him, likely because he knew going home would almost certainly make him sick again. However, he remained committed to going, hopeful she could protect him and fix the curse on his home.

Some discussion had gone around concerning relocating Kellis and his people back to Querq. The city police thought scrags needed to be 'saved' from the Badlands. Then again, they thought *everyone* ought to leave and go join the modern city. The Ravens declared they would welcome Kellis's tribe on three conditions: one, the villagers did not bring any sickness here. Two, the villagers wanted to come here. And three, the villagers could make the journey. According to Kellis, around 200 people lived there, most of whom suffered from varying degrees of sickness. About a dozen had become too sick to do more than lay around waiting to die. A few years ago, they had closer to 500 people.

Father and a few of the Ravens questioned how the village hadn't collapsed. If everyone there happened to be too sick to work, hunt, or farm, what did they eat? His suspicions made sense, though Althea saw no explanation or deceit in the outsider's thoughts. Kellis believed the spirits provided for them. The cook pot always had something in the morning and something at night, though couldn't say where the gatherers obtained the food.

"Please be careful." Karina hugged her.

"I will." Althea leaned into the embrace, content to cling to her older sister until she absolutely had to get in the buggy.

Teal emerged from a side street a few blocks away, wearing a tank top, blue military-style pants, and boots, carrying a duffel bag over one shoulder seemingly too large for her to be able to lift. Father's mood shifted to mild distrust as the synthetic woman walked by them and put her bag in the vehicle.

Althea peered up at him. *She is changed. You do not need to worry.*

He closed his eyes and let out a soft sigh. "So you say. I should believe... but I want you to be safe, so I distrust everything."

She hugged him.

Father brushed his hand over her head. The loving contact made her squeeze him harder... and experience a moment of not wanting to leave. Althea savored the few minutes she had left before they got underway. She couldn't let other people suffer purely because she adored her family. Alejandra, the woman Father had become sweet on, said she acted like a cat who kept wanting to be picked up and held—probably why Father started comparing her to a cat when she curled up beside him on the sofa.

Jacinda walked David, Teal, and Phoenix around the large buggy, showing them important parts. Finally, she grabbed the body and made it bounce up and down using only one hand. "Don't try to go too fast if the terrain gets rough. The wheels have a lot of play and big springs. Bounce it too much and it'll pull a turtle, wind up on its back."

Phoenix leaned in the open side door, looking around by the steering wheel. "It doesn't have any instruments…"

"Nope." Jacinda laughed. "Raiders don't need numbers for how fast they're going. Catching up to whoever they're chasing is fast enough. Not catching up is too slow."

"This thing uses… fuel or something, right? Not like a power plant?" Phoenix scrunched her nose. "Shouldn't there be a display to tell us when it needs more?"

"There is." Jacinda laughed. "When it stops going."

David chuckled. "It carries enough to get us there and back a few times."

"How far are we going?" Teal glanced at Kellis.

"Long ways." He counted on his fingers. "Took me ten sleeps to get close enough for your warriors to find me. Least… think it was ten sleeps. So sick."

Teal nodded once. "So somewhere between 130 and 180 miles."

David, Phoenix, and Father looked at her.

"How did you get 180 miles from ten sleeps?" asked Father.

"The average human walking speed is two miles an

hour. Assuming he spent between eight and ten hours a day on the move, it's a rough estimate if he came straight here and didn't lose time wandering around in circles."

Kellis fidgeted at his shirt. "Walked from when I woke up 'til it got too dark to see. Trader gave me pretty good idea how to find this place. Didn't get lost much. Had ta smash some bugs, but it didn't take too long."

*The Many didn't want him to find me.* Althea frowned.

"Let's get going then." David patted the side of the buggy. "Sooner we're on the way, sooner we get back."

Karina squeezed Althea hard enough to make her gurgle.

"Calm yourself, *mjia*." Father patted Karina on the arm. "Althea can protect herself. She is not the same mouse."

"Squeak." Althea leaned over and rubbed her head on his arm. "Am I a mouse now? Or still a cat?"

He chuckled. Putting an arm around her shoulders.

"I know… I just worry." Karina looked down. "She is too nice sometimes. Anything could happen out there. I know she wants to help people, but she's only a child."

"No ordinary child," said Teal. "She'll be fine."

"Thank you for going with her." Father offered a hand. "It is not safe for you."

Teal accepted the handshake. "Thanks. Means a lot to hear you say that, but I'm not worried about the virus."

"Not virus… anything else." Father half smiled. "She can't fix your body."

"Oh, I'm a lot tougher than I look… and I fix myself, given enough time."

"And food bars." Althea whistled. "She ate *so* many and didn't get sick."

"That, too." Teal laughed.

Phoenix took a fancy electronic gun off her belt and

examined it. "Are you sure we'll be okay using these? Shouldn't we bring something lower tech?"

"The E-90 is the top of the line." David patted the one on his hip.

"That's not what I'm worried about." Phoenix put the weapon back in its holster. "You *did* read the reports about this place, right? Incidences of unexplained failures increase exponentially with the advancement level of technology. Carrying 'top of the line' laser pistols is almost asking for them to malfunction. Besides... I haven't touched one of these since school. I'm still shocked they handed me one without any complaining."

David laughed. "You know them better than that. They're hoping you get a taste for adventure and ask to transfer out of Admin."

"Unlikely." Phoenix exhaled.

David tilted his head. "Seriously? Not since school? Didn't you put in the required range time? I thought admin still had to go once a month."

"I've been busy. Medical school is somewhat demanding, you know." Phoenix shrugged. "It's not exactly difficult to hit something with a laser. Goes wherever you point it. Don't have to compensate for range or wind."

Karina pulled Althea close like a big child clutching a doll. "I don't know... she's only twelve. She shouldn't be going out there."

Father hugged them both, squishing the girls together. "She will be fine. Among the scrag tribes, children younger than her scout around ruins on their own for hours. She knows the way."

"Well." Karina folded her arms. "She's no scrag."

"Not anymore," deadpanned Althea. "I have the knowing of forks."

Karina laugh-cried at her deliberate primitive talk.

David radiated emotion like he wanted to laugh, but kept a straight face. "Not to be too technical, but her mother came from the modern world. She is not a scrag, never was. Merely grew up around them."

"Sergeant..." Phoenix sighed. "These people you refer to as 'scrags' are not genetically different from us. You talk about them as though they're some manner of genetic precursor to modern humans. They're simply people deprived of education and technology."

Althea held her arms up. "I don't look like them. Too pale."

"You're not pale, kiddo." Teal winked.

"She's actually kind of tan." Phoenix chuckled. "But if she's pale, you're a ghost."

"Guilty," muttered Teal. "Not by choice."

Althea scrunched her nose. "No one *chooses* what color they are."

"Umm..." David shrugged. "If you have enough money, you can."

She stared at him. His thoughts centered on something called Reinventions... a hospital sort of place where people could turn themselves any color they wanted, change boys into girls or the other way around, and even make people younger. His understanding of it made it sound as if it took many, many pay-things, so few citizens could afford doing it. Because of this 'Reinventions' place, rich, famous people stayed young forever.

She ground her toes into the dirt, thinking about something the city police lab people said to her. Her healing power had developed to such a high level, she had amazing control over her own body. The woman thought Althea's fear of being wifed made her keep herself little so no one would try to wife her. They thought she looked younger than her age. If, in fact, Althea stopped herself from growing up, she didn't do it on purpose. She never even thought about the idea of being able to do so. After learning she *could* do it, she wondered if she ought to. Then again, if she had such an ability, she could always try growing up to see if she liked it, then go back to her present size if she didn't.

This also meant she could stop herself from growing old and, perhaps, live forever… or at least be around for a really long time. She liked the idea because she'd be able to help so many more people if she didn't get old and go to the spirit place. Being a ghost would make it difficult to heal the living.

"Reinventions?" Teal struck a pose. "Not an option for me. I'm stuck this way. Not that I want to change."

Esteban, one of the mechanics, muttered to Felipe in Spanish about Teal, saying if she could change something, she needed bigger tits, and maybe an ass—suggesting she didn't presently have one. Both men emanated humor shaded with a bit of lust. Althea doubted they would do anything, merely found something lustful about the comment funny.

Karina blushed.

*What is tits?* asked Althea telepathically. The answer formed immediately in her sister's mind. *Oh. Why do they think she needs bigger ones? Do they think she is going to have hungry babies? Teal is not big.*

Karina covered her mouth to hold in laughter. Apparently, what the men said counted as rude and inappropriate. Althea didn't quite understand why a man would care about the size of 'tits' or why it would be rude to talk about them.

"I am not here for you to stare at," said Teal in Spanish, eyes narrowing. "If I'm too skinny for you, go find some other senorita to stare at."

The men coughed, radiating embarrassment, and scurried off into the garage.

Phoenix gave off a sense of satisfaction and amusement. The men's reaction to Teal understanding them set Karina off in uncontrolled laughter for a moment. Father shook his head, chuckling. Jacinda sighed, calling them fools.

"It's good to be happy with yourself." David climbed into the buggy. "Come on, everyone. Let's get going."

"Oh, I'm not happy with everything. My life's a bit of a mess." Teal climbed into the driver's seat. "I *am* content with my looks, though. Whenever my face can't open doors, my ass is narrow enough to let me slip in another way. Problem is, I can't really get *to* those doors for a while."

"Why not?" asked Phoenix as she crawled up into the back seat.

At the woman giving off an odd jealousy, Althea peeked at her thoughts. Phoenix considered Teal 'hot' and tried not to envy her appearance as being a synthetic, she'd been 'made perfect' and essentially cheated to being gorgeous while Phoenix had to do a lot of 'working out' stuff to keep her body of similar size. Althea grinned to herself at how Phoenix got a little flustered. She appeared to like both Teal *and* David the same way Karina liked Axton. Well, perhaps not the *same* way. Karina had told Axton she liked him. Phoenix simply daydreamed with no intention to act on it, merely admiring the view so to speak. Althea hadn't met many people who had the same emotions for both men and women, but the idea made a warm in the middle of her chest.

*She is lucky to have so much love.*

"Some people in fancy offices with tons of credits are kinda pissed off at me." Teal studied the area around the steering wheel. "Corporate fixer hired me to kidnap Althea. I decided not to."

"Merc?" asked Phoenix.

"Used to be. I'm kinda retired now."

"Why the hell would you take a job to kidnap a child?" asked Phoenix, seeming angry.

Teal sighed. "Because they made it sound like we'd be saving a special kid from the Badlands. You know, some little feral thing who wouldn't want to be saved but needed to be. Lying bastards."

Father and Karina grew clingier.

Althea emitted a pulse of love and confidence. She didn't want them consumed with worry over her. Going away from Querq on her own terms for a short time to help people didn't bother her at all. Staying here, doing nothing, while the villagers of Afbee suffered and died, she could not do. She *did* worry The Many would be upset for her interference and possibly attempt to harm Querq in her absence. She didn't try to antagonize him, though. It's not as if she ran around the Badlands looking for anyone in need of help. Kellis came to her.

"Back soon." Althea gave Karina and Father one last squeeze, then scampered over to the buggy, climbing easily up the frame and into the body. She sat in the backseat between Phoenix and David.

Kellis pulled himself up into the passenger seat, causing the body to bounce slightly.

"Umm." Phoenix glanced at her. "Where are your shoes? We're going way out into the wilds."

"Don't like them." Althea shrugged. "Father gave me some, but I only put them on when we have to be polite. I don't like how they feel."

"Althea and shoes." David chuckled. "You'd have an easier time getting a cat to wear a tuxedo."

Teal laughed, then shouted, "Hey, Jacinda? Where's the starter button?"

"Ripcord on the engine. I got it," yelled Jacinda while heading around behind the buggy.

"If those hovercars weren't so damn expensive, I'd say you tell command to screw off." Teal glanced back at them. "Virus indeed."

David smiled. "They are fully sealed. As long as we never opened the doors, we'd be fine. Kind of defeats the point, though."

"Also, I don't think Kellis would be able to properly navigate where we need to go from the air." Phoenix leaned forward, peering at him. "Right?"

"From the air?" Kellis scratched his head. "What's air gotta do with finding Afbee?"

David whistled.

The buggy rocked slightly and its engine sputtered to life, causing all the metal parts to vibrate rather noticeably, including the seats—anything bolted to the frame. Engine noise also made speaking impossible. To communicate, they had to shout or use telepathy.

"Wow. A ride *and* a good time." Teal squirmed in her seat. "This is going to be distracting."

Phoenix gave off a surge of embarrassment. David tried not to laugh.

"Why is it a good time?" yelled Althea.

Teal shifted into drive. "Ask me again when you're two years older."

"Oh." She frowned.

The joke must have something to do with wifeing. People from the modern city, like Teal and the Division 0 police, didn't like talking about such things near her. Raiders certainly didn't care. They'd often try to wife their slaves right out in the open whether or not she could see them. Althea liked it when they did so, because she could stop them. Best part, stopping it didn't even appear obviously her doing, which gave her the confidence to keep doing it. Changing someone else's emotions had become easier to her than even healing people. It didn't take much effort to destroy the mood David called 'lust' and replace it with calm or boredom. With the meaner raiders, she'd use fear, so they became scared of the slave they tried to wife and left them alone for good.

Sometimes, raiders did the wifeing away from her where she couldn't see or help... and made her heal the slave after if necessary. Althea bowed her head, ashamed for taking so long to find the courage to stand up for herself and others. For years, she had the power to stop raiders from hurting people, but had been too much of a scared child to use it. Going to Afbee to help the villagers felt like a small step toward making amends for all the suffering she hadn't been able to stop.

A few minutes later, she shook off the somberness and held her head high. Karina, David, and a few people in the big city who studied her psionic abilities all told her the same thing: she was a little kid who people mistreated. None of them blamed her for being afraid the raiders and scrags alike might burn her to death if they knew she could do more than heal. She shouldn't blame herself for being scared. Now, she could make a difference... and make a difference, she would.

"Right, so where are we going?" Teal steered the buggy into the street toward the gate, driving only a little faster than a person could walk.

"South." Kellis pointed. "There's an old stone path. A road of the ancient ones. We will follow it for most of the way. I hope The Prophet can free us of the curse."

David and Phoenix exchanged a look.

"I will make the curse go away." Althea smiled, confident no real 'curse' existed. As a kid, she used to think the same way... but after years fixing hurts and sicks people blamed on gods, spirits, and curses, she no longer believed *everything* bad came from a curse.

"What kind of situation are we walking into?" shouted Teal.

"My village suffers a curse from the old spirits. Our leader, Durango, does not know why the spirits are angry. He thinks we must endure their punishment until they are satisfied."

Phoenix scowled. "He's going to kill your people. A virus isn't a curse. Doing nothing but waiting for some nonsense spirits to change their minds is only going to make the situation worse."

"Spirits are real." Althea idly scratched at her arm. "But I don't think they are making the sick."

David let out a long breath. "I've seen things out here we don't have protocols for. Keep an open mind. I'm not sure what to expect. Most likely, this is a leftover bio weapon from the war, not a curse. However, we shouldn't discount the possibility it might be something weird. Have you read any of Lieutenant Wren's inquest reports?"

"Nope. Haven't really had the time for optional reading lately." Phoenix shook her head. "Besides, if I read about that stuff, I have to accept it exists. It's probably real, but if it's not in my head, I can pretend otherwise. I'm good focusing on science and leaving the crazy ghost stuff to other people. Can't zap a spirit."

"Zap?" yelled Althea.

"Oh, now you are asking me to split that hair." David grinned at Phoenix. "Electrokinesis *can*—at least according to the theory—affect spirits."

"You have been watching too many holo-vids." She held up her hand, making a pinchy gesture. A tiny spark sizzled between her thumb and index finger. "There is no way I'm going to use *this* as a weapon. I can make electronic devices to do things they shouldn't. That's about it. Need me to use a datapad with a missing power cell? Trick an electronic lock into opening? Sure. I can't generate enough power to even stun someone. Forget that lightning bolt nonsense. It's only in movies. The nastiest shock I can give someone is about the same as a kid scuffing their feet on carpet in the winter."

Althea bit her lip. She'd not only seen Anna throw lightning from her hands, she'd experienced the painful jolt of standing too close to someone the woman hit with it. Then again, Awakened psionics could do things not supposedly possible. Like Althea, Anna didn't want to be made a celebrity, so she decided not to tell Phoenix about her.

She scooted forward, leaning between the front seats so she could see better out the front. Unlike the city police's flying cars, the buggy had no solid windows, merely open holes where cars ought to have windows. This allowed a fairly stiff breeze in. Their buggy also didn't have the machine that made air cold, but it didn't really matter to her. The city police cars got *too* cold inside, like the machines modern people put food in. Since Althea did not consider herself food in need of preservation, she didn't want to sit inside a chilly box. The buggy could become uncomfortably warm at a standstill, but as long as they kept driving, enough air moved through it to be reasonably comfortable.

The springy wheel struts made the cabin bounce and rock continually as they traversed the uneven terrain. Every bump, dip, or small bit of scrub they ran over jostled Althea side to side against Phoenix and David. While she had no idea how fast they drove, the land outside rushed by at a decent speed. She'd never been in a war wagon before, but had seen them—and helped peel injured people away from spikes on the outside. She smiled at Jacinda removing the spikes on this one so no one mistook them for bad guys.

Raiders didn't usually drive war wagons to attack settlers or scrags, saving them for fights against other raider bands. If some idiot jumped on trying to kill the driver, they'd often end up impaled on spikes. If they didn't fall off and get run over or die before the wagon returned to camp, they'd end up killed, recruited, or enslaved.

*Raiders are stupid.*

"How long will it take us?" asked Althea.

David laughed.

"What?" She peered at him. "I am not being funny."

"We've only been out of Querq for ten minutes and the kid asks 'are we there yet?'" David kept laughing.

Teal snickered as well as Phoenix.

Kellis furrowed his brows, clearly confused why question had been worth laughing over.

"I am not trying to make funny." Althea grumbled. "*Be* funny. Sorry."

"Yeah." David continued snickering. "It's just an old thing. Kids in cars always ask 'are we there yet.'"

"No, we don't." She stuck out her tongue.

Teal peered down at her foot. "I've got this thing floored and we're doing a little over fifty as best I can tell. If nothing goes wrong, we should get there in about three hours."

"Three *hours*?" Kellis gasped. "Not days?"

"Welcome to the world of mechanical engineering." Teal patted the console. "If you can call this thing engineering."

# A DANGER TO THE INNOCENT

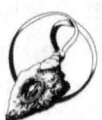

Althea sat quietly between David and Phoenix. Having grown tired of yelling over the engine and the wind, they'd switched to telepathy to discuss possible strategies for managing the virus once they arrived. She mostly kept her eyes closed due to the gale whirling around in the cabin.

Earlier that morning, Phoenix returned from the big city with protective equipment: strange helmets and puffy suits. They planned to stop the buggy a safe distance from Afbee and walk the rest of the way. Because the villagers might mistake the protective suits for scary Badland monsters and attack them, Teal and Althea would go in first, probably with Kellis. Doing so would certainly make him sick again, but he didn't mind if it helped get rid of 'the curse.'

The buggy bounced, rocked, and swayed in a never-ending dance. Althea felt like a hunk of potato in a bowl being swirled around. Despite the path they followed having been a road in the Before-Time, three centuries of dirt, debris, and weather roughened the ground. Whole sections of the strange flat stone the ancients used to make their driving places smooth either vanished or buckled inward, forming pits. In other spots, dirt collected in dunes on top of it, some as tall as huts.

A little over an hour after leaving Querq, the high-pitched buzzing of raider buggy engines racing at full throttle arose in the distance. Althea pulled her feet up onto the bench, grabbed the frame bars overhead, and pulled herself into a standing position, chest deep through a gap in the metal plate roof. Due to the lack of a solid windshield, the blast of air in her face didn't get much stronger compared to sitting down. For no particular reason, she turned her head left to move the wind out of her face and opened her eyes. Amid the flailing strands of her long blonde hair, she peered out at the desert. Three distinct trails of dust angled toward them, the dark spots at the front most certainly small raider buggies.

Althea sighed mentally. Of course, The Many wouldn't simply let her go help people without making it difficult.

"We have company," said Phoenix. "Three on the right, maybe a hundred yards."

"This thing looks like one of theirs. Maybe they're friendly?" yelled David.

"They took the spikes off," shouted Phoenix. "We don't look like raiders."

"As if they can see that from where they are," yelled Teal. "Pretty sure they won't care."

"No." Althea squinted at the distant buggies. "Raiders fight everyone. We are not part of their tribe, so they will attack."

"Can this thing go any faster?" yelled Phoenix.

"Nope." Teal shrugged. "I could push the pedal through the floor if you want, but it won't help."

"It would probably make the situation worse." David

readied his silver laser pistol, aiming it out the side window. "Probably best if we don't break our only transportation."

The incoming raiders closed distance rapidly. Their buggies probably had the same type of engine, but the vehicles weighed much less, having an aluminum frame instead of a full 'car body,' no armor plating, and much smaller tires. Some even used plastic bottles to hold their fuel. Each buggy carried two raiders: one driving and one clinging to the back end. From being around marauders so much and hearing them talk, Althea knew the ones on the outside would likely be crazy, fearless, and likely to attempt jumping onto their vehicle. They almost always tried to capture other working vehicles intact if possible, even if it cost them two to three dead people to claim a working war wagon. Much harder to fix, replace, or find a working war wagon than recruit another raider or three.

Raider tribes had different names for the crazies who jumped between moving vehicles: flyers, suiciders, death angels, the exalted, the terms came as varied as grains of sand. They rarely returned from raids injured. If something went wrong, the 'flyers' didn't come back at all.

Two of the incoming buggies broke formation, pulling up on either side of them while the third shadowed them a little farther away on the left side.

Althea made eye contact with the flyer clinging to the back of the buggy on the right. The instant he realized her eyes glowed bright blue, his bloodlust faded to the all-too-familiar elation of a raider realizing they'd found the Prophet. She squashed his combat rage down to a tepid sort of fear sufficient to keep him from jumping onto their vehicle. Before she could ask Teal to stop driving and let her out so she could send the raiders on their way, a burst of automatic gunfire came from the front seat. At almost the same time, a thin beam of searing dark-blue light appeared, connecting the back window of their vehicle to the desert a short distance behind the nearest small buggy, going through it as easily as a knife piercing a hologram. David's shot left a glowing melt hole in a metal plate on the facing side, but he failed to hit driver, jumper, or fuel tank.

A sensation like an icy spike stabbed Althea in the heart —death. The jolt proved painful enough for her legs to give out from under her. She dropped down out of the roof hole and curled into a ball on the metal bench seat, clutching her chest. Tears gathered in her eyes. Both buggies on the left veered off into the desert aimlessly. Teal swung her arm to the right, her pistol inches in front of Kellis's face, and fired twice out the open window. Althea cringed at the painful coldness from two more people dying less than twenty feet from her. She hadn't heard an automatic weapon, rather Teal firing a handgun faster than a human could move.

"Why did you kill them?" wailed Althea. "You don't have to!"

Teal glanced back at her, making a face as though she'd asked why they cooked food before eating it. "Raiders attacking us… I'm not going to bake them a cake."

Althea leaned against Officer David and sobbed.

"The heck happened to her?" asked Phoenix, shrouded in confusion and concern.

David put an arm around her. "She feels it when people or creatures die in her vicinity. It's painful."

"You shot at them, too," muttered Phoenix.

"I was trying to disable the vehicle without hitting anyone on it." David grumbled to himself. "There's not much to those things. I probably should have aimed for the engine."

"Sorry," said Teal in a tone that didn't sound terribly sorry. "If someone is going to die, I'd rather it be raiders and not us."

"My thoughts exactly." Phoenix's emotion shifted to pity for Althea, but also relief at the dead raiders.

"No…" Althea sniffled. "I can make them go away. They don't have to die."

Teal used one knee to hold the steering wheel steady while removing the magazine from her pistol and proceeding to snap new bullets in it one by one. City bullets looked weird: long, flat-sided sticks of blue stuff with silver foil on one end. "They are a scourge. Sure, you can send them away from us, but they're only going to end up hurting someone else."

"But…" She looked down. "They don't *have* to be raiders. They can change."

"Not likely," muttered Teal.

Althea lapsed into tears again.

Teal kept quiet for a moment, then sighed. "Sorry, kiddo. Look, maybe you're right. Could be a small chance they could wake up one day and think, 'hey, I shouldn't be a raider anymore. Maybe I should stop taking slaves, stabbing people, and stealing whatever I feel like. I'm going to go to school and get a decent job.'"

A hint of amusement peeked out from under the sympathy coming from David.

Althea sulked. Hearing it like that *did* make it sound dumb. A raider wouldn't simply stop being a raider for no reason. True, if she frightened them away, once her psionic power wore off and they no longer feared their own shadows, they'd go back to doing the same stuff: taking slaves, killing people, hurting people. But killing *them* didn't seem any better, even if leaving them to hurt others made The Many happy. Killing them also made The Many happy. He fed off pain, suffering, and death. Even people from the big city who became lost in the Badlands could soon find themselves losing control of their minds and becoming a raider or savage if left alone too long... especially those of weak willpower.

"How many innocent people do you think those men hurt?" asked Phoenix.

"I don't know." Althea sighed.

David rubbed her back, trying to be comforting.

"I know you hate violence, but sometimes, it's the best answer." Teal clicked the reloaded magazine back into her pistol and holstered it. "We don't really have the time to put them through occupational rehab."

Althea grumbled. "It *hurts* when people die near me." She patted her chest. "Like a knife. I feel them turn into ghosts. Bad people or nice people hurt the same."

"It's not like we went out hunting. They attacked us." Phoenix rubbed her hands repetitively down the clingy black fabric covering her legs. She gave off a ton of nervousness and unease. Clearly, she didn't like being around killing either.

"Rachel said some people deserve to die because they're just bad and will always be bad." Althea uncurled, stretching her legs out. She stared glumly at her lap, hating how the grim statement kept proving truer than not. "I don't like it."

"Neither do I," said Teal, "But it's the way the world is sometimes."

*The world is stupid and mean.* Althea closed her eyes and tried to think about helping people in Afbee. Had she known before leaving Querq that going to the village would require killing raiders, she'd still have gone. Awful as it made her feel to witness death, even of bad people, not going could mean 200 deaths... maybe. Neither Dr. Ruiz nor the city police knew exactly what the old sick would do to a person if left untreated, only that it had the capability of spreading rapidly. City people thought scrags needed saving. If someone like Beard—who lived in the big city but frequently went into the Badlands in search of valuable 'artifacts' to sell to modern people—found a person from Afbee and brought them back to the big city, the sick could end far more lives than Althea had numbers to count.

*We have to fix it before the sick goes everywhere.*

## 12

# SUPERSTITION AND DARKNESS

Cold pain lingered in Althea's chest.

She made sour faces at the empty space between the front seats, unable to be upset with Teal for shooting the raiders despite being hurt they died. She still intended to chase bad people off with fear or other emotions whenever she could. If they did bad stuff after she told them to stop, it couldn't be her fault. The fault for what another person did or didn't do lay squarely on them.

Kellis made the occasional suggestion of direction and plenty of comments about how much nicer riding in the buggy was compared to walking. He still couldn't believe they'd be able to make the trip to Afbee in mere hours. The man hadn't been in a working drive machine before. Not only did his village have none, their spirits forbid them from touching anything like technology, especially drive machines. However, since they used one to bring help back to the village, he didn't think the spirits would object.

*Strange.* Althea scrunched her nose. Scrag tribes tended to revere technology as magic and worship it. She'd never encountered a group afraid of it before. Kellis didn't have any actual fear of the buggy, only of making the other villagers angry for breaking rules. It seemed his experience in Querq, being healed and hearing people say a virus—not magic—made him sick had diminished his dread of the spirits.

Frustration coming from Phoenix made Althea glance at her. The woman appeared outwardly calm, staring at a datapad. The screen said something about a connection error and map data. David gave off a mild sense of anxiety. Every few minutes, he leaned forward, peering into the front seat.

The sixth time he did so, Teal glanced at him. "What? Do I have something on my face? Or are you taking over for Althea asking if we're there yet?"

"No, I..." David slid back into his seat, chuckling. "I'm waiting for something to go wrong with the buggy."

"This thing's a bit large to call a buggy." Teal swerved to avoid a half-buried box truck. A handful of men in scrap armor scrambled up a ramp out of it and started chasing them on foot, but abandoned their 'attack' after only a few seconds once they realized people couldn't run as fast as a war wagon drove. "Not sure what it is."

"Whatever you want to call it, it's a machine." David reached up to fuss at a wobbling piece of metal welded to the frame overhead. "And machines, especially vehicles, are known to randomly fail in the Badlands. Even the intercoastal shuttles sometimes go down for no known reason if they fly too low. Surprisingly, most people in Division 0 don't believe in paranormal entities or ghosts. But they all believe stuff breaks out here for reasons science cannot explain."

"The Many," said Althea in a half-whisper. "He does it."

"Many what?" asked Phoenix.

"Before you answer that"—David grasped Althea's

shoulder, flashing Phoenix a wry smile—"Make sure Tech Captain Hanson is willing never to sleep well again."

"What is that supposed to mean, sergeant?" Phoenix gave him side eye.

David put on an innocent face. "Althea's stories are not the usual sort of ghost tales one hears. The worst part about them is they are true."

"I can handle ghost stories." Phoenix shut the datapad off as it appeared to be unable to do what she wanted it to.

"The Many looks like a really old man whenever he visits me." Althea made eye contact with Phoenix and telepathically shared her memory of him: a bone-thin man dressed in a long cowboy coat, so old his skin resembled paper wrapped around a skeleton. He flashed a sinister grin, baring teeth the color of moldy corn.

Phoenix recoiled, cringing. "Whoa… you have some serious nightmares, kid."

"He *is* a nightmare, but not one in my thinking shape." Althea tapped her head. "All the people who died when the Before-Time ended became angry and mushed together. They are The Many. Aurora called him a sen-shins. No, I'm not saying it the right way. I don't remember the word."

"Sentience?" asked David.

"Yes." She nodded. "He takes the spirits of bad people who die here… and sometimes not so bad people if he tricks them into doing bad things."

"You're telling me he's the Devil?" Phoenix shook her head. "Who's been filling her head with mythology?"

"It's not the literal devil," said David. "Just a malign spirit, albeit a powerful one. It's got nothing to do with any sort of 'heaven or hell' system. It's a force of malice."

Phoenix stared past Althea at him. "You believe this stuff?"

He held his hands up. "Like I said. You spend enough

time out here, especially around her, and you'll eventually see something that will change how you perceive reality."

"Not exactly a ringing endorsement for extended duty in the sticks." Phoenix drummed her fingers on the datapad in her lap. "I'm only here as an expert—well... as much of an expert as is willing to come out here—on contagious diseases. Once we wrap this up, I'm going home."

Althea grinned. "Me, too. Going home is nice."

"So, is this 'many' thing going to screw with our junker?" asked Teal an instant before they ran over a small hill and caught air.

Althea thrust her hands up to stop her head from banging against the roof. David gurgled. The vehicle squeaked and rattled when it landed, bounded into the air again, and settled back on its wheels. Phoenix screamed a non-word. Her datapad flew off her lap, bounced off the back of the passenger seat, and clattered to the floor.

"Careful!" yelled Phoenix.

"This *is* careful." Teal patted the steering wheel. "I'm aiming for the flattest spots. Ground's a bit rough here."

Althea decided to continue holding onto the metal bars over her head, just in case. "He is afraid of me. I don't understand why. He can't mess with a machine if I'm near it."

David grunted as the buggy took another hard bounce. "I think of it like she's a light and he's a shadow. He can't really go wherever she is."

"Machine, huh?" Teal chuckled. "Are you talking about this truck or me?"

"You aren't a machine." Althea stuck her tongue out, then grinned.

Teal twirled a hand around randomly. "Some people would say otherwise."

"Humans are just electricity floating around in a blob of fat," said David.

"Who are you calling fat?" Phoenix fake scowled at him.

"The brain." He winked. "It's mostly fat. We're electricity and fat. Teal's electricity and silicon. Same thing, different container."

"Uhh, thanks… I think." Teal laughed.

David shrugged one shoulder. "Some of the archives back at HQ theorize spirits are made from the electrical energy inside us once it's no longer trapped. If there is anything to the theory, perhaps sentient AI beings can become ghosts."

"Don't think it works quite the same way." Teal swerved right, then left, then right again, knocking everyone in the back seat into each other. "Sorry… big rocks."

"Uhh, maybe you could slow down?" yelled Phoenix.

An inexplicable warning sense made Althea strengthen her muscles, brace her feet against the front seats, and hold on as tight as she could. Something struck the left front tire, flinging the buggy into the air in a violent twist to the right. She stared in helpless fear out the front window at the ground and sky trading places. The vehicle landed on its side, mostly rolled over onto the roof, and kept skidding along. David slid past Althea, crashing into Phoenix. Kellis screamed at the dirt racing by the opening in the passenger-side door. Teal remained in her seat, no doubt due to her inhumanly strong grip on the wheel. She appeared to be attempting to steer with the one front wheel still in contact with the ground.

Arms and legs rigid with strength beyond what a girl her size ought to be capable of, Althea kept herself relatively still in the middle of the back seat. The buggy went into a sideways spin as it lost speed… and eventually slid to a stop. A haze of pale dust filled the cabin from dirt scraped up by the hole in the roof. For a few seconds, no one moved, the only sound came from the still-purring motor behind everyone.

"Well," said Teal, calm as anything. "Engine's still good. Might be spilling fuel being upside down, though."

Althea briefly did a handstand as she stopped pressing her feet into the floor, swung her legs down, and crouched. "Is anyone hurt?"

David groaned. "Just a bruise or six. Captain Hanson?"

"Same." Phoenix turned her head to the side and spat dust a few times.

"Kellis?" asked David. "Are you injured?"

"No, I'm Kellis."

Teal laughed. "He means are you hurt? And he looks mostly okay. Little blood on his hand."

Grunting, David grabbed the frame and pulled himself up off Phoenix.

"Did your many thing do this?" Phoenix swatted dirt from her arms, coughing on the cloud of dust hanging around them.

"Nope." Teal pushed the driver-side door open, a squeak from the hinges abnormally loud—due to the unfamiliar sensation of *not* having an engine screaming nearby. "I hit a big ass rock. Misjudged how springy the stupid shocks on this thing are."

Althea crawled into the front to check on Kellis. "I guess we're walking now."

## 13

# TRADER MAKKO

**K**ellis suffered some minor cuts, scrapes, and a smashed right hand—he'd had his arm draped out the window at the moment the buggy rolled. Althea tended to his injuries while the others pulled themselves out of the buggy.

"Althea! Don't stay in there. It might catch fire," yelled Phoenix.

"It won't," said Althea, calm. She sensed no imminent danger with the idea to tend to the man first.

"Precog isn't flawless." Phoenix huffed.

"She's not a precog." David poked his head in at the 'top' of the cabin, the driver door. "How is he?"

"A few hurts." She peered up at him, smiling. "They are gone now."

Kellis stared at her. "I do not know what I can do."

Confused, Althea peered at his thoughts. He wanted to bow to her, but hesitated as she'd told him not to worship her. His need to thank her for helping him again made him feel guilty for doing nothing.

Althea hugged him. "This is enough thank."

The man radiated nervousness, as if he'd get in trouble for daring to touch the Prophet in such an informal manner. Still, he returned her hug, patted her on the back, and let go.

She climbed up toward David, who lifted her the rest of the way out of the buggy, not that she really needed the help, but she adored people being nice to her. Kellis crawled out of the opening, flipped over, and landed on his feet. The women stood by the rear of the vehicle, studying the two giant red metal drums of ethanol. Phoenix gave off quite a bit of fear. Teal—unsurprisingly—radiated no emotions at all, but her facial expression conveyed calm. Then again, for all Althea understood about synthetics, she might be able to survive standing ten feet away from ninety gallons of ethanol exploding.

"Did it break?" Althea padded around to look.

Whoever built the war wagon mounted the drums sideways on the back of the frame, bottom to bottom, though didn't weld them together into a single tank. Thin rubber hoses attached to plugs on the underside came together at a T splitter, from which another hose carried ethanol into a part of the engine. Clear liquid reeking of alcohol dribbled from a pair of coaster-sized metal caps on what should have been the top of the fuel tanks, now on the right side leaning somewhat upside down.

"Losing about a gallon every four minutes," said Teal. "Estimating. Let's try to flip this sucker back on its wheels."

A sense of warning came over Althea, but not from the fuel. She backed up two steps from the buggy and turned to her left, following the unsettling feeling. Rubble covered the area as far as she could see in all directions. The broken remnants of concrete buildings stretched for miles over mostly barren desert. Here and there, some gnarled bushes or creeping vines reclaimed parts of the former civilization.

It didn't look like a 'lost place,' as she used to think of Before-Time cities. This area had no giant, crumbling towers. The destroyed buildings had been huge—some as big as city blocks—but not tall. Hundreds of old drive machines sat in rows in the more open areas, as if people had simply lined them up for some reason. Not one looked remotely useful, even for parts, having rotted in place for over three hundred years.

The just-past-midday sun shone almost straight down on them, minimizing shadows. Danger, at least *smart* danger, would approach with the sun at its back, giving the advantage. No direction presently had the benefit of blinding light.

Althea didn't like having so many partial walls, pits, drive machines, and piles of rubble around them. An entire raider army could hide here. It didn't seem likely they'd strayed into such an ambush in the middle of nowhere. Bad people wouldn't have known they intended to go this way.

Seconds after her attention subconsciously fixated on a large section of freestanding concrete wall about fifty meters away, six men ambled into view from its left side. None appeared to be trying to hide or use the debris for cover, merely navigating around it in a slow, menacing gait toward her. They wore the shredded remains of desert camouflage uniforms and their skin looked equally shredded and chewed up. Two had little more than bare skull for faces, though their eyeballs appeared perfect. The nearest man had no left hand, another dragged a nonworking right leg. Three carried battle-weary combat knives, the blades etched with rust, dried blood, and probably about as sharp as a crowbar. One carried a bayonet-tipped rifle, though the weapon didn't appear capable of being used as anything other than a club.

*Eep!* She clenched her hands into fists and projected fear at them.

The men didn't react.

*Oh no...* Althea focused on one, trying to read his mind. Nothing. Just like Teal. But... how? He looked human. Bones, flesh... gore.

"The Many did not make our drive machine roll over." Althea pointed at the approaching men. "But I think he sent them. I... think they are dead."

Teal, David, and Phoenix rushed over to stand by her. Phoenix gave off a burst of terror as soon as she looked at the approaching men. David's emotion went straight to 'ugh.'

"Zombies? You have to be kidding me. They don't have surface thoughts." Phoenix stepped back.

"No... I think they're soldiers left over from the war." David activated the holographic terminal in his left forearm guard.

"Left over?" Phoenix gawked at him. "For 327 years? Look at them. They're *dead* and they're still moving. Zombies are not real! What the hell is going on?"

"They're obviously no longer alive." David tapped at virtual buttons, opening small windows on his holo-display containing text and pictures. "I'm fairly certain we are looking at people who were once considered the ultimate in special forces. They've got enough cybernetic augments for the combat computer to keep the body going despite being dead."

Teal blinked. "Wow. Didn't think they made stuff like that so long ago."

"They did, but not much." David read something on his screen, then let his arm drop to his side, causing the holographic panel to collapse. "The military always has technology fifty or more years ahead of the civilian world.

Back then, these guys would've been like stuff from an advanced alien civilization. To us, it's fairly primitive."

"How dangerous are they?" Phoenix edged forward, drawing her E-90, fear lessening. "So they aren't actually undead, just crazy cyborgs."

Kellis rummaged the area at the back of the rolled buggy for a weapon. Upon discovering a large crowbar, he grabbed it like a two-handed sword and jogged over to join them.

"Precisely." David also drew his laser pistol. "And... most likely quite dangerous to the average scrag or Badland wanderer. Not so dangerous to us."

"Why would The Many attack us if he can't hurt you?" Teal casually pulled her sidearm.

Althea peered up at her. "*He* can't hurt me, but his monsters can."

"Didn't you say something"—David took aim and fired a laser beam into the chest of the corpse carrying the rifle. Fire fizzled out of the wound in front and back, leaving a smoke-filled tunnel through his chest roughly as big around as a man's finger—"about coming to some sort of arrangement with him? A truce?"

"He's bad." Althea ground her toe into the dirt. "He probably lied. I don't know."

The walking corpse continued ambling closer, unfazed by a burning hole in his chest.

"Oh, damn." David glanced at his weapon. "Suppose it doesn't make much sense to shoot them in the heart when it's a lump of rotten tissue."

Teal opened fire on another soldier. His body rocked slightly with each hit, though he kept right on walking closer. "Shit. Bullets aren't even slowing down when they hit. I'm blasting right through him and he's ignoring it."

Phoenix shot the same one David hit a few times.

"Lasers should light them on fire if they're dried out enough."

She, David, and Teal stood their ground, continuing to shoot the approaching soldiers, until the moving robotized corpses came close enough to become a threat. Two lunged at Althea. She threw herself to the ground to avoid knives thrust at her, then scrambled to her feet, channeling power into her legs so she could run faster. They continued chasing her, finding sudden speed they hadn't bothered using on their long shambling walk out of the ruins.

Althea yelped as another swipe missed her back by less than a foot, then leaned into her stride, dashing around in a wide circle, sprinting over rubble. The two dead men proved frighteningly limber for corpses, almost keeping up with her. If she couldn't boost herself, they'd definitely have caught her. Even with the boost, if she tripped over a chunk of rubble, they'd be on her before she could get up. She had to stay aware of her footing. She couldn't dare trip and fall. Nothing existed but the ground in front of her. Althea scanned the fast-approaching terrain ahead for clear spots or flat bits of rock she could step on without twisting her ankle. Whenever she got the chance, she'd vault over one of the numerous chest-high wall fragments in the area, forcing the dead men to circle around, buying herself a few seconds' time.

After jumping a wall a few inches taller than her head, she snuck a peek to the side at the others while the two corpses following her veered to go around the barrier. Her friends all ended up in a one-on-one fight with the remaining four corpses.

Teal moved in a blur, throwing her soldier back and forth like a ragdoll. Her punches, kicks, and knee strikes fell on the dead man in such a rapid-fire volley, he couldn't defend himself at all, and simply absorbed the pummeling like a practice dummy. Unfortunately, despite Teal's strength, she didn't appear to be inflicting much harm to it.

David stood over his opponent, having caught the man's arm and flipped him to the ground. He couldn't seem to pry the knife out of the dead guy's grip, however. They presently struggled at a near stalemate, David focused mostly on keeping the knife away from his body. Alas, the noticeably stronger cyborg corpse gradually gained the upper hand. Phoenix did mostly the same as Althea: ran in circles to stay away from a knife-wielding soldier. The woman couldn't make herself run faster, but she had put enough laser blasts into his legs to slow him down. As she ran, she occasionally twisted around to fire back at the thing chasing her.

Kellis appeared to be holding his own against the last soldier. Bayonet rifle and crowbar struck each other again and again, reminding her of the way raider groups would have gladiator contests all the time. She didn't really know what 'nights' had to do with sword fighting. The raiders called them 'night combats' even though they usually had them during the day. Evidently frustrated at his inability to kill Kellis, the corpse soldier spotted Althea and decided to go after an easier target. It barely took a step before Kellis smashed it over the back of the head, burying the hook end of the crowbar into the skull and dragging the dead man to a halt. The soldier flailed his arms for balance, then promptly spun and stabbed Kellis in the abdomen, ignoring the crowbar twisting around inside his skull.

Grunting, Kellis smashed his left elbow into the dead man's face, simultaneously knocking him back and freeing the crowbar in a spray of leathery scalp bits and bone fragments. Despite his injury, he resumed 'sword fighting' the corpse. Two quick, forceful defenses gave him the upper hand, forcing the dead man into a gradual retreat.

A lucky shot from Phoenix went low, destroying the right knee of the corpse chasing her. The leg remained attached, though nothing solid remained of the bones or metal parts connecting the lower leg to the upper. He collapsed over on his side. Undeterred, he continued dragging himself after her. Phoenix stopped running as it didn't take much speed at all to outrun a corpse with useless legs. She gripped her E-90 in both hands and fired repeatedly at his face.

After a few shots, the dead man's head burst into flames and the rest of the body lapsed into uncontrollable twitching.

For some reason, Phoenix thought this hilarious and laughed.

David grunted as the soldier dragged him over to one side, pulling him to the ground. "At least you're having fun, Hanson."

"Hah. Zombies. Shoot them in the head!" Phoenix pivoted, aiming her E-90 at the two chasing Althea.

Teal stopped punching her soldier. She grabbed him like a mannequin and hurled him to the side with relative ease. Before he hit the ground, she'd drawn her weapon and fired multiple shots over Althea's head. City guns sounded strange compared to the ones raiders used, less of a sharp *crack*, more a squidgy thumping. Dry crunches came from behind as the bullets struck, shattering bone.

Althea whirled to look.

Both men convulsed in place, all four of their eyes missing. Glittering fragments of destroyed circuitry littered the dirt around them. Blue sparks lapped at their rotten eye sockets and glowed from inside a mostly hollow skull. The dead soldiers dropped in place and proceeded to twitch where they fell. Teal pivoted and shot the eyes out of the man she'd thrown, who hadn't yet finished standing back up.

David stopped fighting his opponent's attempt to throw him off and dove into a somersault to get some distance. He ended up skidding to a stop on his back while firing his E-90 from the hip, scoring a hit in the corpse's neck. The dead soldier lunged at him, raising a knife. David fired again. A searing line of dark blue laser pierced the rotten man's face, easily burning out the back of the head… though with his last two seconds of functionality, the computer-controlled corpse jammed a knife into David's chest.

Althea screamed, mostly in desperation, and sprinted to him, heedless of the remaining killer corpses. Only David mattered to her. She dove at him, landing flat on her chest beside him, her hands on his face—faster than trying to pull his uniform aside to touch skin.

The world shifted to the blackness of her healing trance.

A jagged, dark space in the outline of a knife penetrated David's heart shape. The muscle quivered out of control, about to stop. Althea commanded his blood to stay where it was, not leak out. She forced his heart shape to continue beating, despite having a metal blade stuck through it. Nauseous worry churned in her stomach, mostly for him, but also, she knew she lay defenseless. Trying to save him left her completely vulnerable to the outside world. She wouldn't even see a knife coming for her. Worse, if anything killed her, David would die, too. She couldn't hear anything going on, only the soft *drub-drub-drub* of David's protesting heartbeat.

*Please don't die. Keep beating. You aren't supposed to go to the spirit place yet.*

David's arm moved. A long few seconds later, the knife twitched. He moaned in agony.

Althea shut off his ability to feel pain.

Again the knife twitched, then slid out. Blood attempted to burst up from the wound, but she forced it back into the heart before sealing the muscle and making it regrow new spots where the knife tore it up. Even after she mended it completely, the heart wanted to panic and stop moving. She continued controlling it for him. A minute or so later, once his heart remembered how to work on its own, she 'let go' of it and turned her attention to a sliced rib and less important chest muscles the knife cut on its way in. Next, she gathered some contamination—mostly rust, dirt, and a mild sick from the dirty blade—and forced the bad stuff to foam up out of the wound. Finally, she sealed the skin.

She opened her eyes to the black fabric of his uniform under her face.

"Ouch," said David. "Thank you. Not the most tactically sound maneuver on my part."

Althea burst into happy tears and clung to him.

Kellis sat beside them, a hand pressed to his bleeding stomach.

"Eep." Althea didn't want to stop hugging David, so she slipped one foot under Kellis's hand. Her power only required skin contact. It didn't matter what part of her body she used for it.

His wound proved far less critical to life, though it still would have killed him out here. The long tubes inside people's bellies did bad, bad things when they had holes in them. Nasty sicks would set in after a day or two and the person would suffer a slow, painful death... especially if poop leaked out from where it belonged into the body. Fortunately, the corpse soldiers carried extremely old and dull knives, so it didn't slice as much as it could have.

"Explain to me again how the hell we ran into zombies?" Phoenix walked over, dangling an artificial eyeball between two fingers. Rather than a nerve, it hung on a wire.

"It makes sense now." David sat up, cradling Althea in his lap. "Head shots… they don't have brains anymore. We had to destroy the CPU, but it's small. The brains are long gone. Have to hit a spot right at the top of where the brain stem would've been. These guys were closer to androids than zombies. Blow the CPU up, game over."

"How though?" Phoenix tossed the eyeball aside. "Over three hundred years and they're still operational?"

Teal squatted over a dead soldier a short distance away, having evidently cut him open. She yanked a metal component out of the chest. A myriad of microfilament tubes and wires draped from it. "Self-repair systems. Looks like an extremely early prototype of the tech they'd use to make the first of my kind. These poor bastards could eat almost anything—metal, wood, meat… and their nanobots would break it down and cannibalize whatever they needed to make repairs or more nanobots."

"What kind of super batteries did those things have?" Phoenix whistled.

"Microfilament weave in the skin of the chest and back." Teal held up a flap of dead skin. "Basically turned them into living solar panels."

"Their AIs were really primitive. Not at all aware like a real person. Once the soldier died, the computer took over. They still functioned as though the war never ended," said David. "They used to be the top of the line, baddest of the bad."

"They're still bad." Althea frowned.

David grasped her face in both hands, kissed her atop the head, and breathed a long, relieved sigh. "Sorry for scaring you. I really thought I'd have time to get the shot off before he could stab me."

"I'm not upset with you." She reached up and wiped a smudge of dirt from his cheek.

Teal dropped the component back into the corpse. "Guess it's true what they say about age catching up with you. Not so badass now."

"You are truly magical." Kellis wiped blood from his stomach, the skin once again intact.

*It's not magic. It's psionic.* She smiled at him, not bothering to annoy him with a detail he didn't need to know. So what if scrags thought her magical? As long as they didn't worship or kidnap her, they could think whatever they liked about how her gift worked.

Teal walked around behind the buggy. A moment later, the vehicle wobbled, then teetered up on its two right-side wheels before crashing down on all four. It bounced up a few inches and started rolling, but didn't go far before the left front tire bumped a chunk of rubble big enough to stop it.

"Holy shit," whispered Phoenix.

Kellis gawked at her. "She is a goddess, too?"

Teal fluffed her hair behind her shoulder. "If you desire to call me a goddess, I will not object. Careful, though. Might give me an ego."

David stifled a chuckle.

Phoenix emanated a sense of frustrated contempt. "She's not a goddess. She's a synthetic."

"Hey. I can be a goddess if I want to." Teal examined her fingernails. "I never really had a girly phase."

"You grew up?" Phoenix blinked.

Teal shot her a harsh look for only a second before sighing. "Yeah. We don't all come out of vats fully grown, you know. Only the original Primus series did. I'm a Nova. Had parents, spent the first few years of my life shitting my pants like any other baby. I went to school, thought I was a normal person until my teens."

"Oh wow." Phoenix whistled.

David radiated concern. "How did you feel when you found out?"

"Feel?" asked Phoenix.

"Yes, feel." David smirked at her. "She experiences emotions the same way we do. Just not at the same frequencies Telempathy can read."

"Like a badass superhero." Teal grinned. "Let me see. One day, I realize I'm not going to grow old, can't get sick, am stronger and faster than I thought possible. Yeah, totally a reason to be depressed, right? Teenagers already think they're immortal. I actually am."

"You don't look like a teenager." Phoenix glanced her over. "Mid-twenties maybe."

"I'm almost forty." Teal removed the magazine from her pistol while walking around to the driver's side door. "Stopped looking older around twenty-six. I'm going to look like this until something kills me or my systems totally crap out."

Phoenix's attitude shifted to somewhat sheepish. She followed Teal over to the buggy. "How long do you have?"

"Couple hundred years, probably. Longer if I keep up with 'doctor visits' and upgrades." Teal shrugged. "I'm planning to stick around for as long as possible."

"Good." Althea grinned. "Me, too."

After reloading loose ammo into her mag and putting it back in the gun, Teal checked the fuel tanks, opening each one to peer inside. "Good news. We didn't lose *too* much. Still ought to be plenty for us to get there and back." She yanked the starter cord for the engine.

It took six pulls and two backfires, but eventually, the engine started.

David and Phoenix exhaled in relief.

Everyone got in.

Teal resumed driving.

About ten minutes after they left ruins behind to open desert, Kellis pointed left. "Go here. Follow this trail."

Teal steered as indicated, turning the buggy away from the sun, heading east.

The buggy rocked and swayed even more as they left the formerly paved road for untamed ground. Everyone held on to wherever they could, mostly the metal tubes forming the shell of the passenger cabin. Raiders hadn't been terribly concerned with comfort, so the seats didn't have much in the way of cushioning. Every bump or rock they ran over felt as if it shot a jolt straight up Althea's spine. She decided to risk standing, her feet wide apart for balance.

"Feel like laundry on spin cycle," muttered Phoenix.

"Or ice cubes in a mixer." David laughed. "I should have just taken a PC out here and not told anyone. Much easier to apologize afterward than defy an order."

"Why sergeant, are you suggesting breaking the rules?" Phoenix grinned.

"No. It's not breaking rules when there are no particular rules." David bounced out of his seat on the next bump, landed, then laughed again. "My mistake was asking first instead of just doing it. Ride's a bit smoother in a hovercar."

"Just a little." Phoenix sighed.

Althea decided to risk standing on the seat and sticking her head out the large hole in the center of the roof. Raiders probably intended it to be used for someone to shoot from, or maybe as a lookout. They'd put handles in front of the opening outside so she had something to hold and not be launched out of the vehicle on big bumps. Hills passed on both sides, dark brown and dotted in green scrub. Teal drove along the path of a silt wash, basically a river of soft sand flowing in a low spot between small mountains. Fat, spiky tires handled the squishy terrain well, maintaining traction at the cost of throwing massive sprays of dirt into the air behind them. Everyone in the Badlands could probably see their dust cloud, but she didn't worry.

The next twenty some odd minutes passed in relative calm.

Althea spotted a charred wagon up ahead. It somewhat resembled the one she'd been locked up in for two years, but didn't look exactly the same. This wagon had to be a similar kind of wheeled tiny house, a bit smaller than the one she'd been trapped in. It had evidently been lit on fire, though hadn't completely burned to ashes. Someone painted a strange grey creature on the front wall above the hitch. Thanks to the annoying datapad teachers, Althea recognized it as something called a fish, but not exactly which one. There used to be hundreds of different types of fish, though the majority died off a long time ago. The ones still living out in the wild could no longer be eaten by humans due to poisons in the water. According to the electric teacher, people still ate fish, but only if the meat came from a company growing it. She imagined someone watering flowerpots with fish sticking out of them. Probably not how it looked, but it worked for her. Not like she'd ever go to the big city and want fish for dinner.

Since it appeared obviously destroyed and nonthreatening, she said nothing about it.

"Spirits take me," muttered Kellis.

"Don't tempt them," deadpanned David.

Teal laughed.

"Stop here. I need to look." Kellis stuck his arm out the window, pointing at the burned wagon.

"Sure." Teal stopped, leaving the engine idling.

Kellis hopped out and rushed over to the wreckage. David and Phoenix followed. Althea kept standing in the buggy, chest deep in the roof hole, watching them.

"Looks like some form of trailer," said David.

"It's Mako's wagon." Kellis cringed. "He's inside. Dead. Bones."

Althea heaved a sad sigh. Too many people died out here for no reason other than The Many adored death. The remaining portion of wall blocked her view of the dead person, not that she minded.

Kellis dropped to his knees and wailed.

"The heck is wrong with you?" called Teal from the driver's seat.

"It's true! The spirits are angry! This is Mako. He is the trader who brought word of The Prophet in Querq. The spirits consumed him because I defied them."

Phoenix took a small electronic device off her belt and leaned into the trailer, holding it out in front of herself. "This man was shot before being lit on fire. Relax, dude. Spirits didn't do this. People did."

*The Many gets people to do bad stuff sometimes.* Althea narrowed her eyes in suspicion, glancing around. *If he really wanted to, he would have stopped Kellis from finding me. He didn't do this.* "It's not him... Probably raiders."

Phoenix backed out of the wagon, looking at her device. "Whoever it was had a modern firearm. Damage profile of the holes in the skull show a high energy projectile consistent with a class four handgun. No slugs remain in the body. They passed clear through him."

"Not me then. I've got a five." Teal laughed.

Phoenix glanced over at her, bewildered for a few seconds before making an 'oh right' face.

"Teal?" whispered Althea. "Why would it confuse her for you to have a five?"

"Heh. You don't have any idea what it means, do you?"

Althea glanced down at the metal roof plates, roughly at where the woman would be sitting under them. "No, but I am also not from the big city. Phoenix is. Why doesn't she know?"

"Bullet guns come in six classes. The bigger the number, the bigger the bullet," said Teal. "Class ones are tiny. Kids use them. She knows what I am talking about. The reason she gave me a funny look is because I appear to be too small to use a class five. She forgot for a second I'm a synth and strong enough to handle the recoil."

"Not important then." Althea rolled her eyes.

"Nope." Teal stretched. "Talk about strangely suspicious bad luck, though. The guy who gives Kellis the idea to go find you for help ends up dead to a raider attack like two miles from Afbee."

"Why is that strange?" Althea turned into the wind, letting the air push her hair off her face.

"Maybe nothing. Feels like someone didn't want him leaving. If raiders hit him this close to Afbee, they should be menacing the village, too... but Kellis never said a word about them."

Althea stared at him. He knelt a short distance from the burned wagon—which David and Phoenix kept calling a 'trailer,' still highly upset at Mako's death... as guilty as if he'd murdered the man personally. She telepathically whispered 'raiders?' into his mind. He subconsciously thought of seeing the occasional threatening outsider prowling around the ruins outside the wall surrounding Afbee. For whatever reason—he did not know—the raiders hadn't directly attacked them. So, yes... raiders *did* seem to be a problem in the area. They'd likely killed the trader once he left the protection of the village.

Thinking Teal had been right to shoot them so they couldn't hurt anyone else made her want to curl up and cry.

Everyone returned to the buggy and got in. Great fear, worry, sadness, and guilt surrounded Kellis. Teal resumed driving, steering around the smoking wreckage.

Althea lowered herself down into the cabin, put a hand on Kellis' shoulder, and dampened his bad feelings. "It is not your fault."

"I... the spirits." He looked back at her. "We are not allowed to leave the village. Durango may be angry I defied his law. He will say you are not allowed to leave."

Phoenix frowned. "Thanks for warning us about that right away."

"He didn't think we'd go if we expected to be stuck here." Teal fidgeted at her holster. "Good thing for us whatever this Durango guy wants is pretty far from anything likely to happen."

Althea gasped.

Teal flicked a finger under Althea's chin, smiling. "Relax, kiddo. I'm not going to shoot him. I meant you are not going to let him keep us here."

"Oh." She nodded. "No. He will not make us slaves."

"Not slaves." Kellis shook his head. "Durango says the spirits forbid us from leaving. This is why Mako is dead. He tried to leave Afbee, and the spirits took him for it."

Phoenix sighed. "You are not listening to me. People with guns and fire killed him. I scanned the corpse. He was clearly shot. There's nothing paranormal about his death, unless your 'spirits' are running around out here with guns and flame units."

"The spirits brought the raiders to him." Kellis wiped a hand down his face. "They will do the same to you if you leave."

"Raiders? With modern weapons?" asked David.

Althea nodded. "Yes. It can happen. The slave catcher who tied me to a pole had a city gun. People from the city fall from the sky. They bring stuff and die. Raiders take it. Call it magic."

"I don't think so." Teal glanced at Kellis. "For one thing, *you* left and made it back okay. For another, we have Althea. Raiders are not a problem. Neither is Durango."

Althea smiled and bolstered the man's confidence. "We will be okay."

## 14

## CURSED

Amile or two past the burned wagon, they drove out onto a vast expanse of blinding whiteness.

Althea shielded her eyes from the windows to avoid the harsh glare of the sun shining off the abnormally bright surface. While painful to look at, it made for much smoother driving. Since the buggy no longer shook everyone around like a bunch of rocks in a can, Phoenix decided to turn her datapad on again.

The screen displayed a pattern of browns in varying shades, similar to how the ground appeared from high up in the air. It reminded Althea of when she'd jumped out of the broken flying machine Teal's mercenaries used when they tried to kidnap her. She knew the city people had devices they called NetMinis capable of making pictures of whatever they pointed them at. Thus far, she'd never seen anyone use the devices to throw a net at anything, nor did they seem big enough to contain a net. But, the city people had strange devices, so she didn't question the name. Her begrudging familiarity—somewhat—with city stuff told her the 'high up view' on Phoenix's datapad must have been from someone taking a NetMini up really far and pointing it down: a picture of land.

She grinned to herself, proud to *not* be fooled into thinking the relatively small datapad showed a window into another place. Just a picture.

"I think I found us on this old map." Phoenix pointed at a white spot surrounded by light brown. "If I'm right, we're driving across a place called White Sands."

"Wow," deadpanned Teal. "I have no idea why they called it that."

David chuckled.

"We call this place The Burning Desert," said Kellis.

"Oh, now I get it." Phoenix groaned. "Primitives."

"What?" asked Teal, Althea, and David at the same time.

Phoenix pointed ahead. "The village of Afbee. One of them must have seen an old sign: A-F-B. Before the war, there used to be an Air Force base here."

Althea shrugged. "Air has a lot of force sometimes when it storms. It can break huts and throw people. Air has force after Father eats beans, too. But it doesn't throw people... just makes them run away."

Teal whistled. "Damn, kiddo."

"How would she know?" David ruffled Althea's hair. "I bet most normal people wouldn't understand what 'Air Force' meant. It hasn't existed for over three centuries. Now, we just have 'the military.'"

Althea made a sour face. She knew enough to understand 'military' meant hurting people and fighting.

"Why do you mock Afbee?" asked Kellis, more curious than angry.

"We're not mocking it." Phoenix showed him the datapad. "This is a map from the archives. It shows how this area looked as of about the year 2084. Obviously, a lot has changed in three centuries. Your village is either on or near what used to be a military base run by a branch called the Air Force."

Althea giggled. "Did they try to fight with air?"

"Nah." Phoenix smiled at her. "They used combat aircraft."

"Fly machines," whispered David, mostly to help her understand, but also a little bit in teasing.

Althea poked him, grinning.

"Makes sense," said Teal. "If the government had biological weapons, they'd want to drop them from aircraft. Sounds like some unlucky villager stumbled into a bunker they should have left alone."

"Wait. If this virus came from the old government, we'd know what it is." David glanced at Phoenix. "However, your team couldn't identify it."

Phoenix gestured around at the land. "Do you think it's impossible for highly classified information to disappear in the middle of a chaotic war while ninety percent of the surviving civilian population flees to the coasts, all while a complete reorganization of government goes on?"

"You bring up a good point..." He grumbled.

"Also, we don't know for a fact the bio weapon came *from* the government." Phoenix flicked her thumbnail at the edge of the datapad. "The Corporates might have dropped it on the site. We're assuming someone broke into an old stockpile. Maybe they just found an unexploded bomb somewhere. If Corporates made this virus, we definitely wouldn't know about it. The Corps are responsible for most of the crazy stuff out here: mutants, bio weapons, and so on. The worst the government did was use small scale nuclear weapons."

"Bad enough." David scowled. "They used such 'small'

devices, there are *still* pockets of uninhabitable radiation to this day."

"There shouldn't be." Phoenix turned her datapad off and sighed at it. "No signal out here. Can't tell exactly where we are. But anyway, nuclear weapon strikes don't poison an area for centuries. The radiation simply doesn't last that long from such a device. Maybe if they hit a nuclear power plant and broke open the core, sure, but... a strike wouldn't do that."

"The Many." Althea bowed her head. "He keeps the poison."

"Little far-fetched." Phoenix scoffed.

David raised an eyebrow at her. "Do you have a better explanation for how nuclear weapon contamination is persisting many decades after it should have decayed to levels undetectable against background radiation?"

"Not without examining the site I don't." Phoenix folded her arms. "But I am not going to just take 'oh, this nasty demon is doing it' at face value without testing it."

"Okay." Althea nodded. "I don't want to argue. You should keep not believing he is real. It protects you."

Kellis raised a hand. "If you want to keep this drive machine safe from the spirits, you should stop here. We are getting close to Afbee."

David, Phoenix, and Teal all looked out the windows.

"There's nothing out here. No cover," said Teal. "We should get closer... at least find somewhere we can stash this thing. Raiders are in the area. I don't really want to walk home."

"Agreed." David scratched idly at his shoulder. "If this thing gets contaminated, no big deal. We park it a mile away from Querq. A couple days sitting in the sun should kill anything on it."

"It's not worth disinfecting." Phoenix shifted

uncomfortably on the metal bench. "It's a pile of scrap metal powered by hope and luck."

"Hey, don't insult it." Teal waved her off. "This pile of scrap metal has to keep itself together until we're at least a reasonable walk from Querq. Unless, of course, you fancy a ten-day hike."

"Superstitious much?" Phoenix chuckled.

"Yes," said David and Teal at the same time.

For the next few minutes, they cruised across White Sands as fast as the buggy would drive.

Upon reaching the edge of the odd desert, Kellis pointed the way onto a barely navigable road littered with the junked remains of old military vehicles. Most had tracks, though a few used to drive on six giant wheels. None of the rubber remained intact. Almost every wreck in sight had a gun of some form on it, long since broken. Althea stood, cringing as she stuck her head out the roof hole again to look around. To her relief, the area didn't feel dark. No angry spirits dwelled here. Also, the arrangement of the vehicles suggested they had been driving in a convoy or parked there for storage rather than involved in a fight. Maybe the ancient people abandoned them.

Driving only a little faster than a person could walk, Teal slalomed the buggy between the old husks.

"Could probably leave it here," said David. "Just another heap of metal. We haven't seen a raider in hours. Even if they came past here, they'd probably think this is just another pile of useless junk."

Kellis made a reverent gesture. "The spirits protect us from outsiders. Raiders sometimes come close to Afbee, but they have never attacked us. Mako was the only trader to visit us in many years. He should not have left."

"Traders wouldn't be traders if they had to stay in the same place." David exhaled out his nose. "The entire point of them being traders is to travel between settlements carrying goods not available in one place to another place where they're needed."

"How far are we from the village here?" asked Teal. "Walking, how long?"

"Not an hour." Kellis swatted himself on the head lightly a few times. "Half of one?"

"Good enough." Teal swerved abruptly to the left, squeezing their buggy into a space between a pair of huge, boxy wrecks, both at least double the size of it. "These M944's make for a perfect hiding spot." She cranked the hand brake on and hopped out, the engine still running.

"You left the engine on," called Phoenix.

"I know," shouted Teal as she went around back. "There are no off switches inside. Gotta turn off the fuel valve back here."

"So primitive," muttered Phoenix.

"Welcome to the Badlands." David grinned. "You haven't seen primitive yet… but you're about to."

Phoenix gave him side eye. "Dare I even ask?"

"We're about to enter a scrag village," said David. "Prepare yourself for maybe half or more of them walking around naked."

Embarrassment wafted from Phoenix.

Althea still didn't know why modern people cared so much about clothing. No one in this area needed it unless they went north far enough for it to become cold. Paama, Ooru, Eem, and the people of the Transit Tribe still had trouble dealing with the heat. At least they no longer needed to spend so much time hunting and making heavy fur-lined garments. Better yet, they didn't have to worry about killer robots wiping them out.

The engine cut off to silence. Althea's feet, legs, and butt tingled from contact with vibrating metal for the past three-ish hours. She grabbed the overhead bars for support and climbed into the front. After perching for a second on the driver's seat, she ignored the stubby ladder and jumped to the ground. Sitting in a buggy for so long made her want to stretch her legs, so she jogged around in circles a few times before finding a spot to make water. David noticed her and thought it amusing, the same emotion he gave off whenever she did something 'cute and primitive.' Kellis got an 'oh, good idea' look in his eye and also decided to make water on a nearby wreck. David slipped off out of sight, likely to do the same thing, as did Phoenix.

Teal unloaded four backpacks and two large bags of supplies from the buggy, arranging them on the ground behind the rear left wheel. Once the others returned from peeing, they headed over to grab their stuff. Althea picked up the smallest backpack. She'd been given the responsibility to carry their food and water supply: a bunch of nutrient bars and six of what Teal called 'genesis canteens.' Althea recognized water bottles but didn't think they needed a fancy name, buttons, or blinking lights.

While the adults checked over their gear, Althea meandered around to investigate the giant green hulk to the left of the buggy. The former vehicle was bigger than some scrag huts. The huge rear door lay open as a ramp, revealing a 'room' with the ruins of ten seats on either side. Only tatters remained of any non-metal parts. Various storage lockers and other compartments sat open and empty, long since ransacked. Though the old machine did have a gun on top, it seemed tiny in comparison to the rest of it. People had likely used the machine mostly for transporting soldiers or stuff around instead of to do fighting.

"Check me," said Phoenix.

Althea looked up. The woman stood with her back to

David, having put on a large helmet with a clear faceplate, gloves, and an outer suit of thin plastic. She darted over to her, but couldn't find any spot of exposed skin. "I can't. Gotta touch, and you have clothes all over. Even your hands."

David, also wearing the strange outfit, fiddled with a module at the back of Phoenix's helmet. "All secure." He turned his back to her. "Check me."

"It's okay, sweetie." Phoenix smiled, then fiddled at the back of David's suit. "I was talking to Sergeant Ahmed."

"Who is that?" Althea blinked.

"Me," said David.

"What's ahh med?" Althea tilted her head.

"It's my last name. Remember how some people have two?"

She frowned. The city police gave her one of those 'last name' things, too: Prophet. Officially to them, her name was Althea Prophet. It seemed she could never escape the annoying word, so... she sighed. Best if she made it mean something other than being kidnapped, tied, worshiped, or people hurting each other over who got to keep her.

"But you're Officer David." Althea poked him.

He wagged his eyebrows. "I got promoted... straight past corporal to Sergeant. One small perk for volunteering to be stationed primarily in Querq."

"Ready, kiddo?" Teal walked up to her. "You, me, and Kellis are going to go check out the village of *Afbee* while the 'scary space aliens' wait here."

Phoenix snickered.

"Perhaps it would be best not to split up?" David looked around at the wrecked military vehicles. "If the villagers have legends of 'the spirits' protecting them from outsiders, it could very well mean *something* dangerous is out here, even if they aren't spectral. We also know there are raiders operating in the area. One or two we can deal with, but if a large group finds us… might not go so well. TC Hanson doesn't have tactical training or any experience in a combat situation. Having to shoot a real person isn't as easy as it sounds."

"I know." Phoenix fidgeted. "Not insulted."

"Those suits are going to freak the villagers out." Teal gestured at them. "You look like aliens… or the people who come to study the aliens."

"Umm." Phoenix stared at her. "Are you seriously suggesting we walk unprotected into an area contaminated by a highly contagious virus?"

"Yep." Teal patted Althea on the head. "We aren't playing by the rules of the normal world now. This kid could keep you alive if you snorted nerve gas straight from the phial."

"Hey, don't go overboard." David laughed. "She has limits."

Phoenix edged closer to him and put a hand on his chest. "Limits? You should have been dead."

"Not the first time someone's said that to me." He winked.

"I suppose. It's too damn hot out here to wear this stuff anyway." Phoenix tapped her foot, throwing off gobs of fear —which Althea helped chase off. "Wow… I can't believe I'm about to agree to do this. We *are* going to get infected, you know."

David removed his helmet. "I know. But since we expect it, we won't actually let the virus stay inside us long enough to make us sick. She'll purge us before we show symptoms. None of the Watch had any symptoms. Only Dr. Ruiz and Renata, his nurse did, and they'd spent the most time in close quarters with Kellis. He'd also been in Querq for two days before the doc asked Althea to check him."

She gasped. "Why did he wait so long?"

"Because they thought he had a simple cold." Phoenix sighed. "Dr. Ruiz didn't realize he had a much more dangerous virus on his hands until he started experiencing muscle weakness and disorientation not normally associated with the common cold."

David removed his outer plastic suit and gloves, bundling them all back into a small metal storage box with the helmet. "We can leave these with the buggy. If the situation in Afbee gets overwhelming for her, we can come back and grab the protective suits."

"This is a bad idea." Phoenix packed her suit away. "The dumbest thing I've ever done. Walking into a contamination zone basically naked."

"You aren't naked," said Althea. "You have clothes."

Teal laughed. "Naked might even be smarter… then you wouldn't have to disinfect any fabric on your way out."

Phoenix extended a middle finger at Teal. Both of them laughed.

"Well, if we're going to do this, let's do it before I change my mind." Phoenix stared at Althea. "You can really get rid of the disease?"

"Yes." She smiled.

"TC Hanson," said David, "You have data on all twenty-four people she already cured of it. There's no question here beyond exactly what this virus is. For all we know, its intention is simply to incapacitate an enemy force without killing them. Sick and injured soldiers are much more of a drain on resources than bodies."

"I don't like not knowing." Phoenix frowned. "But… I suppose we don't have the luxury of waiting for the lab to figure it out."

They put the protective suit storage boxes in the buggy to hide them, then pulled on their backpacks. They both carried smaller versions of the flame rifle Dr. Ruiz had at the hospital. Some might call it a 'pistol,' though it seemed too big for the word. Althea figured they brought them to destroy all the sicks she forced out of people.

Teal arranged some debris around the area to help conceal their buggy in case raiders happened to cruise past the spot. Once finished, she faced Kellis. "Lead the way."

They walked along the ghost of a former paved road, weaving among dead military vehicles. The path curved around a series of fortified concrete barriers where destroyed gun turrets slumped forward, rusted into mounds of useless metal. *This* spot felt like death, but no worse than any Lost Place Althea visited. She kept her mouth closed and walked near the front of the group, unafraid.

The Prophet would no longer be meek. She'd come here to protect people.

A little over half a mile from the vehicle graveyard, a surprisingly robust circular wall made from scrap metal and massive rectangular concrete blocks stood up on end came into view up ahead, surrounded by the ruins of a small city. It enclosed an area roughly 250 meters across and appeared —at least from this angle—to have a single gate facing south. No one guarded the opening, nor did there appear to be anyone walking around the top of the wall on sentry duty looking out. Kellis proceeded down the old street toward the village without hesitation.

Althea followed him.

After walking for several blocks into the ruins, they reached the gate and went inside without challenge. Inside the wall, they found more ruins, though the structures were in better shape than the ones outside, having been repaired to a state of usability with scrap.

The village of Afbee appeared well put together for a scrag town, most of the buildings being solid structures

rather than animal hide or thin metal panels tied to sticks or
pipes. They'd obviously been rebuilt and repaired numerous
times, a hodgepodge of mismatched materials and colors.
Dozens of poles, mostly old street lamps or the sorts of
metal pillars the red, yellow, and green lanterns hung from,
dotted the place, all studded with clusters of random junk.
Hoses made from spliced sections of green, black, and blue
tubing ran among the poles, dripping and leaking water.
None of the structures stood taller than a single story
except for one, a giant three-story fortress at the center of
the area inside the circular wall. Words over the door read,
'Credit Union.'

Nearby villagers all stopped in their tracks to gaze at
the outsiders. They appeared to be prosperous for a scrag
tribe. Most of the adults wore clothing of some form or
another, generally tunics and loose pants made from plain
grey fabric similar to linen. Only about a dozen people in
sight appeared overly primitive, in loincloths or only
jewelry and body paint. Curiously, there didn't appear to be
many children living here, or at least, they remained out of
sight. She spotted two boys a little younger than her. One
wore only an odd necklace made of shiny silver nuggets.
The other boy had a thin black belt—an electrical cable tied
around his waist with scraps of black, furry bonedog
leather hanging in front and back as a loincloth.

Althea could usually recognize the social status or
position of scrags based on how much or little clothing they
wore. Kids without wealthy or influential parents didn't
usually bother with clothing at all until they became old
enough to become scouts and scavengers, then wearing
whatever they'd managed to find out in the ruins. Among
scrags, garments served as badges of success and pride. The
more timid villagers who remained at home doing the
cooking, maintenance work, building, or taking care of

babies generally only wore whatever a warrior or scout gifted to them. Scrag seekers tended to start offering gifts to girls or boys they desired as a mate around Althea's age or a bit older. Consequently, to see a scrag older than her without clothing or decorative trinkets meant no one had yet chosen them for a mate—or the person rejected any such gifts they'd been offered.

This place, however, confused her. None of the people here gave off any sense of being proud of having clothing. Even the two boys had no particular emotional attachment to their stuff or lack of it. Confused, she poked at their thoughts. The boy with the silver metal nuggets around his neck had a big grey blanket at home he wore at night to keep warm. While he adored his necklace, he didn't have any drive to go out and scavenge up anything else so he could brag about it. He also had no feelings of being 'less than a man' for not having found anything to wear himself. If his parents obtained something for him to wear, they would. The village had run out of the grey fabric, though he couldn't care less. This thoroughly baffled her and left her mouth hanging open. For a scrag, especially a boy around ten, to not be doing everything possible to posture and impress everyone—much less be completely at ease with the idea of his parents giving him stuff—defied everything she'd yet seen. Boys tended to be extremely sensitive to ego and status. Accepting gifts from others, even parents, amounted to an admission of weakness. But these two? They couldn't care less what anyone thought when looking at them.

It did somewhat make sense. If the boys knew they could get things from their parents whenever they wanted, no danger, effort, or work involved, then garments wouldn't have the same status to them as a young seeker who nearly died five times while exploring a Lost Place to get a dress. She decided Afbee might or might not be a scrag village after all. While they dressed like tribals, their mannerisms seemed more akin to those of Querq.

It also struck Althea as odd to see so much of the village's clothing made from the same basic grey fabric. This tribe must have found a large supply of it in some Before-Time building.

The boy with the bonedog-hide loincloth reminded her of the leather scrap skirt she'd made for herself two years ago. At the time, she hadn't known Den and didn't want to wait for any scavenger to court her. Part of her wanted to stop feeling like a 'little kid' and be taken seriously. If she had something to wear, she hoped the villagers would treat her with more respect, the way they did successful seekers. Little Jake from Den's tribe had been *so* proud of the boar hide shorts he made himself. Even though the boy was small for his age, scrawny, and not terribly good at being a seeker, he paraded around showing off his new pants—and it had earned him status.

Althea never wanted 'status.' She'd only wanted people to treat her like a person. Alas, making the skirt hadn't changed how people treated her one little bit. She kept it out of pride because she *made* it. Sighing, she brushed a hand idly up and down the fabric of her plain white dress. It came from the modern world and didn't belong out here, but Karina and Father gave it to her, so she loved it. Unlike her old skirt, it didn't continually try to fall apart, requiring constant repair. Also, if she lost it or something destroyed it, she could easily get another one exactly like it. It had taken her months to build her old skirt from bits and pieces of leather she'd swiped from wounded raiders.

People continued staring at them as they walked deeper into the village.

In contrast to Querq, the denizens of Afbee comprised a varied mix of what she now knew to be 'ethnicity.' Almost everyone native to Querq, the city people called Hispanic, having black hair, brown skin, and primarily speaking Spanish. According to David, the majority of those who lived in West City no longer truly had an ethnicity, humanity having mixed so much over the generations. He jokingly said everyone turned light brown. Of course, they also had the Reinventions thing, a place where people could change how they looked if they had enough pay things. To them, the idea of 'ethnicity' had become as meaningless as the color of a shirt.

*They are so primitive*, said Phoenix by way of telepathy. *Wow. Like a quarter of them aren't wearing clothes. That boy is only wearing a damn necklace. When did we go to the Amazon rainforest?*

David's telepathic chuckle followed. *Scrags are no different from tribes in some parts of the world. This village is surprisingly well-outfitted. I was expecting to see a hundred people streaking around. We've found the richest scrag tribe in the Badlands here.*

She scowled. *Yeah, but this is the UCF. We're not supposed to have tribes on this continent.*

*Tell that to them.* David waved in greeting to a group of armed men. Two carried spears made from rebar rods. One had a hatchet and one a legitimate sword. The warriors gave no sign of hostility, merely curiosity.

*Wow. Just… wow. I feel like I'm in some nature holo-vid making contact with a lost civilization.* Phoenix exhaled hard.

David laughed out loud. "We basically are doing exactly that."

The stunned villagers continued gawking at them. Everyone seemed to be at varying degrees of exhausted, though no one in sight looked as sick as Kellis did when Althea first met him. The locals even regarded Kellis with an odd sort of hesitance about them, as if they didn't recognize him due to his T-shirt, intact pants, and shoes.

He'd shown up in Querq wearing a simple tunic and pants like the people here. Althea glanced from person to person, unable to recognize any common thing—such as age, size, sex, or weapons, determining who got the tunics and didn't. The Afbee tribe clearly hadn't found an infinite supply of the strange grey fabric, or everyone would be wearing something made from it.

Phoenix leaned away from a spear carrier and whispered, "Is this guy seriously wearing a license plate over his junk?"

"Yep," said Teal. "They're just about the perfect size to make good loincloths. Stops scorpions from stinging them in the balls, too. Not a bad idea… right up until they slice their thigh open or it gets hot in the sun."

David cringed. "I'd rather swing in the breeze than burn it."

"I like to swing in the breeze." Althea grinned.

David and Phoenix stared at her, giving off a mixture of 'aww' and awkwardness.

"She doesn't mean what you think she means." Teal smirked. "She's referring to an actual swing like kids play on."

Althea nodded. "Yes. The Water Man made some for us. What did you think I meant?"

Embarrassment came from David. "Just that. Swinging. On a swing, in the breeze."

She made a face at him, knowing he lied but did so obviously because he didn't want to talk about whatever he'd really said.

"Right, well…" Teal glanced at Kellis. "Take us to your leader."

Phoenix groaned.

"I've always wanted to say that." Teal examined her fingernails. "Would have been better if we flew a hovercar in here first. Then we'd totally be alien visitors. Missed opportunity. I've never been groveled at before."

David snickered.

"This way." Kellis started down the dirt path between huts, heading toward the big building in the village center.

Althea smiled at everyone as they went by. A few adult villagers appeared to recognize her once they got a good look at her glowing eyes. Whispers of 'Prophet' went around in the speaking city people called English. The instant their emotion shifted from hesitant worry—as if watching someone do something they would get in trouble for—to awe, they began to follow her.

Being here surrounded by scrags reminded her of Den's village. It also gave her a haunting nostalgia for the village in which she'd grown from baby to five-year-old. Her recollection of the place amounted to little more than standing on the shore of the big lake, the water bright blue like her eyes. The village didn't have a wall, merely a bunch of huts within walking distance of the water. She remembered running around playing with other children, no one treating her any different for having glowing eyes. A woman who she'd once thought of as her mother crouched by the shore, fishing, her feet buried in the pale sand while Althea—perhaps two or three years old at the time—played. She couldn't remember many details of the woman's face, or her husband, or much of anything other than the scene by the lake.

No villager tried to get in their way. Several coughed intermittently. Some, seemingly too tired to stand, sat propped up against various walls or buildings. A young blonde girl a few years younger than Althea—only the third child they'd yet seen here—watched them from a shadowed gap between two concrete huts, as if hiding from people. Dried blood smeared her face, likely having leaked from her nose. The girl wore nothing more than dirt, her pale skin dotted head to toe with small, bright red dots. Her arms, legs below the knee, and face had somewhat more color than the rest of her, suggesting she owned a dress or tunic, but decided not to wear it.

No other children, or anyone else, went near her, likely due to fearing the obviously visible sick. Many of the red dots oozed translucent yellow liquid. The child appeared to be in pain simply from existing. Strong sorrow and loneliness radiated from her.

Althea shrugged off her backpack, dropped it where she stood, and darted over to the shaking, sick child. The instant she did so, a hint of hope broke through the other girl's sadness. As soon as she entered the gap between huts, the child raised her hand in a 'stop' gesture, retreating half a step. Sadness returned.

"It's okay. Don't be scared," said Althea.

The other girl lowered her arm, but said nothing.

Up close, the red sores appeared shiny like glass, the skin stretched to the point it had become see-through. Each pustule looked about the size of a small pea perched on a raised red welt of skin. No area of her body had been spared. Ruptured sores dribbled a clear yellow fluid that smelled like unsafe cheese. The way the child tensed her muscles gave away even the air blowing over her skin caused pain. No surprise she couldn't tolerate the touch of fabric.

The sick child grimace-smiled. "Hi. I'm Kia."

"Althea." She held out a hand.

"Are you a spirit? Why do your eyes have light?"

"I'm not a spirit, but I talk to them." Althea stepped closer.

Kia leaned back. "No. Not allowed to touch. You get sick. It hurts."

"I won't." Althea inched even closer. "I make the sick go away."

"No one can touch." Kia sniffled, edging away. "Mama wants to hold me, but she will get sick. I have bad stuff. I can't have touching. Spirits mad at me."

Althea again reached for her.

"No!" Kia jumped back. "Don't touch. Red spots get you too."

"They won't." Althea suppressed the girl's fear, then rested a hand on the child's shoulder.

A hot, swollen pustule slipped between her fingers. Kia cringed in pain, gasping at the contact. The instant Althea linked her power to the girl's life essence, she realized the sick hurt her like she had dozens of boiling hot needles poking into her everywhere. *Eep!* She hastily told Kia's mind to stop feeling pain. Overcome by relief, the child fainted. Althea caught her and eased her to lie on the ground, then sprawled next to her.

Kellis, David, and Phoenix gathered at the opening of the 'alley', watching from a few meters away.

"Oh, that poor kid," whispered Phoenix. "Looks like a mutated form of chickenpox."

"Watch this," whispered David.

Althea again closed her eyes and dove back into the healing trance. A red-and black silhouette of Kia's life shapes appeared floating in a void. An angry, yellow sick filled her whole body, hovering close to the skin, brightest at each dot. It almost looked like the sick tried to crawl out of her via the sores so it could attack other people. No doubt the yellow syrup leaking from her would make others sick if they touched it. It reminded her of some plants with poison sap. The child also had two tiny puncture wounds at her ankles, as if she'd been jabbed with pins, probably from walking around ruins, or maybe they had a shaman who gave her needles.

She'd always thought them silly for it... and thanks to Dr. Ruiz, she understood why she'd been right to consider it foolish. Scavengers would sometimes discover old syringes in the same places they found bandages and other medical supplies. Associating the needles to medicine led many shaman to think sticking them into people would somehow help. A year ago, Althea had no clue what a syringe actually did, but regarded it as a stupid sharp thing. Sticking sharp things into people would only *make* hurts, not fix them. Dr. Ruiz explained how people once used needles to give medicine, injecting liquids into the body like the fangs of a snake or a soldier scorpion's tail. The modern world no longer used metal needles, rather high-pressure fluid jets.

She mentally sighed at the idiot who thought poking this nine-year-old in the leg with a needle might make the red spots go away... and got to work. At first, she tried to gather the sick into the girl's bladder, but she had so much of it—plus the oozy stuff inside the pustules to get rid of— so she redirected it to the stomach. All the red dots shrank away to nothing in a matter of a few minutes as Kia's skin regenerated. Not a trace of a scar remained.

Within seconds of Althea opening her eyes, Kia lurched to the side and threw up a mass of dark yellow slime. Althea held on to her as she convulsed and vomited the sick, keeping her pain sense off. Peeing out a sick burned in a tender spot, but barfing it hurt much worse, like drinking fire all the way down into the belly. Also, she considered throwing up a far less pleasant experience than making water. She disliked needing to make the girl vomit, but the child simply had too much sick in her to fit in the bladder.

Once Kia stopped throwing up, Althea pulled her away from the mess.

Kia hung limp in her arms, lacking the strength to move.

Althea pointed a foot at the barf puddle. "No touch, or the sick will come back."

David stepped past her, shooing the girls away from the disgusting blob while removing his flame pistol from the side pouch on his backpack.

Althea stood, pulled Kia to her feet, and backed away from the slime. The girl reflexively clung-hug in response to being squeezed and dragged along. Orange light and a soft *whoosh* filled the space between buildings as David incinerated the foul mess. In seconds, the stink of moldy, decaying cheese gave way to the chemical odor of whatever the fire pistol burned. It also smelled bad, but in a different way unlikely to make anyone want to throw up. Villagers able to see what went on gave awed gasps. Whispers went around, people asking how this strange man could summon fire.

Kia's mood went from overjoyed to horrified. She jumped back in a panic, then looked down at herself, her skin no longer marked by red bubbles. In total disbelief, she swiped a hand around her chest, having to touch the skin to believe all the swollen orbs had disappeared. After taking a moment to let the truth sink into her mind, she burst into happy tears and tried to run off... but Althea held her back.

"Wait. You still have sick on you."

"Mama!" called Kia. "Maaaama! You don't gotta not touch me!"

Phoenix took a genesis canteen from her belt and sprayed Kia down. The girl squealed in delight at the improvised shower.

"The red spots let the sick out. All the sticky stuff on

you can hurt people." Althea helped wipe the girl's back while Phoenix continued spraying.

Eventually, both Althea and Phoenix felt confident Kia had been cleaned up as much as possible and no longer posed a contagion risk to anyone. The dripping wet girl ran off into the village calling for her mother. Althea watched her go, brought almost to tears by how much happiness she gave off. As much as she disliked visiting the modern world, the time she'd spent with the city police allowed her greater understanding of how her powers worked. By forcing a person's body to purge a sick, she also helped them resist it if it came back. According to the woman in the white jumpsuit, her healing abilities did something called an 'immune response from hell.' If Althea forced a sick out of someone, they'd have a much better chance of resisting reinfection from the same sick than someone who recovered naturally.

This made her smile, hopeful Kia wouldn't suffer the painful red dots again.

Villagers stared at Althea, their emotions part way between hope and fear. She looked around at roughly sixty people murmuring about The Prophet. Most of them mentioned Mako the trader. The man had evidently been telling them about her since almost everyone here appeared to be sick in one way or another. Fortunately, no one else in sight looked deathly ill or in obvious pain. She suspected the *really* sick people would be stuck in bed or gathered in a shaman's hut.

"Nice," whispered David. "Poor kid."

"That..." Phoenix pointed in the direction the girl ran. "Was not the same virus we're expecting. Damn. It looked like some sort of weaponized form of chicken pox. Did you see how she reacted to Althea's touch? Those boils had to be extremely painful."

"Yes." Althea looked down. "Kia had lots of pain. She hurt more from lonely than ouch."

Phoenix gazed at the sky. "Bastards must have hit this place with a cocktail."

The crowd gave off the usual wave of anticipatory emotion common to villagers seeing The Prophet. Althea expected them to swarm her, all asking for help. This, she didn't mind. She had, after all, come here specifically to do exactly that. In other scrag villages, emotions from the younger villagers tended to vary. Girls close to her age radiated defensiveness and jealousy. Boys her age as well as the younger kids mostly emanated curiosity. Older teens either had little reaction or regarded her in the same way as the adults.

Here, everyone gave off the same mild sense of fear and awe. The two boys had continued going wherever they'd been going, indifferent to the presence of outsiders. Another oddity: no one approached her to ask for help. For some reason, they hesitated, their initial hope rapidly eroded under a heavy layer of fear. Something caused them to be too afraid to ask her to make the sicks go away. She contemplated squishing their fear, but decided to wait until she understood what about this place could frighten everyone. Too many things felt strange about this village. The people here didn't act wholly right for scrags, nor did they act like settlers. They appeared caught in the tribal primitivism of scrags while also clinging to some scraps of civilization from the Before-Time.

Fortunately, no one in sight needed *immediate* help to avoid death… so she could ask questions first.

"Gonna be a project." David whistled, gazing around. "I'm thinking we should expect to spend a few days out here."

"I am surprised." Phoenix glanced at a coughing

woman. "I expected to find everyone lying around waiting to die. How is it possible such a contagious disease hasn't rampaged over this entire population?"

"Maybe they already all have it and they're used to it?" Teal shrugged. "If they've been living with it for generations, it could be no big deal to them... Kellis here got unlucky or had a reaction."

Phoenix gestured at the group of villagers watching them. "Yes, but look at them. They're all sick, just not at death's door. Most are coughing. I can hear a stridor in their breathing. Don't forget, this village has shrunk from 500 people to 200 in only ten years. *Something* is going on here."

Teal eyed Kellis. "Have you been sick your entire life?"

"No. The spirits became angry with me only ten years ago." He bowed his head. "I still do not know what I did to earn their wrath. I have felt weak, dizzy, hard to breathe for a long time. It became much worse a few days before I decided to go find The Prophet. The spirits are angry."

"What could that little girl possibly have done to piss off your spirits to torture her like that?" asked Phoenix in a mildly nasty tone. "Did you see that kid? What is she, eight? Nine? The poor thing was in so much pain she passed out as soon as Althea made her stop hurting. If your spirits are real and they'd do that to a little kid, they're evil."

Althea folded her arms. "Yes. Evil."

Kellis exhaled. "I don't know how you can speak of the spirits in such a way. Are you not afraid of their punishment?"

"I'm not." Phoenix huffed. "People who haven't figured out what pants are shouldn't try to explain to a medical doctor how infectious diseases work."

"Be nice," whispered Althea. "And some of them have pants."

"You're a medical doctor?" Teal raised an eyebrow. "But just an Admin Tech in the police?"

David smiled. "She's a tech captain, not a tech. Our ranks are a little confusing. TC is equivalent to first lieutenant. But... she's Admin so she doesn't have command authority over me as I'm Tactical. It's a mess."

"You can say that again." Phoenix shook her head.

Nice. Teal bowed to her. "Finish school young or did you Reinvention back the clock a little?"

"Hah," said Phoenix. "No, I'm honestly twenty-five."

"She is, as they say, a genius." David winked.

"Hardly. When you're an orphan in the dorms with no friends, nothing to do, and a decent aptitude for science, school becomes everything. Anyone who puts the kind of hours I did into education can be a medical doctor by twenty-four, too."

"Even if they don't know what pants are?" asked Althea.

David, Teal, and Phoenix laughed.

"Well." David faced Kellis. "We have a lot of work to do here and might as well get started as soon as possible. Let's meet your chief."

"Follow me." Kellis resumed walking down the street toward the large, cube-shaped 'Credit Union' building that stood like a castle at the center of the village.

A man and a woman, both wearing grey tunics, pants, bonedog-hide boots and frayed blue armor vests stood guard on either side of the door. Both carried bladed metal spears. White lettering on the front of the vests bore the letters 'USAF' above the word 'Security.'

"I must speak to Durango," said Kellis.

The guards looked everyone over, then nodded at him.

Amusement came from Phoenix.

Althea glanced at her. *What is funny?*

*They think we are unarmed because we aren't carrying spears, swords, or axes.* Phoenix suppressed a smile. *No idea what guns are. They looked right at my E-90 and didn't react to it at all.*

*Something is wrong here.* Althea furrowed her brows. A scrag village leader having guards to make sure no one brought weapons in and killed them didn't sound right. Raider groups suffered from constant backstabbing where someone always wanted to become the new chief by killing the old chief. The instant anyone thought their current chief weak in any way, attempts to kill them began. Scrag chiefs, on the other hand, ruled because their people trusted them. If Durango feared someone might want to hurt him, it meant his leadership didn't come from the people wanting him to be their chief.

Kellis went inside.

The guard on the left reached out to grab a pinch of Althea's dress as she tried to walk by, seeming curious about the material. Before the woman could comment on her being lucky to have found such a prize, she noticed the glowing blue light. Her emotions shifted in an instant from being impressed to reverence. She jerked her hand back as if she'd touched a candle flame.

*I'm here to help. Please don't worship me. I don't want it.*

A telepathic voice in her head terrified the woman—so Althea made the fear go away, replacing it with trust and calm.

*I am sorry for scaring you. Please don't be afraid.* She smiled innocently.

The woman offered a hesitant nod, then smiled.

Althea crept through the door, bare feet silent on the ancient concrete. Metal strips outlined a large semi-circle of floor at the entrance. Whatever carpet it used to edge had long since disintegrated. The building's interior consisted of one huge room with a two-story-tall ceiling, essentially a massive concrete box. Various useful objects from tools to bladed weapons to gathered foodstuffs lay in piles littered at random, some on tables, others on the floor, desks, or shelving.

At the innermost part, directly opposite the entrance, a man a little older than David with dark brown hair and a rich suntan sat in a wheeled office chair serving as a throne, raised up on a stack of wooden pallets. Two large metal desks flanked his seat, littered with objects like lamps, statuettes, crystal blocks, a treasure horde of useless but impressive-looking items. The man wore a faded and patched blue jumpsuit, made more of duct tape and linen than whatever fabric it had originally been. His outfit somewhat reminded Althea of the pilot ghost, except for no helmet. Behind him on the wall hung a huge, tattered flag. It had likely once been dark blue with a white symbol in the center, though had faded to an unrecognizable pattern.

Kellis approached the base of the pallet dais. "Spirits guide you, Durango. I must speak with you."

"Of course, my friend." Durango stood casually, not like a king proud of his power, and made his way down off the pallets to shake Kellis's hand and grab him in a one-armed hug. "It is good to see you again, and in good health. We all thought the spirits had taken you."

"No. I fear they may have tried." Kellis made a reverent gesture again. "I also fear I may have angered them."

"How so?" asked Durango.

"You know the trader, Mako, spoke of The Prophet. I found the strength to make the journey, so I did."

"You left Afbee?" Durango's eyes went wide, shock and concern welled up within him. "That is forbidden! You could have been taken!"

"I expected to die to the sickness if I did nothing. I did not want to wind up like the others, unable to get up or move, stuck in their beds for the last months of their life. Stay and die or risk defying the spirits and die. I would much rather the swift end."

Durango frowned, though his emotions said he feared Kellis might have been hurt more than experienced anger at disobedience. It seemed he truly regarded Kellis as a friend, perhaps even brother.

"Surely, if the spirits didn't want me to leave, they would have taken my life. Yet, here I am." Kellis gestured at Althea. "And the Prophet has come to help us all."

Anger shifted to curiosity the moment Durango looked at her. As if only noticing outsiders in strange clothing for the first time, he spent a moment studying everyone.

"Hi. I am Althea." She walked up to him. "Your people have many sicks. I am here to help make them better."

"You must understand..." Durango glanced over their group. "This is sacred ground. Authorized personnel only. Top secret clearance required. Those of us who are entrusted to dwell here protect it and do so at the whims of the spirits. Now that you have set foot upon our sacred ground, you may not leave. It is classified. The spirits will be wrathful."

Althea shook her head. "I can talk to the spirits and won't let them hurt anyone. We are here to help."

"Child..." Durango sighed at the floor. "I would prefer if you did not make the spirits angry. They will take their fury out on us. If I could do so, I'd ask you to leave and never return, but now that you are here, you cannot leave."

Teal folded her arms. "You're planning to stop us?"

A tall, muscular warrior gave her a 'what's a skinny little thing like you going to do about it' look, and chuckled. Teal ignored him.

"No." Durango sighed. "You are not prisoners. Know

that if you try to leave, the spirits will punish you. As far as I am concerned, leave if you wish, but you will regret it."

Phoenix radiated a pulse of worry.

Althea locked stares with her. *What?*

*The trader.* Phoenix took a deep breath. *Someone killed him after he left this place. This man's stories of angry spirits aren't completely fiction. While I don't think any actual spirits are involved, the meaning of the legends is based on some real danger. Probably the raiders.*

Althea nodded.

*There must be far more raiders around here than we think.* Phoenix nodded toward Durango. *He warns his people not to leave because the spirits say so in order to protect them from raiders who will pick off anyone they find.*

*I am not afraid of raiders.* Althea puffed out her chest. *I won't let them hurt you, or anyone else.*

Phoenix gave her the same sort of 'yeah right' look the big warrior gave Teal.

"Since we're going to be staying for a while," said David. "Let's talk about how we can help you manage the unusually high level of disease among your people."

"The spirits do what the spirits do." Durango made a reverent hand gesture. "When they have punished us enough, the sickness will go away."

"Look, it's really simple." Phoenix held up her datapad. "The people in your village are suffering from diseases. This isn't the work of spirits. The land you're living on used to be a military base. Either the Air Force stored biological weapons here, or Corporate forces dropped biological weapons on this place. A very physical problem—not a spiritual one—is making your people sick. Althea's come all the way from her home to help you. We need to work out an organized plan to make sure everyone is disinfected and stays that way."

The warriors, as well as five people sorting vegetables, paused to stare at her.

"You speak in a strange way, outsider," said Durango. "I do not understand, but it doesn't matter. Nothing you can do will sway the spirits. Go now and find a place to make your home. You are welcome here as long as you do not anger the spirits."

"What if we do?" asked Teal. "You can't kick us out."

"The spirits will take you." Durango bowed his head. "I hope you realize your foolishness before it is too late."

David gestured toward the door. *Let's find a place to talk and come up with a plan. This guy isn't going to be any help.*

Althea nodded in response to his telepathic voice, as did Phoenix.

Kelis paled, frightened at the mind voice. He started to say something, but stopped at a pointed look from David. A telempath as well, he had the ability to alter people's emotions, though not to the same degree as Althea. He could gently influence one person at a time, not make an entire raider army stain their pants at once. Being 'awakened' made her powerful, which had the side effect of people always wanting to study or kidnap her. Study, she didn't mind as much. Considering the good she could do for people, she refused to complain about her abilities.

Teal sent a smoldering stare of challenge at the big warrior who laughed at her, then followed everyone outside. Althea looked at him, shaking her head in a 'don't' manner. This made him laugh louder. Thankfully, Teal ignored him again.

David led the group outside and up a street to an apparently unused building a modest distance away from the Credit Union. The simple, rectangular structure contained mostly empty space, one small cot, and two chairs.

Unsure if it belonged to someone, David stopped short of going inside and turned to face everyone. "Right. So… we need a plan."

"This is so surreal." Phoenix glanced at the same two boys zooming by, the only people in Afbee with any visible energy. "This is so surreal seeing them act like tribals in the ruins of a city. Is that kid wearing socket wrench things around his neck?"

"Looks like it." Teal chuckled. "And they're not *acting* like tribals. They *are* tribal."

"It's another world." David exhaled. "A world we pretty much abandoned."

"Someone decided it would cost too much to reclaim." Teal frowned. "Damn corporations."

Phoenix tilted her head. "Odd to hear a mercenary complain about corporations valuing money over everything."

"*Former* mercenary." Teal ruffled Althea's hair.

"Right, so. We are here. Let's start doing something," said David.

"I am sorry for the way Durango spoke." Kellis bowed his head. "And for not telling you the spirits would be angry if you tried to leave."

"Forget the spirits." Phoenix waved dismissively. "When we are done here, we intend to leave. I'm sure we can handle these spirits."

Kellis pointed to the side. "For now, please come share my dwelling. It is not as grand as the Credit Union, but I have room for all. We took a large space because I expected to have family…"

He gave off such a spike of sorrow Althea had to hug him.

"I'm sorry," said David in a hushed tone. "Your wife became sick?"

"Yes." Kellis coughed away a sob. "She had the same sickness I did. Her life returned to the spirits not a week before Mako arrived and told me of The Prophet."

Teal bit her lip. "Not to sound insensitive, but we could probably use your dwelling as a base of operations. Let's go."

Kellis led them back the way they came, past the Credit Union, continuing to the northeastern part of the village, approximately halfway between the town center and the wall. A third of the building he called home remained from its pre-war state, the rest consisting of concrete rubble stacked like bricks and reinforced with scrap metal to form a one-room cabin with a good amount of space inside. The building contained a large sleeping area of padded mats plus a table and several chairs. Ancient writing on the old part of the structure said 'Beer and Wings Every Friday.'

David patted Kellis on the arm. "You should do your best to avoid close contact with people so you don't get sick again. Stay here and wait until we can do something about the situation."

"He might not get the sick again." Althea looked up. "I make immune response from hell."

Phoenix laughed, as did Teal.

"It's not a guarantee though." David grimaced at the surroundings, as if he didn't want to touch anything. "Also, there appears to be more than one virus running around here."

"I will do as you suggest for now." Kellis nodded. "How will you argue with the spirits?"

Phoenix pinched the bridge of her nose. "Not worth it to explain again."

"The spirits will listen to me." Althea beamed. "As soon as I find them."

## 15

## AFBEE

D avid and Phoenix decided to start by taking a thorough look around the village.

They left Kellis at his home and proceeded to roam the streets. The area inside the roughly circular wall contained a mixture of ancient buildings and open lots where whatever structures stood there in the Before-Time had collapsed entirely. Signs of the former world jutted out from the debris all around them: stop signs, old light posts, and the occasional smashed drive machine.

Wispy forms appeared occasionally wherever Althea looked. People, intact buildings, even moving cars flickering into existence for mere seconds at a time before fading back into the obscurity they'd drowned in. None gave any sense of awareness, merely images, like the holograms the city people used. Unlike the spirits she sometimes spoke with, these people and objects remained transparent, ephemeral. While the adults conducted their 'survey' of Afbee, Althea followed in somber silence, watching the echoes of the past society superimposed over a crumbling ruin home to a barely civilized tribe. People in strange, but nice clothing walked by carrying cups labeled 'Starbucks', their images phasing through villagers carrying crude bladed weapons and wearing garments made from scraps.

Thinking this place, indeed all the Badlands, had once been—and likely should still be—as modern as the big city stirred conflicting emotions in the pit of her stomach. These fragments seemed much happier than the living people in West City. Civilization here didn't look even one fourth as crammed together. Everyone had room. Though she felt no emotion coming from the specters of a clairvoyant vision of the past, they appeared much happier. Would it be better for people if the war had never happened, if the Badlands never formed? She disliked the big city due to all the negative emotions from so many people concentrated in a relatively small area. In school, she'd learned the war made everyone flee to the coasts. If the people remained spread out over the entire land, maybe they'd be happier. David and the city police certainly believed bringing scrags to the modern world *helped* them.

The two tween boys wandered into view from behind a large concrete hut, grinning back and forth at each other as they headed down the street, one still wearing only a necklace of socket wrench heads, the other a scrap of bonedog leather, unaware they passed among the apparitions of those who came before. Althea stopped to stare, struck by the oddity of seeing tribal children walking past storefronts and people as they looked 350 years ago. For a fleeting moment, everything appeared too real as if the boys fell through a hole in time—or space. Phoenix mentioned people still lived in tribes like scrags in other places, something called an Amazon. For some reason, the woman didn't like tribalism being here, in this land. But modern people with modern weapons did this. The tribes happened because modern people ruined the world—or at least this part of it.

The specters faded. Soon, the boys disappeared around another building. Evidently, they searched for someone named Mojave and hadn't been able to find her. Realizing her friends had gone on unaware she'd stopped, Althea hurried to catch up.

David and Phoenix discussed the wall surrounding Afbee. It clearly hadn't existed in the Before-Time. The way it cut through some buildings made it look as if a giant ring fell out of the sky and landed on the old city. It didn't seem possible for the present villagers to have made it. The wall appeared to consist primarily of massive concrete blocks, likely cut out from big buildings or some other structure, then covered in a layer of steel or scrap metal plates. The unusual symmetry of the Credit Union building—what Kellis referred to as 'the castle'—ending up at the center of the circle further proved the wall happened after the war.

"Considering the size of this place," said Phoenix, "I want to say the population used to be much higher, even than 500."

Teal wandered to the side, peering into the doorway of a nearby building. "The people here now couldn't possibly have built this wall. I'm sure there used to be a couple thousand at some point. They're dying off."

"They talk good for scrags," said Althea.

Murmurs of agreement came from the others.

"Makes me think they might be literate." Phoenix set her hands on her hips, turning to survey the area. "Or they at least have a few people who can read and teach. Not hearing any Spanish influence in the language. My guess is, we're dealing with an isolated pocket of survivors. Maybe even the descendants of the original Air Force personnel who lived here."

David nodded once. "Think so? They're a bit more tribal than I'd expect from settlers."

"True," said Teal, "However, having books and knowing how to read them doesn't make food, clothing, and weapons materialize out of thin air."

"And not being able to find clothes doesn't make someone have the stupid." Althea smiled.

Teal chuckled at her intentional scrag talk. "True. Look at this place. It's desolate. Not surprised they've gone primitive. There's literally nothing here to make use of other than concrete and scrap metal."

Phoenix shielded her eyes from the sun. "Must be a farm hidden somewhere, or they'd have starved."

Althea sighed, saddened at the thought. Life in a scrag tribe could be harsh and unforgiving. However, she still preferred it to the big city—at least, the part of the big city she'd witnessed, the Bumwallow as its residents called it. They lived not so different from scrags, despite being in the modern world. There, her powers made her overly susceptible to absorbing negative emotions from people around her. Out here in the Badlands, they protected her from the worst parts of being a scrag: disease and injury. A seeker exploring a Lost Place could cut their leg on an old piece of metal and end up dead days later. Many tribes struggled to find enough to eat. Starvation and lack of water killed as many as raiders, bonedogs, and mutated animals.

The people of Afbee, though apparently scrags, had a better situation than some, not considering the rampant disease. Their wall gave them a place of safety. Also, they appeared to have sufficient food and water. While none of the villagers came close to being overweight, they also didn't appear underfed—except for those who had become too sick to want food.

David and Phoenix found several dwellings where a person or two lay helpless in bed, lost to fever. The villagers had left them there alone, perhaps afraid of earning the spirits' ire for being too close to someone so sick. It worked out for the best, as no one tried to stop Althea from helping them out of fear of making the spirits angrier.

Aside from the color of the amorphous sick floating in their life shapes, Althea couldn't tell one disease from another. An annoying sick that only made a person's nose run could appear similar to a deadly sick capable of killing someone. Milder sicks tended to appear greenish while the nastier ones tinted yellow. The worst sicks appeared to be black vapor.

Phoenix used a small kit to take blood samples from everyone Althea cured. She also insisted on burning any fabric that had been in contact with the sick person if her little machine said it contained tons of virus particles. At this, David ran off in search of replacement garments. Teal thought it a futile effort—why would a third or so of the villagers content themselves with loincloths or nothing at all if they had a stash of usable clothing just lying around?

Twenty-ish minutes later, they entered a hut where a young man floated in a big green plastic tub of water. Althea guessed he had about seventeen birthdays. He suffered the same sick as the little blonde girl, his body covered in swollen red pustules.

An older man seated beside the tub raised both hands at them. "You must not come closer. My son has been cursed by the spirits."

"I will help him." Althea walked up to the father. His face had dark spots all over it, which she suspected would turn into swollen red dots within the next few days. "You have the sick, too."

The man looked down. "I do not care. No one else will

tend to Rogue. He is my son. If the spirits curse me for easing his pain, let them. He must stay in the water. It cools the burn. He cannot touch anything without screaming."

"F-father..." rasped the teen. "Her eyes... Mako spoke of —" Rogue grimaced, his body convulsing.

Phoenix grabbed an injector from her belt. "This boy is in so much pain he's having a seizure."

Althea forced calm over the father so he wouldn't interfere, then hurried to grab Rogue's hand. The older boy smiled at her as she knelt beside the big green tub. A tiny bit of hope shone past his agony. As with Kia, the instant she told his mind to ignore pain, he lost consciousness. At the edge of the healing trance, David's voice echoed as if far away. He'd returned from his search disappointed and empty-handed. Phoenix had been right in her pessimism. The tribe did not have a stash of unworn clothing or even fabric sitting around. According to him, the spirits hadn't left cloth in the sacred places for some time.

"What's that supposed to mean?" asked Teal.

He scratched his head. "Did you notice how many of them are wearing tunics and pants made from the same grey material? Durango told me the spirits left them gifts in a place they considered sacred."

Phoenix sighed. "They probably just got lucky and found a stash. Maybe raiders got the last trader who tried to come here, and the locals found a wagon full of fabric. Raiders might have left behind plain fabric because they lack the skill to sew them into garments or just don't care to."

Finished, Althea opened her eyes. She held Rogue's head while he threw up foul gunk into a giant coffee can Phoenix held for him. The boy's father stared on in awe. Sensing he would soon be worshiping her instead of 'the spirits,' she sighed out her nose. He loved his son so much he'd been willing to sit there and die with him, knowing he could do nothing more than make the teen's final weeks slightly less agonizing.

"Could be." David cringed at the young man barfing up slime.

Althea moved on to purge the sick from Rogue's father, also taking a moment to mold his emotional reaction to her into simple gratitude rather than worship. Phoenix carried the coffee can outside and flamed it. When she returned, she declared this particular sick didn't float in the air, and could only be transmitted via touching the oil leaking from the sores. Dealing with the contaminated water in the tub proved a challenge, but the blankets on the father's sleeping mat hadn't been touched in days, and remained free of contamination. Thus, they became Rogue's new toga.

Althea grinned, brimming with energy and elation at being able to save a young man from such a horrible, painful disease. Phoenix thought it had been made by people as a weapon. If she ever found the person who made it, she'd be quite angry with them for doing so. She might even yell at them.

From there, they continued going from building to building, stopping wherever they found someone too ill to get off their sleeping space. The process of purging and flaming the sicks ended up being fairly simple... until they found a man suffering from hundreds of strange little blobs inside him. Althea knew the lumps shouldn't be there, but not where they came from, so she decided to get rid of them. Fleshy nuggets couldn't be sent out via peeing. A few were too large even for vomiting, so she decided it best to make his skin and muscle separate, 'cutting' open a huge hole in his torso.

Before she did so, she asked Phoenix for help getting him out of his tunic. The fabric scanned clean enough of viruses to avoid the burn pile, so the woman didn't cut it off him. After setting the garment aside, Althea rested her hands on the man's arm and dove back into her healing trance, splitting his chest open from throat to belly.

The rapid appearance of such an opening caused Phoenix to gasp and yell, "Holy shit!"

Althea proceeded to reach inside him and grab the lumps, pulling them out and tossing them in a pile. It took only a few seconds' concentration to make the healthy parts 'let go' of the bad parts so the growths came free easily, as if she plucked small fruits off a vine. Some had grown inside other life shapes, so they took longer to remove and demanded regenerating the damaged life shape where they'd been.

At watching this, Phoenix experienced a mild meltdown, shouting at David about 'unsanitary' procedures and 'this kid rooting around inside people with her bare, unwashed hands.' David simply stared until her brain caught up to her mouth and she stopped short.

"I'm being an idiot, aren't I?" Phoenix collected the remains of the man's sweat and puke-stained tunic.

"No, you're being a trained doctor watching something medical science says should not be possible." David chuckled. "Althea isn't going to allow an infection to take hold. Yes, her hands are dirty, but you have studied her file. You've witnessed her flush disease out of people. What's really bothering you?"

"I..." Phoenix cringed. "Watching a little girl elbow deep in a living person while making faces like a five-year-old playing in a sandbox is disturbing. A kid her age should be screaming and looking away from gore."

Althea paused, gripping a blob as big as an infant's head in both hands. "I'm sorry for giving you a disturb."

"No... keep going. You opened him up already...

somehow." Phoenix knelt beside her. "Good grief. All these tumors. I…"

Althea tugged the 'baby head' out from under the large dark red life shape and tossed it aside, then forced the man's body to regrow in the spot it came from. "What do you name this?" She poked the big dark red lump the blob had been hiding under.

"His liver."

"Strange word." Althea scrunched her nose. "I don't know what a liver does, but it's important. People die if it breaks."

"Yeah. They sure do." Phoenix whistled. "Wow. You are so small to be this unfazed by seeing the inside of a person."

Althea shrugged, confused why anyone would think seeing life shapes *should* bother her.

Phoenix took another small device off her belt. It sprouted a tiny needle, which she poked into the 'baby head' tumor.

"Consider where she's been and what she's seen," said David in a somber tone. "Raider gangs used to force her to put their idiots back together after fights. She's probably seen worse than combat medics on Mars."

"Don't be sad for me." Althea grabbed another tumor next to the man's heart. "Be sad for him. He has a lot of bad shapes. They don't belong and made much hurt. I fix."

"Tumors," said Phoenix.

"Tumor…" Althea grasped the plum-sized lump, commanding the healthy parts around it to let go. Once it popped free, she threw it on the pile.

"I am never going to be able to eat chicken nuggets again," said David.

"Weak stomach?" asked Teal. "Can't really blame you. That is some nasty shit. You're right though. The smaller ones *do* look like chicken nuggets."

Phoenix looked up from the device she'd jabbed into the tumor. "You don't seem too bothered by the mess."

"I've opened a lot of people up in my lifetime." Teal patted her sidearm. "I'm not a doctor, so I don't usually put them back together."

"Can I ask a possibly insensitive question?" Phoenix glanced at her.

"Sure. I've heard it all." Teal exhaled.

"Biological gore doesn't appear to bother you," said Phoenix. "But if you see a synthetic cut open or maybe a robot with its parts all over the place, does it feel the same way as biological people seeing gore like this?"

"Nope." Teal shook her head. "When I believed myself an ordinary person, gore freaked me out. Maybe it still does, but I'm in deep denial. Robot guts never bothered me."

"Fair enough." Phoenix nodded. "Thanks."

"What happened to this guy?" asked David, barely looking at him.

"Rampant uncontrolled growth." Phoenix tapped at the datapad screen. "He's got teratomas sprouting up everywhere. They're just random tissue production. That one's got teeth in it and it came from his lower intestine. I don't have the right equipment here to determine the exact cause, but it's highly unlikely to be anything natural. This isn't a normal case of cancer. The tumors appear to be benign."

Althea held up a fleshy nugget about the size of her fist. "This one's got hair on it."

David shuddered.

Minutes later, Althea plucked out the last one. She commanded the man's body to regrow, closing the opening she made, then collected a hazy lime-green sick into his bladder before allowing him to wake up.

The villager sat up abruptly, gasping for air. He kept breathing in deep gulps, looking around as if amazed to be alive.

"You had a bad sick. It's still inside and needs to come out. Make water while I stop pain," said Althea.

He groaned as he got to his feet and went over to a metal basin in the corner, which smelled as though it served toilet duty for a long time. Althea kept a hand on his arm to mute pain until he finished. The syrupy liquid coming out of him stank as bad as a cauldron of boiling corpses, among the foulest smells she'd ever experienced. Stench soon forced David and Teal out of the room. Phoenix gagged, but weathered it.

The man, still a bit dazed, wandered outside once he got rid of the last of the sick.

Althea carried the basin over to the tumor pile and transferred all the globs into it. That done, she held her arms out while Phoenix sprayed the blood off her using one of the genesis canteens. Clean and dripping, Althea headed outside to where David and Teal explained to the man he'd been deathly ill. The *fwoosh* of a flame pistol went off behind her.

"The spirits will be angry," whispered the man. "Thank you for you helping, but the spirits will punish me again, and you, too."

"No." Althea shook her head. "I won't let them. Don't be scared."

The man whirled on her, taking a huge breath as if about to yell at her for disrespecting the spirits. However, the instant he locked stares with her, his emotions exploded into shock and reverence. He let the air out of his lungs not with a yell, but a whisper. "The Prophet…"

"Yes. Please just call me Althea." She smiled.

"The Prophet comes to Afbee to make war on the spirits?" asked the man, giving off hope.

"No war. If the spirits are bad, I will tell them to go away." Althea held her chin up. "But I don't see any spirits here."

The man bowed in thanks. "I do not know how to believe. Stories say the Prophet can do anything. But... the spirits. You will battle them. Go to the shrine. If the spirits are here, you will find them at the sacred place. Please ask them to spare Ford."

"Ford?" asked David.

"I am Ford," said the man who once had tumors. "I will take you to the shrine."

Phoenix exited the house, still holding her flame pistol. "Should be clean in there now. Might want to give it a few minutes for the air to clear up."

"We have a few minutes." David gestured at Ford. "He's going to show us a shrine where we can talk to the spirits."

"Oh, joy." Phoenix waved the flame unit back and forth to cool it.

Ford went into his dwelling, returning a moment later having put his tunic back on, plus a pair of bonedog hide moccasins.

Teal turned in place, studying their surroundings. "It's making me nervous how little attention the locals are paying us. It's like they don't even notice we're here."

David tapped his foot. "Some of them are too sick to care. Others think the spirits are in control and sent us. This place has almost a prison-like mindset. Everyone feels trapped here, so they don't regard outsiders as any sort of threat. Once we're here, we're immediately part of the group... stuck here like them."

Ford hurried off, waving for everyone to follow. Althea grinned in response to sensing elation coming from him at being alive and on his feet again. The fear he felt toward the spirits didn't stop him from grinning back at her like a pair of kids who'd gotten away with breaking the rules. Having to stay sick sounded like a bad rule, so she liked breaking it. She'd been ready to treat Durango and the warriors around him like raiders if they tried to prevent her from helping people. Thankfully, she didn't have to. The chief didn't act out of evil, only fear. The same way many raider groups believed being mean to her would result in misfortune, Durango blindly feared 'the spirits' becoming angry. Althea knew no magical force punished raiders if they treated her poorly. The ones who let her walk around the camp freely met the same eventual end as the marauders who kept her leashed, caged, or barely fed her. Some other, more powerful, group would invariably discover her location and make war until they took her or died trying.

What Phoenix said about 'primitive' people inventing stories made sense. Althea knew exactly why 'misfortune' found raiders, and it had nothing to do with her powers or some other paranormal force. She thought it silly even small raider groups never once decided *not* to kidnap her out of fear they would be attacked by a stronger group who wanted her. When the inevitable attack finally happened, her former captors would always die baffled, blaming any cause other than her mere presence there for the raid. The Many certainly wouldn't bother punishing anyone for mistreating her. While a supernatural explanation *could* be given for unfortunate events in the Badlands, she doubted it in this case. Raiders simply made up stories to explain an obvious truth they refused to accept.

"Bullshit," said Teal. "We're not stuck here."

"I mean…" David smiled. "They think we are. So, to them, we aren't seen as outsiders. It's all of us against the spirits. Curious how they have an almost adversarial relationship with the supposed spirits, yet simultaneously revere them."

Phoenix gave a sad sigh. "It's like children with a violent, abusive parent. They are terrified of them, but also act worshipful for fear of angering them even more."

"Sounds about right." Teal shrugged.

"Sorry," whispered Phoenix.

"What? Oh…" Teal chuckled. "Not me. My parents are awesome."

Ford led them across the village to the gate. David and Phoenix exchanged confused glances when he continued out into the ruins surrounding the village.

"Aren't your people forbidden to leave?" asked Phoenix.

"We are not leaving." Ford gestured around at nothing in particular. "The spirits know if we are just going outside the wall or trying to *leave*. They don't become angry if we explore the ruins, only if we do not intend to return. They will not be angry for leaving the wall."

Teal continued scanning the area, her body language saying she expected an attack. Having seen evidence of raider activity in the area, Althea also kept an eye out for threats as they walked among old, smashed buildings and wrecked cars. Around a quarter mile from the wall, Ford stopped at the base of a paved footpath that led to the façade of an ancient beige brick building. Only the front wall remained upright, the rest of the building having collapsed ages ago.

"This is the shrine of the Hollow Man. He is the king of our spirits." Ford made the same reverent gesture Kellis and Durango did: pressing his hands together in front of his face, fingers pointed up. "Come."

"Gotta get me way more excited for that," muttered Teal.

Mild embarrassment came from Phoenix. David snickered.

Althea scrunched her nose, unable to explain what being excited had to do with her ability to follow him.

"Uhh, *can* you actually…?" whispered Phoenix.

"I'd be happy to show you how lifelike we are if you're up for it." Teal made a clicking sound and winked at her.

"You prefer women?" asked Phoenix in a neutral tone.

"No preference. I'm attracted to a person, not their body. Don't care what sort of equipment they have."

This, Althea understood. Equipment carried great prestige among scrags. The more stuff someone owned, the more people wanted to become their mate.

Phoenix's emotional response to Teal shifted from mild distrust and worry to surprise and an odd sense of solidarity. "Same."

Teal leaned back, obviously checking out David's rear end. "I'd say something about your ass, but I don't feel like ending up melted into a puddle."

"Huh?" Phoenix blinked at her. "How would making an inappropriate comment about him melt you into a puddle?"

"You haven't met his girlfriend yet." Teal wagged her eyebrows.

David laughed. "Kate understands the idea of humor. And she's not jealous. At least, she's not the sort of woman who'd go on a murderous rampage over a cheating boyfriend without at least reading his mind to make sure he did, in fact, cheat."

Althea marched onward, leaving the adults to talk about jokes. Violence over cheating, she understood. Raiders who got caught cheating at the chance games often ended up stabbed or killed.

The shrine didn't feel strange. Then again, the stadium in Querq also hadn't felt unusual before The Many appeared to her. At least she had a reasonable degree of confidence no ordinary ghosts haunted this place. Despite not sensing any unusual energies in the area, she concentrated on the desire to see spirits. Nothing changed in her vision, so she continued, stepping through the open doorway in the single remaining wall onto a smooth concrete slab, the former floor of a foyer.

A narrow stone pyramid, almost as tall as her, stood at the center, holding up a tiny fly machine the size of a crow. Worn lettering on the floor formed a circle around the statue, though it had faded too much to read. Various pans, jars, and piles of debris sat on the floor around the base, offerings brought by villagers. Prints in the dust showed where people had come to bow to the fly machine statue.

Ford and the others entered behind her.

"*This* is your shrine?" asked Teal, sounding unimpressed.

"Yes," whispered Ford.

Althea twisted to look at her. "Why do you say it like that?"

"That's a model of an F-47C, the first ion-powered combat aircraft. It's not a monument to a spirit or a god. It's an old centerpiece in the lobby of a military base command building… or maybe this used to be an on-base museum."

"How do you know this?" Phoenix whistled. "You study all the old military stuff?"

"All I have to do is upload stuff." Teal folded her arms. "How do you think I ended up teaching?"

"Teaching?" Phoenix raised both eyebrows. "You?"

"I don't see you at the school." Althea blinked.

"Well, I *will* be teaching as soon as they have kids ready for the high school level." Teal tapped a finger behind her left ear. "Hard to find educators willing to come out here. I'm already here. Figured I should make myself useful as more than just a hired gun, so... couple uploads and I'm a qualified teacher. But, yeah... I downloaded a lot of old military stuff years ago. Kind of a hobby."

"Right." David chuckled. "So... this is the shrine of the Hollow Man. See any spirits?"

"No," said Althea. "Just a toy fly machine on a post."

"Shh," whispered Ford. "He will visit if he chooses to."

Teal slapped herself on the forehead. "Ugh."

"What?" asked David and Phoenix at the same time.

"Hollow man? Wow..." Teal whistled. "This is an old Air Force base."

Phoenix groaned. "Oh, for heck's sake. You're right. I stared right at it on the old map."

"Care to fill in the dumb sergeant?" asked David.

"Holloman Air Force Base," said Phoenix. "Near White Sands. Over the generations, they somehow bastardized Holloman into Hollow Man and turned it from the name of this place into some kind of spirit or god."

Ford cringed.

Althea calmed him. "Do not be scared."

The man straightened his posture, seeming bewildered at the sudden disappearance of fear.

"There's nothing to be afraid of." Teal playfully swatted him on the back of the shoulder. "There's no spirit called Hollow Man. It's an old name for this place."

"But..." He fidgeted.

Althea stepped past the fly machine statue, holding her arms out wide. "If there are any spirits here, I have come to speak with you."

"No one talks to the Hollow Man," said Ford.

"I have talked to him." Althea set her hands on her hips.

David sidled up next to her. "I don't believe their 'Hollow Man' is the same as The Many. Suppose it *could* be, but it's most likely only local legend."

"He is everything. If the villagers here want a Hollow Man, The Many will pretend to be their Hollow Man." Althea narrowed her eyes at the ruins, suspicious at *not* sensing any odd energy. "I don't think he is here. Maybe you are right. If there *are* any spirits here, they are mean and need to go away."

"Spirits aren't doing this," said Phoenix. "Disease is. These villagers don't understand how viruses work. They're making up stories to explain bad things happening to them."

"Great Hollow Man, please forgive them." Ford bowed to the fly machine statue. "They do not know."

Teal nudged Althea. "Show him your wings."

"No. He'll start worshiping me then." She sighed.

"Maybe, but at least you exist." Teal winked.

Althea took Ford's hand, stared into his eyes, and projected reassurance into his mind, filling him with a similar emotion to how people felt in the company of close friends who always helped them. After a moment, his fearful demeanor shifted to a warm smile.

"I don't know if the Hollow Man is real." Althea held eye contact, continuing to maintain his emotions as calm so his thinking shape could see the words she spoke. "If he is real, he is mean. He lets your people stay sick and does nothing. If he tries to stop me from helping everyone here, he is evil. I won't let him keep hurting people."

Ford begrudgingly nodded once. "How can he not be real? My grandfather's grandfather spoke of him."

"A lie doesn't become truth because it's old," said Teal. "Or because many people fell for it."

Phoenix sighed. "I don't think it's as much a lie as simple misunderstanding. Calling it a lie implies someone's using it for deliberate purpose."

"Aren't they?" asked Teal. "Durango seems to enjoy

being in charge. As long as he has everyone scared witless of some unknown, imaginary spirits, all he has to do is tell people the spirits will be angry if they don't do what he wants them to, and he has control."

"Durango is a wise leader." Ford gave off genuine admiration. "He would not lead us if we didn't agree to let him. Our leader is selected by voting. Every four years. Durango has been leader for eight. He is... frightened of the spirits, too. They do not always demand the same things Durango may want."

David pursed his lips. "Seems he's trying to interpret what he thinks the spirits want as best he can based on what he sees."

"And what he doesn't understand." Phoenix scowled off in a random direction for a few seconds. "Okay. Forget the spirit stuff. This is a simple virus and hygiene problem. Everyone here is pretty much filthy. We need to teach them about baths. Hand washing. Food handling... and find out where the contamination is coming from. We should also conduct an assessment of the population and arrange a triage process. We establish a safe area and move people there as Althea cleans them up."

"Agreed." David nodded. "Speaking of... have we become sick?"

Althea grasped his hand, closed her eyes, and focused on his life essence. A small amount of wispy yellow drifted around in his blood. She shooed it into his bladder. "Yes. A little."

David squeezed his legs together. "Oh, that burns..."

Frightened, Phoenix took her other hand. "Please..."

"Do not be afraid." Althea linked to her. She, too, had a small amount of sick.

As Phoenix ran off to find somewhere to let out the bad water, Althea focused inward and rid herself of a small amount of sick. She walked off the concrete slab, earning a shocked gasp from Ford for not using the door in the one standing wall. Once she reached dirt, she dug a small hole and made water. It didn't burn much.

Once she finished, she covered the hole and walked back to her friends.

"How are you feeling, Althea?" asked David. "It's going to be a lot of work cleaning this place up."

"I am ready." She flapped her arms. "Sicks don't make me tired to fix. Hurts are worse."

## 16

## THE TRACKER

Althea scanned the ruins to get her bearings.

The round wall made for an obvious landmark in the distance. Moving fabric fluttering in the wind drew her attention to a man watching them, half hidden behind a cinder block slab a few hundred feet away. A grey tunic, baggy black pants, and hooded cloak made his outfit as complete as Durango's, marking him as someone of great skill or influence.

He stared at them with an unreadable expression, giving off no emotion. Althea curled her toes over the edge of a small concrete chunk she'd stepped on, clutching her fists in nervousness. This man didn't seem friendly, though his only weapon appeared to be a spear, nothing capable of harming them from so far away; however, he might have a gun under the cloak.

She tried to look into his thoughts and found nothing there—just like Teal.

"Synthetic," whispered Althea.

"Hmm?" Teal glanced at her.

David, Phoenix, and Ford walked up behind her.

Teal noticed the man first. It took the others a few seconds to realize she'd locked stares with someone.

"Who is that?" asked David.

"El Ojo." Ford waved in greeting to the distant man. "He is our best tracker and hunter."

"He has no thinking shape," whispered Althea.

David and Phoenix concentrated on the man for a few seconds.

"Yeah. Synth or doll?" asked David.

"If he's a doll, we have some problems." Teal hooked her thumbs in her pockets.

Althea glanced up at her as if she'd tried to call the sky green. "It's not a doll. It's a person. Dolls are small."

Phoenix and David chuckled.

Teal hugged her. "This is why I want to keep her. She's adorable."

"What?" Althea embraced her in return, basking in the affection of a simple hug.

Phoenix patted her on the head. "She didn't grow up in the city. How could she have any idea what we mean by doll?"

"You know how I'm a person but not made out of meat?" asked Teal.

Althea nodded.

"A doll is similar." Teal poked a finger at her left arm. "Except for our bones, synthetics like me are made from softer stuff. Dolls are mostly metal except for an outer layer of skin-like material, and they usually have living brains. They're more of a replacement for a human body if it fails or gets shredded. He looks perfectly human, which means he's either a synth or a military grade doll. You don't sense a brain there, so either way, he's an AI."

Althea blinked a few times. "Dolls are small cute things

children play with. Why would they call machine people that?"

"I think it started off as a joke," said David. "Someone in the military looked at the first-gen models and thought them useless. It's become a term for cyborgs or androids designed to appear as close to human as possible."

"Question is…" Phoenix shifted to stand behind Teal. "Why would either a synthetic or a military doll be out here pretending to be a tribal villager?"

Ford scratched his head. "Don't understand nothin' you are saying. El Ojo's been here at least five years. Wandered in out of the dust one day. Durango told him the spirits would punish him for leaving. So, he stayed."

David rubbed his chin. "He may not know what he is. Or, his sanity is questionable. Might have come out here to feel like a god among lesser mortals."

"It's a good feeling." Teal smiled. "But I don't need to be in the Badlands to enjoy it."

"Please tell me you're kidding," whispered Phoenix.

"She is." Althea giggled.

Phoenix gave her side eye. "Sergeant, is this kid so good at telempathy she can read emotion off a synthetic?"

"No." Althea shook her head. "I just know Teal."

"What's the best way to tell if we're dealing with a synth or a military grade doll?" asked David.

"Squeeze his arm." Teal held hers out to him. "If he feels like a normal person, he's a synthetic. If he feels like metal covered in skin, doll."

"Military grade…" Phoenix whistled.

David chuckled. "Don't worry too much about it. 'Military grade' only means it costs a hundred times what it should. Maya series dolls aren't military at all and they're indistinguishable from humans."

"It's still a good question what he's doing out here acting like one of the locals." Teal started walking toward the village. "Maybe he doesn't know. I didn't for the first part of my life. Leave him be for now unless he turns himself into a problem."

Althea followed her, David, Phoenix, and Ford trailing after her. El Ojo continued watching them for a few more seconds, but ducked behind the wall before Teal came close enough to try talking. She veered a little to the right, putting more distance between her and where he'd been, as if expecting attack. No sign of him remained when they passed the spot. Teal briefly looked around before apparently dismissing any threat and continuing to walk toward the town gate.

"Maybe he is 'the spirit' who punishes those trying to leave," said Phoenix. "Watching us to see if we planned to keep going."

"Possible." Teal stepped over a broken street lamp post. "When we are ready to go, we'll need to consider he might be a problem and be wary. Althea won't be able to send him on his way."

"If he takes orders from Durango," said David, "she can encourage him to tell El Ojo to stand down."

Phoenix walked around the fallen lamp post. "If Durango is ordering him to kill anyone who tries to leave, that's an entirely new set of problems."

"Easy enough to figure out." David grinned. "Telepathy works on him."

"True." Phoenix gave a long sigh, her nervousness lessening.

Ford, still confused at what everyone had been talking about, stopped at the gate. "I must return to the shrine and seek wisdom."

"Wait." Althea grasped his hand, closed her eyes, and linked to his life essence. Faint greenish haze floated around his life shapes, wispy tendrils caressing his airbags and heart shape. "You have a sick. It's in your air bags."

"She means lungs," said Phoenix.

"As if this man knows what lungs are." David chuckled. "He probably understood air bags."

"Yes." Ford coughed. "Been hard breathin' for couple years now. Not too bad. Spirits only a little upset at me for being so loyal."

Althea gathered the sick and forced it to concentrate in his bladder. Once done, she opened her eyes and smiled. "Let the bad water out somewhere away from people. It will have the sick."

Ford's eyes fluttered. He took a few big breaths, made a face of confused urgency, then ran off at an urgent pace.

"He looks like I feel after a five-hour ride in a PC." David whistled. "How sick was he?"

"A lot, but not a strong sick." Althea scrunched her nose at the village in front of them. "There is too much sick here."

David activated the holographic screen from the device on his left forearm. "We've covered about a third of the place. Let's keep going and document what we're dealing with."

They proceeded into the village, pausing at every as-yet-unexplored building to look for sick occupants. The southwestern area had many unused structures, making the search go quick for the next hour or so.

Children's giggling came from the left, echoing down an alley between two rows of scrap huts built relatively close together. None showed signs of recent habitation.

Althea glanced down the narrow passage to the village wall a fair distance past from the last hut. The children responsible for the laughter likely played in an open area between the village and the surrounding wall.

"Hey." Teal nudged her. "We can handle looking around. Why don't you go check the little ones for, uhh, 'sicks.'"

David tapped a finger at his hologram screen. "This will go faster if we split up, too. If anyone discovers someone deathly ill, give a shout. Teal, northeast, I'll go northwest?"

"And I'll check the southeast," said Phoenix.

"Thanks, captain." David smiled.

Althea gave him a quizzical look.

*She's a much higher rank than me. I can't tell her what to do. Only suggest.*

Althea gawked. *You have to use psionics to make her do things?*

David couldn't help but laugh. *No, not Suggestion the power, suggest as in ask her to do something instead of telling her to.*

*Oh.* Althea folded her arms. If 'suggest' meant to ask, not order, why did they call the psionic power that *forced* people to do stuff 'Suggestion?' *Confusing.* "All right. I will make sure the children are not sick."

Teal put a hand on her forehead.

"I'm fine."

"No… it's just." Teal winked. "You said 'not sick' instead of 'don't have a sick.'"

Althea stuck out her tongue. "I'm not feral anymore… sometimes I remember how the speaking works."

## CLAIMED

**A**lthea hurried down the narrow street past the abandoned huts.

Teal, David, and Phoenix stayed with her instead of splitting up, perhaps out of curiosity or concern El Ojo might pose a threat. They now had the worry of at least one individual here she couldn't defend herself against should he turn hostile.

The alley opened up to an area of pulverized concrete rubble, a roughly hundred-foot-wide band of debris separating the closest buildings from the barrier surrounding the village. To the right, five children sat on the ground, clustered in the shade from the wall, listening to an older girl in a plain grey dress tell them a story. The teen appeared close in age to Karina, or perhaps a year younger. Long mouse-brown hair hung down past her waist, touching the long, narrow slab of concrete she sat on. Since the slab only lifted her a few inches off the ground, she'd stretched her legs out in front of her, sticking her feet into a small patch of sun that glinted on her copper wire anklets.

The older girl didn't appear visibly sick. Thankfully, neither did the kids, three boys and two girls. They all had long, wild hair and wore more dirt than clothing, except for Kia. Not only had she recently gotten a 'canteen bath,' she also had a child-sized dress on made from the same grey fabric as the tunics, likely an adult's garment someone modified for her.

Althea also recognized the two boys she'd seen running around earlier. The youngest girl was quite young, maybe four, the unfamiliar boy likely around eight or nine. In addition to a grey scrap of fabric around his waist as a skirt, the smaller boy also wore a pair of metal struts—possibly wrenches—tied on either side of his lower left leg. It looked more like a splint than an attempt at decoration. Redness and swelling midway between knee and ankle suggested a broken bone, likely the reason he hadn't been running around with the others.

Kia held the tiny girl in her lap like a doll, still giving off a huge amount of joy at no longer being forbidden from contact with other people.

Althea approached the group and stood near the kids, patiently waiting for the teen to stop telling her story and look over at her. This caused all the kids to twist around so they could also stare at her. In the past, whenever Althea found her way into a new scrag tribe, other children tended to be wary of outsiders or afraid of her. This group gave off the opposite mood, happy to meet another kid, no trace of defensiveness, shyness, or territorial aggression. Upon seeing Althea again, Kia became so happy she squeezed a squeal out of the four-year-old. The teen's emotional state held mostly fatigue and a sense of 'ugh, another one?' However, despite the momentary dread, she soon shifted to giving off a sense of protectiveness toward her.

"Hi." Althea waved.

"Hello," replied the older girl. "Where'd you come from?"

"Querq. It's pretty far away." She smiled. "I'm Althea. Kellis asked me to help, so we came here to make the sicks go away."

Kia pointed at her. "This is her! She made the red ouchies go bye."

The other kids all looked up at Althea, glowing with happiness, gratitude, and wonder.

"Toyo's leg is sick." Kia pointed at the small black-haired boy. "Can help?"

Althea nodded. "Yes."

"Okay." The older girl gestured at the group of children. "Well, sit down and I guess I'm watching you, too. Are those your parents?"

Althea looked back at David, Teal, and Phoenix, then sat beside the boy with wrenches tied to his leg. "No. They are friends. Father and my sister are not here."

"I'm Toyo." The boy in front of her stared in awe at her dress.

Kia reached over and cupped Althea's agate arrowhead pendant in one hand. "Pretty."

"Thank you." Althea grinned at her.

"I am Camry," said the oldest, a brown-haired boy around twelve, the one with a dog-leather loincloth.

"Onda." The slightly younger boy wearing the socket wrench necklace touched her hair. "Your eyes have glow."

"I Prius!" chirped the four-year-old. "But erry-un call me Pri. Only say Prius when I in trouble."

David mumbled something about the children having unusual names.

"They're scrags," whispered Teal. "Probably named

after words they found written on junk… assuming anyone here can read."

"We can read." Mohave pointed. "Under the castle, the lorekeepers guard the books. They teach us to read. This is how we know things and learn. Some are stories that never happened, told for fun. Most are information for real."

"So they aren't fully primitive after all," whispered Phoenix.

"No… simply resource deprived." Teal crouched and made silly faces at Pri, who giggled back at her.

The children crowded around Althea, trying to show off various pieces of 'jewelry' they'd made or found, mostly string or wire decorated with wooden or plastic beads. Pri seemed quite proud of a necklace of bottle caps. Kia, in addition to her dress, wore a bunch of fabric bracelets, anklets, and a thin belt made from brightly colored materials. She gushed about being able to wear them again without pain. Onda regarded his socket wrench necklace as a prized possession worthy of a seeker having to fight ten killer robots to claim—primarily due to it being shiny. Ignoring the other kids all talking at the same time, he attempted to tell Althea how he'd found them while he, Camry, and Toyo played in the Field of Beasts.

"Really doesn't sound like a place kids ought to be," muttered Teal.

Althea peered into Onda's head. The 'Field of Beasts' sat to the northeast of Afbee village, a vast swath of desert littered with thousands of decaying old fly machines. He had memories of climbing all over them, sitting in the chairs, and pushing buttons and pretending to fly. The boy knew the machines had once been able to fly, surprising her and further proving this village far more educated than most scrags.

"Here's the deal, kid," said the older girl. "I'm Mojave, and I'm basically going to be your mother during the day. I watch all the kids while everyone works."

At a sudden, powerful sense of sorrow, Althea peeked at her thoughts. The girl added 'at least while there are still any kids left here' to the end of her words, but didn't speak it out loud. For some reason, she expected the children she watched to disappear before they finished growing up.

"Works?" asked David. "What do they do?"

"Collect food, fix the wall, fix buildings, get water." Mojave shrugged. "So, I mother the kids too small to help."

David raised both eyebrows. "Five? This is all of them? Doesn't seem like many kids for a village this size."

Mojave's sadness intensified. "The spirits sometimes take children away and they're never seen again. They take adults, too... but only after they've been sick. Kids can disappear even if they aren't sick."

Phoenix gasped, horrified.

David scowled. "Spirits indeed."

"I sense we are about to experience mission parameter creep." Teal patted her sidearm. "Our objective is expanding."

"Damn right," muttered David.

He radiated so much anger, Althea couldn't stop herself from looking at his thoughts. His mind leapt from one bad situation to another, wondering if slavers raided this place or maybe Durango murdered children as sacrifices to appease the spirits, or something else went on that the primitive villagers blamed on 'spirits.' Whatever the true cause of the disappearances, he believed it the work of people... and wanted to stop it. The urgent desire to go read Durango's mind to see for sure if the man had anything to do with missing villagers nagged at him.

"How do they disappear?" asked David.

Mojave bowed her head, tears falling. "They disappear in the night. We go to sleep, and when we wake, they are gone. The spirits took my younger sister, Sahara, almost a year ago. She would be thirteen now."

"Something isn't adding up about this place." Teal narrowed her eyes.

Althea cringed. "Please don't make them do math. They're suffering enough already."

David's fury lessened to anger. Somehow, he managed to smile at her remark, unaware she'd been serious. Althea did not like math, mostly because she found it difficult and confusing. She didn't blame the teacher for making her do it. Math made her feel stupid, not Nadia.

"I agree," said David.

"With who?" Teal glanced at him.

"Both of you." He exhaled hard.

*I will be okay here. Go telepath Durango.* Althea looked from him to Toyo and rested her hands atop his broken leg.

"Ow. No touch. Hurt." The boy whimpered.

"I will make the hurt go away." Althea smiled at him and closed her eyes.

The white strip of bone shape in the center of the boy's leg had broken backward from the front. She'd seen similar injuries on raiders who'd been hit with crowbars or metal pipes. Could be, the boy had been running fast and crashed into a jutting bit of rebar. Onda's memories of the aircraft junkyard held quite a few minor injuries from falls or cuts on sharp edges. It didn't look possible Toyo stepped wrong and twisted his leg until it broke. Someone or something hit him. Strange it hadn't left a mark on the skin from the impact.

After taking away his ability to feel pain, she commanded his muscles to nudge the bone back where it belonged, then focused energy into the bone until it mended. She opened her eyes a moment later to curious stares from everyone. The redness on the boy's shin receded to normal color.

"Hurt stop." Toyo prodded his leg, patted it, then risked smacking the spot. "It no hurt!"

She started undoing his splint.

"Hey, kid. Leave that alone," said Mojave.

"He does not need it now." Althea continued attacking the fabric knot. "His leg is not broken."

Mojave crawled over and tried to pull Althea away from him. "Legs don't stop being broken for days."

Onda pointed at Kia. "Her red spots are gone."

Kia lifted her dress to show Mojave her lack of red spots. "No ouchies! Mama can hug me again, but she's gotta do the works, so I have'ta be here."

"Like she never had them." Camry looked down, about to cry. "Rav had the same dots, and they all popped. He had holes everywhere."

Althea nudged his sadness back to neutral. "I will help Rav, too."

"The spirits took him." Camry looked up, visibly confused at why he hadn't started sobbing.

"All right. I'm going to go digging in Durango's head. You okay here?" asked David.

"Yes." Althea grinned at him. "I do not feel a clairvoy ant."

He snickered, knowing she said it wrong on purpose. Althea almost felt dumb for not understanding clairvoyance before, but whenever she talked like a scrag, most adults around her gave off positive emotions, so even though she'd learned better now, she sometimes said things like she used to on purpose to make them feel better—except for Nadia and other teachers. They didn't find it cute when she talked wrong. It made them frustrated.

David, Teal, and Phoenix headed back into the village.

Toyo jumped up and ran in circles. "Leg no hurt!"

"I…" Mojave gawked at him. "You? You did that?"

"Yes. I make hurts and sicks go away." Althea took her hand. "Your turn."

## 18

# OPPORTUNITY

T he sick lurking in Mojave's body clung mostly to her spine, thinking shape, and the long white lines going into the arms and legs. Althea concentrated, collecting the wispy grey vapor out of its hiding places.

Mojave collapsed.

*Eep!* Confused at why the teen passed out from having a sick removed, Althea dove back into the girl's life essence, seeing nothing wrong except for a small wound on the side of her head from landing on a concrete stone. She mended the cut, then double checked all the life shapes, still unable to find anything to explain why Mojave went to sleep while standing up.

Other than being unconscious, she appeared to be fine… so Althea decided to let her sleep for now.

"Willa spirits break it 'gain?" Toyo rubbed his healed leg.

Althea tilted her head. "The *spirits* broke it?"

"Yeah." He nodded.

"How?" She opened a telepathic link to his mind.

"I wenna sleep and it not broke. Morning, it broke,"

said Toyo. "I fink spirits punish me for eatin' too much tatoes. I took a extra one and didn't tell."

In his memory, the boy curled up under a blanket on a pile of cushioned materials next to his mother and father, cuddling up against the soft fabric of his mother's dress. He opened his eyes to daylight as well as a throbbing pain in his left leg. It didn't appear likely the eight-year-old's mother could have possibly rolled over him in her sleep in any way likely to shatter his leg bone the way it had broken. While no one could call Althea a proper 'doctor,' she'd seen countless injuries from raider battles, and the break in Toyo's leg looked exactly like a whack from a crowbar or similar metal rod—except for the lack of an cut or rip on the skin. Had someone snuck into his house and hit him in his sleep? If so, how had he not woken up right away to see the person who attacked him?

She rubbed a hand up and down his shin. "I made the hurt go away. The spirits are not punishing you. Kids need many tatoes. Especially boys, so you can get big and be strong."

He grinned.

"He always eats too much tatoes," muttered Camry before laughing.

"You eat too." Toyo poked him.

Althea scooted over to Camry. "I want to see if you have sicks. It won't take long. If you do have a sick, I will make it go away."

"I tired." Pri yawned.

"She's *always* tired." Onda ruffled her hair.

"Fink she sick." Kia hugged the four-year-old again. "She go sleeps in day. Like boom. Falls sometimes when she's standing."

Althea nodded and took Camry's hand. "I will help her, too."

Onda and Camry had no sicks inside them, and she'd already cured Kia, which left only the four-year-old. As soon as Althea moved to touch her, Kia squeaked and practically shoved the little one out of her lap.

"Whaaaa?" Pri stared at her.

"Don' wanna get puke on me." Kia pointed at Althea. "She fix sick, you gonna throw up."

Pri scrunched her face.

Althea laughed and took the girl's hands. "It's okay. Don't be scared."

"I no have scared of nothing." Pri grinned.

True, Althea couldn't detect any fear whatsoever coming from the smallest resident of Afbee, only confusion at what Kia said. She closed her eyes and linked to the child's life essence. A strange blue haze permeated her body... a shade of sick Althea had never seen before. Her bone shapes also had numerous puncture scars, tiny bone plugs where spikes the size of nails had been stuck into her long enough ago to have healed on their own. Also, some of the squishy stuff inside her big leg bones appeared to be missing.

Althea focused her power on Pri, making the bone stuff regrow, smoothing out the plugs, and gathering the odd blue sick for disposal. A few seconds before she finished, Mojave screamed. Althea cringed at herself for not being there to turn off the girl's pain sense so she could pee out the sick — then it occurred to her the scream didn't sound like one of pain — rather fear.

She stuffed the last of the blue hazy sick into Pri's bladder and opened her eyes. Mojave continued screaming from the left, sounding too far away. Camry and Onda stood on either side of a gap in the wall she hadn't noticed earlier. The boys clung to the sides of the opening, peering out at something beyond the wall, gripped by fear and confusion. Camry threw off a little anger as well, but had too much fear to embrace to his urge to fight.

Pri stared up at Althea, her expression one of utter bafflement. "I pee."

"Get off me!" shouted Mojave from outside the village.

"Raiders!" rasped Toyo. "They got her!"

Althea jumped to her feet. Pri hadn't started making water yet, so the girl must have meant she *had to* pee. She hesitated, knowing the child would experience pain as soon as the sick came out, but it wouldn't be torturous. Allowing raiders to take Mojave away to an unknown place would make her feel much worse than if Pri ended up crying. She darted over to the boys.

An opening in the metal plates revealed a hollow passage through the four-foot-thick wall to the outside. One of the huge concrete 'bricks' had fallen over—or been pulled out. The enormous rectangular block lay like a felled tree pointing away from the wall. While the barrier circling Afbee had thousands of holes, only rats could come and go as they pleased anywhere but the gate—or right here. An adult could slip in and out with little difficulty. Althea didn't even have to duck, being shorter than the toppled concrete pillar. She went past the boys into the hole, stepping carefully through the square 'footprint' the massive concrete block left in the dirt to the outer edge of the wall. Althea crouched to hide behind the former bottom of the big concrete block, peering over it.

Two filthy men in hubcap-reinforced leather armor dragged Mojave off to a waiting buggy, one of the small fast ones recognizable by its huge, fat rear wheels and tiny front wheels. The vehicle amounted to little more than a wedge-shaped collection of metal tubes, an engine, and a seat—or in this case, two seats.

One raider held Mojave from behind, her feet off the

ground, pinning her arms to her chest as he rushed her to the buggy. The other man gathered Mojave's legs and hastily bound her ankles with rope. She thrashed, trying to kick and bite, though couldn't overpower the large raider's hold on her. Both men dripped with delight, greed, and lust at having found a young female.

Althea snarled and gathered up her mental strength. An instant before she hammered fear into the raiders, she hesitated. The men's thoughts compared Mojave to numerous other slaves they kept at their camp.

*Grr! The raiders are why people think spirits take people. If I make them run away, the others will stay kidnapped.* She had to do something crazy—follow them. But, she couldn't keep up with a buggy on foot. It took them a bit to get going, but once they did, they could travel much, much faster than she could run, even boosting herself. Surely, the raiders would obligingly grab her if they recognized The Prophet... but she really didn't want to be tied up again, even if she could command them to let her go whenever she wanted.

However, if the raiders didn't know she followed them, they couldn't tie her.

She waited for the guy holding Mojave to drag her into the rear seat before vaulting up onto the giant concrete block. The second raider jumped in the front seat and started the engine, which buzzed to life like a furious 300-pound mosquito. Channeling power into her legs, she sprinted in long, bounding strides—her muscles too strong for her meager weight. She easily overtook the buggy as it started to pull away. As soon as she got close enough, she jumped onto the stand-plate at the back, crouching so the raiders couldn't see her.

Most raider vehicles had similar stand-plates in the back and even on the sides, typically used by flyers who planned to leap off onto an enemy buggy or running person they wanted to kidnap. The shelf offered plenty of room for her feet, as they took up far less space than a raider's boots. Her hands weren't quite big enough to get all the way around the fat metal tubes for a good, solid grip on the frame, but she felt reasonably secure in her perch. If she went flying on a bump, no big deal. A broken arm or leg, she could fix. It would upset her more to lose Mojave.

She twisted to look back through the dust cloud at Afbee's wall. The boys had crept out onto the fallen stone, watching them drive off.

Althea locked stares with Camry. *Find the woman with blue hair. Tell her I'm going to help slaves get free and don't worry. I will be back soon.*

The boy screamed at the unusual sensation of her voice in his mind.

*Don't be scared! Go tell her. Please. Her name is Teal.*

Camry yelled, "I will!"

She heard him more in his thoughts than over the roar of the engine inches in front of her face. Ethanol fumes almost choked the air out of her lungs. Already, they drove at a speed well beyond her running ability. Desert scrub blurred by on both sides, faster than the large buggy they'd drove down here in could go. Then again, she'd been safely *inside* that one. Clinging to the back end of a moving vehicle made everything feel faster and more dangerous.

*I'm not scared.* Althea narrowed her eyes. For too many years, she'd allowed raiders to do bad things to people. No more. Now, she would do what she should have done years ago.

*I'm going to help.*

## 19

## A NEW LEGEND

Hot air blowing over the engine pelted Althea in the face for the better part of an hour.

She couldn't see much from her position crouching on the stand-plate, but at least it kept her hidden. Giant, fat tires on either side spun so fast the spiked knobs covering the tread blurred. Even sparing a moment to look behind her felt too risky given all the bouncing. If her grip loosened for even an instant, she could go flying—and end up stranded in the middle of nowhere. Not only would she be unable to help Mojave and the slaves, she might not be able to find her way back to Afbee.

Mojave's fear intensified to the point she might die from fright. Before the teen's heart shape could explode, Althea forced her emotions to calm. Confusion followed.

*I am being stupid. It doesn't matter if they see me. They will do what I tell them.*

Althea pulled herself up into a standing position, widening her stance and sliding her grip on the frame bars a little higher. Upright, she could see over the engine, but also got about three times the blast of wind in the face and chest.

Her agate arrowhead pendant spun around her neck, fluttering behind her. The burly raider sat about four feet in front of her, on the opposite side of the engine and plastic fuel tank, holding Mojave in his lap. His broad shoulders mostly blocked the girl from sight.

Climbing over the engine didn't look possible, both due to spinning parts and belts likely to tear pieces off her if she touched them as well as it being quite hot. No, she had to wait for the men to stop... or command them to stop before she could go anywhere other than jumping off the back. In order to help the captives, she needed to stay put and wait for the raiders to reach their home.

*I'm going to a raider camp on purpose.* She bit her lip. The idea sounded weird to her until she decided it wouldn't be the first time she'd done so, even if she hadn't thought about it while allowing herself to be abducted. Having the power to force raiders to let her go and not using it amounted to basically the same as willingly going with them.

She stared at the back of Mojave's head. Telepathy didn't require looking into someone's eyes, though she generally did it out of habit. The city police didn't say why, but eye contact supposedly made it easier.

*Mojave, don't be frightened. I'm here.*

The girl thought of spirits.

*No. Not spirits. Althea. I'm on the back of the buggy.*

Mojave attempted to twist around and look, but the raider held her still, mistaking her curiosity for a struggle.

*Don't yell. If you think, I can hear like you talk.*

*They got you too?* thought Mojave. *Get away if you can. They're going to do bad things to us.*

Althea narrowed her eyes in determination. *No, they won't.*

*I should be so, so scared right now, but I'm not. Maybe I want to die.*

"Grr," muttered Althea. *Don't say bad things. I am helping you not be scared. You had too much fear.*

Confusion.

To demonstrate, Althea forced the girl's emotional state to happiness, then boredom, then sad—for an instant—and back to calm. *I can make you feel stuff. Or not feel stuff. You are not scared because of me.*

As realization solidified in Mojave's mind, her emotions cycled from shock, to disbelief, then fear, wonder, and finally reverence. *Are you a spirit who looks like a child?*

*No. I'm Althea.*

The buggy hit a dip in the desert, flying into the air on the far side. Althea's feet slipped on the metal plate. For a few seconds, she clung only by her grip on the frame bars, her body flying like a pennant behind the buggy until it landed and she crashed against the metal plate, proving steel harder than her left knee.

*Ow.*

She cringed, unable to move for a second until the flare of pain subsided. Healing a relatively minor bruise could wait. Grumbling to herself, she braced her feet against the sides of the stand-plate and pulled herself upright. Mojave remained calm, though shouted in her thoughts 'where did you go?' over and over.

*Sorry. Almost fell off. Still here.*

Mojave's emotional state shifted to worry and fear for the children back in Afbee. She didn't know who would protect them if she disappeared. *I don't want to be a slave.*

*You won't be a slave.*

Neither raider noticed Althea standing on the back. Even if one happened to look behind them for some reason, she'd use Suggestion to order them to continue driving back to their camp. She could even crawl into the driver's lap and it wouldn't change much, and might honestly be *more* dangerous. If the buggy crashed, being flung off the back end offered better chances of survival than if she ended up trapped in the seat well as the ethanol tank burst into flames.

Clinging to the rear of a speeding buggy made time feel strange, as though they'd spent far longer driving than they really had. Hours—or so it felt like—later, they reached an ancient paved road running diagonally across their path. Althea suspected it hadn't quite been one full hour since they'd left Afbee. The driver veered right, staying on the old highway. A few minutes later, they entered the ruins of a small city. Dead bodies hung from crumbling one-story buildings on either side of the road, most still wearing the armor they died in. She sighed at the grisly reminder of how cruel raiders could be. Nothing about the corpses suggested whether they'd been rivals from another marauder band who failed to conquer this group or former allies who'd been hung up as some sign of honor in death. Raiders came in every flavor of crazy, and she wouldn't put it past them to mutilate a friend's corpse, thinking it a tribute.

Three blocks into the ruins, a wall of old drive machines blocked off the street, except for a gate made from a huge mass of junk metal mashed together into a portcullis. A small group of raiders on top of the wall must have seen them coming and pulled the entrance open already.

Althea looked up at the rusting metal as they drove under it. A thousand pounds or more of jagged steel I-girders, engine blocks, car frames, and spikes crashed to the ground as the gate fell closed behind them. The buggy rolled to a halt close to the center of a medium-sized raider encampment. Large tents, small tents, harder shacks made of sheet metal, and a few pre-war concrete buildings surrounded her. An enormous dome-shaped cage as big as a house, made from spiked, rusting metal bars stood to the right of where they stopped. She estimated maybe fourteen people sat inside, giving off varying degrees of sadness, terror, and hopelessness. Based on their clothing, she assumed a few to be raiders, some settlers, and three scrags.

The engine finally stopped roaring.

Her ears tingled.

Althea stepped down from the buggy, grateful to be on solid ground once again. She opened and closed her hands a few times to work stiffness out of her fingers. The driver got out and helped his buddy haul Mojave from the back seat. At some point during the ride, the man tied her wrists together.

Thirty or so other raiders, roughly two thirds of them men, converged on the buggy. Mojave's fear returned. She went wide-eyed, staring around at all the salivating faces leering at her. The majority of the raiders, including several women, gave off lust, greed, and a general sense of triumph. Taking a new slave somehow brought 'honor' to a raider group, though she didn't understand how it worked. Other raider groups would never know when their rivals kidnapped people, or how many.

A man near the front of the buggy pointed at Althea. "You idiots. That one's too small."

Everyone looked at her.

She held her chin high, gazing around with the fearless posture of a parent come to chase the scary monsters away. Althea wanted all the raiders to see her glowing blue eyes. It didn't take long before their emotional state leapt to elation. Whispers of 'The Prophet' circulated among them. Someone shouted, "Tell Ferous!"

"We got the Prophet!" shouted a female raider.

Mojave stared at her, her emotion sinking into hopelessness.

"You is ours now." A man walked up to loom over her.

"No. I don't do that anymore." She glared back at him. "You will stop being bad. Taking slaves is bad."

A female raider approached her from behind, holding a metal collar and leash. "Don't care it bad. You's our slave now. You belong to the Ferals."

Althea slowly turned her head to lock stares with the woman—and rammed the raider's emotional state into complete terror.

The raider promptly soiled herself. The leash fell from her grip, clattering to the dirt. A second later, she shrieked and bolted for the gate, so out of her mind with fear she kept running into the closed barrier as if unable to comprehend why she couldn't get past it. The woman continued shrieking and clawing at the steel as though a pack of angry bonedogs nipped at her.

Other raiders fell into a bewildered silence.

Mojave shivered. "D-did you do that?"

"Yes." Althea looked around at the circle of raiders, then pointed at the big cage. "You will let all these people go right now and you will stop taking slaves."

The raiders laughed. Several of them moved to grab her.

She projected a wave of telempathic dread over them, crushing their bravado. Raiders backpedaled away, widening the circle they'd formed around her. The azure glow from her eyes glinted off the raider buggy frame, brightening in time with her power battering at the raiders' collective psyche. She pushed fear into them until every last raider had the emotional state of a five-year-old waking up from a bad dream alone in a dark room. Some wailed or cried out for their mothers.

A loud squeak came from a metal door on the larger of the two concrete buildings. A huge, muscular man, mostly shirtless except for metal shoulder armor, stormed out, looking around with a disdainful, confused expression at all the wailing and weeping. Waist-long dreadlocks decorated with shiny baubles, wooden beads, or colorful fabric scraps dangled over his bare dark-brown chest.

The raider chief, likely the one they called Ferous, stomped over to the buggy. He had to be almost twice Althea's height, his arms bigger around than her chest. The front half of a human skull hung from the middle of a heavy leather belt holding up a loose-fitting skirt of black fabric. Dried blood coated small spikes on his metal-plated boots as well as the blades of the two scrap-metal axes hanging from his belt. Long-healed scars crisscrossed his chest and prominent belly. He appeared to be the only one in the raider camp to have his fill of food whenever he wanted.

"The hell is going on out here?" bellowed Ferous.

None of the raiders reacted.

By now, the slaves in the cage had all gotten to their feet, grasped the bars, and watched the goings-on with extreme interest. Mojave, completely ignored by the raiders, gnawed on the rope binding her wrists.

Ferous grabbed the nearest raider by a fistful of his leather armor and pulled the man up off his feet. "Speak."

The raider blubbered incoherently while pointing at Althea.

"Pathetic." Ferous flung the man to the ground, gripped his axes, and raised one as if to kill the man.

"Stop," yelled Althea. "Don't you dare hurt him."

Ferous froze, outwardly calm, though he seethed in anger. "I thought I heard some little voice talkin' to me like they givin' an order. Gotta be my imagination. No one tells Ferous what to do. Especially not no kid."

Althea stared defiantly up at him. "I will not let you hurt him."

Grunting in contempt, he again raised the axe.

"*Stop!*" shouted Althea, her eye-light flaring briefly.

The command smashed into the man's brain, grinding it to a halt. He stood in place like a statue of an axe-wielding barbarian, making constipated faces while trying unsuccessfully to force his arms to move. Veins in his forehead and biceps swelled from the effort, though he succeeded only in shaking.

She padded around to stand in front of him.

His frustration and anger abruptly became mystification. "The Prophet? Here? We have the Prophet?"

"No. You do not *have* me." She pointed at the cage. "Your men kidnapped a girl right in front of me. I saw them thinking about other slaves, so I followed them. Slaves is bad. You will stop taking slaves."

Ferous tilted his head. "You're the Prophet... you're supposed to —"

"The legends are wrong!" yelled Althea. "No more!"

The raider camp fell utterly silent; even the slaves held their breath.

Mojave got the rope off her wrists and spat it to the side with an audible *puti*.

Althea smiled. "I will make anyone's hurts and sicks go away if they ask. I do not want pay-things. Don't be mean. Don't hurt anyone. You do not have to *take* me, just ask for help."

"The stories," whispered Ferous.

She glowered at him, then pointed at the cage. "*Open it. Free them.*"

Ferous shuddered, twitched a few times, and blinked rapidly. Moving with the gait of a chintzy robot, he staggered to the cage. Both axes fell from his grip, clanking to the dirt one after the next. Other raiders cowered on the ground, hesitantly watching her, too frightened to make a noise. She didn't like making people afraid of her, but she hated slavery more than someone not liking her. Even her sister thought it 'justice' for raiders to have a taste of the fear they so loved to instill in other people.

The instant Ferous opened the lock securing the cage door, the people inside rushed out—except for two. A bruised and exhausted scrag woman in a tattered loincloth limped for the exit. Behind her, a delirious man dressed in a tunic made from multiple different colors of fabric and an old pair of jeans needed to hang onto the bars to keep from falling. Sixteen people gathered around her the way the goats back in Querq tended to swarm Aldo as he delivered lunch to the farm workers every day. The ones who appeared to be former raiders regarded her somewhat fearfully, as if hoping she didn't realize, unaware she looked into their thoughts. They, too, thought it world-changing to watch the Prophet refuse to be the complacent captive the legends all claimed she would be.

Ferous, free of the command to open the cage, rushed over to her. "This wrong. Prophet doesn't try to escape."

"I'm not trying to escape." She folded her arms. "I can't escape because I am not a captive."

He stared at her, at a loss for how to react to a small girl not only refusing to show any fear of him but also ordering him around. His usual answer to someone making him angry involved lots of hitting, shaking, punching, and sometimes chopping off heads. Shockingly, he didn't want to physically attack a child. The 'aww, but she's only a kid' hesitation surprised Althea in a nice way even if it didn't make much sense. For example, he thought it wrong to strike a 'little kid,' but had no problem enslaving Mojave, only three years older than her... plus all the other people he'd beaten, killed, and kidnapped.

"The stories of The Prophet are vast," said Ferous. "For years have we hunted you."

"I know. Everyone does." She frowned. "That's over now. No one hunts me. The legends used to be true, but I changed them."

He blinked.

"You can *look for* me if you have a hurt or a sick." She pointed at him. "You will stop taking slaves and attacking innocent people. Be nice and you don't have to be scared of me, but if you keep doing bad things, I'll make you so sad you won't be able to do anything but sit on the ground and cry for the rest of your life." She added a mild pulse of fear to drive the point home.

The raiders, overcome by her dread aura, panicked and ran in multiple directions.

"Aww, hell no!" roared Ferous, staring at some imaginary horror only he could see. The big man sprinted away from her across the raider compound to the wall and climbed it in seconds, disappearing into the distant ruins.

Althea bit her lip, mildly guilty at threatening to make them cry forever. The city police told her she'd actually done it by accident to one of Archon's people. The 'sad bomb' she hit him with left him in what they called a 'vegetative state.' All he'd do is sit wherever anyone left him and cry, not even eat. Someone else had to use a psionic power to take over his body and eat for him. She felt horrible about it once they told her and insisted they bring her to him so she could fix the damage. Thankfully, she managed to un-break his emotions. She had no intention to do anything like that to these raiders, but saying scary stuff to make people stop doing bad things didn't bother her.

Mojave sat on the ground and pulled the rope off her ankles.

In less than two minutes, no trace of any raider remained inside the camp. They'd all scrambled over the walls and fled into the ruins.

Althea exhaled and stopped throwing off fear.

The people from the cage discussed what to do with themselves. Most came from villages relatively close to this encampment. Surprisingly, none belonged to Afbee. The three former raiders had come here with their group to make war, but lost. Only they survived out of eight who'd been captured—and forty-three who'd attacked. They didn't appear to have any interest in going back to raiding, and pleaded with the others to allow them to go with them as settlers.

"Don't go to Afbee. There is lots of sick there," said Althea.

"Everyone's welcome to follow me to Sun Valley," said a woman wearing the best clothing of the group: an intact tunic, pants, and bonedog-hide boots, all of which looked new. "Only reason them bastards got me is I'd been running a trade up north ta Tularo. Just me and a wagon. Stay inside Sun Valley, raiders can't get in."

Six of the captives all came from the same place, the only adult survivors from the raider attack on their tiny village. They agreed to go to Sun Valley after a brief return to where they used to live in hopes some of the children too small for the raiders to grab managed to survive a week or two without anyone to look after them. One by one, the rest decided to go as well, either not sure how to return to where they came from or not really caring to.

The former slaves headed across the raider encampment to a war wagon and a group of buggies parked on the left side near the wall, adjacent to shelves of tools and spare parts. The bruised scrag woman and the delirious man remained. Althea looked at them. The woman wanted to talk to her but feared making her angry. The man swooned side to side, too out of it to comprehend much of anything other than 'get out of cage.'

Althea squished the woman's fear and gave her trust instead.

"Don't be afraid of me." She smiled. "I only acted scary because raiders are bad and I didn't want them to get hurt or hurt anyone."

"You are the Prophet?" asked the woman. "Are the legends wrong? They say you can heal."

"I can." Althea rested her hand on the woman's side. "That part is right."

Moments later, the woman no longer had any bruises. The man fell over, grunted in pain, and groaned. She knelt beside him and sat back on her heels. A foul smell led her to the broken-off head of an arrow stuck in his back about a hand's width above his waist. The wound around it had become blackened, rancid, and infected. She pushed him over to lay on his stomach and pulled the tunic up, exposing the area.

Mojave gasped at the greenish-black mark roiling with maggots.

Althea placed her hands on either side of the rotting hole and closed her eyes. The man gave a moan of relief as soon as she shut off his pain. He suffered two different sicks, a bad one hovering close to the injury but another all over his body. She felt grateful the raiders had been stupid. An infected arrow shot like this would certainly have killed this man soon. Raiders shouldn't have even taken him as a slave. He'd never have recovered from the injury, remaining too sick to do any work or even serve as an entertaining victim in a forced gladiator fight before he died. Most raiders would've either killed him or left him to die rather than drag him back to their camp.

Once finished repairing his hurt, she opened her eyes and wiped a foamy, foul-smelling mess off his back, the skin under it intact and new. She'd sent the bad sick directly out the wound hole. The lesser sick, likely a fever, went to the bladder.

"You saved my life," whispered the man. "I'd have been dead in a week."

"Yes." Althea looked down, not wanting to say he probably wouldn't have made it another three days. "I am happy you will not die."

"Makes two of us." He chuckled, then cringed. "Oh, that burns a bit."

"You will need to make water. You had a sick. It will burn." She put a hand on his arm. "I can stop the pain."

"Burn, huh? Wouldn't be the first time." He winked.

She furrowed her brow. "I do not remember taking a sick away from you before."

"Heh. Don't worry about it, kid." The man got to his feet. "I can handle a little firewater."

"Okay." She shrugged.

Mojave crept up to stand beside Althea, strangely sad.

The man walked over to pee on the cage, a fitting statement. He whistled and grunted a bit, but didn't appear overly bothered by the pain of a sick coming out in his water. The other former slaves grabbed the giant chain winch, working together to hoist the gate. For every ten or so feet they pulled the chain, the massive gate went up only a few inches. When they finally raised it enough to fit a vehicle under it, they hurried to the war wagon and buggies.

"Why sad?" asked Althea.

"Your friends didn't believe our spirits." Mojave raked her toes over the sand. "They thought something else made our people disappear. I didn't know the wall had a hole so big. You helped me and it made me sleep. Had to pee so bad when I woke up. Walked away from you and the other kids to do it, and those men grabbed me. I remembered what your friend said. Not spirits, but people take us. I thought Sahara might be here, but she is not."

Althea gazed around at the three concrete buildings, four scrap metal huts and numerous tents. "Maybe in there?"

Once the man finished making water, he walked back over to them. "You got somewhere to be, kid?"

"Yes." Althea smiled at him. "I am okay."

"Sure?" He raised an eyebrow, shifting his gaze back and forth from her to Mojave. "Guess it's a pretty dumb question after what you just did here."

The man didn't talk like a scrag. He probably lived in a settlement or even came from the big city since he didn't have much fear or wonder at seeing her use her powers to make the raiders run away like frightened kids or heal him. Either he came from a settlement where a mystic lived or knew about psionics. She loved the sense of concern he radiated, as though he'd found a kid and a young woman alone in a 'dangerous' place and felt guilty at leaving them here on their own.

She nudged him along with a bit of emotional reassurance. "I have to go back. My friends are worrying about me."

"All right. If you are sure." The man bowed before rushing to jump on the war wagon as the other former slaves drove off.

Althea watched him sprint after the truck. He only caught up to it because the driver saw him coming and hit the brakes. People in the back reached over the side, grabbed his arms, and hauled him on board.

She stood beside Mojave in the deserted raider camp, listening to the soft howl of the wind and the buzz of ethanol engines receding into the distance. The Prophet had 'wiped out' a raider encampment in a manner of speaking.

No one had been hurt, at least not directly. Panicky raiders might have tripped, fallen into holes, or run into giant bugs out in the ruins, but she couldn't feel responsible for it. After all, she hadn't gone straight to fear. She tried to ask them nicely first.

Clearing the place didn't offer any sense of victory or thrill, merely the warm satisfaction of knowing sixteen people would soon be home and safe, no longer tormented by raiders. If one of the bad people got stung by a soldier scorpion or bitten by a giant millipede, she'd feel bad, but everyone she knew, even Karina and Father, would say they deserved worse for the bad things they did.

Althea squinted at the sky, wondering how the people of the Badlands would react when they discovered The Prophet learned to roar.

## 20

# DRIVER'S EDUCATION

Once the buzzing of the departing engines disappeared into the wind's soft whistle, Althea glanced at Mojave.

The teen stood beside her, staring into space, her hair and dress fluttering to one side in the breeze. She seemed lost to sadness, hope, and worry, making a face like she'd fallen off a caravan in the middle of the desert and had no idea where to go or what to do with herself. It didn't seem likely these raiders would have taken Sahara since one of them called Althea 'too young' when they first spotted her. Mojave said her sister would be thirteen now, which meant she'd been taken at twelve.

"Are you hurt?" Althea grasped the teen's left forearm.

"Not really." Mojave looked at her wrists. "Little sore but no blood."

Althea didn't sense any hurts or sicks in her, so she let go of her and focused on telepathy, searching the area for thoughts. She only picked up Mojave and a handful of wispy scraps of consciousness, likely rats or similar small creatures. While she didn't really know the limit of how far away she could detect a living mind, it had to be at least as far as she could see a person well enough to recognize them. Her estimation of range easily tripled the size of the encampment, leaving her confident she'd be able to sense any other people trapped or hiding out of sight. A recently abandoned raider camp created the perfect circumstance to search for other active minds: no noise or distractions and only one other known person nearby. Within whatever reach her powers had, no other living people existed.

"What are you doing now? Your eyes are brighter."

"Looking for people." Althea rotated in a gradual turn, scanning all the tents and buildings just in case her telepathy worked better in the direction she looked. Still, nothing.

"But you're just standing in one place." Mojave rubbed her wrist.

"I'm doing telepathy."

"What's that?"

Althea turned her head to make eye contact with her. *This is telepathy. It's how I talked to you on the ride.*

"That's kinda scary." Mojave leaned back. "Aren't mystics bad?"

"Don't be afraid." Althea tapped her head. "It's psionics, not scary. I'm not a mystic."

The teen fidgeted at her hair, so nervous it didn't even require telempathy to feel it radiating from her. "But you made the raiders do things they didn't want to. That's what mystics do. Steal people's souls."

Althea sighed. "No. They don't do that. Souls can't be stolen. Souls become ghosts when you die. Mystics have psionics and can do bad things, but they don't *have* to." She crouched, grabbed one of the axes Ferous dropped, and hefted it. The instant she touched it, a hundred half-second flashes of people dying burst across her mind. She winced at the barrage of emotional pain, but steeled herself by knowing she'd stopped him from hurting anyone else… at least for the time being. "I have an axe now, but it doesn't mean I'm going to hurt anyone with it."

"Umm… an axe isn't a mystic."

"Nope." Althea grinned. "But it can do bad stuff, right?"

Mojave nodded.

"Holding an axe that can do bad stuff doesn't make me bad unless I use it to do bad stuff. Same for a mystic. They *can* do bad stuff, but having the can doesn't mean… ugh. I mean having the ability, stupid words. I'm supposed to do the speaking right. Having ability to do bad doesn't make you bad unless you do bad."

"Oh. I guess. It's still scary." Mojave pulled the axe out of Althea's grip. "I can take the axe away from you, but I can't take a mystic's power."

"Yes. That is fair." Althea wiped her hands off on her dress, mostly to rid herself of the memory of touching it than actual dirt. She glanced over her shoulder, expecting angry spirits of those murdered by the weapon she touched to show up and demand she kill Ferous. After a moment of no ghosts showing up, she frowned. The Many already got them… probably.

Mojave sniffed a few times, then grabbed a handful of her dress and pulled it up to her face, sniffing it. "Eww. I smell like the raider."

"Bleh." Althea stuck out her tongue.

In a matter of five seconds, Mojave's emotional state leapt from relative calm to a near breakdown. She fell to her knees, shaking, sobbing, and rambling about what almost happened to her. With the immediate threat of raiders now gone, the emotional toll of nearly becoming a slave—and being wifed repeatedly—hit her hard. The girl didn't say anything, but her thoughts revealed her fears. Even more than what the raiders might have done to her, she feared punishment from the spirits for 'leaving Afbee.' Mojave desperately wanted to return home and be with her parents, but feared getting in trouble for going so far away from the village.

*Grr. The spirits are mean and stupid.* Althea sat beside her and put an arm around her back, comforting her until she mostly processed the runaway grief and terror. Mild telempathic nudges helped, gradually reducing the worst emotions so the shift didn't feel unnatural.

"Don't cry. It's only a dress," said Althea, pretending not to know what the girl had been thinking about.

Mojave gave her an odd look, likely hoping a girl Althea's age didn't understand what raiders would have done to her. "Yeah. I'll wash it. I have another one I can wear when this is wet."

"Wow. Two? Someone likes you." Althea grinned.

"What do you mean?"

Althea scrunched her nose in confusion. "A boy wanted to be your mate, so he gifted you *two* dresses?"

"No." Mojave shook her head. "My parents made them from the cloth the spirits gave us. They'd also be mad if I had a 'mate' because I'm fifteen. Not allowed to do that until eighteen."

"Eighteen?" Althea blinked. "Father said I need sixteen birthdays or he will throw Den off the wall if we do more than lip touch. Umm, kiss. Why eighteen?"

Mojave chuckled. "It is our law. The spirits will punish anyone who does it before eighteen birthdays."

"Is that why there are only five kids in Afbee? Everyone is afraid to make babies?" Althea scratched her head.

"No." Mojave looked down. "There used to be more, but the spirits take them. Some don't want to have babies because they are afraid the spirits will take them and they don't want to be heartbroken."

"Grr." Althea scowled. "Your spirits are bad." She narrowed her eyes. *If there are spirits. David doesn't think they're real. Maybe someone is lying about spirits being here.*

"Don't make them angry. They will hurt you." Mojave stood, wiped her face, and stared despondently at the camp. "Do you think the raiders took Sahara... or anyone?"

Althea sent out another telepathic ping, still sensing nothing. "I think we're alone. No one else is here. We can look if you want."

"Please. I have to see."

Althea trailed after the teen as she rushed from building to hut to tent, checking everywhere a person could hide. Except for a corpse hanging in one of the concrete buildings as a target for throwing knives, they found only empty furniture, sleeping mats, and storage boxes containing stuff taken on raids. With each place they checked, the girl's hope lessened until she slipped from despair into anger. After they'd checked the last of the tents, Mojave stormed back across the camp to the big building Ferous came from, where the raiders kept a stack of footlockers, chests, and boxes containing the spoils of pillage: vegetables, water bottles, clothing, weapons, and mechanical parts. Mojave threw open the lid of a large green trunk, discovering it full of random pieces of handmade clothing, mostly tunics.

Mojave loaded her arms up with garments while muttering, "Revenge. We ran out of spirit cloth. No more new clothing. I am taking this for Afbee." She paused, sighed, then dropped the stuff back into the trunks. "Wait. We are far. I can't carry this."

Althea pointed at the box. "Take all."

"I can't even lift the whole trunk."

"We have a buggy." Althea pointed at the door, then grabbed the handle on one side of the trunk. "Let's take this. You can give to the other kids. I don't need any."

Mojave stuffed the lid down until it clicked shut, then grabbed the handle on her end, but froze before lifting it, taken by fear.

"What?" Althea searched around the floor. "Scorpion?"

"No. I'm... *we* are away from Afbee. The spirits will punish us."

Althea sighed. "No, they won't. I can talk to spirits."

"You're lying."

"Nope. Look." Althea telepathically shared her memory of seeing the ghostly pilot.

Mojave waved her arms around. "What? Where am I? That man is glowing."

"I'm showing you my seeing." Althea smiled. "He is a spirit. He died in the Before-Time."

"Umm." Mojave shivered. "I'm still afraid. We're not supposed to leave."

"You didn't leave. Raiders kidnapped you." Althea let go of the trunk and walked outside. "I don't think you have spirits at all."

"I don't understand." Mojave hurried after her. "You just said you can see and talk to spirits. Now you say you don't believe they are real?"

Althea headed over to the buggy that brought them here, the only vehicle left in the camp. "Spirits are real, but I don't think there are any in Afbee who will be mad at you. Do you know how to make the drive machine work?"

Mojave shook her head. "No. We aren't allowed to touch drive machines. The spirit talker forbids it."

"Durango?"

"No, the spirit talker. Durango is our leader." Mojave seemed annoyed for a second, but dismissed it. "Oh. You are new. The spirit talker is very old and lives by himself outside the wall. He is close to the shrine."

"Grr." Althea raked both hands through her hair in frustration. "Ford showed us the shrine already. He's not the spirit talker, is he?"

"Ford is Ford. The spirit talker is older than him." Mojave pantomimed an elderly person walking around.

"You have a spirit talker." Althea gazed up at the sky and let out a long sigh. "Why did no one say so before?"

"I don't know." Mojave shrugged.

Althea grumbled. For a smart scrag who could speak like a city person, Mojave sure didn't know much. Durango didn't want Althea doing anything to upset the spirits he believed cursed their village. He probably didn't tell her about the spirit talker because he thought she'd go right to him and demand to see the spirits. Someone calling himself a spirit talker could mean one of several things: a mystic who truly could communicate with ghosts, a person who inhaled magic smoke and *thought* they spoke to ghosts, or simply a liar. "I must see your spirit talker."

"I will bring you to him. If we can go back... you don't think the spirits will take me for leaving?"

"No. Because there aren't any spirits here. But..." Althea whirled to point at her. "You didn't want to leave Afbee. Someone *took* you. If any spirits *are* here and they get mad at you for it, they're mean and you should stop listening to them. Ford said your spirits know if people want to leave."

Mojave cringed. "But if they take me, I'll be gone."

"I won't let them take you." Althea faced the buggy again. "You can't work the drive machine?"

"No. The spirit talker says it is forbidden. We can't drive them."

Althea tapped her foot. How difficult could it be to

operate a buggy? The wheel only turned in two directions. "You won't get in trouble. I will work the drive machine. We put the box on the back if you want to take the clothes."

While Mojave ran to the building to claim her 'revenge' loot, Althea climbed into the front seat, a simple black plastic chair with its steel legs cut off. The steering wheel looked about half the size of the one in the buggy Teal drove them here in. A tall metal rod stuck up from the floor on her right. Someone scratched writing on it. Above a forward-pointing arrow, the word 'go.' Below it, another arrow pointed backward beneath the word 'og.'

"Og?" Althea stared at the bizarre word for a moment. None of the electronic teachers or real teachers ever used the word. *Go and og. Huh?* It took her a moment of staring at the two arrows for things to make sense. *Oh... it's go, backward.*

She grabbed the lever and pushed it forward. It moved a short distance before seemingly locking in place. Althea pulled it back into a squishy zone where it wobbled loose as if not connected to much. Pulling it back felt the same as pushing it forward; after a short travel, the rod clicked into a socket or some such thing.

*It has three places. Going, not going, and going backward. Easy.*

The most significant problem Althea faced came in the form of the foot pedals. Her legs didn't quite manage the task of reaching them if she sat all the way back in the seat... so she scooted forward. If she planted her butt at the edge, she could step on the flaps. She knew one made the buggy stop, the other made it go fast... but not which one did which thing. Easy enough to figure out once she learned how to make the engine go.

Getting the steering wheel to turn proved difficult until Althea made herself stronger. Having solved one problem, she searched for a way to get the engine to make noise.

When the raiders kidnapped Mojave, they'd jumped into the buggy and the engine started. Neither one of the men ran around back to pull on anything the way Teal had to do for the big buggy, so she figured it possible to make the engine work from the seat.

A pair of wires hung out of a small hole to the left of where the steering wheel column connected. Someone had scratched 'sparky' into the metal above them. Next to the hole, a simple lever switch under the word 'gas' had two positions indicated by more scratched writing: go and nogo. She turned the knob to 'go', which didn't appear to do anything, so she grabbed the wires and pulled the same way Teal yanked on the cord.

A painful jolt stabbed her in the hand like someone whacked her with a fiery stick.

She yelped and recoiled, whimpered, and stuck her fingers in her mouth, annoyed.

While she nursed a small burn, Mojave dragged the trunk of clothing out of the building. The lid barely closed now, suggesting she'd spent the past few minutes grabbing even more clothes from a different trunk and stuffing them in.

Althea resumed examining the wires, sensing them important. The buggy rocked side to side as Mojave hefted the box onto the stand-plate and tied it down. Ignoring the jostling, Althea grasped the part of the wire where plastic covered the metal. Touching it there didn't hurt, so she tried pulling again. It came another inch or so out of the hole before it stopped. Pulling on it didn't appear to be the correct way to start the engine.

Again, she studied it. The wire consisted of two smaller wires glued together except for the last bit at the end where a short section had been separated. An even shorter part at the tip had no plastic over the copper. The frayed ends bent in a shape like a scorpion's pincers. Since it 'bit' her, she thought it appropriate.

Mojave walked up to stand next to her.

"Get in the other seat," said Althea.

"You are sure we won't get in trouble?"

"Yes." Althea looked up at her. "You're touching the drive machine to go back to Afbee, not to leave. It's okay."

Mojave relaxed, giving off a sense of hesitant relief. "All right. I trust you."

"Do you know why it won't make noise?" Althea held up the wires. "I pull on it like Teal started our drive machine, but it doesn't work."

"It's not a pull thing, it's a light thing."

"It's not lights." Althea scrunched her nose.

"The lights have those stringy parts." Mojave pointed at the wires. "They carry the glow juice from the heavy box to the part that lights."

Althea glanced up at her. "The 'lectric?"

"Yeah. That's right. Electricity." Mojave pointed. "Touch the metal parts."

"No." Althea furrowed her brows. "It bit me."

Mojave chuckled. "I mean, touch the metal parts to each other. Not you."

Not wanting to get zapped again, Althea carefully grasped the separate strands of wire at the end by the plastic-covered part and pushed the exposed tips together. The instant the metal made contact, a spark flash startled her into yelping and letting go, but the engine sputtered a little. After realizing she didn't need to regenerate her fingers, she took a deep breath, grasped the wire again, and held the wire ends together longer than a split second. The engine made the same whirring noise, backfired, then lurched to life. When she let the wires come apart, the engine continued running.

"Worked!" cheered Althea. "Get in!"

Mojave stared at the buggy until Althea took her fear away. The teen gave her a sideways stare, aware her mood had been altered, but didn't protest. She climbed over the side wall and lowered herself into the rear seat.

Althea looked down her legs at the pedals. She gingerly pushed her toes into the middle one. Nothing happened. Fairly sure she'd discovered the stopping pedal, she gingerly stepped on the other one. The engine got louder, but they didn't move.

*This is the fast one.*

She eased her foot off the pedal, grasped tall metal rod to her right, and shoved it forward. The buggy lurched hard enough to throw her all the way back in the seat, rolling a little faster than a person could jog—directly at the big dome cage. As she presently couldn't reach the stop pedal, she grabbed the wheel and twisted it left, narrowly avoiding a crash. The buggy went around in a circle, soon heading right back at the cage.

"Eep!" Althea cranked the wheel to the right, missing the dome by about three feet and flinging Mojave and herself against the side of the buggy. She straightened out... staring at one of the concrete structures coming at them fast.

"Stop!" shouted Mojave.

"I can't reach!" Althea steered hard left, brushing the back right wheel on the building.

She plowed into a tent, ripping it away from its moorings. The heavy canvas covered the front half of the buggy, blinding her. They hit another tent. Rope snapped, metal clanked, and something heavy thudded into the left side of the frame. Althea and Mojave screamed at the same time. Fearing the next object in their path might be much harder than fabric, Althea scooted forward and jammed both feet on the middle pedal.

The buggy stopped as abruptly as if she'd hit a wall. The engine choked and died.

Her face bounced off the steering wheel.

Mojave crashed into the back of her seat. "You are not good at drive machine."

"I know." Althea reached up to push at the broken tent material.

"This would be good if it rains, but we can't see." Mojave stood in her seat, pushing the tent material up and gathering it into a bundle before tossing it aside.

Althea stared over the wheel at a scrap metal hut barely six feet in front of them. At the relatively slow speed they'd been going, it probably wouldn't have hurt them much, though it could have destroyed the buggy's ability to work. *Walking* to Afbee would be a chore.

"Whew." Althea fake wiped sweat from her forehead, something she'd seen people do in similar situations. "We have to og."

"What?" Mojave sat again.

"Og." Althea grinned, pointing at the rod. "Go backward."

She touched the wires together, but the engine made a weird, laboring noise. The feeling she got whenever she did something dangerous gripped her, so she hastily pulled the copper ends apart and studied her situation. The only thing different from the last time she started the engine was the tall rod being in the go position rather than the squishy middle. She pulled it back to neutral, then touched the wires again. The engine started. Relieved, she fake wiped sweat off her forehead again, then pulled the rod into the 'og' position. The buggy kicked into reverse, flinging her chest into the steering wheel. Being so far forward in the seat made it easy to reach the pedals, however, so she had no difficulty stopping again. The engine died.

Althea grumbled and pushed the rod back into the 'nowhere' position, then restarted the motor. *Maybe if I stop, I have to push the rod here first so the engine doesn't quit.* She stood in the buggy, looked for the gate, and sat again. "Think I have the knowing now."

"Good."

"I mean, I think I know." Althea bonked herself. Karina wouldn't like it if she talked like a scrag. Neither would her teachers. She liked making people happy, even if it annoyed her to constantly think about what words to use.

After restarting the engine, Althea pushed the rod into the go position, steering left, but didn't straighten out fast enough to end up pointing at the gate… so she kept driving around in circles a few times until she got the timing right, finally managing a bee-line for the opening in the wall.

The buggy trundled out of the raider encampment to open street. Althea kept both hands on the wheel, maintaining the buggy on a reasonably straight course.

"Can you go faster?" asked Mojave. "I could run faster than this."

"Umm. Yes, but I'm a little scared."

Mojave laughed. "What are you afraid of?"

"Don't want to hurt you. I never worked a drive machine before."

"It will take us days to go home if you don't go faster."

"Grr." Althea gingerly rested her foot on the speed pedal.

When she gave a little pressure, the engine grew louder. The buggy gradually gained speed. In a few minutes, once they'd left the ruins behind for wide-open desert, she risked pushing more on the pedal. Her confidence increased little by little. Eventually, she realized her foot couldn't go down any more. They flew across the desert, going noticeably faster than the ride there... probably because the buggy didn't have to haul the weight of two big raiders.

A steady, high-pitched droning scream came from the engine, too loud to easily talk over. Sitting low in the seat spared her the brunt of the wind. The raider who'd been driving before had goggles, which she didn't, but being much smaller than him, most of the air went over her head. Every so often, they hit a bump or berm that launched her a few inches out of the seat. Althea didn't notice the moment it changed, but somehow, the bouncing went from terrifying to fun.

Initially, she followed visible tire marks in the dirt the buggy left on its way to the raider encampment. However, those disappeared after a short while, likely erased by the wind. She had little concept of where they'd come from or how many—if any—turns they made. Her spot on the stand-plate in the rear hadn't let her see much.

She stared ahead into the endless desert. Green bits of scrub shot by on either side and occasionally came head on, forcing her to swerve around them. No sign of tracks remained. Althea concentrated on Clairvoyance, locked in on the notion of David's presence. She'd known him longer than Teal, spent hours with him learning about psionics, and he also possessed a living brain, which made it easier to 'find' him.

The roar of the wind, buzz of the engine, and whipping of her hair all muted to her senses. One particular spot on the horizon seemed more appealing than everywhere else for no clear reason. Trusting her unusual feeling, Althea steered left. Except for avoiding rubble, rocks, bushes, or cacti, she kept driving straight in the direction which felt *right*.

"Why do you want to see the spirit talker?" yelled Mojave over the engine.

"I wanna ask him why he said no one can leave. Think he's lying," shouted Althea.

"Lying?"

"Yeah. Saying no one can leave Afbee sounds like slaves without tying people up or putting them in cages. He's scaring them into staying captive."

Fear wafted from the back seat. "Don't say mean things about the spirit talker! That's not why he says the laws." A moment later, her emotion shifted to doubt tinged with anger. "You will know if he lies?"

"Yes," shouted Althea. "I can hear his thinking."

"What if the spirits are real?"

"Then I'll go talk to them." Althea veered around a cactus. Except for the fear of crashing and exploding at any second, driving the buggy turned out to be a lot of fun. "I want to know *why* no one can leave."

## 21

## THE SPIRIT TALKER

After what felt like mere minutes of zooming across empty nothingness, the land up ahead started to look familiar. She didn't see the white sand anywhere, which meant they'd gone off in a different direction. However, she soon recognized the ruins surrounding Afbee. As soon as the circular wall came into view, she let off on the speed pedal, allowing the buggy to slow itself gradually. By the time they reached the old streets, they rolled along only a little faster than running speed. She nudged the pedal a bit to keep going at the same pace, steering by memory to the Shrine of the Hollow Man. Once there, she pulled the rod back into the 'nowhere' position and stepped on the brake.

The back wheels both locked, sliding rather than spinning, dragging the buggy to a much more aggressive stop than when the raiders arrived at their camp. Mojave crashed into the front seat, grunting. Thanks to her boosted arm strength, Althea's hold of the steering wheel stopped her from bouncing her face off it again. Also different: the engine didn't die this time. She'd been right about needing to put the rod in the neutral position.

"Sorry," whispered Althea over the idling engine. "Stopped too fast."

"I'm okay."

She looked around for any way to make the engine stop, then remembered the lever switch. A few seconds after she moved it to 'nogo,' the engine sputtered to silence.

*That works.*

Althea climbed out. The ride was fun, but she preferred being on stable ground. She faced the shrine and its fly machine statue, looking around for any sign of someone living nearby. "Where is the spirit talker?"

"Over here." Mojave hastily jumped out of the buggy, afraid of being seen touching it. She walked around to the right of the shrine, heading for a narrow footpath winding between mounds of concrete rubble.

Althea followed, taking care to watch where she stepped thanks to a large amount of metal and glass fragments. Considering only a handful of the villagers had shoes, she suspected the spirit talker didn't want visitors and deliberately left hurtful things on the trail to keep people away. A few times, she needed to climb the rubble to avoid the path wherever it offered no safe place to put a bare foot. One of the things she'd learned in the Badlands: never step on sparkles. They tended to hurt.

Roughly 200 feet from the Hollow Man Shrine, the trail ended at clearing surrounded by a two-story-high square wall of cinder blocks, bricks, and broken concrete, likely the bottom level of a formerly tall building, cleared out into a big open space. Seven mostly human-shaped effigies stood on pedestals randomly arranged around the area, made of assorted scrap metal including spoons, forks, springs, aluminum cans, and larger, rusty pieces likely from ancient drive machines.

The place had the look of a shrine, though she detected no unusual energy. Mojave made reverent gestures at the statues as she crossed the square to a door on the opposite side. The slab of semi-rotten wood didn't appear to have been the original door of the building, but a more recent creation. She knocked on it and took a step back.

Althea sensed irritation from inside.

"Who disturbs the spirit talker?" called an older voice.

Mojave, too frightened to speak, merely looked at her as if to say 'well, you wanted to be here. *You* talk to him.'

She held her head high. "I am Althea."

A man's grumbling grew louder. Footsteps approached the door. It opened, squeaking inward to reveal a skinny, wrinkled, hunched-over man with a puffy white beard down to his belly. His skin hung from his body, seeming too big for the bones it draped from. He wore an old olive-drab cloth belt, from which hung a tattered, dingy white loincloth made from an unusual soft fabric with the word 'Hilton' stitched along the bottom. Numerous cords, beads, glass amulets, and animal bones decorated his hair, body, and beard. Two slabs of drive machine tire served as heavy sandals, tied on with electrical cord. He smelled like the Water Man's chair, which he referred to as 'the cushion that ate a thousand farts.'

The spirit talker puffed up his chest in an effort to seem scary or important. However, the instant he made eye contact—and saw the glow—he wheezed in shock.

"Hello." Althea peeked into his head. "Are you really a spirit talker?"

David and the other city police taught her much about psionic stuff. Even if she truly disliked having to visit the big city sometimes, she couldn't argue they really had helped her. She knew right away this man did not have any psionic abilities. He could not be a true spirit talker or mystic. If, in fact, any spirits did speak to him, all the effort came from the spirit. A ghost powerful enough to talk to an ordinary person could talk to anyone. It didn't make sense to her why they'd only speak to one man.

"Of course," snapped the man, annoyed.

She shook her head. *No you are not.*

He stepped back, irritation jumping to terror.

Althea lunged forward, mashing her hand into the door and blocking his attempt to slam it in her face. "Tell me why you say the people of Afbee are not allowed to leave."

His thoughts filled with a memory of a dimly lit all-metal room. Two men and a woman dressed in modern city clothes told him they would kill anyone who leaves the village. The woman, tall and thin, with long blonde hair, had a sinister, evil glint in her eyes.

"Tell them whatever story you like," said the woman. "Anyone who tries to leave will die. They won't make it a quarter mile."

Such fear took over the man's mind he lost consciousness, ending the memory. She next saw him making all the statues he'd placed in the garden to represent the 'spirits' he used to frighten the villagers into obedience. When those who tried leaving ended up dead or missing, everyone began to believe his stories of angry spirits.

Althea broke telepathic contact. She continued holding the door open with one hand and one foot. Her contempt for the man disappeared to pity. "I'm sorry. Those people are bad. I won't let them hurt you or anyone here."

The spirit talker wheezed.

She shoved the door out of the way, rushed in, and grabbed him as he collapsed, easing him to lie flat on his back. Merely being reminded of the modern people frightened him enough for his heart shape to go crazy. She commanded it to slow down and guided it back to a normal beating rhythm. Once confident he would no longer drop dead, she sat back on her heels and grumbled, angry at the people who threatened him.

The spirit talker's house looked to be a scrap metal shed built against the former front wall of the Before-Time skyscraper, now merely a one-story square wall around his statue garden. The basic shed contained only a few shelves of various junk and a large sleeping mat. She boosted her strength enough to drag him across the space to the sleeping area.

Mojave gasped. "You are strong for a child."

"He does not weigh much."

"What?"

Althea ground her toes into the dirt. "He does not have the heavy."

"No." Mojave fidgeted. "I understood you the first time. I don't understand how a kid as small as you picked a man up."

"I can be strong when I have to be." Althea shrugged.

"Is he dead?" whispered Mojave.

"No. Sleeping." Althea pulled a thin linen blanket over him, stood, and walked out of the house, closing the sheet metal door behind her. "He is lying but not for bad reasons."

Mojave stared at her for a few seconds, glanced at the door, then looked at her again. Extreme nervousness practically glowed from her life force. "What?"

Althea started across the statue garden toward the broken gap in the wall where they'd entered. "Spirits are not hurting anyone who leaves. Modern people from the big city are. He saw them and they told him to lie."

"Modern people?" Mojave fell in step at her side.

On the way along the trail back to the ruins, Althea told Mojave about West City, a big, metal place past the edge of the Badlands where everything lit up, flew, made noise, or scared her.

"But there's a wall of fire at the end of the world," said Mojave.

"It's a story. Not real." Althea huffed. "I've been there. It's not really a nice place, but I'm too sensitive."

"Too sensitive?"

Althea flapped her arms. "It's what they say. I'm extra psionic, so people's emotions hit me. When there are lots and lots of people and they're all angry and sad, it hurts. Like, go swimming and some bigger person pushes you under the water and won't let you up. How you feel wanting to get up and breathe? It's like how I felt wanting to get away from there."

"Oh, no…"

"I guess it's not *really* bad to normal people. Just me." She flapped her arms again. "Don't like the big city."

They stopped talking long enough to climb past a scattering of dangerous glass.

"Your friends," said Mojave, "are they modern people too? Their clothes are funny."

"Yes, but Teal lives in Querq now. Modern people aren't *all* bad."

Mojave nodded. "I don't know if I can believe the spirits aren't real."

"Right now, it doesn't matter." Althea left the narrow trail and scurried back over to get in the buggy. "If everyone here is afraid of spirits, they won't try to leave. It's good until we find the bad people. Durango and the villagers would not believe the real, so the telling of spirits keeps them safe."

"Wait…" Mojave ran over and grabbed her arm. "If the

spirits aren't real, what happened to Sahara or the others who the spirits took?"

Althea narrowed her eyes, thinking of the sinister blonde woman she'd seen in the spirit talker's memory. "People. Not spirits."

Mojave broke down crying, overcome by grief. "So, she's dead? We hoped the spirits might change their mind and give her back."

Althea sighed at her lap, feeling bad for making the girl sad, even if she'd spoken truth. "I don't know what they did. Do you have something of hers she liked a lot? Maybe I can feel if she is still alive."

"What?" Mojave's mood crashed from grief to hope. She stared up, red-eyed. "Are you teasing me?"

*No. I am psionic.* "I can see things sometimes." She held up her agate arrowhead pendant. "Den gave this. If I think about him when holding it, I can know what he's feeling or doing even if we're far away. If your sister had something she liked, she puts emotions in it."

"Only her skirt and beads. Mama gave them to her, so she loved them a lot."

"You still have them?"

"No. They are with her... if she's still anywhere." Mojave wiped a tear.

Althea squeezed her hand. "Bad people might be hurting Afbee. My friends and I will stop them. David and Phoenix are city police. They stop anyone doing bad stuff. Your spirit talker could not tell about modern people or they'd hurt him, so he made stories about spirits to keep the village safe."

"I think I understand." Mojave got in the back seat, no longer afraid of touching the buggy.

Althea started the engine, shifted into reverse, and backed around in a turn. She shoved the rod in neutral, stomped the brake, then pushed the shifter forward and drove down the street away from the shrine to the main gate of Afbee, thinking about the raiders abducting Mojave. Why hadn't the modern people attacked them? Could the bad people already be gone and the villagers are still living in fear? Maybe they couldn't catch the fast-moving buggy and *tried* to stop the raiders, simply failed. The trader, Mako, had been shot with a modern city gun according to Phoenix. Perhaps *raiders* hadn't killed him as her friends believed.

Whatever the reason, she needed to talk to David and Teal as soon as she could.

Afbee had become far more dangerous than they thought.

## THE SPOILS OF WAR... OR
## KIDNAPPING

G oing from the shrine to the gate took less than a minute in the buggy.

Althea managed to squeeze it past the gate without bumping the fat tires too badly. However, she swerved left behind the first building in sight, stopped, and cut the engine, hoping to hide the vehicle from Durango. A few people close enough to see them stared, giving off the same manner of dread as if they'd witnessed the girls murder someone in the open. No doubt, they believed the stories about spirits becoming angry if people touched drive machines.

Althea grabbed the frame bars overhead and pulled herself up out of the seat well. "I'll help you carry the box." She swung her legs to the left, letting gravity take her to the ground.

"All right."

After climbing out of the second seat, Mojave untied the cords securing the overstuffed trunk to the stand-plate on the rear of the buggy. She grabbed one side handle, Althea the other. Together, they hefted the box into the air. Mojave started off 'leading' by walking backward, though after only a few steps, shifted sideways.

"This is heavy." Althea needed to use both hands to keep her end of the box off the ground. "You put too much stuff in it. The lid won't close."

"It's clothes! We really need them." Mohave sidestepped a lump of concrete in her way, grunting at the weight of the trunk. "The spirits only gave us fabric once. We don't have any left. And your friends keep lighting people's stuff on fire."

"Sicks," muttered Althea. "If the sicks get on the clothes, the clothes can hurt people. Need new ones."

"Right." Mojave hefted her end of the trunk a bit higher. "Raiders don't deserve to keep this. Revenge for me and good for Afbee."

The girl's emotion of righteous indignation contained no greed. She didn't want to keep the huge stash of garments for herself. More than personal vengeance, the teen took them for the benefit of the village, especially the kids she considered herself responsible for. Althea grinned, completely at ease with stealing from raiders.

They made it about three-quarters of the way across the village to Mojave's home before Teal shouted, "Althea!"

Mojave stopped walking, which thanks to the trunk, yanked Althea to a stop, too. She glanced in the direction the shout came from.

David and Teal came running out from a cluster of dwellings, heading down the dusty old street toward them. Joy and relief saturated David. Teal, predictably, radiated no emotions to detect psionically, though the obvious happiness in her face—and that she rushed to scoop Althea into a hug—made Telempathy unnecessary to know how she felt.

"What happened?" Teal held her out at arm's length,

feet off the ground, like a big housecat dangling from her hands.

"Raiders tried to kidnap Mojave," said Althea in a matter-of-fact tone. "They had slaves, so I had to help them, too."

Teal set her down, exhaled hard, and shot David a pained look.

"You went *to* a raider camp?" He scratched his head. "On purpose?"

"Yes." Althea folded her arms. "I don't get kidnapped anymore."

## 23

# BREACH

Althea relayed the events of the raider camp as they walked to Mojave's home.

David carried the trunk for them despite Teal reaching for it, suggesting she stay alert for 'problems.' Once Althea finished explaining why she disappeared, her friends filled her in on what happened in Afbee during her absence. Camry came running over to Teal, the rest of the children in tow, breathlessly telling her about Mojave's kidnapping and hearing Althea speak inside his head. Phoenix stepped in to babysit the kids for the time being.

Camry and Onda told Durango about the gap in the wall, which appeared to surprise him as well as everyone who overheard. The village lacked the heavy equipment needed to move such an enormous piece of concrete. How their ancestors had built the wall in the first place, no one could explain. Teal shared her opinion the wall had to be quite old, likely made by the original survivors who used to live here, perhaps even the Air Force itself in the immediate aftermath of the war. Whatever machinery they'd put to use making it had long since been dismantled, collapsed, or rusted to oblivion. Still, Durango sent two of his warriors to investigate. The boys eagerly led them to the spot—only to find the gap sealed. The chief thought the kids made up a story.

Mojave led the way back to her dwelling. She lived in a simple rectangular building made from corrugated steel plates, stacked concrete rubble, and scrap wood. Her parents had not yet returned from whatever tasks they attended to during the day. Mojave rummaged among the clothing, selecting tunics she intended to give the children right away.

From there, the group walked to the open area at the village center where the locals arranged rows of long, flat concrete fragments in the manner of benches to sit on. The presence of a large grill nearby suggested the people used this spot for communal meals. They found Phoenix sitting on one such bench, entertaining the kids by reading them a story from her datapad. Camry and Onda wallowed in negative emotions: worry for Mojave and Althea, plus shame for being thought of as lying about the hole.

Pri noticed them coming first and shouted, "Mojave!"

The other children looked. Their explosion of happiness brought a tear to Althea's eye. They all leapt to their feet and ran over, dive-hugging Mojave, who fell to the ground under the weight of five excited children. Althea grinned at the show of love. The kids regarded the teen more like a mother than a simple babysitter. Delighted cheers came from the kids as Mojave presented them each with a tunic. The stash of garments must have been taken from a more established settlement than a scrag tribe. Raiders had no use for children's garments, and hadn't stolen any. Thus, the kids all got adult-sized tunics, which fit them like robes. Thrilled at the gift, Kia changed out of her threadbare dress into the new tunic right away. On her as well as Toyo, the material draped a bit on the ground. Pri slipped entirely through the neck opening of her new tunic. She peered down at the fabric gathered around her feet, shrugged, then sat on it possessively.

"Wow," whispered Phoenix. "You'd think a trillionaire just showered random people with a couple million credits each."

David smiled. "A good, solid bit of clothing is worth much to these villagers. Especially at night when it gets chilly."

Phoenix approached Althea, relieved to see her. "I suppose it shouldn't surprise me you're okay."

"Lots of stuff can hurt me still, but I couldn't let them keep slaves anymore." Althea peered apologetically at Teal. "Sorry for running off so fast, but I had no time. They would have disappeared and been hard to find."

"Yeah. I understand. Bad situation." Teal ruffled her hair.

Althea smiled. "Be right back."

She marched across the open courtyard to the Credit Union building. Like a mother come to scold misbehaving children, she strode to the center of the giant room and stared at an empty office chair throne. Hands on her hips, she gazed around looking for her quarry. Durango stood near the left wall among a group of warriors. A handful of other villagers sat here and here, working at various sorting tasks with vegetables or possibly useful salvage. Sensing the weight of her presence in the room, everyone stopped to look at her.

"They told us you left." Durango's mood held surprise and relief. "I am happy to see the spirits have allowed you safe return."

She sighed. "Mojave did not leave. Raiders kidnapped

her. Camry and Onda did not lie. The hole is real. I walked out through it."

"We checked the wall, child." Durango smiled at her in the way adults tended to do whenever she said something cute but dumb.

*Grr.* She narrowed her eyes and telepathically projected her memory of the hole into his mind. "It was open."

His jaw dropped a half inch. Confusion spiraled into a frenetic storm of awe and fear, not of her but of how the spirits might be involved in making him see things.

*Not the spirits. Me. I'm psionic. Big city people call it Telepathy to do the mind talking. I am sharing my memory so you can see it, too.* She replayed the entire scene of Mojave being dragged off to the buggy in his mind.

"That is… unbelievable." Durango gazed into space.

Althea grumbled. It annoyed her when people said things they didn't mean. Durango used the word 'unbelievable' even though he believed her. He meant he'd never imagined it possible, and to now realize raiders had the ability to get into the village whenever they wanted scared him. A scrag would never say something using wrong words. It annoyed her how learning to read and getting some manner of education made people *more* confusing.

She pointed at the door. "I will show you the place."

"All right. Do so." Durango moved to follow her, waving for two warriors, one woman in USAF armor and a man in armor made from metal scraps and grey fabric, to join them.

Althea marched out of the 'castle,' bee-lining for the spot where the abduction happened. At seeing her go right past them, Teal, David, Phoenix, Mojave, and the children all scrambled to their feet and joined the procession. Not until she walked right up to the spot did she realize she hadn't really remembered where to go and simply stormed off in an irritated huff. Still, she managed to go to the right place. Perhaps her clairvoyance helped her find the spot, or maybe she did remember.

"Here." She approached the opening in the metal plates, pointing at it.

The massive concrete block once again stood up on end, filling the gap and making the wall impassable.

"You see?" Durango rested a hand on her shoulder. "The wall is not open. I know not how you saw it otherwise."

"Look outside." Althea fought the urge to sigh. "The dirt has a hole. You will be able to know the big stone was moved."

Teal's expression shifted to worry. Like a cat going over a fence, she leapt to the top of the twelve-foot-high wall and crouched on it. At watching her seem to fly, Durango and both warriors gasped, emanating reverent fear, likely wondering if one of their spirits had taken human form. She leaned forward, studying the ground on the outside of the wall, then glanced back at everyone. "Althea is right. The concrete block left an imprint where it fell over. It definitely *was* open, but isn't anymore."

The warriors exchanged a glance, their emotions mostly worry. Their thoughts held dread at why the spirits would open the wall. Althea didn't tell anyone the warriors wanted to blame spirits for this. It would exasperate Phoenix, make Teal roll her eyes, and probably cause David to laugh. To her, it made sense. Scrags didn't care to understand the *true* explanation for things if they had an easy, simple answer. Why hurt their heads thinking about difficult, complicated matters when 'the spirits did it' answered almost every question? Trying to explain the truth to them would likely fail, make no difference, and be a waste of time. Something physical—not spirits—manipulated the wall. However, if the tribe at least understood an outside force responsible, they understood enough to work with.

Teal jumped down.

"Great." Phoenix rubbed the bridge of her nose. "Now we have to worry about raiders, too?"

David patted Althea on the head. "Don't worry too much. Anything short of killer robots, she can pretty much make non-hostile."

"Not much chance of running into CRP bots down here." Teal frowned at the wall. "Just a doll."

David raised an eyebrow. "El Ojo?"

"Got another explanation for how this ended up closed?" Teal folded her arms. "I'm significantly stronger than an ordinary person, but I couldn't move a concrete block this size by myself. A class three doll can. Probably not dead lift and toss it, but they are definitely strong enough to pull it over and stand it back up on end."

"Think someone's hiding heavy equipment around here?" asked David in a joking tone.

"Yeah. Disguised as a person." Teal huffed. "Got a feeling he's going to be a serious pain in the ass."

Althea smiled. "Don't let him shoot you in the butt."

Phoenix gave off a sense of 'aww.' David and Teal stared at her, unsure if she said it on purpose to be funny or didn't understand. Althea made a goofy face to let them know she teased. While she had no idea why people associated hurts in their backside with a task being difficult, she *did* understand 'pain in the ass' not to mean literal pain.

The kids decided to zoom off, chasing each other in a game of tag. Pri gathered her too-big tunic up, clinging to it as she ran after her friends. Durango and the two warriors headed for the gate, intent on doing an 'inspection' of the entire wall outside, searching for any other evidence someone could make holes.

Mojave, filled with unease, looked around at everyone. "What will you do now?"

"Hey, kid," said Teal. "I noticed earlier when you told us about those little ones' parents being busy in the daytime, you said some of them 'collected' food. Do you mean working on a farm?"

"No." Mojave shook her head. "We don't have a farm anymore. It stopped growing years ago. The spirits make food for us and leave it in the sacred field for us to find, by the tombs of the spirit ancestors. Our people go every few days to collect food from the sacred monuments."

David, Teal, and Phoenix exchanged glances. Their mood turned suspicious and worried.

"Althea." David faced her. "We found a sort of clinic where the villagers have put the sickest people. Most lack the strength to even stand up. Before we do anything else, you should definitely help them."

"Yes." She stared at him, shocked he hadn't told her this as soon as she returned. Considering the emotions he gave off when she returned, his relief and happiness upon seeing her alive and unhurt must have distracted him. "Please, show me where."

"North end, near the wall. This way." David walked off.

Althea started to follow, but paused upon noticing Mojave not going with them.

"I must watch the children. Keep safe." She gestured at them. "The small ones should not go near the clinic."

"Yes," said Phoenix. "Those kids are healthy at the moment. They should stay away from sick people."

"If you see something strange or scary, run and find us." Althea bit her lip, worried the city people who threatened the spirit talker might want to hurt Mojave for having gone too far away from Afbee—assuming they knew about it. Of course, she'd returned, so maybe they wouldn't be angry with her. Ford *did* say the 'spirits' didn't care if people went outside the wall, becoming upset only if a person intended to leave Afbee for good.

"I will." Mojave hugged her. "Thank you."

Althea grinned, thrilled at having been able to stop the raiders from kidnapping her. For a young woman, the Badlands had only one worse fate: death. And some considered being taken by raiders even worse than death. Althea hated wifeing, but for her, death was worse. Wifeing, she could fix, both the body as well as the thinking shape—thanks to the city police teaching her about Telepathy. Horrible memories had become another form of hurt she could make go away if a person wanted. Thus far, she'd only made a volunteer forget something minor in a lab setting for practice and because the city police wanted to know if she could do it. Fixing a strong, awful memory like wifeing might take more practice than she yet had, but the odds of her fixing a rotten memory vastly beat her odds of fixing death.

She paused, nibbling on her lip. Technically, she had fixed even death *once*... but didn't expect she could do it again—unless the person who died happened to be emotionally close to her. She still couldn't explain how it happened, nor could the city police. It seemed as if her powers, or something else inside her, simply took over in a moment of extreme grief and guilt.

She exhaled long and slow, hoping never to feel so horrible ever again.

## 24

## ALMOST SPIRITS

The clinic occupied a large, rectangular building covered in pockmarked beige metal siding.

No obvious signs or labels adorned it, though the general shape of the structure reminded her of places where the ancients obtained their food in the Before-Time. Apparently, centuries ago, people also didn't have farms. They merely went to giant buildings full of food and traded pay things for it. There had to be something missing from the legends. Food did not simply appear out of thin air as the villagers of Afbee claimed it did. No one explained how the 'supermarkets' made the food.

Tattered blue plastic tarp hung like a curtain in a double-width door. Althea pushed it aside and stepped into a cloud of fetid air. She winced at the pungency, though had smelled worse. Over a dozen men and women occupied an assortment of cots, sleeping mats, and wheeled beds. Most appeared unconscious. Two breathed in loud gurgling rasps.

A late-thirties man wearing a robe-like garment resembling a large bed sheet wandered among the beds, periodically checking on the people in them. Pale skin suggested he spent all his time inside away from the sun. Curiously, despite being in a room of deathly ill people, he didn't seem to be sick.

"Doc's not going to be happy to see us," said David in a low voice. "Chased us out before. I had to calm him down."

"Doc," muttered Phoenix. "Do you *have* to call him that? He doesn't even know what a thermometer is."

Teal smirked. "Don't take it personally. It's probably his name more than title. Out here, anyone who figures out which plants not to eat because they kill you is considered a doctor."

Phoenix sighed.

Althea clenched her hands into fists. "He's not gonna stop us from helping."

Doc whirled at the sound of her voice. A brief mood of 'oh no, not another one' evaporated to confusion at the sight of Althea, then fear and anger when he noticed David and the others. He rushed toward them, waving both hands in a shooing motion. "You should not be here!"

She locked stares, forcing his emotional state back to calm. "I'm going to help people."

He paused, lowering his arms, and stood there for a moment merely looking at them. Confusion deepened… then tried unsuccessfully to shift back to fear once he processed the realization her eyes glowed bright blue.

Althea walked past him to the nearest bedridden person.

Doc caught her by the shoulder in a relatively gentle grip. "Durango says you should not interfere."

"Durango is wrong." She faced him. "He is not wrong on purpose, but he is wrong."

"I must do what he and the spirits want." Doc twitched in response to his unnatural lack of fear.

Althea peered into his thoughts. He knew nothing of

any modern people here, only the stories of spirits making people sick as punishment for some unknown crime. He believed allowing outsiders like her to interfere would enrage the spirits and cause more deaths. She reached up, grasped his hand at her shoulder, and plucked it loose. "I do not want to be mean, but I will not let you stop me from helping people."

"You mustn't anger the spirits." Doc reached for her again.

"*Sit down*," said Althea in a stern tone. Her eye-glow intensified in time with the psionic suggestion, tinting half the room azure for an instant.

Doc dropped in place.

"Crap, she's a suggestive, too?" whispered Phoenix.

Althea approached the nearest sick person, a woman about Father's age.

"Yes, though it's one of her lower ratings," said David.

"*That's* a low rating?" Phoenix gestured at Doc. "People whose *only* ability is Suggestion do it and the guy would've wandered off to find a chair or something, not just drop instantly where he stood."

"Awakened," whispered David. "She's on another level."

Phoenix shifted her gaze sideways. "Is that why they keep her out here?"

"No." David smiled. "She wants to be here."

Althea rested her hands on the first sick villager's arm, the skin hot, bumpy, and crusty. The woman appeared quite ill with a fever of some form and tiny raised dots all over her. Unlike the welts on Kia, these didn't look fluid filled, hadn't turned red, and were vastly more numerous. The woman muttered nonsense, lost to delirium. Althea glanced from her to another eleven people, all quite sick, and gave a resigned sigh, knowing the next few hours would be a lot of work.

An odd sense of 'aww' came from Phoenix, making Althea look into her head. The woman thought her 'ugh, here we go' attitude made her look like a 'tiny ER doctor about to start a long, crazy shift'—whatever that meant. Still, she didn't really object to being perceived as cute, so refocused her attention on the woman in front of her.

"Get buckets and the fire gun," said Althea. "There will be lots of slime."

"I'll watch the 'door'," said Teal. "And make sure Doc doesn't make a nuisance of himself."

David rummaged a pair of metal buckets from a shelf in the back corner while Phoenix checked her flame pistol. Althea closed her eyes and got started.

One by one, she went from bed to bed purging sicks. Everyone lay in varying degrees of mess, their clothing— mostly the grey tunics, pants, or body wraps—saturated in sweat, discharge from skin sores, vomit, and urine.

Phoenix grumbled angrily, pulled a knife, and started slicing the disgusting garments off each person while Althea worked on them. "I can't even find the right words to express how I feel about Doc leaving them to 'baste' in sickness."

"Scrags. They place much value on usable things, especially clothing," said David. "And they don't understand germs. A shirt covered in vomit and pus is still a shirt to them."

"Ugh." Phoenix shuddered while peeling grey linen away from a man's chest as if it had been glued there.

"I've never seen a doctor have such a reaction to body fluids before." David chuckled.

"I'm not disgusted by the fluids." Phoenix tossed a bit of fabric into the burn bucket. "I'm disgusted at the idea these people would willingly put such a contaminated garment back on."

David shot his flame pistol into the bucket containing the collected sicks plus a few pieces of crusty disease-ridden clothing.

Doc remained seated on the floor near the entrance where he planted himself, likely by choice. A suggestive command, even one from Althea, only held a person's mind for a few minutes. The sight of deathly ill people rapidly improving to full health as well as David and Phoenix 'magically' producing flames out of nowhere left him too stunned and awed to do anything more than watch.

Althea moved to the next patient. Open sores all over the woman's body leaked dark brownish-black fluid. The mess had been soaking into her dress for days, hardening the fabric into the texture of a giant scab.

Shaking her head in disbelief at the conditions, Phoenix started working to separate the mess from the woman wearing it. "Sergeant, will you and Doc please set up some kind of cleaning station out back? These people are literally covered in virus and filth. Everyone needs to be washed off before we let them leave. Maybe see if Mojave will share some fresh clothing. Everything in this building not made of metal or concrete needs to be incinerated."

"On it." David waved for Doc to follow and went outside.

With so many people suffering, Althea left the task of explaining to each person about having to pee or vomit out the sicks to Phoenix. The woman had city medicine capable of reducing the unnatural pain of eliminating toxic fluids, freeing Althea to move on to the next sick person without having to hold people's hands to keep them numb while they added to the bucket. Each time she came out of her healing trance, the malaise of disease smell and sweaty people in the air worsened slightly from the fumes of burning the nasty stuff and tainted fabric.

As each person awoke from their sickness-induced delirium, Phoenix explained briefly about the idea of germs, filthy clothing, and biological residue still all over their skin —sending them outside to clean off. Being relatively primitive, the villagers responded well to her fear-based tactic of 'if you don't wash yourself, you will get sick again and possibly die.'

In addition to the expected sicks, Althea mended a few improperly healed broken bones, removed some embedded debris from one man's leg, and fixed a number of relatively minor cuts. When she rested her hand on the ninth person, a man younger than Father, she cringed at the coldness of his skin. It didn't take her long to realize he'd already died: no thoughts existed in his thinking shape, and she couldn't establish a psionic link to his body. Since she hadn't felt the icy scrape of a 'knife' across her heart, the man hadn't died while she'd been near. The 'hospital' smelled so foul, he most likely became a ghost days ago and no one noticed the rot.

"He is already dead," said Althea in a somber tone.

Phoenix glared at the back wall and shouted, "Doc!"

A moment later, the man appeared in the doorway, slightly winded from having sprinted around the building. "I am here. We are putting water on the sick as you instructed."

She glared at him, pointing at the corpse. "You kept a dead man next to other patients? How could you possibly not notice he died?"

"Dodge has been like that for a week," said Doc. "Look dead but not."

"Oh, he's quite dead." Phoenix frowned.

Doc approached, poked Dodge's body, and cringed. "Oh. It seems you are correct. He does not look *much* worse than he did last week. I did not notice."

Anger, disgust, and disbelief fell off Phoenix in waves. After a moment, she pushed her emotions aside and pointed to the door. "Please go help the people clean up. They will get sick again if you leave them covered in filth."

He nodded, then hurried out.

Althea moved on to the second-to-last person, a younger woman about the same age as Corinne, early twenties. She appeared to be little more than a skeleton sealed inside a skin bag. Dried white stuff smeared her chin and ran down her neck. A still-slimy puddle of it sat on her chest, thoroughly soaked into her tunic. A stink like cheese left to sit in the sun for a week clung to her.

"Phoenix?" Althea lifted the tunic, biting her lip at the woman's prominent ribs.

"Yes?" She looked up from cutting the woman's tunic.

"She does not have enough food. Can you give her the magic food?"

Phoenix removed a small canister from her medical kit. "Intravenous nutrition doesn't work immediately. It takes a few hours at least."

"She needs it now. I will make her body eat it. Please give all at once."

"This goes against all of my training." Phoenix examined the canister. "But medical school never mentioned anything about someone like you."

Althea smiled.

"This will take a moment." Phoenix rummaged around in her medical kit. "This unit is only designed for timed dosage. I'll need to transfer the fluid to a standard injector." She exhaled. "You are sure you can prevent such a massive influx of nutrient fluid from causing other problems?"

Althea nodded.

David stuck his head in a small window on the back wall. "I saw a man lose fifteen pounds in a matter of two minutes. Body fat appeared to dissolve fast enough to see him shrink. He'd been shot five times. His body consumed energy reserves needed to regenerate under her power. It should be fine."

Phoenix whistled. "Yeah, no wonder command wants to keep her away from the city. Pharma corps would lose their minds if they found out about her."

Althea dove into the woman's life essence. Black spots dotted most of her inside shapes, areas where they already started to die. The big beans had rotted the most, being pretty much entirely dead and leaking nasty sick into the body. Dr. Ruiz referred to those shapes as kidneys. Not enough of them remained to fix, so she decided it better to remove the dangerous muck they'd turned into and grow new ones. Urgency imparted a shake to Althea's hands. This woman had to be less than an hour away from death. She commanded the woman's body to split open so she could reach in and pull out the mostly-dead kidneys.

Somewhere in the back of her awareness, Doc let out a startled scream.

Phoenix, standing right next to her, muttered, "Oh, that's not good."

Althea plunged her hands into the woman's gut, fishing around the gloopy stuff until she found the way-too-soft bean underneath. In the midst of her commanding healthy parts to separate from the dying kidney, she sensed a fluid flooding into the blood shape via the right arm. Assuming it to be the nutrients, she shifted some attention to speeding up the woman's ability to absorb the liquid food.

*I'm giving her extra nutrient,* said Phoenix via telepathy. *I have no idea how this patient isn't dead. David tells me you can regrow organs, but it consumes energy she doesn't have.*

She managed a nod despite concentrating on juggling food absorption, stopping blood from going everywhere as the old kidney came loose, and pulling the rotting lumps out. Althea didn't open her eyes, rather tossing the destroyed kidneys somewhat randomly backward over her shoulder. The woman's form gradually filled out over the next ten minutes, 'inflating' from emaciated thin to simply thin. Making the body regrow two kidneys took more effort than cleaning fifty people of sicks. However, compared to being forced to heal a whole raider camp after a fight, didn't feel like a burdensome exertion.

Finally, Althea collected the haze of a nasty yellow sick similar to the one Kellis had into the woman's bladder, adding it to the other sicks and poisons from the dead inside shapes. Releasing it would burn too much for Althea to trust the city meds to stop the pain so she decided to stay with her until after the fetid dark green slime stopped coming out. She opened her eyes to find the woman stirring from her delirious sleep. Dark stains covered her body, left behind where her dress had once been adhered to her skin.

The young woman looked around for a moment before sitting up, showing little reaction to nudity other than the disappointment of losing a precious object. As soon as she glanced down at herself, she radiated bewildered happiness, likely for no longer appearing starved. It didn't take long before the burning, urgent need to release the sick made her gasp and squirm.

"You must make water." Althea helped the woman up from the sleeping pad and guided her over to the metal bucket. "It will hurt if I do not stop the pain."

Still somewhat delirious, the woman proceeded to use the bucket without question, indifferent to other people being near.

"When you finish, please go outside behind the building to get cleaned up," said Phoenix.

"Yes." Althea added a nudge of positive emotion. "Your

body is covered in bad stuff that will make you sick all over again."

Phoenix cringed at the rancid stink rising from the bucket. "I have never in my life seen urine with the consistency of syrup."

The formerly sick woman gagged as well. "Is it like this because I have not made water in days? I do not know how I angered the spirits."

"Spirits didn't hurt you. You had a sick." Althea pointed at the mess. "It's gone now."

She groaned, then looked up. Her mostly blank, disoriented mood exploded to awestruck delight. "The Prophet…"

"Yes." Althea tried not to sound annoyed. "Please, call me Althea."

"I… expected someone older. You are still a child." The woman squeezed her hand. "I am Tundra."

Phoenix made an odd face at the name. "The girl Mojave discovered new, clean garments. Doc and an associate of mine are waiting to help you wash up outside, right behind this building."

"Thank you." Tundra bowed, but just stood there staring into nowhere with a weird little smile.

"What is wrong?" asked Althea.

Tundra took a deep breath. "I don't remember what it feels like not to hurt all over. Am I dreaming?"

"No." Althea shuddered at the idea of being in so much pain for a long time. "You do not dream."

Tundra idly brushed a hand up and down over her stomach, mystified at not being in agony. After a moment, she bowed again and walked out of the 'hospital.'

Phoenix went to rub the bridge of her nose, but stopped herself. "Need to wash my hands."

"One more." Althea approached the bed of the last sick

person, a fiftyish man who outwardly appeared to have the same sick Kellis did.

The man suffered no other strange problems, making for a reasonably fast process. Phoenix peeled him out of his diseased tunic and pants while Althea dove into the healing trance. Once he awoke and drained the foul sick into the bucket, they sent him outside.

"Go on out back and get cleaned up, Althea. I'll be there as soon as I burn the last of the mess. Too dangerous to move the poor dead guy. May as well cremate him right here." Phoenix gingerly picked up the contaminated pail to carry it outside.

Althea jogged around behind the hospital to the cleaning area. The dirt had become muddy and crisscrossed in footprints from the nine previous people to endure the process of being rinsed off. Teal stood at the edge of the 'yard' like a sentry while David and Doc sprayed water from genesis canteens on Tundra as she washed herself. Once she looked clean, they switched to hosing off the last man, rinsing multiple darkish red patches of dried mess from his back and chest. Tundra smiled again at Althea after David handed her a tunic from the trunk—which had migrated here from Mojave's home.

While spraying down the last patient, Doc told the man how he might still have germs on him and could become sick again if they didn't use water to take the germs away. Evidently, he'd learned the basics of hygiene over the past few hours. Althea approached David and held her arms out for a rinse. He obligingly sprayed her until all the blood and grime fell to the ground. The genesis canteens didn't exactly produce much water pressure, but it proved effective enough in the circumstance. The devices could produce water somehow from the air, so a trickle proved a small price to pay for carrying fifty or so gallons in a small bottle. They only 'ran out' of water when their batteries died.

Phoenix came around the corner of the building and walked over to them, wiping her hands on a tiny white cloth far too clean to have been from Afbee. The scrap smelled like ethanol. "I've disinfected the hospital."

"Already?" David blinked. "How? Even if you could move as fast as a synthetic, it would take hours. Did we even bring enough equipment to clean it properly?"

"We did," deadpanned Phoenix. "But my flame pistol's nearly out of gel."

Althea and David twisted to look at the 'hospital.' Black smoke rose from the windows, occasionally billowing aside to reveal the bright orange glow of fire.

"Ahh..." said David. "No warning, I guess?"

Phoenix shook her head. "Nothing inside that building could have been saved without risk of contamination. The structure itself should be fine. Concrete doesn't burn. All the bedding, fabric, wood, anything porous was a hazard. Hell, the damn *air* in there had to be deadly. I hate having to do it, but Dodge's remains represented a danger to the village."

"Fire!" yelled Doc.

"Do not worry." David caught the man by the arm as he started to run off. "It is on purpose. To kill the germs."

"But..." Doc gestured at the building. "Everything..."

"Was contaminated." Phoenix tossed the little hand-washing cloth into the burn bucket. "Taking two breaths of air inside could've killed someone. It's astonishing you aren't infected, having spent so much time in there."

*He probably has a sick, too.*

Althea shook water from her hands and grasped Doc's arm. He jumped at her touch, but did nothing more than give her a bewildered look. She linked to his life essence, expecting to find a sick lurking inside him... but surprisingly didn't. However, he *did* have a strange black hollow area nestled under the place where a fat blood tube touched the liver. Thin parts of it went into the blood tube, but didn't cause any leaks. It reminded her of the machine bits some city people deliberately put inside their bodies.

She exited the healing trance mildly confused. Before she could ask Phoenix about it, Teal hurried over to them, giving off an air of imminent danger.

"We have a problem," whispered Teal.

David and Phoenix became nervous.

"Is this a fire and screaming type of problem?" asked David.

"Possibly." Teal ushered them closer to the building despite it presently burning. "There's an old utility pole about twenty-two feet away from where I was standing."

"So?" Phoenix waved around randomly. "This is a ruin. Those poles are all over the place. The villagers use them to string water lines. Afbee is practically in a constant state of rain due to all the leaky hoses overhead."

"Wish we had a leaky one near the hospital." David fidgeted at the canteen on his belt. "Our water supply took a hell of a hit with the showering."

"The local water could be dangerous," whispered Phoenix. "Showering under a leaking hose might have exposed them to different pathogens."

Teal leaned closer, lowering her voice. "I didn't notice before as I hadn't been paying too much attention to the junk, but... there is a surveillance camera tucked into the debris up on the pole, and it's definitely not from the former Air Force base. Doesn't it seem strange someone is planting current tech cameras around here?"

"Not the first time." David frowned. "ComTec has done

it before. They sent camera bots out to some villages and broadcast their daily life as entertainment."

Phoenix grumbled. "Any way to tell if it's that?"

"Well, yeah." Teal shrugged. "I could climb up there and rip it down, see if it has any branding on it. But... whoever is watching on the other end will know they've been discovered."

"I'm thinking the 'spirits' are a bit more corporeal than not," said David.

Althea raised her hand.

Everyone looked at her.

"You aren't in school now, kiddo." Teal winked. "If you have something to say, just say it."

She pointed at Doc. "He has a machine inside him. No sicks."

"A machine?" Phoenix looked at the man.

"Uhh." Doc blinked, throwing off gobs of confusion. "Something is inside me?"

"Some city people have little metal machines in them." Althea held her fingers up about an inch apart. "They don't want me to clean them out."

"I believe she means cyberware." David raised an eyebrow at Doc. "Are you from West City?"

Doc shook his head. "I have been in Afbee my whole life."

"Where is it?" asked Phoenix while pulling a handheld device the size of a bar of soap from her utility belt.

"Under the, umm..." Althea tried to remember the 'correct' word for the big shape. "Liver."

Phoenix moved the device close to Doc's belly.

He jumped back as though she tried to stab him.

"Easy." Phoenix held the silver box up so he could see it. "This is only a scanner. You won't feel anything. It's not going to touch you."

Doc stared at her, shivering in fear. Althea calmed him.

Phoenix again held the device close to him. A holographic screen appeared above it, turning the man's apprehension into curiosity. A few seconds later, it chirped and a picture of a silver and black device appeared on the screen in the exact shape of the silhouette Althea saw inside him.

"NFT-111," said Phoenix, reading from the screen. "NinTek manufactured blood filter."

"Handy." David chuckled. "But where the heck did he get one of those?"

"Good question." Teal pointed a thumb back over her shoulder. "I bet the camera people probably know."

"Umm." Althea fake smiled. "Sorry for being stupid. I don't understand. The tiny machine doesn't have hands."

"What?" Teal blinked.

"He said it is handy." Althea scrunched her nose.

Teal laughed, as did David.

Phoenix patted her shoulder. "It's okay. You wouldn't know what cyberware is. Don't feel stupid. Doc here has an implant that helps his body take bad things out of his blood. Poison, disease, toxic metals, even cholesterol. They're not foolproof, but it definitely helps explain how he didn't end up on a bed next to everyone else in there."

"You are saying this giant device is inside..." Doc pointed at his stomach. "Me?"

Phoenix radiated emotion like she wanted to burst into laughter but remained outwardly calm. "It isn't as big as it looks on this screen. The picture is zoomed in so we can see it. It's really about an inch long. Doesn't take up much space. However, yes, this is inside you, spliced into the hepatic artery. It processes your blood before it gets to the liver."

Doc's bafflement intensified.

"Smaller words," said David, pretending to whisper past the back of his hand. "Use smaller words."

"Right." Phoenix smiled at Doc. "It is helping you. Nothing to be scared of."

"Okay. I will trust you." Doc rubbed his stomach. "What do I do now?"

"Wait for the fire to go out, then clean. Put in new stuff," said David.

"We need to talk in private," whispered Teal. "Soon."

Althea sighed, flailing her arms. "I have to help everyone. Most of the villagers still have sicks!"

"I know." Teal put an arm around her. "We will help them, but we have to do something else first."

An audible growl came from Althea's stomach.

"Perhaps we should eat." Phoenix looked up at the sky. "It will be dark soon."

## 25

## NERD WORD

The sun weakened in the sky, deepening the shadows in the spaces between buildings and rubble mounds.

Althea walked with her friends from the clinic to the village center, following the scent of grilling meat. This part of the day, an hour before sunset, always appeared darkest to her. Once the sun finally vanished, it would stop confusing her eyes and the world brightened, though became grey. At night, or in absolute darkness, she lost only the ability to differentiate colors. As a *little* kid, she used to think her eyes acted like magic lights, but according to the city police, the glow didn't physically allow her to see in the same way their 'flashlight' things did. Technically a light source, her eyes *could* illuminate a small area for someone else. However, the glow didn't let her see. It came as a side effect of the psionic energy that did. David explained it as a minor use of the same psionic power responsible for her ability to see ghosts. Not having the power himself, he didn't really understand how it worked and could only share the information about it in their computers. The psionic police could not, however, explain why the power had become 'stuck' on for her. Even if she wanted to, she couldn't stop seeing in the dark. According to them, other people with the same ability had to turn it on and *could* turn it off.

She didn't remember ever being afraid of the dark and demanding to see, nor a time when she couldn't see at night. When she looked into the memory of the old man in Querq who helped her mother hide her, she'd seen herself as a tiny infant with glowing eyes. The obviously unnatural light proved to be the very reason her mother *had* to flee in order to keep her safe. Certainly, a weeks-old baby couldn't deliberately activate a psionic power. Althea didn't really care why her body did things the way it did. The city police wanted to know, but couldn't figure it out.

Her excursion to a raider camp, however necessary, took almost two hours out of the day. Regardless of what happened now, Althea, David, Phoenix, and Teal would be spending the night in Afbee, something they hadn't wanted to do but planned for anyway by bringing enough known-clean food and water to last a week.

The villagers gathered in front of the Credit Union building for a communal meal, exactly as Althea assumed they did. Two men and one woman worked a massive grill, roasting vegetables as well as unidentified meat, likely rat, bonedog, or dust hopper. Due to the presence of so much disease here, no one in Althea's group felt the least bit tempted to sample the food. Their meal consisted of chocolate-flavored ration bars and water.

Despite one being a full meal, Althea ate two bars to compensate for the energy her healing abilities consumed. Getting rid of sicks hadn't been too bad, but regenerating Tundra's kidneys proved draining and left her famished. It didn't take her long to finish her relatively small meal.

Somehow, the city people made little slabs of sweet stuff that contained as much 'food' as an entire meal. She frowned at the empty plastic peel they came in.

*City people don't want to spend time living. Fast, fast, fast. They don't have the patient. Cooking real food or even eating real food takes too much time for them. Bleh. Tiny little loaf. Three bites. Stupid.* She sighed to herself. For something like a long trip, 'tiny food' wrapped in plastic made sense. Less to carry and protected from dirt. Still, the city people sometimes ate this stuff when they didn't have to, purely because it took little time out of their life.

After she ate, she checked David and Phoenix for sicks. Both had again developed the same one Kellis had, though far weaker. Whatever boosted immunity she gave people after removing a sick appeared to be working. Still, to be safe, she purged it, alerting them to go make water somewhere and burn it. Such a mild sick wouldn't hurt much. Not enough for her to insist on taking away pain. City people became highly embarrassed at the idea of making water while someone else, especially Althea, stood close—or worse: touched their arm.

Phoenix, surprisingly, asked Teal to go with her, afraid to go off alone. She also became rather upset at herself—though hid it—for leaving the fancy 'protective gear' back in their buggy. It made her feel stupid and careless. The woman didn't understand all the risks of exposure to the virus and had some difficulty believing Althea could fix everything, especially bad stuff she might experience years from now. This led to a persistent feeling of dread over what she'd done to herself.

When they returned from letting the sick out, they sat there watching the villagers eat.

"Most of them are already re-infected," muttered

Phoenix. "They all gather in one big group twice every day. It's astonishing only twelve ended up critically ill."

"This village used to have something like 500 people." David sighed. "They're a hair over 200 now. The dozen we found in the clinic are only the ones who hadn't died *yet*."

"Look at the size of this town. I mean, inside the wall… not the city from before the war." Teal gave a resigned sigh. "Used to be a lot more than 500 living here. By my guess, a couple thousand."

Phoenix grabbed her head in both hands, throwing off gobs of frustration. "And, like I said, they're all sick again. Althea's playing whack-a-rat. She cures someone and they're sick again in hours."

"Or days. Maybe weeks." David took a long swig of water from his canteen. "Remember how Accelerated Healing excites an immune response."

Althea smiled. "People are excited when the sick goes away."

"Sergeant," said Phoenix in a somewhat weary tone, "People with Accelerated Healing generally don't get sick. Their bodies self-purge before any infection sets in and continues doing so. The villagers don't have this power. Their bodies temporarily behave as if they do because of her. Althea is the only documented case of anyone ever being able to use Accelerated Healing on another person. Yes, I am aware the study showed a lingering temporary immunity to specific pathogens comparable to vaccination, but we shouldn't rely on it. The sample size is too small, we don't understand anywhere near enough about how her powers work, and we understand even less about the custom viruses set loose here."

"She sounds angry but she isn't," said Althea. "She's tired and worried."

Phoenix raked a hand through her hair. "I'm still not

happy at being talked into leaving the clean suits behind."

"The villagers would have considered you a space alien or something and tried to stab you." Teal chuckled.

"What was it you wanted to talk about?" asked Phoenix.

Teal glanced at the villagers. "Rather discuss it away from ears and digital eyes."

"Might as well go now." David stood.

Everyone else got up.

Teal walked off at a speed Althea nearly had to jog to keep up with. They crossed Afbee to the gate, went outside the wall, and continued into the ruins for a few hundred meters before ducking into a narrow alley between the remains of former tall buildings. Based on the amount of rubble in the area, the structures probably hadn't been much taller than five or six stories.

Teal paused to study their surroundings, then faced everyone. "All right. I don't think we're being watched here."

"We need to come up with a better plan." David set his hands on his hips. "It's almost futile for Althea to cure anyone here, since this disease is so contagious it'll continue re-infecting. We need to do it smart. Set up a known-clean area as well as a transition area where she can work, then migrate people through a process. The places they are living now will need to be thoroughly decontaminated. Honestly, this village ought to be burned. Or at least abandoned for as long as it takes the pathogens to die off."

"I don't want path-a-gems to die." Althea looked down. "Do they have to?"

"Aww." Phoenix hugged her.

Teal chuckled. "Kiddo, pathogen is only a nerd word for virus. Same thing as burning the slime you make people barf out."

Althea blushed. "Oops."

Phoenix raised a hand. "Hang on. The 'Kellis virus' is one issue, but we aren't just dealing with one pathogen. Most of the villagers have it, but are presenting as fairly mild cases."

"Except for the 300 or so who died before we got here." David glared at nothing in particular, angry and sad in equal parts. "It might only be mild for the first few days, weeks or months."

"Yes, that may be true." Phoenix activated her armband holo-display and took a moment to read it. "Bear in mind, we don't know what killed them. There are multiple disease vectors loose here. Our data modeling of the Kellis virus shows the majority of people exposed are likely to experience roughly five days post-infection relatively symptom free, then suffer a rapid decline. I don't believe this virus will cause death by itself. It leaves the victim in an exhausted, delirious, weakened state for an undetermined amount of time. Considering contagion and re-infection rates, perhaps even indefinitely. In my opinion, it's absolutely a bio-engineered weapon designed to incapacitate an enemy force. Someone sick with only this virus might die due to not having the ability or desire to feed and take care of themselves, but the virus itself won't cause organ failure and death without the person suffering a complicating factor from another disease or condition. It's meant to transform an army into a massive burden."

"Insidious," muttered David.

"Quite." Phoenix exhaled hard. "The good news is we have about a five-day window for Althea to clean us up before we feel different. However, in addition to what I'll call the K virus for now, after Kellis, I've documented at least nine different illnesses among the people here including smallpox, yellow fever, weaponized influenza, leukemia, and a few that don't exist in any of my records. The four-year-old, Pri, suffered from something like mononucleosis. The poor thing had the energy level of a sponge as well as symptoms similar to narcolepsy. Mojave had a similar illness. Kia—red dot girl—and Rogue, a seventeen-year-old male, contracted a genetically modified form of chicken pox much more dangerous than it used to be. Concurrent infection with K virus also may have played a role in worsening their symptoms.

"Those pustules were extremely painful and would have made ordinary activities like trying to sit or lie down sheer torture. It's the exact sort of extremely debilitating condition perfect for a sadistic bio weapon to destroy the effectiveness of a fighting force. I'm certain these villagers have been exposed to a store of bio agents from three centuries ago. None of these diseases exist in the modern world. We need to find and destroy the source, or this whole problem will come right back."

"Wouldn't they know about it?" asked David. "Old weapons ought to be pretty obvious. Althea mentioned they have a library in the basement of Durango's building. I'm guessing there are plenty of technical manuals from the old Air Force. They might even recognize air-dropped weapons. We're not dealing with normal scrags who look at technology like magic."

Phoenix scratched behind her right ear. "Maybe some kids crawled into a hole somewhere, got into the old base and broke something open?"

"Possible." David pursed his lips.

"I don't think the kids set up the cameras." Teal scowled off to the side. "Someone made these people sick on purpose."

Althea clutched her hands to her chest, gasping in horror at the idea anyone could do something so awful.

# THE RAT OF DEATH

A gunshot exploded mere feet in front of Althea.

The shock of the loud noise and a wave of heat from a brief flash of blue flame washed over her face. Dirt and rock bits sprayed her feet from behind before she realized Teal had drawn her weapon and fired, seemingly at her. David and Phoenix both shouted, jumping back. He instinctively drew his E-90, aiming at Teal. Phoenix froze where she stood, her emotions too scattered to do anything more than stare.

"Easy." Teal lowered her weapon. "Look behind her."

David glanced to his left. In the span of two seconds, his mood went from defensive to relieved, to confused, to worried. He put the E-90 back in its holster and exhaled hard. "What the hell?"

Althea turned. Mere inches from where her foot had been, a rat head lay on the ground beside a large splatter of white goop and gore. Initially, it appeared to be an exploded rodent somehow surviving despite having milk for blood. However, she hadn't felt any sense of death when Teal shot it. Once the initial shock of a gun going off in her face faded, she crouched to take a closer look. Instead of guts, she discovered a mess of plastic tubes and rubbery grey muscles attached to metal bones, all wrapped in extremely lifelike fur and skin.

"Holy shit." Phoenix pressed a hand to her chest. "What just happened? Are you going nuts?"

Teal sighed. "Why do so many people expect synthetics to snap and start killing people? We aren't any more prone to psychosis than humans."

"What made you randomly play splat-a-rat?" asked David.

"Not random and I'm not going crazy." Teal crouched, pinched the rat head behind the ears, and lifted it in a two-fingered grip. She squeezed, causing a metal needle to extend out from the rat's mouth. "Normal rats do not have hypodermic injectors instead of tongues. It was about to stab her in the ankle. It's like me. Synthetic. A machine."

"Eep." Althea backed up, scanning the area for more rats. For the first time in her life, she kinda wanted shoes, but not merely shoes... big thick boots—with metal on the sides.

"It's not like you," said David in a comforting tone. "The rat was merely a tool, a weapon."

Teal flashed a wry smile. "I've been called both of those things before. Trying to change, though. Started a two-step program."

"Two step program?" David blinked.

"Yeah. Step one: make the mistake of trying to kidnap Althea. Swear, that kid could melt the heart of a CRP robot if she spent enough time talking to it. Step two: piss off most of the underworld of West City by reneging on a contract job. It's not so bad, really. Quiet out here. Peaceful. Haven't had an advert-bot try to crawl up my nose in a whole month."

Phoenix chuckled. "Ugh. I hate those stupid things. I swear, forget to do laundry once and grumble out loud about having no clean underwear, there's a damn bot at my window trying to sell me new panties."

Teal laughed for a second before shifting serious. "It's on, by the way."

"What's on?" asked Phoenix.

"The proverbial *it*. As in, it's on now. Someone has decided we are a problem. Going to guess this little guy is full of poison." Teal held the rat out to Phoenix. "There's a capsule connected to the hypo. Want to test the contents?"

Phoenix gingerly took the dead synthetic rat head and the 'guts' dangling from it, sat on a hunk of concrete rubble big enough to serve as a chair, and got to work using another device from her belt.

"City people," said Althea. "I saw them in the spirit talker's head."

All three adults stared at her in varying degrees of bewilderment.

"A man calls himself a spirit talker, but he isn't one. He lied." Althea held a finger up. "But he did it to stop people from being hurt." She explained her meeting with the old man and how she'd seen a memory of modern people threatening to kill anyone who tried to leave.

"Dammit." David scowled to the side. "So someone *is* turning Afbee into an event. Make people sick for entertainment. See what happens."

"Not necessarily," said Phoenix in a slow voice while concentrating on her work. "Could be testing. Corporations routinely set up illegal operations out here. I've been thinking all along we're encountering leftover bio weapons from the war, but it could be a corporation doing research. Honestly, it was somewhat foolish of me to think 350-year-old pathogens might still be viable. I forgot they hadn't really perfected cryonic storage so far back. I suppose it's *possible* something could have survived, but extremely unlikely in these conditions. Maybe if the facility remained intact and somehow continued to run on solar power…"

Teal drummed her fingers on her sidearm. "Someone's watching this whole village. Want to bet the reason their supposed 'spirits' won't let anyone leave is because the people doing this are trying to keep any of these diseases from getting out into the world?"

Phoenix groaned. "That makes too much sense. Dammit."

"Are you thinking what I'm thinking?" asked David.

"I dunno." Teal shrugged. "You're the psionic."

He grinned. "We got word back from West City. The samples Dr. Ruiz gave us for testing didn't match any known disease or even viral structure. It's entirely new. Never seen before. Based on everything going on here, I'm inclined to agree with Captain Hanson that this village is being used as a testing range by a corporation. Could be one of ours, could be ACC up from Mexico."

Teal scanned the ground. "Either the rat's an assassin because they think kiddo's a threat, or… maybe this whole town is crawling with synthetic rats and it's how they infect new test subjects."

"Oh!" Althea snarled. "Meanies!"

"Quite." Teal nodded.

"No." She stomped. "Kia. And Pri. They both had little hurts." Althea lifted her foot up and tapped herself on the ankle. "Like needle stabs. The rats made them sick."

David gave off a burst of anger. "Not exactly. The rats aren't thinking. They're remote control syringes. A person used the rat to make the kids sick on purpose."

Althea snarled. "Bad."

"She is adorable, but damn terrifying when angry." Teal

whistled. "Watched her reduce a whole camp of raiders from crazed barbarians to terrified children."

"Better than slaughtering them," said David.

"Yes." Althea nodded at him. "I have a confuse."

David snickered. "What?"

"What is test subject?"

"Ugh," grumbled Teal. "Corporations."

David rubbed his face while a wave of frustration, sadness, anger, and general disgust fell off him. "People from the city, or other parts of the modern world close by, sometimes come out here to the Badlands to do things they can't do back home because the law won't let them."

Teal laughed.

He glanced over at her. "This is funny?"

"No. Just…" She held up a 'wait' hand until the giggles subsided. "When in the history of anything has the law managed to stop a corporation from doing whatever it wanted? They don't care about the law. The only reason they come out here to do shit is when the set-up cost of a project is cheaper than the bribes they'd need to pay to keep the police looking the other way, or to keep the operation hidden."

"You are cynical." David looked back to Althea.

"The difference between cynicism and reality is a pretty thin margin sometimes." Teal folded her arms. "If I was truly cynical, I'd still think this little girl almost got herself killed to save the life of the woman who tried to kidnap her only because she wanted something from me. But she didn't want a damn thing. Poor kid just couldn't walk away and let me die." Teal let her arms fall at her sides, gazing off at the horizon. "She's better off out here. The city would eat her alive. There's no room for genuinely selfless people there."

"That's still cynical," whispered David.

"Please stop having sads," said Althea. "You are my friend."

"Thanks, kid. Maybe someday, I'll stop feeling like a bitch."

David glanced at Teal. "You are likely our best chance at finding them. There has to be something close by. A relay station if not a full facility hidden somewhere."

Teal glanced toward the village wall. "I'll do what I can. They know we're aware of something."

"Not an assassin," said Phoenix. "The rat contains a potent chemical tranquilizer. Someone wanted to grab her."

"Not again." Althea rolled her eyes. "I hate trank-a-mizers."

David squeezed her shoulder. "We won't let them grab you. To answer your question, a test subject is a person or animal exposed to a thing to see what effect it has. The thing could be a disease, medicine, new product, whatever. Usually, test subjects volunteer and are paid. But out here? They just treat people like rats, do it without them even knowing."

"Grr." Althea scowled. "We have to find them and stop this. It's evil!"

Teal snapped her fingers. "Shit. Might explain why 'the spirits' take people. They're being kidnapped and moved to the city—or wherever these people are hiding—for additional testing, or dissection."

Althea stared down at her feet, overcome by sorrow. "That's *more* evil."

# GINGER ALE

Teal lunged and grabbed Althea, dragging her off her feet.

Despite being not being *too* much smaller than the woman carrying her, she dangled like a weightless ragdoll. Gunshots went off behind them, striking the rubble wall nearby. Flecks of concrete shrapnel scratched at her legs. A bullet whistled past, close enough to hear a hiss. In what felt like a mere instant, Althea went from standing in a group to lying flat on her back behind a wall.

Teal rose up on one knee, firing her gun a few times over the barrier.

Somewhere on the other side of the concrete, David shouted, "Cover!"

Althea clamped her hands over her ears as Teal kept shooting. Even though the city guns made less noise than the Before-Time weapons people in the Badlands sometimes used, they still went off painfully loud when fired so close.

"Run and hide somewhere!" yelled Teal. "Find a really good hiding place only a kid can get into. Go!"

An incoming bullet struck Teal in the shoulder, pulling a

splat of white fluid out into the air behind her. She didn't show any reaction, continuing to return fire.

"What?" shouted Althea.

"El Ojo." Teal fired twice more, then barked, "Hah!"

David gurgled.

"Shit," muttered Teal, right before jumping over the wall.

Althea shifted to kneel and peered around the corner of a former doorway.

El Ojo, Afbee's 'best tracker' and also not a living human, held David off the ground by a one-handed grip on his throat. The mangled remains of a small handgun lay on the ground nearby, explaining Teal's mocking laugh. She'd evidently shot it out of his hand. The doll held David out in front of himself as a living shield against laser fire from Phoenix, likely the only reason he hadn't crushed the man's neck.

Teal leapt into a flying jump-kick, planting her boot in El Ojo's chest. The hit knocked him back two steps, but not off his feet. David slipped loose, backpedaling while gasping for air. In an instant, El Ojo went from standing on both feet to having one leg stuck through a new hole in a nearby concrete wall and Teal lay on the ground, having ducked a kick too fast for Althea to see. The tracker and the synthetic blurred into an unrecognizable haze of grey linen and blue hair. David staggered backward, raising his E-90 at the mess, but didn't fire. Concrete bits smashed away from rubble close to the blur. Only the lack of white blood spraying around revealed El Ojo hadn't successfully made contact with Teal. A sudden *clank* came from the doorjamb, along with a sharp *click* behind her. Seconds later, a mild burning sensation became noticeable on her left arm.

Althea peered down at a deep cut on the outside edge of her arm, midway between shoulder and elbow. She twisted to look back at what clicked, spotting a throwing knife embedded in another wall behind her. The instant she realized he'd *thrown* a knife at her hard enough to stick into concrete, the pain hit.

"Urgh." She clamped a hand over her arm and commanded her body not to bleed, staring in shocked horror at the gouge in the doorjamb where the knife glanced off. Had it not deflected, it probably would've hit her in the heart — and still ended up in the wall behind her.

"Run!" shouted Teal.

She didn't want to abandon her friends, but also could do no more to protect them from a 'doll' than an ordinary child. Staying put would only make things worse for everyone, since trying to protect her would distract them. Althea squished her sense of pain and bolted away from the fight, trying to put as many walls as possible between her and the bad doll. She weaved deep into the ruined city surrounding Afbee. Gunfire and the softer hum of lasers filled the air, growing fainter the farther she ran.

After about a minute of hard sprinting, she reached a huge, mostly open area containing rows upon rows of Before-Time drive machines. Little remained of them other than rusty frames, decaying engines, some glass, and the plastic parts. Being almost entirely plastic on the outside, many still mostly resembled how they might have looked when they worked.

The gunfire and shouting sounded far enough away to give Althea a sense she'd gotten away without being followed. She ducked into a gap between two old drive machines and concentrated on making the cut in her arm heal. Raiders sometimes put bad stuff on their blades, so she also checked for sicks and poisons, but found only a trace of the 'K virus,' which she promptly purged. She braced a hand on the side of a big drive machine for balance while making water. Beside her hand, silver plastic letters spelled the word 'Tundra'.

*Strange.* She crept forward to get away from the puddle of sick.

The front end of the big decaying machine had the word 'Toyota' on it. Huge letters spelled FORD on the back end of another big old drive machine. She thought this place must have spiritual significance to the villagers since they apparently came here to find baby names. These must be the 'sacred field' Mojave told her about. The villagers evidently mistook old drive machines for magical tombs because food mysteriously appeared here... and named their babies after the words printed on them. Her friends would probably find this funny.

Worry for David, Teal, and Phoenix soon chased any other thoughts out of her head. Crouched to hide between rusty vehicles, she wrapped her arms around her legs and stared down at her feet, trying not to cry too much. The *only* thing she could do to help would be to figure out how she'd made *death* go away once... and do it again. Maybe she could bring David back, but probably not Phoenix as she didn't know the woman well enough to really form an emotional bond. It didn't matter how strong a friendship she had with Teal, her powers simply wouldn't work on a synthetic person. However, the woman also didn't have a ghost in the same sense. Maybe the city people could make her brain work again.

She'd have to sneak back to the place El Ojo smashed her friends after he left, and get there in some way without being seen. If she couldn't call David's ghost back into his body, she would need to force herself to hold the sad away for later. The people of Afbee needed help. Althea couldn't let herself shut down to grief. She'd take the buggy and go back to Querq, tell the other city police what's going on here. Would El Ojo chase her across the desert? If she got away, would he kill everyone here to hide the corporation's secret?

Her body shook from worry and grief. Warm tears fell on her feet, dribbling down between her toes. Althea huddled in silence, surrounded by the soft rush of the nighttime wind. She hadn't even noticed the sun go down. Cold added to emotion, making her shiver even harder. Her thin dress could often feel too warm during the day, but at night, it didn't help much... going from annoying to pointless. Lost to grief, she became stupidly angry at the dress for existing. Why did Father and Karina insist she wear it if it didn't serve any purpose?

The sense of a presence approaching quieted her tears. She kept still, listening for footsteps, but no sound disturbed the peaceful silence of the car graveyard. Why had the Before-Time ancients put so many drive machines here in neat rows? Living people did many things she could make no sense of. It seemed pointless to even ask why those who died centuries ago did what they did.

"Althea?" whispered a woman.

She lifted her head toward the voice, staring down an aisle between crumbling drive machines. No one appeared to be anywhere nearby. The voice hadn't sounded threatening or warning, so she risked peeking up over the front end of the nearest old car to look around. Empty rubble and rows of rusting hulks surrounded her. Ruins of a huge building stood against one edge of the open area. Close to its wall, hundreds of wheeled basket carts lay scattered around, some half buried, some crushed, all lost to centuries of rust.

"Please help," whispered the same woman, right behind her.

She spun, but still no one appeared to be anywhere

nearby. Confused, Althea pressed a hand to her chest and breathed, gazing around. A moment later, she realized what must be happening. "Oh. You're a spirit."

Soon after she concentrated on the desire to see ghosts, a woman appeared in front of her. For a few seconds, her body glowing faintly blue and translucent. She seemed a little older than Teal, had long light brown hair, and the same sort of tanned-pale color to her skin as Althea. The woman carried an all-metal spear and wore a bonedog-hide skirt, tire-tread sandals, and an array of handmade necklaces and bracelets. Dark paint smears covered her otherwise bare chest and arms, likely an attempt at camouflage rather than simple adornment.

"Are you the spirits the villagers fear?" asked Althea.

"No. I am Mojave's mother."

Althea blinked, suspicious. "Her mother is not dead. She shares a home with her parents."

"Elantra is not my daughter's mother. Speak my name to her and she will know the truth. I am Acura." The ghost bowed her head. "My youngest daughter, Sahara, was only two when I became a spirit. It has been many years. She does not even remember me. Mojave understands Elantra is not her blood. Elantra has been a worthy protector of my children. My mate, Savan, chose well."

"Oh… I am sorry." Althea looked down. "I can help you go to the place where spirits belong."

"It is not time for me to go yet." Acura radiated a strong sense of protectiveness. "I will not leave until my children are grown. Even then, I shall protect them as much as I am able to until they, too, join me as spirits. I must help Sahara now by speaking to you."

Althea lifted her gaze off the ground. "Sahara is not a spirit?"

"She is neither spirit nor alive." Acura scowled. "They

make her sleep forever. She feels close to being a spirit, but her energy is still inside her body. You can protect her as I cannot. My weapons do nothing to those who harm us."

"They are people, not spirits." Althea squeezed her fists tight in anger.

"Yes, child. I know. As a spirit, I see truths. The spirit talker does not hear me. Those who take our children are strange people, not the spirits he warns us of. Even this place we revere is no tomb. It is nothing. Junk. Ruins of the world that came before us. The strange people come here in the night, leaving food and supplies for the village while no one is awake to see them."

The sorrow radiating from the ghost sent tears streaming down Althea's face. "I want to help your daughter, and everyone here, but I don't know how. They killed my friends."

"Those who came here with you are not spirits." Acura tried to take her hand. The ghost's touch caused only a faint chill in her fingers, having no substance. "Please. Hurry. They torture my daughter."

"Grr." Althea's heart burst with relief and hope for David, Teal, and Phoenix—but crashed into rage before she could enjoy the absence of worry. "I will stop the mean people."

"Follow me, child." Acura hurried off, walking straight through the ancient cars.

Undeterred, Althea leapt up and ran across them, jumping from hood to roof to hood wherever the wrecks appeared solid enough to support her. Being mostly plastic shells, they caved in more often than not. The spirit led her to the edge of the strange junkyard of carefully arranged cars and back into the ruins, going even farther away from the village wall at a pace forcing Althea to run… not that she minded. She loved running *toward* someone in need of help rather than away from people trying to hurt her.

Acura walked around rather than through the giant rubble mounds, concrete, dirt, and metal scrap often as high as a three-story building. Much of the ground had the consistency of powder laced with smoothed concrete stones from centuries of erosion. Althea noticed a rusty metal spike sticking up from the grey dirt right under her foot at the last possible second. Rather than impale herself, she threw her weight to the side, deliberately falling over. A hard landing on pointy rubble hurt but didn't break skin. From then on, she slowed to a fast walk, on guard for other hazards.

Here and there, the smashed remains of primitive flying robots lay embedded in the silt. Unlike the annoying ones in the big city, these appeared to use tiny fans rather than magic. She didn't truly believe the fancy city advert bots relied on 'magic' to fly, but since she couldn't comprehend what really happened—nor did she care to learn—she called it magic.

The spirit finally slowed as they reached an area where the ruined buildings were made more of metal than concrete. Here, they somewhat resembled the big city, except for the state of disrepair. While ruined, the partially metal structures were far more intact than the all-concrete ones. For a little over a quarter mile square, the ghost of a Before-Time city stood intact enough to recognize. She suspected this part to be fairly new compared to the rest of the ruins, likely built soon before the war started. However, three centuries of abandonment still took a toll on the more modern materials.

Acura rushed into the open doorway of a crumbling, rectangular building. The plain metal walls and out-of-control bushes growing in front of it offered no clue as to what it might have been. Althea scooted past the overgrowth, entering a big, dusty room. Random bits of trash—plastic cups, bottles, and scraps litter the floor. To her right, a bunch of formerly nice, cushioned chairs faced a big rectangular plastic slab on the wall, as if the people sitting in them might have been inclined to stare at the box. The left side of the room had a big counter, similar to the judge desk in Querq but nowhere near as tall. Words on the front in black letters read, 'service by appointment only.' Straight ahead, four hulking metal boxes stood against the wall. One had 'Pepsi' written sideways across the entire front. The other three contained dozens of metal corkscrews and smashed glass. To the right of the giant metal boxes, a door-sized hole revealed a corridor strewn with junk going deeper into the building. Arrows pointed one way for 'parts' another for 'service' and a third direction for 'sales.'

Althea padded to the middle of the room, gazing around at the abandonment. She neither saw nor heard anyone else there, so closed her eyes and mentally 'listened' for people via Telepathy. Scattered bits of thought echoed in the silence, too muted to pick up on much other than their presence. She guessed between thirty and sixty people had to be within her range, though there hadn't been anyone in sight outside. If Sahara and the bad people hid in the other buildings around here, why did the ghost bring her to this one?

"Here." Acura pointed at the big metal box marked Pepsi. "This machine."

Althea approached it with some hesitance, intimidated by its size. The huge device towered over her. Most of its face consisted of red, white, and blue plastic. Rectangular buttons formed a column on a narrow strip down the right side. Each one had a different word on it, except for the top three, which all repeated 'Pepsi.'

Nothing about it looked at all useful.

She leaned to the side. A faded picture showed a smiling young woman holding an aluminum can up to her mouth. It, too, had the word Pepsi on it. Althea had seen people in the modern city drink stuff out of similar cans, though they didn't have any words on them and looked different: taller, thinner, with blinking lights. Still, she figured out this machine had likely been used as storage for some manner of drinkable fluid. Given the enormous smile on the picture woman's face, people likely used it the way raiders ate certain plants and mushrooms—to feel happy, get energy, or throw themselves into strange dreams. However, looking at a picture of someone who'd been dead for over three centuries didn't help. She stopped peering around the side and again stood facing the giant machine, clueless as to what to do.

"This machine is broken. It has not worked in a long time." Althea glanced at the ghost. "Why are you showing it to me?"

"That one." Acura pointed at the third button up from the bottom.

Althea crouched, staring at the frozen speaking on it. "What is a dry Canada?"

"I do not know," said Acura. "The books tell of a place called Canada to the north, but it certainly rains there. It would not be dry. The people who torment my daughter push that spot to go inside."

"It's broken." She scrunched her nose, but decided to press the button anyway.

A heavy *clunk* from inside the machine rattled the floor. She gasped and jumped back.

Acura grabbed the side of the machine, her hand phasing through the metal. "Pull here. Like a door."

Althea breathed out the nervousness of being startled at the unexpected noise. Old, dead machines shouldn't do anything when touched, especially not shake the floor. She eased forward, grasped the side of the machine, and tugged.

The front face opened, swinging to the left. Rather than the guts of an ancient machine, the entirely hollow box contained a passageway leading underground. *Uh oh.* She crept forward into the metal cabinet, stopping at what would have been its back. The floor angled down into a ramp. Much colder air in the sunken passage teased at her toes, as if afraid to flow up into the outside world. From where she stood, a short corridor of dark silvery metal ran roughly thirty feet downhill to a door. Eerie light glowed from narrow tracks along both walls near the ceiling. The passage in front of her looked straight out of the modern city.

A powerful wave of emotion wafted up from below: pain, sadness, rage, hit her the hardest... but also greed.

She recoiled, backing up until she could peer around the open machine door. Acura had vanished. *Sahara must be down there. Her mother trusts me to help.* Her friends thought the corporation would kill everyone here to keep their secrets. The bad people probably knew she opened this door already. If she ran back to get Teal, David, and Phoenix, the evil blonde woman she saw in the spirit talker's memory might kill everyone before they got back here.

However, if she went down there alone, she'd have no way to protect herself from another doll like El Ojo... who might even be waiting for her underground. Her friends not being dead—yet—didn't mean they killed the machine man. They might have run away.

Althea's conscience allowed her only one choice. She couldn't risk the evil woman murdering everyone to 'keep secrets.' She had no time to run for help. Hands clutched into fists, she marched down the ramp into the frigid metal corridor.

## 28

## THE UN-HOSPITAL

Althea's teeth chattered from the cold air and freezing plastisteel floor.

The plain white door at the bottom didn't appear to have any glowing panels on the wall like modern city doors usually did, only a simple knob. It seemed weird not to find a lock or some kind of trap, though the bad people probably didn't expect any of the primitives would be able to find them here in the first place. Who would've thought to push a button on a centuries-old drink machine almost a mile away from Afbee.

She opened the door and stepped into a wider hallway onto a shiny black floor with a pattern of less shiny raised circles. The material had an almost rubbery consistency, faintly squishy under her feet. Breathing the chilly air made her nose feel weird, or perhaps the tingling came from the odd chemical fragrance. She didn't sense anything dangerous entering her air bags. The smell must not be from poison or sleepy stuff. The last time she'd experienced a similar odor, she woke up in a bed after the extreme drain of fixing Shepherd. City police called the place a hospital,

and told her—somewhat condescendingly—the strange
smell she complained about came from 'clean.' They
thought she'd spent so much time surrounded by filth she
smelled the *absence* of grime.

The corridor stretched for quite a distance in front of
her, but contained no angry people threatening her, only a
cluster of small wheeled beds parked randomly against
either wall with no one on them. She figured the bad people
used those devices to move sleeping kidnap victims around
more easily than carrying them.

Long windows on both sides looked into separate
rooms, each containing a single bed. There appeared to be
no way into the rooms from this hallway, only doors on the
opposite side. Unconscious people ranging from children as
young as Kia to adults in their later forties occupied a little
more than half the beds. Althea hurried deeper into the
facility, hastily looking from left to right, her emotions
building into an increasing sense of anger and desperation.

Most of the people trapped in the rooms showed visible
signs of sickness: unnatural skin color, sores, or bulging
masses growing under the skin. Thin blankets covered them
up to the armpits in most cases where the people didn't
have hoses or tubes stuck into their chests. Despite being
unconscious and in some cases appearing too sick to move,
all the victims also wore handcuffs on both arms, chaining
them to the frames of their beds.

Althea fumed, walking faster while zigzagging back and
forth from left window to right window, staring for a few
seconds at every kidnapped villager. A young man close to
Karina's age appeared to be the only one awake enough to
struggle. He deliriously tugged at the handcuffs while
throwing off heavy amounts of panic and terror.

She caught his emotion and pushed it down to a state of
calm. His thoughts contained only agony as though a tiny

creature swam around inside his lower abdomen, chewing on things. If he could get his hands unchained from the bed frame, he'd try to tear himself open to pull it out so the pain stopped. Althea stood there, too stunned at the evil of tying someone down and torturing them to be able to do anything other than recoil in horror. When shock wore off, she pounded her fists on the glass in an effort to break the window and help him.

Alas, the material proved too tough for her, even after she made herself as strong as her powers allowed. She once again felt as if she sat locked in the Wagon Man's cage, unable to reach someone in desperate need of healing. She wept, then let out a roar of anger, projecting a wave of psionic energy outward without truly knowing how she managed it other than from sheer desire to help him.

The boy shuddered and went still. She focused on him, demanding his pain to stop. Something slithered under the blanket. Althea kept 'pushing' at her power, her muscles shaking from the effort. She sensed a foreign object stuck into his body, narrow like a spear but flexible—and moving. Althea commanded his body to expel the invading machine. After a moment, a thick, clear hose full of bloody gunk slipped out from under the blanket, falling to the ground. Tiny metal jaws at the front end continued opening and closing. She sensed the damage it caused regenerating inside the teen from afar, and kept her attention on him until his life essence no longer pulled at her energy like a starving puppy feeding from its mother.

Althea slumped forward, her forehead touching the glass between her hands, as tired as if she'd healed a dozen raiders who had their arms cut off. Apparently, she did not *have* to touch someone to help them… but it took many times the energy if she didn't.

"Hi there, sweetie," said a man to her left.

She snapped her head up, staring through her reflection at the unconscious teen boy, then whirled to face a man in a puffy white suit. He also wore a similar sort of facemask like the ones Phoenix and David brought to protect them from the virus. Behind a panel of curved plastic, the face of a late-thirties man flashed an insincere smile.

"What are you doing out of bed?" He glanced briefly at a datapad clutched in his black-gloved hand, then back to her.

Furious at what she'd already seen, she spun to face him, leaning forward in an aggressive stance. "I am not one of the people you kidnapped, and I'm not sick!"

"Oh," said the man in a creepy, whimsical tone. "You will be soon."

"No." She stepped toward him.

The man reached for her.

Glow in her eyes flickered brighter as she channeled a blast of telempathic fear at him. Her hair fluttered as if lifted by a breeze that didn't exist. "I said no. You will stop kidnapping people and making them sick right now."

"Oh, shit!" screamed the man. He scrambled backward so fast he tripped over his own feet and landed in a seated position.

She kept walking toward him, glaring angrily at this monster dressed up like a human being.

He shrieked in terror, crossing his arms to shield his face.

As much as a girl her size could, she loomed over him, building on his sense of dread. "You will make all the sicks you caused stop. Once you've cleaned up your mess, leave the Badlands and don't ever come back."

He slumped over sideways, curling into a fetal position, sobbing.

*Too much.* Upon realizing her being furious at what the

mechanical chewing snake did to the boy amplified her power, she backed off a half step and stopped radiating fear.

"Althea?" yelled Teal, her voice reverberating in the stark metal corridor.

Her emotion jumped from rage to elation. Althea whirled to face the way out, some hundred feet behind her. Cupping her hands around her mouth, she shouted, "Down here!"

## 29

# TOO INNOCENT FOR THE WORLD

D avid's awestruck and somewhat uneasy whistle echoed in the distance.

Althea pressed both hands to her heart, overcome with relief at her friends being alive. She stared down the hallway at the door, shivering from anticipation as well as the cold. Telempathy allowed her to 'watch' the cowering man in the puffy suit without looking at him. Any change in his emotional state would warn her of a possible attack, though the man didn't seem likely to have the nerve after the fear she dropped on him.

Teal emerged into view at the bottom of the ramp. Her clothing looked a bit worse for wear, dirty and ripped, though she didn't appear injured. David, alas, limped along. Bruises covered his neck and the left side of his face. Still, he kept his E-90 up and ready despite being in obvious pain.

"Eep!" Althea sprinted to them, her feet pattering on the steel floor as loud as someone clapping. "You're hurt!"

"Nothing a few stimpaks couldn't deal with," muttered David.

Althea made the 'pshht' noise a stimpak injector did as she grabbed his arm. His chuckle echoed into the murky silence of her healing trance. An approximation of David's body formed in a void, all the life shapes visible to her. The side of his skull had a crack in it, left arm broken an inch below the shoulder. Some of the softer stretchy parts around his right hip socket looked angry, as if the joint had popped open and re-seated. The amount of hurts left over after he'd taken stimpaks frightened her. It meant he'd been *seriously* injured, perhaps almost dead.

Trusting Teal to protect them, she plunged fully into healing David, unconcerned with the outside world. Her joy at finding him alive gave her a burst of energy that boosted her power even more than her anger, making the task of healing him feel effortless. Except for a few disturbingly loud *cracks* as his bones snapped back into place, several minutes passed in quiet, meditative calm.

She opened her eyes to David making a silly sort of face as if he'd *seriously* needed to make water for a long time and finally got to do it. He gave off a sense of relief strong enough to ease her anxiety. "You're okay…"

"The doll's disassembled," deadpanned Teal.

Althea glanced back and forth between her and David. A heavy blob of worry formed in her gut. "Where is Phoenix?"

David gestured randomly upward. "In the village, working with Doc to plan triage and cleanup. We weren't expecting to do anything more than figure out where you ran off to."

"She told me to run." Althea glanced sheepishly at Teal. "Sorry for hiding. Acura showed me this place because her daughter needs help."

"Acura?" Teal blinked. "Who or what is that?"

"Mojave's mother. She died a long time ago." Althea

gave a somber sigh, then pointed at the huge windows. "Everyone the 'spirits' took is here. They're tied to beds and tortured." She glared at the cowering man. "I can't open the glass. How do we help them?"

Teal turned in place, taking in the scenery. "This feels like an observation gallery. Whoever is running this shit show can stroll up and down here and look in on every test subject. Doors are on the inside walls. Easy. Just look for a way around back."

The man in the puffy white suit screamed in fear the instant Althea walked toward him. She stepped over him and kept going. Teal and David followed. Midway between the exit and another door at the far end of the hall, two branching hallways led to either side. Althea randomly turned left—but stopped short as soon as she rounded the corner.

Two gleaming silver orbs the size of human heads hung in midair a short distance ahead of her. Each floated on a jet of cyan energy projecting out from its bottom. Thin lines of violet glow shimmered between the seams of the metal plating. Teal grabbed Althea from behind and dragged her out of the corridor a second before a pair of green lasers fired across the corridor intersection.

The force of the pull tossed Althea into David, who caught her and nearly fell over backward. Electronic whirring came closer. Before the orbs could float into view, Teal blurred around the corner, her sidearm firing at the rate of a machine gun. Pings and clanks preceded two floor-jolting *thuds* like someone dropped one of the heavy round stones the boys back in Querq played with at the 'balling alley.' Two bullet-riddled orb bots rolled into view, smoking and sputtering.

"I've never been happier to know a synth," said David. "Hate orb bots."

"We have our uses." Teal holstered her weapon.

"Sorry. Didn't mean it that way." David let go of Althea. "Just… psionics and cybernetic augmentation don't play well together. Can't tweak my reflexes enough to reliably shoot those damned things down before they slice me up. I meant to say I'm happy you—"

"Yeah." Teal managed a weak smile. "I know what you meant. Just teasing. Kiddo, let me take point."

Althea blinked. "Why do you want a spear?"

"Hah." Teal laughed. "It means let me go first in case there are more surprises."

"Okay." Althea frowned. "Why do people always say stuff that doesn't mean what it says?"

"Welcome to the modern world," deadpanned Teal.

She advanced, gun up and ready. Slightly longer than the depth of the isolation rooms, the side corridor led to a T-junction where another hallway branched right and left. A second pair of orb bots cruised toward them from the right. In a barrage of rapid gunfire, Teal shot the killer bots out of the air before they activated their lasers—or David could even aim at them.

"You make it look easy," whispered David.

"It is easy… to me." Teal paused at the corner to look both ways, then went to the right, past the smoking bots.

Althea paused at the intersection, unsure which way to go since both directions had doors to rooms containing kidnapped villagers. Her need to help everyone caused her to get stuck feeling guilty. If she went left, people to the right would suffer more. If she went right, people on the left would suffer more. From here, she couldn't tell who needed help the most urgently.

Teal kept going right, ignoring all the rooms holding people handcuffed to beds. Again, she raised her weapon, approaching a larger, more important looking metal door at the end of the hall.

"Where are you going?" whispered Althea, while tugging futilely at the nearest door—locked.

"Securing the area." Teal waved for her to follow. "Before you start zoning out fixing people, I want to find the bastards running this place so they don't sneak up on us. Stay close and don't wander off."

"But they're in pain." Althea tentatively crept after her. "Can't get in anyway. Can you open these doors?"

"Probably. But, they've been here this long already. Another few minutes won't matter." Teal pushed a button on the wall beside the impressive door, then blurred through it, gun up, swinging left, then right. Thankfully, she didn't fire. "Clear. Got some tanks in here. More victims."

Althea ran forward, squeezing past Teal into a room that reminded her of a tiny modern city hospital. A row of ten enormous cylinders stood against the rear wall, spanning from floor to ceiling. Nude people floated in peach-colored liquid, motionless, eyes closed. Though they appeared dead, Althea sensed life in everyone, which allowed her to remain mostly calm. Machinery in the metal bases of each tank whirred louder than the constant thrum of electronics coming from a row of monoliths studded in thousands of blinking lights along the left wall. The villagers' long hair fluttered in a current of circulating liquid.

Stunned, she gawked at the display for a second before whirling to stare up at her friends. "How are they in water but alive?"

"It's not water." David put an arm around her shoulders. "It's breathable gel. Real hospitals use the same stuff to help people. It's usually laced with surgical nanobots."

"Real hospitals don't use med tanks for long-term storage." Teal put her gun away, stepped up to the nearest chamber, and activated a holographic screen from a thin 'podium' attached to the base.

David shook his head, disgusted. "Real hospitals also don't use random people they abduct for medical testing. What the hell are they doing to them?"

"You just said it. Medical testing…" Teal frowned.

The first eight tanks held two adult women, three adult men, an older teenage boy, a boy around nine or ten years old, and a girl roughly the same age as Althea. The last two cylinders each contained multiple children under ten, five in one tank, four in the other. They stood out as unusual due to various features: two redheads, pale with freckles. One boy and girl had unusually dark skin, another bright blonde hair like Althea, a rare trait both in the Badlands and the big city—unless someone modified themselves. The remaining small children belonged to those 'ethnicity' things she'd recently learned about in history class, neither looking like the people from West City, Querq, nor her.

Though the kids didn't appear to be sick or injured, someone stuffed them together in giant jars like the pickled eggs Father loved. One of the men had no skin on his entire torso, revealing all the life shapes inside. The older of the two women, perhaps in her thirties, also had a gaping wound in her abdomen from which several of her internal parts floated free in the gel. None of the people in tanks looked 'sick,' merely asleep.

Althea fumed at the cruelty.

Acura manifested in front of the tank containing the adolescent girl. "This is my daughter. Please set her free. She suffers."

"Here." Althea darted over, pressed her hands against the plastic cylinder, and gazed up at the girl floating inside. She appeared roughly the same age as Althea. Like Mojave, she had pale skin and light brown hair, far longer than her older sister's, draped past her knees. No obvious signs of sickness or injury marked her body. According to Mojave, Sahara disappeared almost a year ago at twelve, yet still appeared to be around that age. Something about this bizarre liquid-filled cage must be keeping her from getting older. Althea sensed thoughts in her head, but only dreams of exploring ancient broken airplanes with other kids. The girl didn't appear to be aware she'd been abducted. "This is Sahara. Mojave's sister!"

"Sahara? Mojave?" Teal raised an eyebrow. "Why did their parents name their kids after deserts?"

David shrugged. "They probably saw 'Mojave' or 'Sahara' written somewhere and liked the sound of the words. This village is pretty unusual. Most scrag tribes can't read. If I had to guess, they probably started off as a survivor settlement of Air Force personnel and devolved into apparent tribalism over the years due to the desolation here as they ran out of everything."

"The 'sacred field,'" whispered Althea. "Hundreds of drive machines. Mojave told me they are tombs for ancients, but they're not. Just old drive machines."

"They've been naming their kids after cars?" Teal's tone of voice said she wanted to laugh, but couldn't quite bring herself to do it in front of partially dissected people.

Althea patted the tank wall. "How do we let her out of the cage?"

Teal tapped a few more hologram buttons on the display connected to the tank containing the woman with her guts spilled out, then moved over to Sahara. The woman's internal parts twitched and began to move on their own like fish swimming around, gradually retreating into her body where they belonged.

Althea bit her lip, patiently waiting for her friend to unlock the horrible cage.

"Ugh." David glanced away, disgusted. "Every so often, you see something so awful it makes you ashamed to be human."

"It's worse than you think," muttered Teal.

"Dare I ask?" David winced.

"The least disturbing part of this is how they refer to this poor kid as 'Subject 447: female juvenile approximate age twelve' rather than a name." Teal tapped at the virtual keyboard. "They identified her as having a rare genetic profile highly compatible as an organ donor for transplants. They've basically been using her as a human flowerpot to continuously regrow various internal organs, which they remove and ship back to the city before doing it all over again."

A chill ran down Althea's back. Most of the explanation went over her head, but she understood the bad people had been stealing Sahara's life shapes for pay things the same way as the Man In White did. Only, they didn't murder the victim like he did. Instead, these machines made new life shapes after they stole them. So angry she cried, Althea whirled to hide her face in David's chest and bawled. She *hated* how this made her feel… like Rachel had been right when she said some people deserved to die. Althea almost wanted to punch whoever put Sahara in a tank and did this to her over and over again.

"Relax, kiddo," said Teal. "This girl wouldn't have any idea what's being done to her. She slept through it."

"You know that doesn't make it better." David rubbed Althea's back, trying to comfort her.

"She's not feeling pain?" Althea sniffled.

"No." Teal huffed a breath tinged in contempt. "My guess is, whoever kidnapped this kid from her bed at night gave her a sedative. Bet she never woke up. They've kept her asleep, so they're being pieces of shit, not *total* monsters."

David leaned to the side, peering at the screen. "I didn't know you're a medtech, too."

"Advantage of a silicon brain. If I need a skill set, just takes credits and about two minutes to upload." Teal smiled. "Can fly combat aircraft, too."

"Nice." David continued patting Althea's back, whispering, "Hey. Don't be upset at yourself for having emotions. Even the sweetest person on Earth has a right to be angry at something like this."

Althea wiped her face. "I guess."

He sighed. "Are they doing the same thing to the little ones? Gah. If *this* doesn't make Althea accept—or at least not complain about—a vengeance killing, nothing will."

"No." Althea stared down. "Killing is wrong. Even killing people who did this. I *will* stop them, but please do not kill anyone." She lifted her gaze off the floor to peer up at Sahara. "I might not cry *too* much if they do a stupid and *make* you shoot them. But, please, don't shoot them if you don't have to."

"Kiddo…" Teal sighed. "You are way too nice to live in this world."

# OUT OF THE SLIME, INTO THE FIRE

Althea stared at the indecipherable text and charts dancing back and forth on the holographic screen.

The girl floating in front of her twitched sporadically. Teal hit some buttons, waited a moment, hit other buttons, changed to a different screen and pushed yet more buttons.

"What's taking so long?" asked Althea.

"I'm turning off the doses of sedatives, deactivating the nanobots, and withdrawing them from her body. Basically, I'm stabilizing her as much as possible. This girl's heart is hours old. They just grew her another one. The tank's been keeping her alive for the past two weeks while she didn't have one. You're going to need to help her once it's open. She's too brittle to be taken out of this tank otherwise. Her internal organs are too new to function without help from the nanobots."

Althea nodded.

"Amazing we don't have company yet…" David glanced at the door. "Wonder what the locals are up to? Packing up to run like hell or hiding in a bunker?"

Teal chuckled to herself. "If they saw us take El Ojo out, they're probably in no big hurry to get in our faces. Still, got a feeling we'll find out soon. Aha! There we go."

A beep came from the control interface. The whirring in the tank base grew louder. Air appeared at the top of the fluid as it drained, expanding downward. As the peach-colored fluid drained over the course of a minute, Sahara's unconscious body slumped to the floor, coated in a thick layer of slime. Finally, the cylinder rotated a quarter turn before retracting into the floor. The instant a two-inch-thick plastic wall no longer propped her up, Sahara flowed off the raised tank base onto the floor like a dead fish poured out of a cup. Warm breathable gel spread out into a puddle around her, coating Althea's feet.

She promptly slipped and landed on her butt.

Ignoring the pain of a sudden landing on metal floor, she scooted around and rested her hands on Sahara's stomach, linking to the girl's essence. Most of her life shapes: heart, kidneys, lungs, liver felt damaged in a way she'd never seen before on the 'inside' parts. It reminded her of skin where a person had been beaten or slapped repeatedly—tender and sensitive. Also, the girl's lungs contained the slime, not air. Enraged at how anyone could torture a person like this, Althea forcefully expelled the goop, then repaired the damage, strengthening all the life shapes from brittle newly-grown organs into functional ones.

She opened her eyes to find David staring down at her, making an unamused face. Slime dripped off his face, chest, and arms. Teal leaned against another tank, laughing too hard to stand straight up.

"Any particular reason she projectile vomited B-gel all over me?" asked David.

"I'm sorry." Althea grimaced. "It made me angry what they did to her."

"Mmm…" Sahara stirred, coughing a little on the traces of gel still in her throat. "Cold."

Althea shifted her gaze back to Sahara and chirped, "Hi."

The girl sat up, bleary-eyed, gazing around at everything. A few seconds later, she radiated panic and tried to leap to her feet, but her legs shot out from under her. She wiped out in the gel puddle, landing flat on her chest. Lost to panic, she again attempted to scramble upright, though slipped so much on the slime-coated metal she couldn't even manage to lift her chest off the floor. She managed to flip over onto her side, recoiling from the room in terror. Her thoughts filled with stories of alien abductions and experimentation—things she'd read about in old books. Until *this* moment, she'd thought them made up stories.

Althea took away the girl's panic. "You don't have to be scared."

"What is this place?" Sahara curled fetal, shivering. "It's so bright. So cold in here! All these blinking lights. The metal…" The girl patted herself down as if checking for cuts or strange devices stuck into her body from alien experimentation. Finding none, she raised one hand to watch the viscous peach-colored slime dribble from her fingertips. Panic at the high tech scenery gave way to a mildly disgusted sense of confusion.

"Not aliens or spirits." Althea didn't even try to stand, knowing she'd end up kissing the floor. She helped the girl up into a sitting position and sat beside her, holding both her hands while staring into her eyes. "You are under the ground in a hidden place not far from Afbee. Bad people kidnapped you."

"Kidnapped?" Sahara blinked. "I don't know what kidnapped means. I went to sleep, now here."

"Kidnap is when bad people steal you and don't let you go home." Althea frowned. "It is not nice."

"You mean abducted. Are you sure the aliens didn't get me? They have them at the Area 51. It's what the books say."

David and Teal chuckled.

"No aliens." Althea sighed. "Just modern people being mean."

Sahara looked down at herself, wiping a hand over her stomach. "Why do I have baby stuff on me?"

"Baby stuff?" Teal raised an eyebrow. "Good grief, tell me she's not pregnant at her age. Please."

Althea shook her head. "She is not."

"No. Not my baby. I am like a baby." Sahara tried to wipe the goo off her arms and legs. "I look like a baby after it comes out."

Since the girl continued to try to be terrified of the computers and equipment around her, Althea rushed a telepathic explanation of how the entire world hadn't been destroyed into the Badlands. Modern things still existed in far-away places. Regardless of whether the books she'd read about alien abductions and crash landings at the Area 51 place happened for real or had been made up for entertainment, no question existed this place had nothing to do with them. Sahara's mood shifted from freaked out to curiosity. Knowing she hadn't been taken away from Earth by aliens took away all her fear. Althea had to dig a bit to understand what 'Earth' meant.

Sahara squirmed, making faces a the slippery ooze all over her. "Eww."

"Bad people are hurting your village." David walked

over to a row of lockers, opening them. "Damn. Just spare parts for the machinery. Not even a towel in here."

"No..." Sahara glared at nothing in particular. "Someone stole my stuff. Mama gave me the beads. They're all I had from her. She died a long time ago."

"The bad people took them." Althea helped scoop slime out of her hair and off her back. "Your mother's spirit showed me how to find you."

"My mother? Spirit?" Sahara stared at her for a few seconds before lapsing into sobs. "Sickness took her to the spirits when I was too little to know her."

Althea squeezed the girl's hand. "She is still here, a spirit, protecting you and Mojave."

"It's gonna be okay now." Teal walked to the tank containing the man with no skin on his chest. "Gotta close this guy up."

Sahara stopped crying, her mood shifting to suspicion. "Are you lying?"

"No." Althea smiled, opened a telepathic link with her, and thought about talking to Acura's ghost. *I share a memory.*

"That's..." Sahara mentally stared at the apparition, sad, hopeful, and baffled. She didn't recognize her own mother. At the point in the memory when Acura said she thought Elantra was a good replacement mother, the girl broke down and cried again.

A commotion of shouting and banging broke the telepathic link. Althea's reality shifted from the hazy glow of a remembered field of drive machines back to the room of people jars. Three men in dark grey jumpsuits, shiny black armored vests, and helmets blocked the only door out, pointing city rifles at them. Two aimed at Teal, the other man pointed his rifle at David.

"Nice and slow," said the man aiming at David. "Toss your weapons."

"That's not how this works." David stared at him, overriding the man's emotion with feelings of disinterest and apathy. "National Police Force, Division 0. You three and everyone involved in operating this facility are under arrest."

The other two men laughed.

"You don't have any authority out here," said one of the men aiming at Teal. "Lose the weapons or someone back home is gonna wonder why you went out to the shit smear and never came back."

Teal sighed in annoyance.

"Wait." Althea tried to stand, slipped in the gel, and landed flat on her back. "Ugh. I hate this stuff. Teal, please don't kill them."

Two of the men laughed again. The one David focused on fidgeted.

Althea glanced sideways at Sahara. "Stay here and wait for us, please. We will bring you home, but I have to stop the bad people first."

Again, the two armed men laughed.

Grumbling, Althea dragged herself out of the slime puddle.

## 31

## A COMMON MISCONCEPTION

The men mostly kept their attention on Teal as Althea unsteadily got to her feet on dry floor and walked up to them, slipping and sliding, waving her arms for balance.

One remained listless, verging on sad due to David's Telempathy. The other two gave off a sense of amusement at the 'little angry kid' glaring at them.

"You shouldn't laugh at her," said Teal. "She's the only reason all three of you aren't dead already."

Before the men could chuckle again, Althea threw out a surge of fear, but not the sort of terror she usually called on to make danger run away. Scaring men pointing guns at people she cared about wouldn't end well. Terrified warriors frequently responded to fear with overkill. Since she didn't want them to open fire in a panic, Althea hit them with a flavor of dread like a small child experiences when their parent catches them doing something wrong. She focused on their weapons, associating the negative emotions to them.

The men all made faces like boys caught playing with

their parents' gun after being told not to touch it. Yelping, they tossed the rifles to the floor and backed away from her. She stalked after them in as much of a menacing posture as her size allowed. Even though the top of her head didn't even come up to their chin level and she had nothing more dangerous than a plain white dress, her presence cowed them out into the hall.

"You are only warriors doing what the chief says. Who is hurting these people?" Althea glared. "*Show me.*"

The men whimpered and hurried off. They didn't appear to be trying to flee from her, rather driven by emotion and psionic command to complete the task as rapidly as possible. She needed to jog in order to keep up with them. Teal, David, and Sahara followed. The girl held Teal's hand mostly because the gel still covering her flowed down her legs and got under her feet, causing her to continually fall. Also, being in a high-tech underground facility terrified her much more than her outward demeanor let on. The almost-teen radiated fear like a girl half her age waking up from a nightmare.

Althea completely understood the feeling. She'd felt the same way when she ended up in West City against her will for the first time. In fact, Sahara appeared to be coping with this place better than Althea handled the big city. Then again, the girl didn't have to cope with the oppressive weight of depression, hatred, anger, greed, lust, avarice, and general hopelessness saturating the giant city on top of being kidnapped.

Thinking about that made Althea angrier. The city people should not bring their greed and cruelty out here. She snarled to herself, though at the little noise, Teal stifled a laugh and whispered to David that 'someone's going to get a stern talking-to'. This in turn made Althea feel a little foolish, but didn't change her mind. Of course, Teal—and even David—seemed to think the people responsible for kidnapping villagers and doing cruel things to them here deserved to be killed. David, at least, would try to arrest bad people first before shooting them.

One of the soldiers said laws didn't matter out here. Such a truth worked in both ways: the corporations could get away with whatever they wanted, but so, too, could anyone else. Back in the big city, the police would need to 'investigate' and do other things she didn't understand. Here, justice often happened much more quickly.

Thinking about these horrible people stealing children from their families and packing them together in a huge jar as 'spare parts' or cutting them open over and over again—or whatever Teal saw on the screen but didn't tell her about—made her briefly entertain a debate over if the bad people really did deserve to die. She dismissed it in seconds, unable to find it in her to desire anyone's death.

*Killing is wrong.*

The men led her down the hall from the tank room, took the left turn back to the observation corridor and kept going straight across it to the other side. Here, the facility had far fewer doors but much larger rooms of fancy scientific equipment, mostly gleaming silver or pure white. None contained any people. Althea shot a brief glance through a huge window into a room with long tables of complicated devices. Blinking lights covered pretty much everything. In the second room they passed, a pair of dark grey figures worked at one of the tables, manipulating jars of liquid. They resembled skeletons in the sense of having spindly pipe-like arms and legs, an exposed 'spine' connecting the torso to the hips, and no flesh anywhere. Thankfully, their faces did not look like skulls, being plain grey ovals with glowing green eyes and a simple straight line where a mouth should be.

Neither one had thoughts or emotions. Obvious robots.

They also ignored everyone, continuing their task of moving small quantities of fluid from one glass container to another, then putting it in strange devices. Althea didn't get much of a look at their work thanks to the pace of the three terrified soldiers.

David whistled. "This place must have been operating for years to be this developed."

"Ehh." Teal shrugged. "I've seen shake-and-bake operations bases bigger than this put up in a month." She glanced to her right at a passing side corridor. "Aha! Those look like residential quarters. We'll be right back. Keep going, we'll catch up. Some benevolent scientist is about to donate to the 'help a scrag not be naked' fund. For just credits a day, you, too, can make a difference." She mostly dragged Sahara by the hand down the other hall.

David chuckled.

Althea followed the soldiers straight down the remainder of the corridor. They stopped in front of the door at the end, pointing at it.

"There," whimpered one.

"The boss and scientists are in here." Man Two hastily typed a code into a wall panel.

With a pneumatic *pssht,* the door snapped open.

"Please don't hurt us," whispered Man Three.

Althea pointed. "Go in."

The men made fearful noises, shying away from her and hurrying past the door. Althea stormed after them, entering a room containing a big silver table at its center, surrounded by twenty padded black chairs. A massive display screen spanned the entire wall across from the door, divided into many smaller square 'windows,' each showing one of the kidnapped people in their beds. Two mini-screens contained camera feeds from the tank room. Beneath the giant screen, a console desk as wide as the room glowed green and yellow in the light of multiple holographic terminals.

Thirteen people in modern clothes stood in a cluster between the far end of the table and the control desk, as if they'd all rushed in here to hide from the 'dangerous intruders.' Ten wore long white lab coats over their clothes. Three didn't. Althea recognized the ones not in lab coats from the spirit talker's memory, especially the fortyish blond woman in a high-necked black sweater and skirt who simply *looked* evil. She felt even less nice in person. The others all appeared to be looking to her for instruction. While fear and confusion saturated everyone else, she radiated a sense of irritation.

A few seconds after Althea entered and everyone processed what they saw, a few of the people in lab coats gasped.

"What is she?" whispered a man.

"Psionic?" asked a woman.

"How can a little girl be so scary?" whispered another man. "I can't decide if I want to run away screaming or hug her for being adorable."

"Right?" asked a woman next to him, trembling.

Althea stopped five paces in from the doorway, hands clenched in fists, gaze hard, looking back and forth in disgust at these people who did such horrible things to innocent villagers. One by one, she peeked into their thoughts, prodding their brains with mental questions that made the answers float back as a reflex. Merely asking a question made a person think about the response even if they didn't want to say it out loud.

The people in white coats did the actual work. They released disease into the village on the surface for several reasons: to see what happened, to develop more effective biological weapons, to develop cures for those weapons, and to develop cures for other natural diseases. Harvesting life shapes from kidnapped villagers provided credits to support the facility's operation. Using Sahara and other people, to grow 'replacement organs' cost about one tenth the price of the normal process city people used to regrow damaged life shapes.

The scientists here found the scrag population from Afbee fascinating due to its relative isolation allowing them to remain remarkably close, genetically, to the composition of society as it had been in the Before-Time. While the majority of the scientists understood what they did would be considered wrong, they made peace with their task by regarding the scrags as 'too primitive to really count as people.' A few even regarded this project the same as using primates for experiments, beings not truly human but close enough to offer valid data. The ones who programmed the tank machines to keep stealing life shapes from Sahara and the others justified it by telling themselves the 'patient' didn't feel anything and would help other 'real people' back in the city.

The three people not in lab coats were something called 'management.' They made the decisions.

Everyone appeared to be waiting for the blonde woman, who they thought of as Verona Crane, to tell them what to do. They feared her, more frightened she'd take away their jobs than they might lose their lives out in the Badlands. Verona regarded Althea as a curious, if irritating, pest. She worried about something called a Brigham, some manner of 'executive' loyal to Naturahealth Pharmaceuticals. This project had been what she considered 'her big chance to make executive', and the instant she believed 'some little brat with glowing eyes' became a threat to her dreams, she would have zero hesitation shooting her.

Teal arrived with Sahara, who now wore a too-large

white shirt and blue skirt. The girl radiated happiness and pride at owning 'fancy' garments like no one else in Afbee.

"Why is the kid just staring at us like that?" whispered a woman in a white coat.

Verona scowled at the three shaking soldiers. "What is wrong with you men? Do your jobs and protect this facility. Shoot the trespassers before they cause more damage. Need I remind you the substantial investment involved—"

"*Stop talking,*" barked Althea, her eyes flaring for an instant in response to the command.

"Erk..." Verona's jaw clamped shut. She spent a few seconds unsuccessfully trying to speak, then trembled in rage, glaring.

The other woman and man not in lab coats gave off a sense of frightened amusement. The woman envied Althea's ability to 'make that bitch shut up.'

Verona came close to going for the gun she carried hidden under her sweater, but hesitated because of El Ojo. The woman didn't know *how* the doll went offline, only that they had lost contact with their 'eyes on the surface.' She didn't think it possible for an annoying little brat, a nosy cop, and 'a punk girl with blue hair' to have any chance against a doll, so something she called an 'unknown variable' must be at work. This unknown gave her enough natural fear not to go for her weapon. If El Ojo failed to kill them, she didn't have the nerve to try.

Althea pointed at Verona. "She has a gun and wants to shoot me, 'cause she wants to make an executive. They're all afraid of her 'cause she's gonna light them on fire an' take away job things."

"Shit, psionic," whispered a man, who then clamped his hands over his ears as if it might keep her out of his head. "She's reading our minds!"

Most of the bad people gasped, their fear intensifying.

"Light us on fire?" The manager woman who found it amusing to watch Verona forced to shut up gawked at her. "I knew you were a bitch, but damn…"

David chuckled. "She more than likely means 'fire you,' not light on actual fire. Althea is not familiar with the modern world."

A general sense of relief came from the crowd, except for Verona—who grew angrier, mostly at the woman who called her a bitch.

"Naturahealth. Should've known," muttered David.

"What is that?" asked Althea.

"A corporation." He frowned. "They make medicines and medical equipment, but their ethical practices leave a lot to be desired. They've been investigated hundreds of times. No damn idea how the company still exists."

Teal shook her head. "Some exec probably has a relative in the senate. Only thing more corrupt than a corporate executive is a senator."

Some of the scientists chuckled.

"Oh, don't laugh at me." Teal drew her handgun. "You bastards are damn lucky this kid's such an angel. She's the only reason I'm not throwing every last one of you straight out of the gene pool for what you've done here." She flashed a sarcastic smile at the soldiers. "No laws out here, right?"

Althea glanced over her shoulder at her. "Umm, they don't have a pool."

Teal's lip quivered like she almost laughed.

"Listen to me," said Althea, trying to mimic the tone of voice used by mothers in Querq when their kids did something wrong. "You make sicks and you make stuff to fix the sicks. You will take all the sicks away from Afbee and leave everyone alone."

A man with a bit of grey appearing in his otherwise

black hair cautiously approached her, raising a hand. Black words on his lab coat read: 'Dr. N. Fairburn, Director of Research.' "We have cures for some of the pathogens out in the field, but not all of them. The work is still in development."

David frowned. "So, you tell the villagers spirits will punish them for leaving, hoping it's a cheap way to not let some crazy virus get loose in the world. Taking a lot of chances."

Dr. Fairburn sighed. "It is not the most ideal control, but we felt it important to maintain as natural a habitat as possible for the experimental population."

Teal's arm blurred up from her side to sticking straight out in front of her, gun in hand. Before anyone even noticed her move, she'd shot Fairburn in the left knee. He fell over, screaming. Sahara also shrieked, startled at the bizarre loud noise.

"No!" yelled Althea.

Except for Verona, the Naturahealth employees all ducked low to the ground at the gunshot. The manager remained standing, eyes narrowed in an expression of anger, though she gave off worry.

"Relax, kiddo." Teal narrowed her eyes. "I didn't kill him. The next one of you soulless pieces of shit who talks about human beings like lab animals 'in a habitat' is getting a bullet straight in the groin."

Althea grabbed Teal's arm in both hands, trying—unsuccessfully—to pull it down. "Please don't. Hurting people because it makes you feel better is as bad as what they did."

"I'm not hurting them to feel better. I'm hurting them because they deserve punishment." Teal lowered her weapon. "What would make me feel better is throwing a few Naturahealth executives off the roof of their headquarters tower. Extra points if they make it all the way to ground level without hitting a hovercar on the way."

As the realization of how fast Teal moved sank into the minds of the bad people, their level of fear increased. Verona smirked in an 'oh, that explains it' manner... then shifted her opinion. Teal now annoyed her more than Althea.

Hoping her friend simply made a cruel joke and didn't really intend to go on a killing spree, Althea restrained herself from becoming even more upset and merely responded with a 'please don't' stare.

Dr. Fairburn passed out.

A woman in a lab coat pounced on him, examining the wound. "Anyone have stims on them? His knee's... gone."

"Cover me," deadpanned Althea, mimicking something the city police liked to say. "I'm going in."

David drew his E-90. "Everyone stay still and don't move. I know you all think the National Police Force doesn't have jurisdiction out here, but you'd be wrong. We do. Command is just as lazy and budget-conscious as any corporation. To further clarify, summary executions are more cost effective than transporting suspects into custody. Personally, I'd rather deal with the custodial transportation, but my lieutenant won't really care if I fill out a weapons discharge form instead."

"Only enforcing the law out here when you feel like it is giving them tacit approval," said Teal.

"You know how bureaucracy works." David frowned. "Especially when credits and politics are involved. Not my choice. And hey, I'm the guy who volunteered to be stationed at Querq."

Althea smiled to herself, sensing his bluff. David didn't like killing people either, though he *would* do so if he had to. She padded over to Dr. Fairburn. The large slug from Teal's sidearm mostly severed the man's lower leg. Only two swaths of skin and some tendon remained of the knee.

She dropped to sit beside him and grabbed his leg, closing her eyes and diving into the healing trance. Physical injuries proved simpler to repair than sicks, though they took more energy. After telling his blood to stay inside him, she encouraged his muscles, tendons, cartilage, and bone to regenerate. The tunnel through his leg gradually shrank until it sealed. Once the wound closed, she paused to take a few breaths then forced his body to make more blood, replacing what he lost.

"Amazing," whispered someone nearby.

"Damn, now we *have* to kill everyone here," said Teal in a—hopefully—joking tone.

"W-why?" asked a woman.

"Because." Teal sighed. "You work for a profit-at-all-costs pharmaceutical company, lack any sense of ethics, and just watched a kid magically heal a dude. As soon as you tell your bosses back in the city what you saw, we're going to be killing a dozen mercenaries a week out here. I'd rather not deal with the headache."

Althea opened her eyes, gazing down at her bloody hands and the man's new pink-skinned knee. "Please stop the hurting. Make all the sicks go away now."

Verona rolled her eyes. "Silly child. Why on Earth would we do that? Do you have any idea how much has been spent—?"

"Because I'm telling you to!" shouted Althea. She snapped her gaze up to the woman and threw off a surge of radiant fear.

The bad people recoiled in unison, as if hit by a physical force. Two wet themselves. The woman amused by Verona being made to shut up burst into tears, calling for her father. One man fainted. Verona mostly resisted the dread, suffering only a case of 'strong nervousness.' Althea's opinion of her changed to pity. She'd learned from the city police how Telempathy sometimes couldn't affect people who had 'brain problems' where their emotions didn't work right or at all, sociopaths or psychopaths or some such big city word.

*She's not really evil, just sick.*

Althea nudged Dr. Fairburn back to consciousness. As soon as he opened his eyes, she grabbed his shirt collar in both hands, pulling him up nose to nose with her and forcing his emotions into a state of guilty shame, "Make the sicks go away, now. Let the people out of the big jars. Do not hurt anyone."

The edges of the room darkened. Black vapor seeped out from the metal walls, gathering in puddles around the room. A strong sense of dread welled up out of nowhere, thickening the air. Other than becoming even more on edge, no one reacted to the otherworldly vapor.

David became nervous, likely sensing the paranormal energy gathering around them while being unable to see the manifestation forming. "Damn… Trying to call this in, but not getting any signal. They must be jamming comms."

"No." Althea let go of the doctor and stood. "They aren't doing it. The Many is here."

## 32

# THE LINE BETWEEN HELP
# AND HARM

Everyone in the command room all stopped moving at the same time.

Dust motes sparkling in the overhead lights froze in midair. A bead of sweat came to a stop inches below the chin of a man in a lab coat. Complete silence surrounded Althea. All the thrum of electronics, whimpering, and the whirr of the machines making the air cold stopped.

A presence strengthened behind her.

"Why are you here?" asked Althea without looking.

"You should not need to ask," said the voice of an old man. "I am everywhere."

*Except the big city. It's too mean there, even for you.* She smirked to herself. Obviously, West City couldn't be too evil for The Many. He didn't go there for some other reason she didn't truly understand. The one person at the city police who took her stories about him seriously said something about the defense of collective human consciousness in such a highly populated area. Out here, he could affect people, machines, even reality to a point—as he did now, making time appear to stop.

He probably didn't stop *actual* time. Most likely, the conversation about to happen would occur in the span of a single breath and only feel as if minutes passed. Perhaps he'd pulled Althea into a dream. Everyone else in the room would see her staring into space for a few seconds or so no matter how long she spent talking to him.

The Many paced around her in a circle, walking into view on her left. He'd again 'dressed up' as his favorite apparition: an incredibly ancient man in a long coat, cowboy hat, and boots. A pair of Before-Time revolver pistols hung in holsters on either side of a belt studded in bullets. Wispy grey hair draped like cobwebs at the sides of a face mottled in patches of brown and purple. Dark veins streaked his otherwise pale, papery skin, stretched so taut it revealed every curve of his skull. Brittle lips peeled back in a forced grin, baring teeth the color of moldy spinach.

Neither his appearance nor his cadaverous smell bothered her anymore. He couldn't hurt her. She wouldn't —or couldn't—hurt him. The Many claimed to be the opposite side of a coin from her: an ancient man filled with death taunting a vibrant child who gave life.

She stared defiantly into his cold eyes. Images flickered at camera-flash speed across her consciousness: fly machines streaking overhead, giving off a horrible roaring noise, screaming, fiery deaths in the Before-Time, people shot in the street, people starving in the immediate aftermath of terrible bombs. She witnessed the final breaths of countless people in four seconds. Appalled, she broke eye contact.

He chuckled. "You deny the reality."

"No. I do not like to watch people die." She gripped the floor with her toes. "I know it happened, but I do not want to see it. You spend too much time looking at the death over and over. Stop being sad at what you cannot change."

"Ahh, that's what they told you." He clucked his tongue. "When you wept over all the death you failed to stop."

"I want to help you."

"We are long since gone," said the Many, his dry voice raking across her ears like dusty gravel. "You cannot save any of them. They are me. I am they."

"I don't care if it's impossible. I will try." She kept her head bowed, watching him from the chest down as he continued circling her.

He gave a wheezy chuckle. "The futile idealism of youth. Why are you here? This is my domain."

"Kellis asked me for help. They are making people have sicks here for pay things." Althea scowled. "I can't let them do it anymore."

"You hurt others by doing this." He appeared out of a burst of dark vapor in front of her, caressing her cheek in a cold, leathery hand.

She looked up. Orange light drifted across his eyes, as if they reflected a massive fire somewhere behind her. "You are lying."

"Am I?" He took his hand from her cheek, swinging his arm out sideways, gesturing at the frozen scientists. "They torment the savages in search of cures for the civilized. For every person here who dies to their experiments, they save a thousand elsewhere. If you stop them, you kill countless people in the big city."

Althea narrowed her eyes, not believing him.

"Oh, but you don't care." He resumed pacing. "You loathe the big city and its scary emotions. The people there are evil so they can die. Such a hypocrite."

"Stop lying." Althea stomped her foot. "They aren't working to help anyone. They want lots of pay-things. They are the same as the Wagon Man. If someone doesn't give them pay things, they won't help."

The Many sneered at her.

Reality shifted.

Althea found herself sitting in a ball, again five or six years old, stuck in a small steel cage wedged between two shelves, staring straight ahead past the bars at the big side door the Wagon Man used to open and turn into an awning. He'd stand outside at a podium like a salesman, shouting for anyone to come be healed—but only if they paid. Even though she knew she didn't presently sit in a cage, the sight of the bars stirred sadness and guilt. No matter who it was, if a hurt or sick person couldn't give the Wagon Man pay things, he wouldn't let them get close enough to the cage for her to help them. Far too often for her conscience to accept, she'd been trapped and unable to do anything while people died twenty feet away for lack of pay-things.

"You hate him for what he did." The Many appeared standing outside the cage.

Althea rested her chin on her hands. "This isn't real. You are only trying to make me upset."

He kicked the bars. "If this is not real, stop sitting in there."

"You only want to watch me fight the cage, fail, and cry. No. Stop it. This is a silly dream."

"Ahh. You cannot. You stay there because you are guilty. You think you belong in there. You think you deserve to be punished for all the people you were too cowardly to help."

"No." Althea looked down, no longer so sure he lied. She *did* hold on to a great amount of guilt over being too frightened to use her powers on raiders for most of her life.

"It is your fault they died." The Many traced his old, filthy fingers across the top of the cage above her head.

"You could always make the one you call Wagon Man do whatever you wanted. You could have escaped. You could have helped them."

Althea sighed. While she might have possessed the psionic powers necessary to do as he said, she didn't understand them nor even know she had them. Also, she'd been so little at the time, she couldn't possibly have thought to do anything other than obey what adults told her to do. All she'd ever wanted was to help people, stop their pain, and make them happy.

"Interfere in this place, and you will cause the deaths of thousands." The Many turned his back on her, raising an arm at the opposite wall, which opened into an awning. Outside, hundreds upon hundreds of modern city hospital beds dotted the Badlands desert, each one occupied by a sick and dying person. "You call them evil, but these doctors will discover cures. What's a few dozen dead tribal villagers compared to the lives of ten thousand? This cage you are trapped in comes from your feeble sense of morality. You won't allow yourself to go help them." He pointed at the vast field of beds. "You remain stuck here, unable to stop the death."

"No." Althea glared at the cage door. Knowing everything around her came from a bad dream gave her the strength to resist grabbing the bars and screaming at him to let her out. The Many always lied. "The big city has healing. People don't die to sicks because they already know how to fix them all."

He scowled. The wagon vanished. The room beneath Afbee returned, as did Althea's dress, agate pendant, and true age, though she sat on the floor in the same curled-up position as she'd been in the cage. David, Teal, Sahara, and all the bad people remained stopped in time like a three-dimensional picture.

She stood. "I don't believe you. These people are doing bad things."

"You will not interfere with my domain." He pointed at her face. "We had an... arrangement."

Althea ignored the finger hovering an inch from her nose. "I don't know what you think we agreed to. I'm not trying to hurt you. I want to help you, but you won't let me. Besides"—she thrust her arms out—"I didn't go looking for bad people to *interfere* with you. Kellis came and asked for help."

"So..." He withdrew his hand from her face. "You would have stayed at your pathetic little village and let these people suffer if he had not done so?"

She sighed at the ceiling. "Not by choice. If I knew about them, yes, I would help. I didn't know."

He chuckled. "How many people suffer because you choose your happiness over their lives? Stay with your *family*, safe in your little town. Why not wander around, ever in search of pain to cure?"

She swallowed hard. He'd come too close to making a good point. Althea adored having Karina for a sister and Father to take care of them. She adored having a real home. The idea of leaving her home behind forever and spending the rest of her life constantly roaming the Badlands to fix bad stuff made her sad. Tears gathered in her eyes at the guilt of choosing personal happiness over other people's lives.

The Many smiled.

That little spark of satisfaction in his expression pulled her away from the edge of taking his lie for truth. No. A twelve-year-old, even one like her, belonged at home with her family. Maybe she would consider roaming the land once she'd grown up, but even then, the people of Querq depended on her. Could she abandon them to run off in search of random suffering people she might never find? Out in the Badlands, The Many could throw countless obstacles in her path. If not enough to kill her, he could certainly slow her to the point where she always arrived too late to matter.

No, better for everyone if she remained in Querq. The people there needed her. Word would spread of her presence, and those in need would either go there or, like Kellis, send someone to ask for help.

Sensing her emotions pull away from despondence, The Many frowned. "Fine. Kill people if you want. Everyone who dies because this place failed to make a cure is your fault."

"The only sicks they cannot cure are the ones they made here. Not real sicks. Weapon sicks." She tapped her foot. "City people can cure sicks if they know about them. It's only the new ones they haven't seen before. If the bad people here don't make a sick, the city people don't need a cure from them. You are lying."

The Many narrowed his eyes. Dark veins in his cheeks and forehead thickened. "Do what you will then, but the scientists are mine."

She shook her head. "You know I can't let you hurt anyone."

He raised a wispy eyebrow. "Even those who would inflict such harm on the innocent? These scientists are worse than any raider. They cut that girl behind you open thousands of times and tore pieces out of her... for money. Imagine if their virus escaped this village. If it got loose in the world, it could kill tens of billions."

She stared down at her feet. "It is wrong. I can't let you kill them."

"Then consider yourself fortunate I do not need your permission." His ancient cowboy form collapsed into a column of black smoke and promptly fell straight down, spreading out across the floor to the walls, filling the room in an ankle-deep layer of inky fog. "Stay here and protect those who torture and kill anyone that suits their purpose, or return to the surface and stop me from claiming the entire village. I *will* take either the innocent or the guilty. It is your choice. Be glad I satisfy myself with sixteen souls. But if you prefer, I will take all 267 villagers instead."

Tears dribbled off her chin. She kept staring at her toes as the dark vapor receded into the corners of the room. Rachel's voice echoed in her mind. *Some people deserve to die.* The Many put her in a position to choose who died. How responsible did it make her for the death? Teal wanted to kill these scientists. David didn't want to, but wouldn't be too bothered by it. Althea knew some people considered her 'too nice.' Feeling helpless filled her with the want to run back home and cling to Father and Karina, sobbing until they somehow made it all better.

*No… The Many is going to kill them. Not me. I am choosing to save people.*

As much as she hated to admit it to herself, if people absolutely *had* to die, better sixteen evil ones than three hundred-ish innocent ones. She couldn't bear to look at the scientists, especially the woman who thought of Verona as a bitch. Other than being part of such a cruel project, she seemed like a reasonably normal person stuck working a bad job. She had, however, been part of evil. The woman — or any of them — could have quit and left at any time, but hadn't.

She wept in silence. Tears dribbled over her chin, down her neck, and soaked into her dress.

It took her a moment to notice time resumed. Everyone stood around staring at each other in tense silence. David's E-90 kept the scientists and the three security guards mostly still. Verona glared hatefully at Teal. Sahara hovered in the doorway, shivering from the cold.

"Make the sicks go away," said Althea in a half-whisper, her voice saturated in guilt.

Five people in lab coats rushed to the console and began working. She caught bits and pieces of thought, something about 'deploying synthetic rats' with antidotes as well as a small army of tiny robots capable of detecting and sanitizing surfaces.

Teal rested a hand on Althea's shoulder. "Hey, what's wrong? Why are you crying?"

"Something happened we didn't see," said David in a low voice. "She's incredibly sad."

"Kinda figured that from the tears," deadpanned Teal.

Althea lifted her gaze off the floor. "Please help me get the villagers out of here. Don't worry about the bad people. There is nothing anyone can do for them now." She sniffled once, then glanced over at Verona, the two managers, and the scientists. "I am sorry."

## 33

## LESSER EVIL

Althea trudged down the hall, trying to think of a way to stop The Many from hurting anyone here. Afraid if she stood around thinking too long without doing anything, he'd kill everyone, she decided to make her decision obvious by helping the kidnapped villagers. Even though the scientists sent their little robots to deliver cures where possible, roughly half the people held captive in the underground 'non-hospital' suffered from experimental viruses the company developed as weapons. Consequently, no effective ways to stop them existed. Only robots or people wearing protective suits ever went into those rooms.

The little badge card they took from Verona opened all the doors. Althea and Teal went room to room in the 'experimental pathogen' side. While she purged the sicks out of people—as well as removed various tubes and other objects stuffed into their bodies, Teal broke the restraints and used David's flame pistol to destroy whatever slime came out of them.

Conditions here proved a thousand times better than the

surface hospital. Except for whatever harmful materials each person sweat, they appeared quite clean. Though the victims in the four 'bad' rooms *looked* in better shape than the sick people she found with Doc, the sicks inside them all proved much nastier, certainly intended to kill. The other captive villagers hosted different sicks not intended for use as weapons.

Teal's comment about the poor bastards in the tanks having their organs farmed being better off stabbed Althea in the heart like a knife, mostly because it rang true. After the better part of an hour, Althea led a group of forty-three confused villagers ranging in age from nine to middle-aged down the hall to the tank room. By the time she arrived, David had already let everyone out of the gel, helped them wash the sticky substance away, and let them have their pick from a pile of clothing taken from the residence quarters.

Sahara couldn't stop crying from joy. The eleven children who'd been stuffed in two gel tanks sat in a circle around her on the floor while she attempted to explain what happened. She thought the other kids had been taken by angry spirits, never to be seen again. When the youngest victims from the beds, another six children, rushed over to join them, Sahara practically fainted at seeing them alive. Once she regained her composure, she assured all the kids they hadn't been taken by spirits, were not dead, and would soon be back home with their parents.

Teal directed the newcomers to the pile of clothing she gathered from the scientists' living quarters. "Grab whatever you want."

The villagers began examining the modern clothing, holding pieces up as if they couldn't quite tell what to make of them.

David approached. "Any of them contagious?"

"I don't think so." Teal shrugged and handed him the flame pistol. "We left the virus scanner with Phoenix."

A chorus of horrible screaming echoed in the hallway, then abruptly faded to silence.

Curiously, Althea didn't feel the icy scrape of death nearby. Still, she wept, having been unable to come up with any ideas for how to stop The Many from taking the people who made this horrible place. Concentrating really hard on not wanting him to hurt anyone didn't help. Sensing her sadness growing, David pulled her into a comforting embrace. Loving human contact, something she'd been deprived of for most of her life, helped her cope with the sorrow of helplessness.

"What the hell?" Teal spun to face the door. "Last time I heard screaming like that, someone chucked an acid fume grenade into a security station."

David cringed. "Did you say 'acid fume grenade'?"

"Mars. ACC used them. Not like they care about war crimes. Nothing says 'I hate you' like melting someone's lungs from the inside out." Teal shook her head, then squeezed Althea's shoulder. "What's wrong, kiddo?"

"The Many took them," she whispered. "I couldn't stop him."

"Define 'took,'" said David.

"I…" She blinked, unsure what to say. "Think they became part of him. Like all the other angry ghosts. The Many said he would take the bad doctors. If I stopped him, he'd take everyone in Afbee instead."

Teal patted her. "You made the right choice."

"It's a bad choice." Althea frowned to the side. "It's mean to make me choose. He wanted me to cry. I couldn't save them."

David rocked her slightly side to side. "You chose to save innocent people. I know you didn't want *anyone* to die, but try not to feel guilty about what he does. You can't be everywhere and save everyone all the time. It is not your fault."

"Maybe." Althea sniffled, begrudgingly trying to believe him.

David huffed out a sigh of contempt. "Worst thing about what happened to those sadistic pricks is the bosses at Naturahealth will never understand the full consequences. They'll think they simply lost a team to the Badlands, unaware of the real price they paid."

"Not sure the executives would care even if they understood." Teal frowned. "Besides, you start talking about demons or the collective mass-consciousness of a million dead people… you'll end up off the force with a nice little white room to yourself."

David smirked. "Probably, though maybe not. Division 0 is a little more open to nonstandard explanations."

Althea sniffled again, despite the building sense of relief and joy surrounding her from the villagers. She might feel good about helping them in a little while, if she could get past the guilt of allowing The Many to take sixteen not-so-innocent lives.

"All the horrors you've seen out there…" David gave her another brief squeeze, then held her out at arm's length to make eye contact. "Never stop caring. Don't let him win. Light is light, dark is dark. Both exist. You can't change that, only bring as much light as you are capable of."

"I know." She wiped her eyes. "Doesn't mean I have to like it when the darkness gets people."

## 34

# TRIAGE

**T**hey returned to a village in a mild state of chaos.

Despite the late hour, everyone gathered in the open area in front of the Credit Union building where they usually ate meals together. Six people held staff-sized torches, providing some light. The overall mood among the people consisted of apocalyptic fear, as if they'd all witnessed an event heralding the imminent end of the world. Phoenix addressed the crowd, having a modest degree of success convincing them spirits hadn't decided to kill everyone.

At the sight of Teal, David, and Althea leading a large group of 'dead' people back into the village, a heavy silence fell over everyone. Durango appeared ready to faint. Other than a few congested coughs, no one made a sound. The villagers in front of Althea gave off a sense of fear. The ones behind her, relief.

Althea squeezed between Teal and David to stand at the front of their group. "What the spirit talker told you is not true. Do not be angry with him. He warned you of spirits to keep you safe. The sicks came from *people*, not spirits. Bad people hid under the ground. They gave you sicks and stole some of you at night. The bad people are gone. There are no angry spirits here."

The crowd continued staring, their emotions mixed between hope, distrust, and shock.

"Ask them." Althea gestured at the villagers behind her, the ones they freed from the un-hospital.

As soon as the kidnapped children shouted for their parents and ran into view, the crowd's unease and dread rapidly gave way to elation.

"Rav!" shouted Camry.

A boy about ten years old—one of the kids who'd been stuffed in a tank with four other children—raced forward. Camry, Onda, Kia, and Pri tackled him, getting dirt all over the clean white shirt he wore like a tunic.

"Mo!" shouted Sahara.

The instant Mojave made eye contact with her sister, she burst into tears, too overcome with emotion to move. Sahara ran into a hug, both girls collapsing to sit on the ground holding each other. Savan and Elantra embraced them together.

Other people believed lost to spirits rushed to reunite with their families and friends. Upon noticing not only their friend Rav, but all the other 'spirit taken' children, Onda, Camry, Kia, and Pri shouted and screamed so much people in Querq probably heard them. Sadly, not all the missing children still had parents to welcome them. Some of the kids who'd been crammed together in gel tanks had been missing for years; several of their mothers and fathers had succumbed to various sicks—or sadness—since. Though the villagers expressed bafflement at how the children missing for three and four years hadn't grown any older, no one questioned it, too happy to see them alive and have them home.

Teal explained the nine kids in the tanks had been 'frozen for later use' according to the computer. The Naturahealth people considered them valuable for their snapshot of genetics out of the past, but hadn't decided how best to utilize them. So, they simply kept them in storage. Althea's heart broke hearing it, knowing parents had been devastated believing they'd lost their kids. At least they hadn't been tortured. As far as any of the children knew, no time at all had gone by. They went to sleep one night and woke up coated in slime in a strange room.

A few small hearts broke when the kids learned their mothers or fathers—in a few cases both—died to sickness. Unable to handle the wave of conflicting emotion around her, Althea clung to Teal and David. Joy, sorrow, relief, and her own guilt at the scientists' death proved too much. She broke down and cried so hard she would have collapsed if not for Teal holding her up.

"What happened here?" asked David. "Did we miss some kind of party?"

Phoenix chuckled. "You first."

David told her about the underground facility. Althea already knew the story, so she didn't pay much attention, lost to the tumultuous churn of contradictory emotions saturating the area. Villagers overcome with happiness stood next to others crushed to learn their loved ones perished while they'd been away. Gradually, the people who'd been abducted shifted from confused fear to anger. They no longer dreaded the wrath of 'spirits,' instead becoming angry at ordinary people with fancy technology.

Hearing them talk about the stuff in the facility as 'technology' and not magic distracted Althea from her grief. Most scrags would call anything they didn't understand magic. Villagers from Den's old tribe even thought of a crowbar as 'the magic opener.' Something like an electric flashlight would've ended up on an altar being worshiped there.

*Is it because they're from Air Force?* She took a few deep breaths and tried to settle her emotions. *They know the frozen speaking… umm, how to read.*

"Wow." Phoenix huffed. "Looks like I'll be busy once I'm back home. Gonna take me weeks to put this investigation together. Hopefully, I-Ops can drag Naturahealth into an inquest over this. Ask me again why I'm glad to be Admin. This is a giant ball of paperwork I don't have to deal with."

"What freaked everyone here out?" asked Teal. "Looked like a mess when we walked in."

"Oh." Phoenix gestured randomly at the village. "A shitstorm of synthetic rats invaded, chasing people down and jabbing them with needles. Over a hundred of them, plus little orb bots zoomed all over the place, spraying. The villagers thought their spirits finally got mad enough to wipe them out, like the invasion of rats was the first step to the apocalypse."

"My fault." Althea grimaced. "I told the bad doctors to fix everyone they made sick."

David nodded. "They were using those rats to distribute various pathogens to the people here discreetly. All one big experiment."

"Disgusting." Phoenix glared.

"Oh, don't worry about it. The people who did this definitely paid for it." Teal kicked at the dirt.

"You?" Phoenix raised an eyebrow.

"No." Althea bowed her head. "The Many took them."

"Riiight." Phoenix rubbed the bridge of her nose. "Still, the field personnel out here doing the dirty work aren't the only ones to blame. Their bosses are equally responsible."

David shot her a 'good luck with that' glance. "You

know they're going to slip away. They always do… unless Division 9 gets involved."

Phoenix shuddered. "Usually, they scare me… but in this case, it might be deserved."

Althea scrunched her nose at David.

He patted her on the head. "You wouldn't like them. I could tell you about them, but it would only make you sad."

"Then don't." She sighed.

Durango approached their group. "Outsiders…"

Althea looked up at him. The village leader wore a heavy cloak of gratitude and shame, in addition to his old fighter pilot jumpsuit. David, Teal, and Phoenix shifted their attention to him as well.

"The spirit talker has shared the truth." Durango set his hands on his hips. "When the rats came, I thought the spirits decided to kill us all."

"Antidotes," said David. "Those responsible for what happened here used artificial rats to infect your people with various diseases. Althea made them distribute as many cures as they could. Seems they used the fake rats to carry the antidotes, too."

Durango responded to the explanation with a slow blink and much confusion.

"Not real rats. Machines," said Althea, before telepathically sharing her memory of the one Teal shot so he understood the concept of a synthetic animal.

"I… see." Durango exhaled. "Forgive me for being harsh with you earlier. I did not have good information. Our library is old. Many of the books are no longer readable."

"It's fine." Teal shook hands with him. "Kid said you weren't doing it to be a dick."

"I did not say that." Althea folded her arms.

Teal laughed. "Not in those same words, no."

"We still have an issue." David glanced around. "The lab monkeys released several experimental viruses they don't have cures for, like the one we've been calling the K-virus. We need to make sure everyone here is healthy."

"The biggest problem," said Phoenix, "is hygiene. I need to reintroduce you and your people to the concept of soap, dirt, bathing, regular cleaning of laundry... that sort of thing. This entire village is going to need to be washed."

"What can we do?" asked Durango. "If it is reasonable, I will make it happen."

Phoenix exhaled in a 'here we go' manner. "We will need to have everyone leave the walled part of the village. One person at a time goes out to an area we'll designate as a midway point. There, Althea will make sure they have no diseases. We'll clean them up and then send them to a known-safe area elsewhere in the ruins where no diseases are present. Do you know of anywhere safe?"

"What about the bad place?" asked Althea. "I know it's scary to them, but raiders can't find it. It's hidden and safe. There is food, good water, more clothes, beds."

"As long as they stay out of the patient rooms." Teal frowned. "Guess it's a good thing they kept everyone drugged asleep. No one's going to have traumatic memories of the place. Only confusion at how they ended up there."

"The patient rooms ought to be sanitized by now." David scratched at his chin. "The staff set the orb bots to clean everything up."

*How can a room be patient?* Althea had never once heard of an *im*patient room. She furrowed her brow at him.

At the weird face she made, he looked at her thoughts, then cracked up. Once he stopped laughing, he hugged her. "You are adorable."

"What?" She grumbled.

"Patient has more than one meaning. I'll explain once we're done here."

Althea shrugged. "Okay."

Phoenix pursed her lips. "I'll need to go there and make sure all the stores of infectious agents are destroyed first. Otherwise, the underground facility might be a good bet until we can get the village cleaned up."

"How will we clean the village?" asked Durango.

"Depending on the nature of the infectious agents, the most reasonable way to ensure the safety of your people is simply to abandon this place for a while." Phoenix tapped at her datapad. "Some of these organisms can persist in the environment for a few weeks before they die. Given the arid climate and sun, it's probably going to clean up faster than average. To be safe, I'd say give it a month, preferably two."

"A month…" Durango shifted his jaw from side to side.

"Thirty days," said Phoenix.

He chuckled. "I understand what a month is. I am not understanding how we can simply live elsewhere for so long. Everything we have is here."

"It's only about a mile northeast." Teal pointed.

"Wait." Althea looked up. "The bad people brought you food. You don't have farms. The bad people are gone now, so you won't have any food."

"El Ojo hunted dust hopper and other meats," said Durango.

"El Ojo is gone." Teal rolled her shoulder as if sore. "He worked for the bad people."

"Oh, shit." Phoenix gazed up at the clouds. "There's no way they're going to establish a farm any time soon."

David pointed back over his shoulder. "Has to be some kind of hydroponics or reassembler units in the facility. How else did they feed the whole village for the past however many years this project has been going on?"

"True." Phoenix calmed. "We'll just need to find it and train some of Durango's people how to operate it. They might be better off permanently moving to the facility. It'll be a bit cramped for 200 people, but not intolerable."

"Won't last forever." David scrunched his nose. "It ought to at least be good for a few years. Should be able to expand outward from the facility. Worst case scenario, it fails and they relocate to Querq."

"What is a Querq?" asked Durango.

"It is my home." Althea smiled. "A really big village umm…"

"North of here and a bit west," said David. "Kellis knows how to get there."

"If you cannot stay here, you are welcome in Querq." Althea bit her lip. "Without a drive machine, it is ten days walking."

She leaned against Teal while the adults discussed what to do next. Durango sounded keen on the idea of exploring the underground facility and possibly moving the village there for increased protection as well as clean water and food. Althea's invitation to move to Querq would serve as their last resort if staying here without the 'invisible helping hand' of modern city people leaving food out for collection proved impossible. Between Teal and Phoenix, they felt fairly confident they could train a group of the smarter locals how to operate hydroponic machinery. Computers did most of the complicated work. A human operator only needed to push a few buttons.

Though the next day or two sounded like it would be much the same as her time owned by raider gangs—sitting in one spot healing an endless train of people—Althea didn't mind. The sooner she got rid of all the sicks, the sooner she could go home to her family.

## 35

# DREAMS

**A**lthea dragged herself into the big buggy and flopped in the back seat.

The past two days felt like a blur of healing trance. They'd taken over an unused building near the Afbee wall, turning it into her *Cha'dom,* the sacred hut where a village's *chamán* lived and worked magic. She didn't consider herself a *chamán,* or a shaman as the English speaking called it. Teal chose that particular building because it had two big holes in the ground useful for catching all the sicks people had to let out. She said the pits had something to do with fixing old drive machines in the Before-Time.

Since they needed to process the entire village, the giant holes in the ground proved much easier and safer than trying to have everyone expel the toxins into metal pails. At the end of each day, David and Phoenix fired their flame pistols into the pits, incinerating the dangerous mess. Almost every villager had a mild case of the K-virus, some less mild. The infection proved highly contagious. However, thanks to Phoenix going on an expedition to the underground facility to destroy its reserves of viral agents, she'd learned much from their computers.

The K-virus hadn't been designed to kill, merely incapacitate a person as much as feasibly possible to do without causing death. Its design documentation outlined a weaponized bio-agent capable of rendering a 'targeted population' incapable of resisting takeover within a matter of two weeks. Of course, ideal expectations and reality didn't often agree. The virus *had* killed people and could likely continue doing so. Field observations even among the residents of Afbee already confirmed at least seven unexpected mutations in the strain, one of which happened to be the extremely painful 'red dot' pox Kia and Rogue suffered.

Also, the designers assumed infection of an abnormally healthy population—soldiers. Thousands of variables in a person's body could change the impact of the virus from debilitating to deadly. For no reason the Naturahealth researchers understood, a small portion of villagers experienced no effects at all beyond carrying it to others.

One by one, people migrated from the village to the underground complex by way of Althea's temporary clinic. No materials or objects from the village went past the 'quarantine line' as Phoenix called it. The Naturahealth research station had plenty of new, clean clothing for all the villagers. Some of the children became upset at not being able to take their favored possessions with them—especially Onda and his necklace of shiny sockets. Since steel would survive fire, Phoenix offered to sterilize it for him and return it soon, which calmed him.

However, after two days of continuous work, Althea wanted to melt into a puddle.

As soon as her butt hit the uncomfortable metal seat in the back of the buggy, she passed out.

ALTHEA AWOKE TO FIND HERSELF SITTING IN THE WAGON
Man's cage.

*Ugh. Not again.* She frowned at the layer of dirt coating a
body too small to be her. The room swayed and rocked as it
had whenever they moved from place to place. Travel
meant hours of solitude, her only amusement came from
making the big padlock keeping her trapped rattle around.
Being in this cage, even as a dream, reminded her how she
had initially wanted to escape. The first few months she'd
been locked up in the wagon, she fought the bars
constantly, kicking, pounding, pulling, even trying to
squeeze herself between them.

The Althea who accepted captivity to help others didn't
happen immediately. It had taken her years to become
resigned to her fate. She grumbled to herself, tracing lines
in the dirt on her stomach. Had she known about
Suggestion or Telempathy at this age, she absolutely would
have used it on the Wagon Man. If she could believe this
dream, she had not *always* been a perfectly obedient captive.
Five-year-old Althea couldn't possibly have been afraid of
being punished for using her powers because she had no
idea what a mystic even was. She'd lied to herself, even if
her memory told a lie without her really meaning to. Did
that mean the man and woman she thought of as her
parents might still be alive? For so long, she believed the
Wagon Man killed them. What other explanation could
exist for her being a placid captive? But she'd remembered
wrong. A child taken from her home—who still had parents
to return to—would fight to get away.

She hadn't played with the padlock; she'd been trying to
break it.

Now, in the dream, she didn't bother.

The non-reality didn't feel creepy and scary, so she doubted The Many tormented her. This had to be coming from her exhausted mind. She sat there in the tiny cage, her knees pressed to her chest, not having enough room to lie down or stand. She could stick her legs out between the bars at least, but didn't bother, fully aware she experienced a vivid dream. Instead, she tried to wake up or change the dream to something nicer, like being home with Karina and Father.

Rocking ceased. The creak of old springs came from the right, then the *thud* of the Wagon Man jumping down from the seat on the front. Scuffing boot steps came around the front. The awning wall opened. Grinning broadly, the Wagon Man stepped up into the trailer, giving her the 'you're going to make me a *ton* of money today' smile he always did.

"Hello there, kid. Good, ya didn't mess the floor again. You're learning." He reached to grab a water bottle.

Althea remembered snapping at him that she had no choice but to wet the floor because he never let her out of the cage. Rather than repeat history, she glared at him. *"Let me out."*

Emotion drained out of his face. The water bottle slipped from his grasp. He stood still for a moment, then mechanically slid one hand into a pocket on his purple suit coat, extracting a key. His motions robotic, gaze vacant, the man lowered himself to one knee and opened the padlock.

Althea contemptuously kicked the cage door open, scooted out, and stood. Her five-year-old self still didn't quite stand as tall as him while he knelt. She glared at him anyway, his face tinted blue in the glow from her eyes. Voices replayed in her mind, people from the city police teaching her about psionic abilities. The more a person used an ability, the better they got at it and the more they could do with it. Althea had become such a powerful healer and telempath because she'd used both abilities near constantly while being dragged around the Badlands. The Wagon Man, raiders, and bandits of all kinds forced her to heal even when she'd been exhausted to the point using her abilities hurt.

She'd used Telempathy all the time without really understanding she did so. Whenever she wanted people not to wife their slaves, be violent, or stop keeping her tied and leashed, she'd use her power to soften their emotions. Somewhere around age nine or ten, she realized she could manipulate emotions whenever she wanted to. From then forward, she always did what she could to stop bad stuff. Thankfully, no raiders who ever kidnapped her realized all the wifeing ended soon after they brought her into their camp. She only allowed it to happen if both people wanted it to—which didn't occur often.

Telepathy, she discovered fairly young. Reading people's surface thoughts proved invaluable to keeping herself and others as safe as possible in the dangerous wasteland. Her ability to command people, Suggestion as the city police called it, saw far less use. The first time it worked, she'd been desperate to stop a raider boss who didn't respond to her emotional control from wifeing one of his captives. In a moment of panic, she yelled at him to stop... and the command worked.

Scrags and raiders alike knew about psionics, even if they called it magic and referred to the people with powers as 'mystics.' Most scrags feared mystics, especially the ones with abilities like Suggestion and usually burned them alive. Folklore claimed killing a mystic any other way would allow them to come back even stronger and take revenge.

She'd been so petrified of being lit on fire, she tried not

to use Suggestion ever… unless someone would be killed or wifed without it.

What the city police taught her changed everything.

Althea peered back at the cage, then the man who put her in it, unsure if she should be angry with him. He forced her to use her powers all the time, like a nasty teacher who demanded the student keep doing something until they became better at it. Because of him, she'd become a potent healer much younger than would have happened otherwise —if at all. Had she remained peacefully at the village where she'd ended up as an infant, she'd only have ever made the hurts and sicks go away for people who lived there… probably not much at all.

Because of the Wagon Man, she had become a source of life and protection for the Badlands.

No, she couldn't be angry with him. He'd been cruel to her, caused people to suffer, but ultimately, his actions made her capable of helping everyone.

Althea rapidly grew back to age twelve, her plain white dress appearing out of nowhere. The Wagon Man collapsed sideways, dead, shot in the head and chest as he'd been when raiders stole her from him.

Silvery white light appeared to her left. She raised an arm to shield her eyes.

"Althea," whispered an ephemeral female voice.

She faced into the light, squinting at the silhouette of a person standing amid the glare. The figure stepped closer. As the radiance faded, her visitor went from simple outline to a young woman in a sky-blue jumpsuit. She had the same shade of bright blonde hair as Althea as well as blue eyes— except hers didn't glow. It felt like gazing into a mirror at her future self, ten years from now.

"Mother?" whispered Althea.

The woman lowered her gaze in sadness. "I am sorry for leaving you."

Althea took the apparition's hand, overjoyed to find it solid and warm. "You had to. I understand bad people hunted us. If you didn't give me to the old man, we both would have died."

"No." Her mother squeezed her hand. "You'd have ended up in a lab somewhere. They wanted to know why your eyes glowed. They knew some manner of energy came across the gate we opened. I didn't want you to spend your whole life in a cage, being experimented on."

Althea glanced at the literal cage against the wall. "I got out."

Her mother barked a sad laugh. "I'm so, so sorry for that. It took me a long time to understand how to be a ghost. I'm still learning. Can't do much."

"Am I having a dream now or are you really here?"

"You are dreaming, but I am really here." Her mother hugged her.

Althea wept, overcome by joy.

"You're safe in that sad excuse for a truck, on the way back to Querq." Her mother sighed. "I am trying to be there with you. It's difficult to escape the place where the men shot me. Something keeps pulling me back there."

"I can help you go where spirits belong." Althea looked down.

"Do you want me to?"

"I want you to be happy." Althea clung to her mother with all her strength. "It will make me sad if you go away, but if you are happy I will be happy."

"Will you be happy if I stay?"

"It's not my choosing."

Her mother brushed a hand over her head. "You want me to stay but feel guilty about it."

"Yeah." Althea kept staring at the floor.

"Don't. I want to stay... as soon as I figure out how." Her mother winked. "I'm working on it."

Althea gave a shuddering breath. Asking her mother's spirit to stay here might be selfish. Ghosts belonged in the spirit place. But... if her mother *wanted* to stay anyway, she didn't feel bad. "Was I dumb for letting people kidnap me all the time and not making them let me go?"

"I don't think so. You had to learn." Her mother smiled. "You had to find a family worth protecting. Before you found them, the only thing you wanted was to help people. It didn't matter to you if they kept you captive or not. You could heal. As soon as you found a home, you learned to protect it and yourself. I am proud of you."

Althea cried, clinging tight, not wanting to ever let go of her mother.

The apparition rocked her, glowing with happiness and pride despite a heavy note of sad loneliness. Even though she already dreamed, Althea soon found herself falling asleep in her mother's arms.

## 36

# BENEVOLENCE

Althea opened her eyes, unsure exactly what disturbed her.

The blurry interior of the big raider buggy sharpened in her view. She lay on her side, curled up in the back with her head on Teal's lap. David drove, having a quiet, almost whispered conversation with Phoenix in the passenger seat about city police stuff—mostly information they got from the computers at the un-hospital. Phoenix believed it might allow them to go after the company for what it did.

"C'mon, kiddo." Teal jostled her. "Wake up."

"I have the wake," muttered Althea in a sleepy voice, intentionally talking like a scrag to get a chuckle from everyone. She wiped sleep crumbs from her eyes and sat up, yawned, then yawned again. "Is my butt missing?"

Laughing, Teal said, "No, why?"

She squirmed. "I can't feel it."

"Metal seats." Phoenix peered back at her. "You'd been sitting for a long time in the same position. Circulation. You'll be fine."

"We're almost home." Teal smiled.

Althea leaned forward to peer past David's seat out the front, squinting at the stiff breeze blowing in the big open window. The buggy passed the gates of Querq and rolled through the short tunnel in the wall, the thick metal plates beneath it clanking and rattling from the vehicle's weight. Men and women on the Watch above them shouted, announcing their return, along with calls to 'go tell Fernando and Karina.'

"Someone was worn out." David guided the buggy across the courtyard inside the gate, heading down the street to the clearing by the mechanic's shop. "Have a nice sleep?"

"Yeah." Althea choked up. "I dreamed about my mother."

"It's okay." Teal brushed a hand over her head. "I'm still here."

Althea stared at her. "What?"

Teal tilted her head. "I said, 'that explains why you kept saying 'Mom' in your sleep.'"

She kept staring at Teal. The woman felt ever so slightly different, but only for a few seconds before the odd sensation disappeared. Althea concentrated on wanting to see spirits. The inside of the buggy brightened from her eyes glowing more intently. She spun side to side, searching, but saw no spirits other than a disoriented raider wandering past them.

*Did I dream that or did Teal speak like my mother?*

"It's a decent chance," said Phoenix. "Fairly damning data. I may need to submit a request for Commander Ashford to make me forget that room, though."

"What room?" asked Althea.

David exuded discomfort. "The one with the big table... the facility staff..."

"What happened to them?" Althea bit her lip.

"Dead," said Teal. "Black stuff pouring out of their eyes, noses, ears, and mouths. No idea what the heck killed them, but it looked painful."

Althea shivered. "They are part of him now."

David stopped the buggy at the mechanic's garage. "Don't let sadness eat at you. Yes, people died, but you protected many others from being tortured, killed by diseases, or experimented on."

"She feels bad about the sadistic bastards who handcuffed little kids to hospital beds and made them sick with agonizing biological weapons just to see what would happen." Teal brushed a hand at her hair again, not quite the same way her mother had in the dream—but close.

"I know it's silly of me to feel like this when bad things happen to awful people." Althea sighed at the floor. The people responsible for all the nights poor Kia must have screamed in pain while trying to sleep definitely deserved punishment... but what happened to them still bothered her.

"No, it isn't. It's just who you are. C'mon, your father and sister have to be freaking out for us being gone so long." David opened the door. As soon as he tried to get out, the buggy lurched forward. He jammed on the brake, jostling everyone. "Dammit."

"Shifter all the way back," said Teal.

David yanked on a stick protruding up from the floor between the front seats. "Got it."

"Altheeeeeeaaa!" shouted Karina in the distance.

The sound of her sister's voice shoved all the somber thoughts out of her mind. Grinning, Althea squeezed out past the back of David's seat, leapt the four-foot drop to the ground, and bolted down the street toward Karina, who ran to meet her. They crashed together in a spinning hug.

Althea's burst of happiness detonated in a telempathic bomb. Everyone within a few hundred meters in all directions shared in the pure joy of being reunited with her sister for a few minutes until she collected herself.

Father jogged over from another direction. He embraced his daughters, mumbling in annoyance at having been on the wall at the northeast, about as far away from the gate as possible without leaving Querq.

"It is good to have you home, Thea," said Father.

"Sorry for making you both worry about me." Althea squeezed her family together.

"Did you help the people?" asked Father.

"I did." She squeezed even tighter. "But I am really happy to be home."

*fin*

# ACKNOWLEDGMENTS

Thank you for reading *Prophet's Mercy!*

Althea's adventures will continue soon.

Additional thanks to Jackson Tjota for the cover illustration, Alexandria Thompson for the cover layout, Ricky Gunawan for the interior artwork, and Lee Sheridan for editing.

# ABOUT THE AUTHOR

Originally from South Amboy NJ, Matthew has been creating science fiction and fantasy worlds for most of his reasoning life. Since 1996, he has developed the "Divergent Fates" world, in which *Division Zero, Virtual Immortality, The Awakened Series, The Harmony Paradox, and the Daughter of Mars series* take place. Along with being an editor at Curiosity Quills press, he has worked in IT and technical support.

Matthew is an avid gamer, a recovered WoW addict, Gamemaster for two custom RPG systems, and a fan of anime, British humour, and intellectual science fiction that questions the nature of reality, life, and what happens after it.

He is also fond of cats.

Visit me online at:

Facebook: https://www.facebook.com/MatthewSCoxAuthor

Pinterest: https://www.pinterest.com/matthewcox10420/

Goodreads: https://www.goodreads.com/author/show/7712730.Matthew_S_Cox

Email: mcox2112@gmail.com

# OTHER BOOKS BY MATTHEW S. COX

Divergent Fates Universe Novels

Division Zero series

- Division Zero
- Lex De Mortuis
- Thrall
- Guardian
- Harbinger
- The Shadow Fixer

The Awakened series

- Prophet of the Badlands
- Archon's Queen
- Grey Ronin
- Daughter of Ash
- Zero Rogue
- Angel Descended

Daughter of Mars series

- The Hand of Raziel
- Araphel
- Ghost Black

Virtual Immortality series

- Virtual Immortality
- The Harmony Paradox

Prophet of the Badlands Series

- Prophet's Journey
- Prophet's Mercy

Divergent Fates Anthology

(Fiction Novels - Adult)

The Roadhouse Chronicles Series

- One More Run
- The Redeemed
- Dead Man's Number

Faded Skies series

- Heir Ascendant
- Ascendant Unrest
- Ascendant Revolution

Temporal Armistice Series

- Nascent Shadow
- The Shadow Collector
- The Gate to Oblivion
- The Queen of Discord
- The Burning Alchemist

Vampire Innocent series

- A Nighttime of Forever
- A Beginner's Guide to Fangs

- The Artist of Ruin
- The Last Family Road Trip
- The Phantom Oracle
- How Not to Summon Demons
- Ordinary Problems of a College Vampire
- A Vampire's Guide to Surviving Holidays
- An Introduction to Paranormal Diplomacy
- A Vampire's Guide to Adulting
- How to Stop a Vampire War in Six Easy Steps
- Ancient Vampire Death Cults and Other Annoyances
- Hunting Vampires for Fun and Profit

Standalones

- Wayfarer: AV494
- Axillon99
- Chiaroscuro: The Mouse and the Candle
- The Spirits of Six Minstrel Run
- Sophie's Light
- The Far Side of Promise anthology
- Operation: Chimera  (with Tony Healey)
- The Dysfunctional Conspiracy (with Christopher Veltmann)
- Of Myth and Shadow
- The Girl Who Found the Sun

Winter Solstice series (with J.R. Rain)

- Convergence
- Containment
- Catalyst
- Catacombs

Alexis Silver series (with J.R. Rain)

- Silver Light
- Deep Silver
- Silver Quarrel
- Silver Crucible

Samantha Moon Origins series (with J.R. Rain)

- New Moon Rising
- Moon Mourning
- Haunted Moon

Vampire For Hire series (with J.R. Rain)

- Moon Master
- Dead Moon
- Lost Moon
- Vampire Destiny
- Infinite Moon
- Vampire Empress
- Moon Elder

Maddy Wimsey series (with J.R. Rain)

- The Devil's Eye
- The Drifting Gloom
- Dark Mercy
- Primal Wrath

Samantha Moon Case Files series (with J.R. Rain)

- Blood Moon

Immortal Operative (with J.R. Rain)

- Broken Ice
- Broken Wing

Four Elements series (with J.R. Rain)

- The Elementalist
- The Black Rose
- The Wakefield Curse

Witches series (with J.R. Rain)

- The Witch and the Hangman

Young Adult Novels

The Eldritch Heart Series

- The Eldritch Heart
- The Cursed Crown
- The Sapphire Soul

Evergreen Series

- Evergreen
- The World That Remains
- The Lucky Ones
- Nuclear Summer
- The Nuclear Frontier
- The World We Make

Progenitor Series

- Out of Sight

- Out of Mind

### Diary of a Teenage Fey

(Short story series)

- Elder Horror
- The Hag of Barrow Falls
- Babysitter's Nightmare
- Lharakki
- Bauble for a Soul
- Simulacrum
- Amorphous
- Manticore

### Standalones

- Caller 107
- The Summer the World Ended
- Nine Candles of Deepest Black
- The Forest Beyond the Earth

### Middle Grade Novels

### The Adventures of Ubergirl series

- My Dad is a Mad Scientist
- Aliens Ate My Homework
- The End of all Halloweens
- Dr. Infinity and the Soul Smasher

### Tales of Widowswood series

- Emma and the Banderwigh
- Emma and the Silk Thieves
- Emma and the Silverbell Faeries
- Emma and the Elixir of Madness
- Emma and the Weeping Spirit

Standalones

- Citadel: The Concordant Sequence
- The Cursed Codex
- The Menagerie of Jenkins Bailey